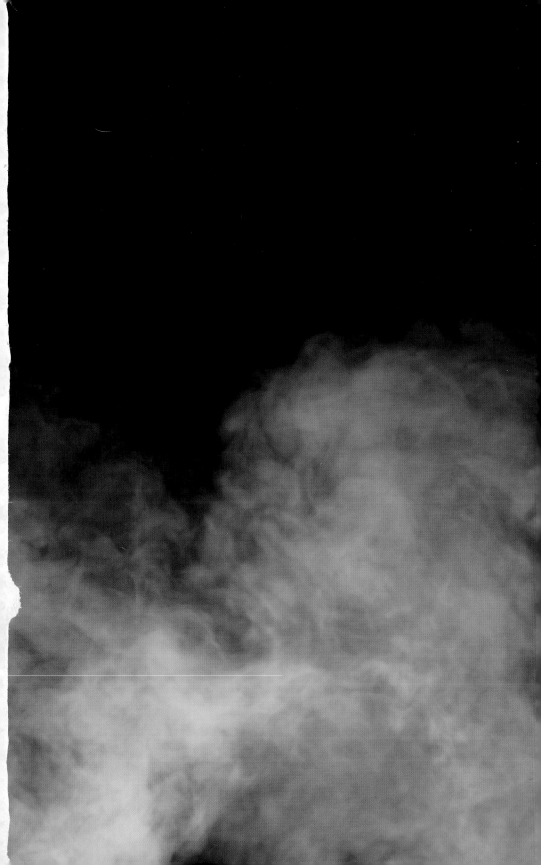

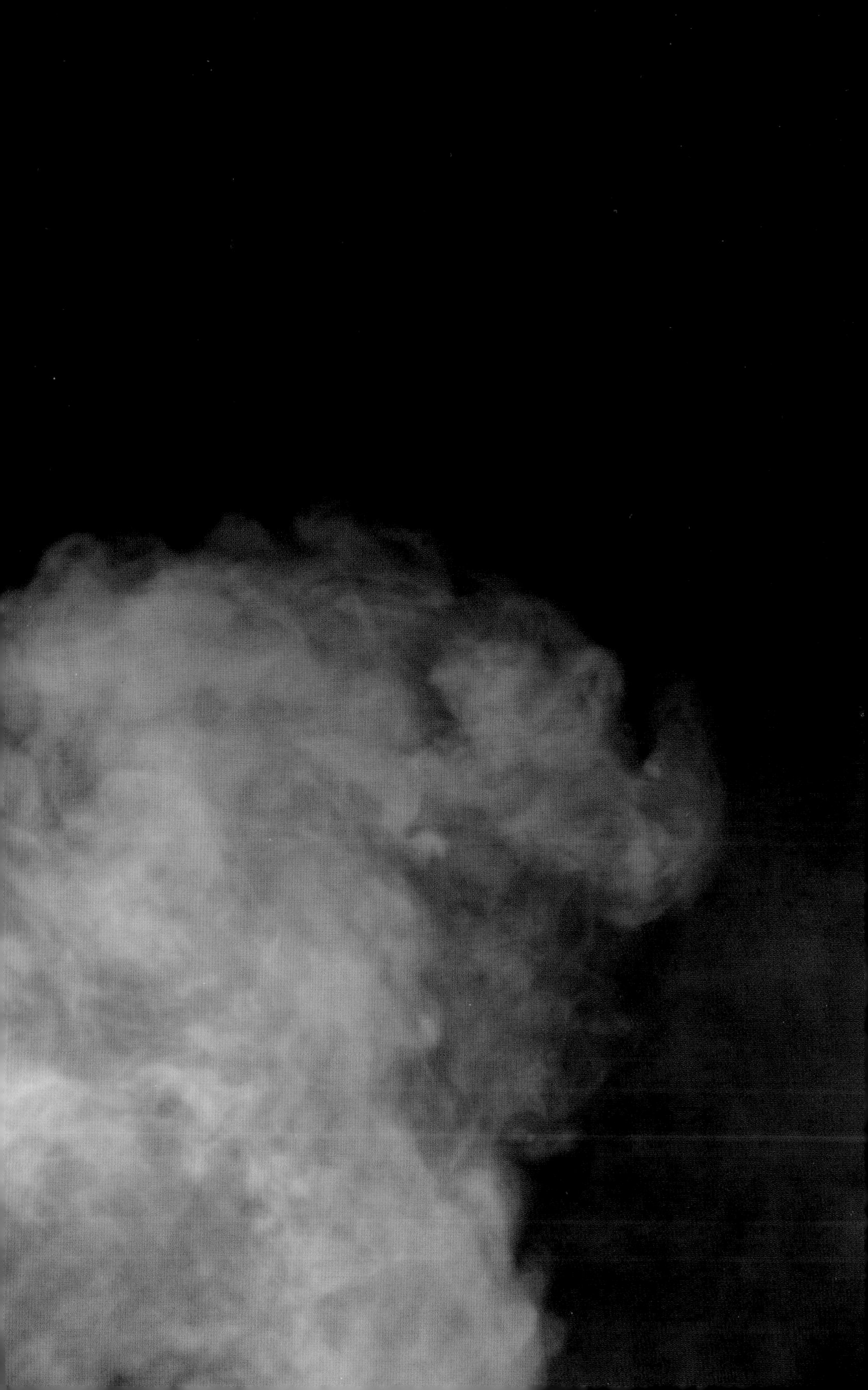

SIMON SPOTLIGHT
An imprint of Simon & Schuster Children's Publishing Division
1230 Avenue of the Americas, New York, New York 10020
This Simon Spotlight edition December 2022
Copyright © 2022 by Simon & Schuster, Inc. All rights reserved, including the right of reproduction in whole or in part in any form. SIMON SPOTLIGHT and colophon are registered trademarks of Simon & Schuster, Inc. YOU'RE INVITED TO A CREEPOVER is a registered trademark of Simon & Schuster, Inc. For information about special discounts for bulk purchases, please contact Simon & Schuster Special Sales at 1-866-506-1949 or business@simonandschuster.com. Designed by Nicholas Sciacca. Text by Matthew J. Gilbert. Based on the text by Heather Alexander. Art Services by Glass House Graphics. Art by Giusi Lo Piccolo & Onofrio Orlando. Lettering by Giuseppe Naselli/Grafimated Cartoon. Supervision by Salvatore Di Marco/Grafimated Cartoon. The illustrations for this book were rendered digitally. Manufactured in China 0922 SCP
10 9 8 7 6 5 4 3 2 1
This book has been cataloged by the Library of Congress.
ISBN 978-1-6659-1570-0 (hc)
ISBN 978-1-6659-1569-4 (pbk)
ISBN 978-1-6659-1571-7 (ebook)

YOU'RE INVITED TO A

# CREEPOVER®

THE GRAPHIC NOVEL

## READY FOR A SCARE?

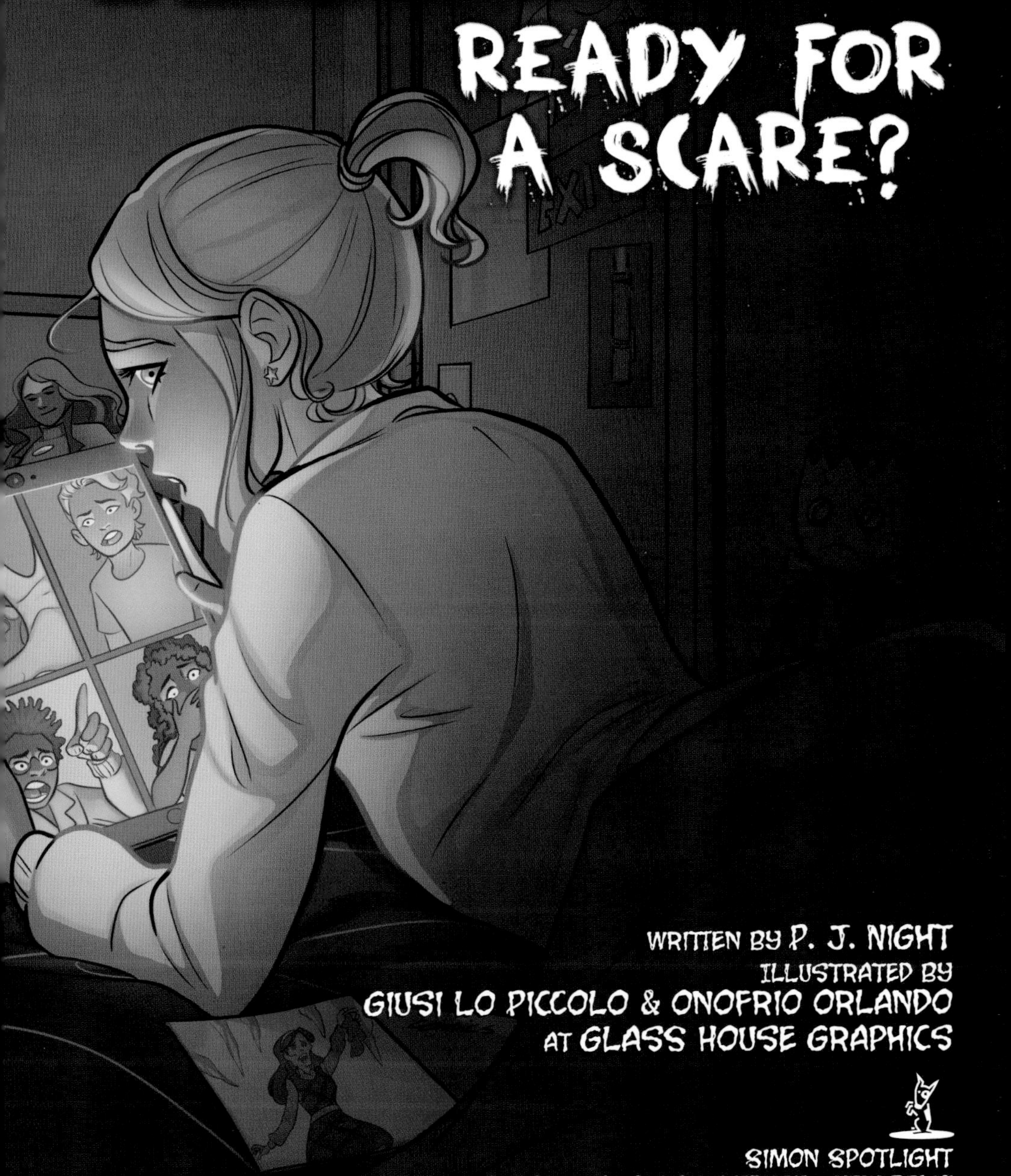


WRITTEN BY P. J. NIGHT

ILLUSTRATED BY

GIUSI LO PICCOLO & ONOFRIO ORLANDO

AT GLASS HOUSE GRAPHICS



SIMON SPOTLIGHT

NEW YORK LONDON TORONTO SYDNEY NEW DELHI

# PROLOGUE

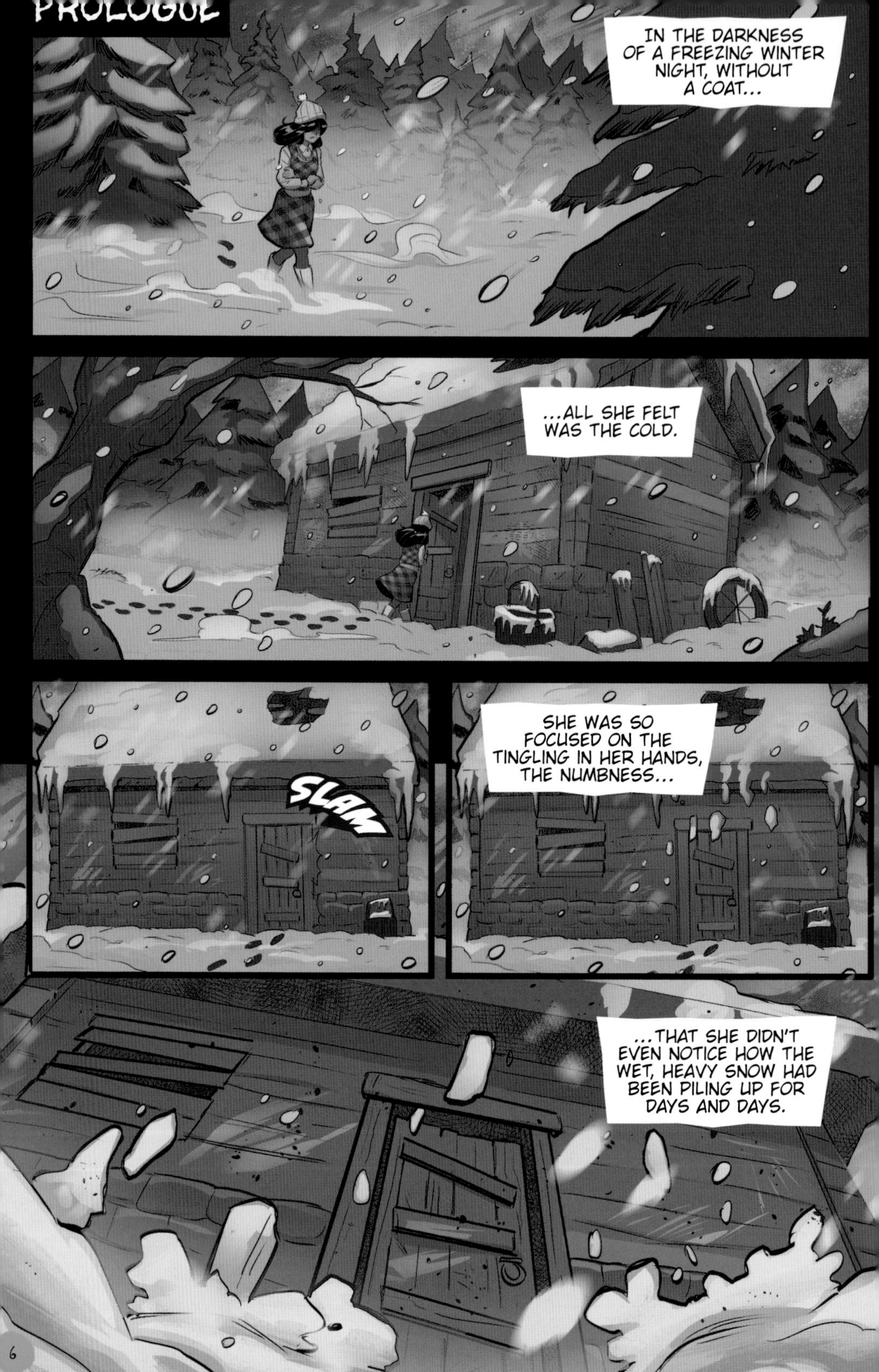
IN THE DARKNESS OF A FREEZING WINTER NIGHT, WITHOUT A COAT...
...ALL SHE FELT WAS THE COLD.
SLAM
SHE WAS SO FOCUSED ON THE TINGLING IN HER HANDS, THE NUMBNESS...
...THAT SHE DIDN'T EVEN NOTICE HOW THE WET, HEAVY SNOW HAD BEEN PILING UP FOR DAYS AND DAYS.

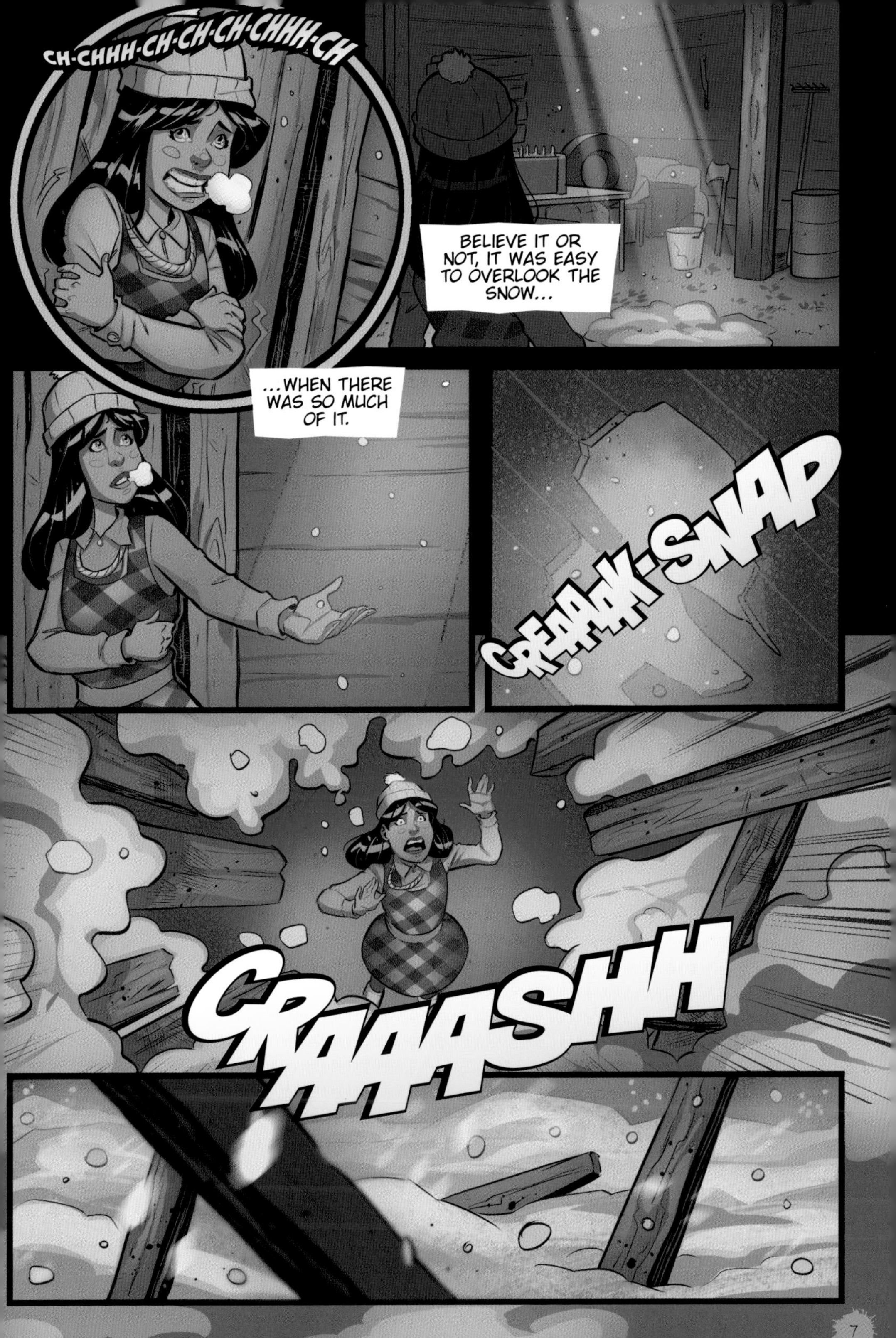
CH-CHHH-CH-CH-CH-CHHH-CH
BELIEVE IT OR NOT, IT WAS EASY TO OVERLOOK THE SNOW…
…WHEN THERE WAS SO MUCH OF IT.
CREAAK-SNAP
CRAAASHH

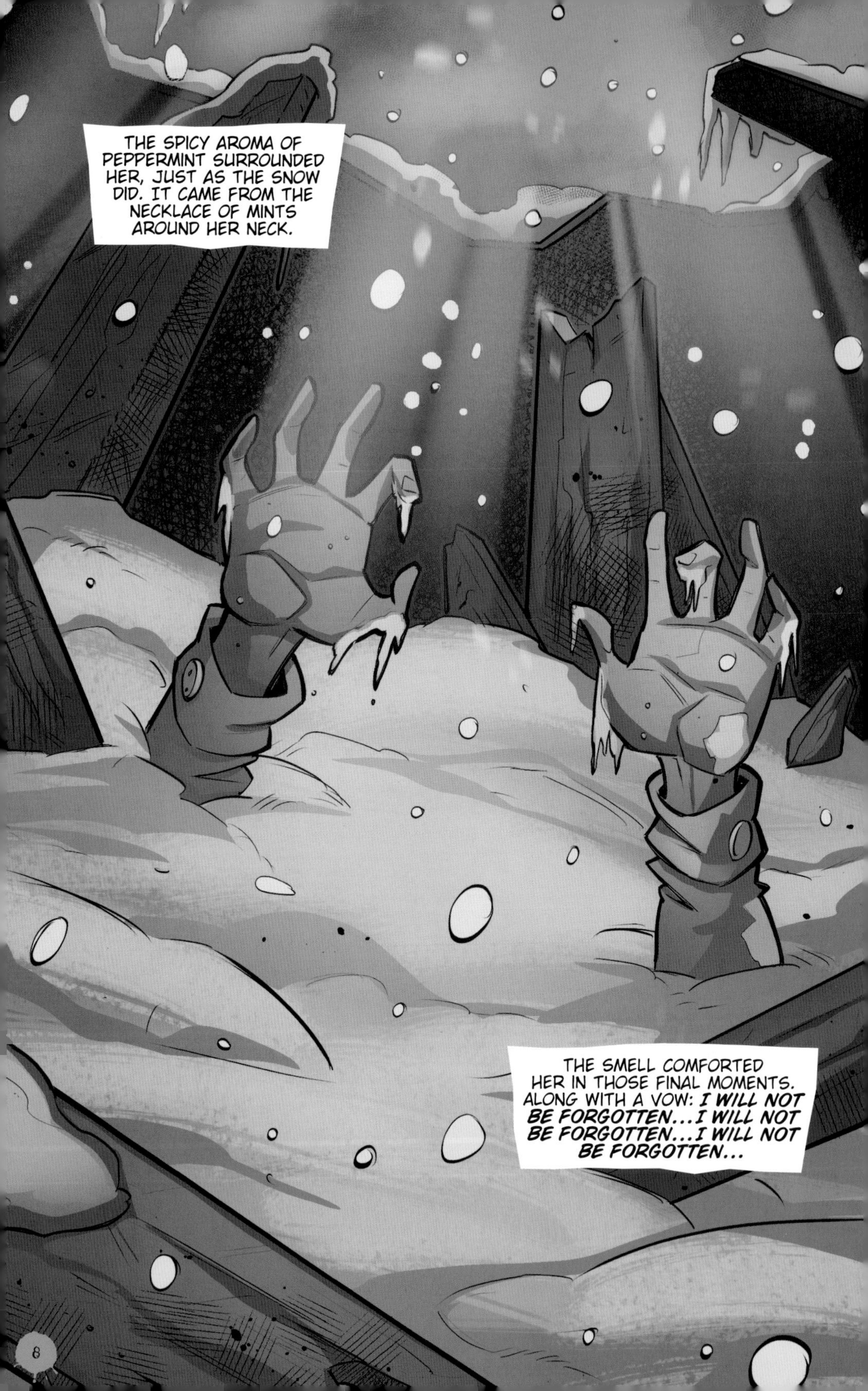
THE SPICY AROMA OF PEPPERMINT SURROUNDED HER, JUST AS THE SNOW DID. IT CAME FROM THE NECKLACE OF MINTS AROUND HER NECK.
THE SMELL COMFORTED HER IN THOSE FINAL MOMENTS. ALONG WITH A VOW: *I WILL NOT BE FORGOTTEN...I WILL NOT BE FORGOTTEN...I WILL NOT BE FORGOTTEN...*

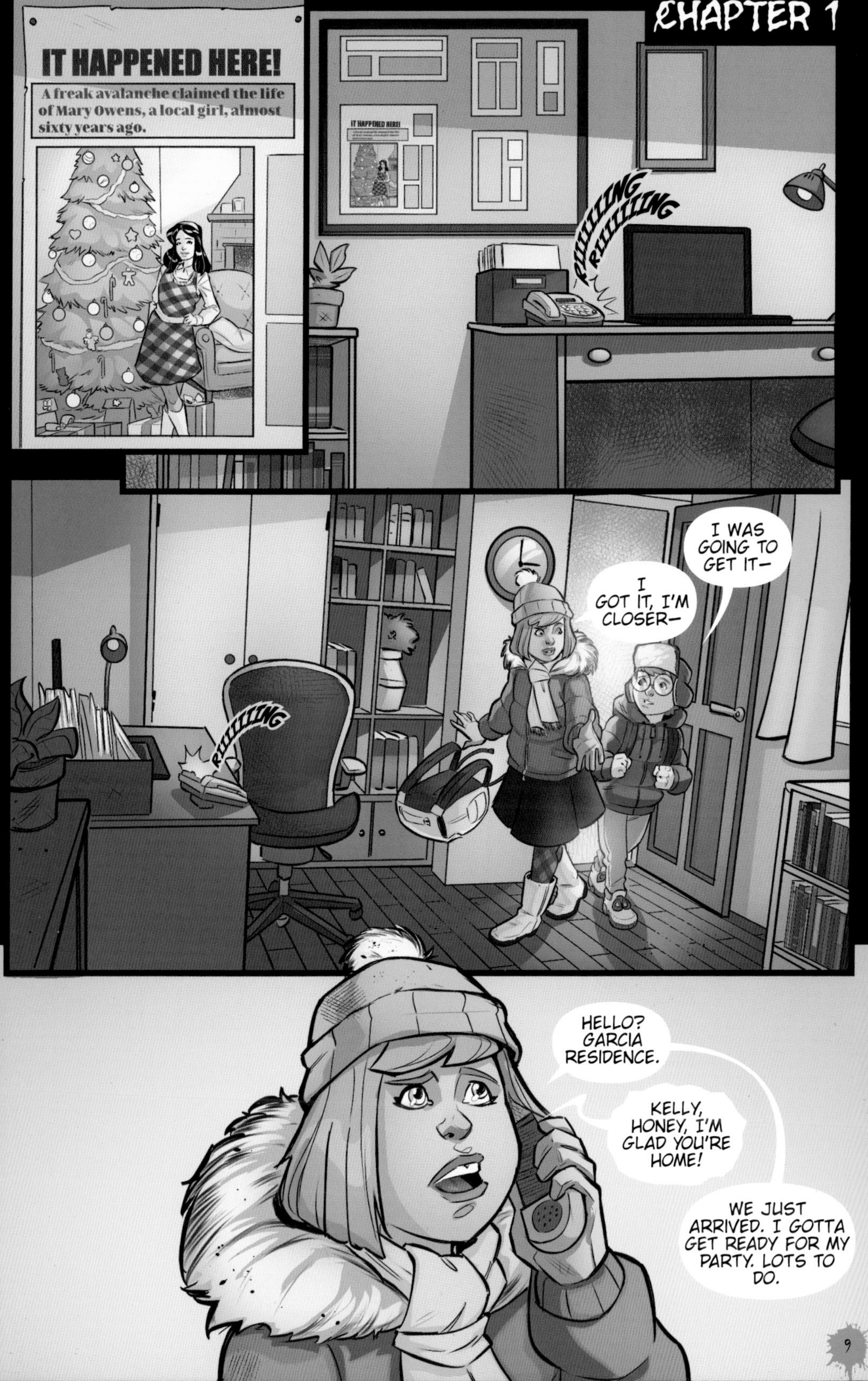
CHAPTER 1
IT HAPPENED HERE!
A freak avalanche claimed the life of Mary Owens, a local girl, almost sixty years ago.
RIIIIIIING RIIIIIIING
RIIIIIIING
I WAS GOING TO GET IT—
I GOT IT, I'M CLOSER—
HELLO? GARCIA RESIDENCE.
KELLY, HONEY, I'M GLAD YOU'RE HOME!
WE JUST ARRIVED. I GOTTA GET READY FOR MY PARTY. LOTS TO DO.

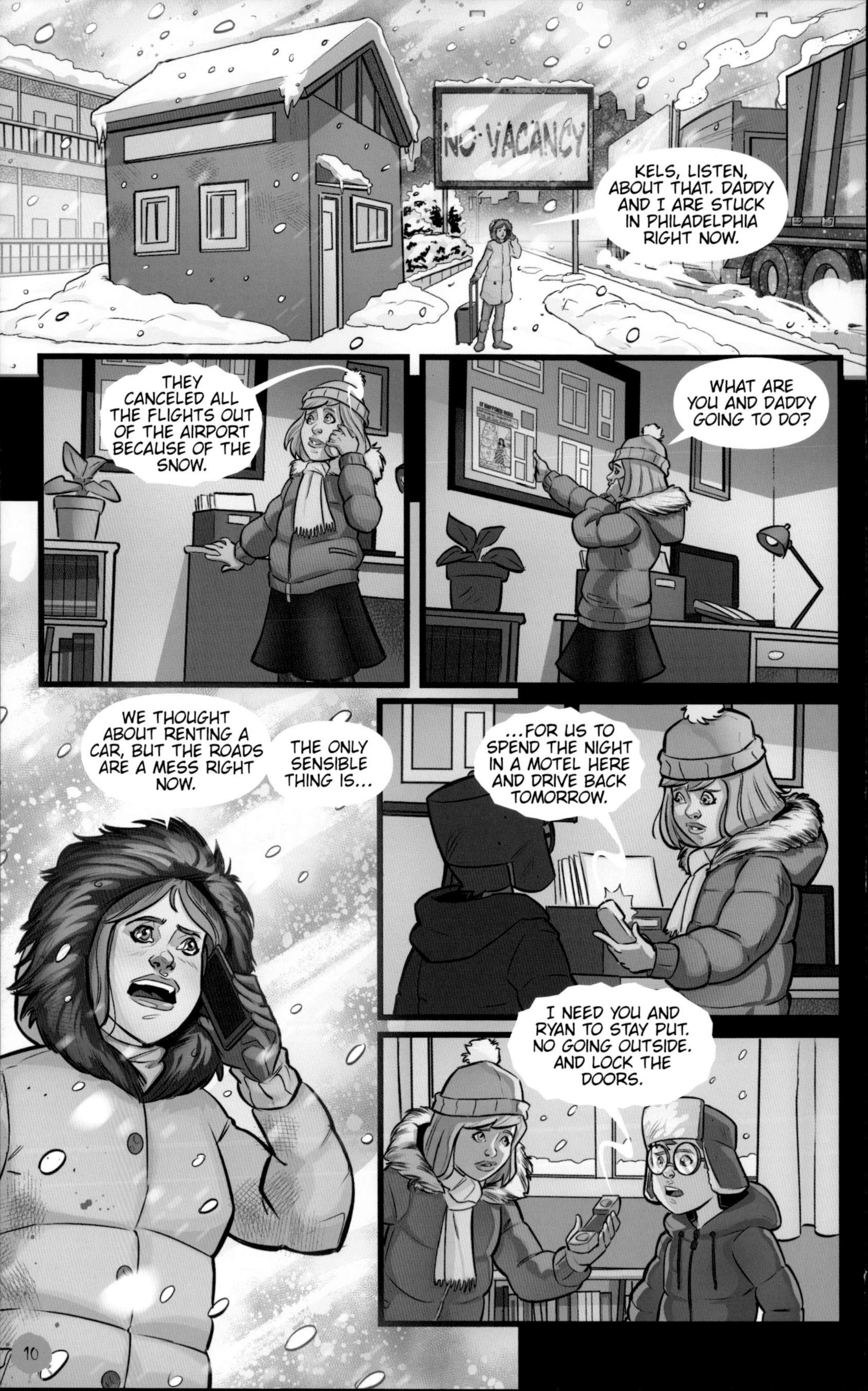
NO VACANCY
KELS, LISTEN, ABOUT THAT. DADDY AND I ARE STUCK IN PHILADELPHIA RIGHT NOW.
THEY CANCELED ALL THE FLIGHTS OUT OF THE AIRPORT BECAUSE OF THE SNOW.
WHAT ARE YOU AND DADDY GOING TO DO?
WE THOUGHT ABOUT RENTING A CAR, BUT THE ROADS ARE A MESS RIGHT NOW.
THE ONLY SENSIBLE THING IS...
...FOR US TO SPEND THE NIGHT IN A MOTEL HERE AND DRIVE BACK TOMORROW.
I NEED YOU AND RYAN TO STAY PUT. NO GOING OUTSIDE. AND LOCK THE DOORS.

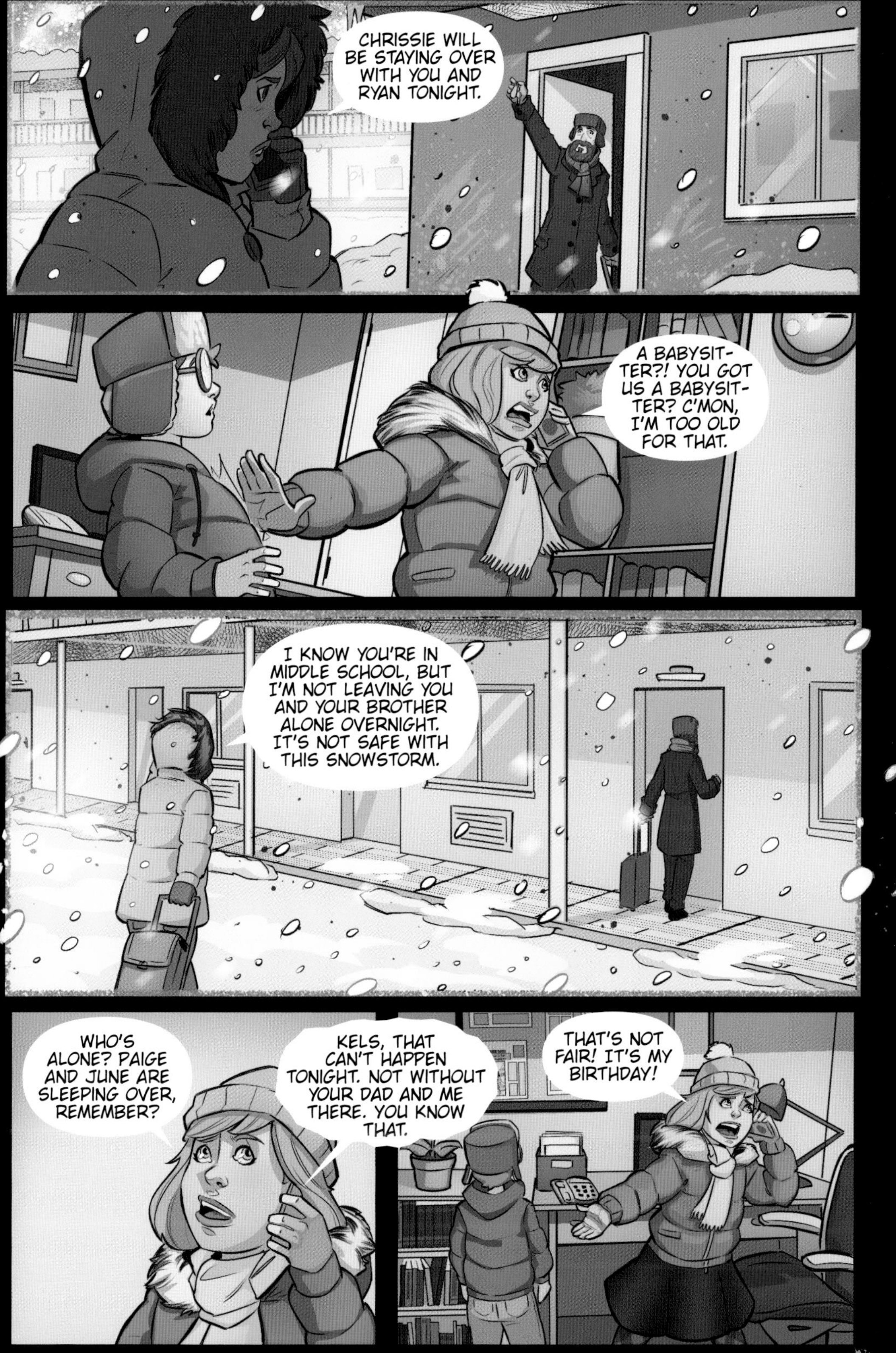
CHRISSIE WILL BE STAYING OVER WITH YOU AND RYAN TONIGHT.
A BABYSIT-TER?! YOU GOT US A BABYSIT-TER? C'MON, I'M TOO OLD FOR THAT.
I KNOW YOU'RE IN MIDDLE SCHOOL, BUT I'M NOT LEAVING YOU AND YOUR BROTHER ALONE OVERNIGHT. IT'S NOT SAFE WITH THIS SNOWSTORM.
WHO'S ALONE? PAIGE AND JUNE ARE SLEEPING OVER, REMEMBER?
KELS, THAT CAN'T HAPPEN TONIGHT. NOT WITHOUT YOUR DAD AND ME THERE. YOU KNOW THAT.
THAT'S NOT FAIR! IT'S MY BIRTHDAY!

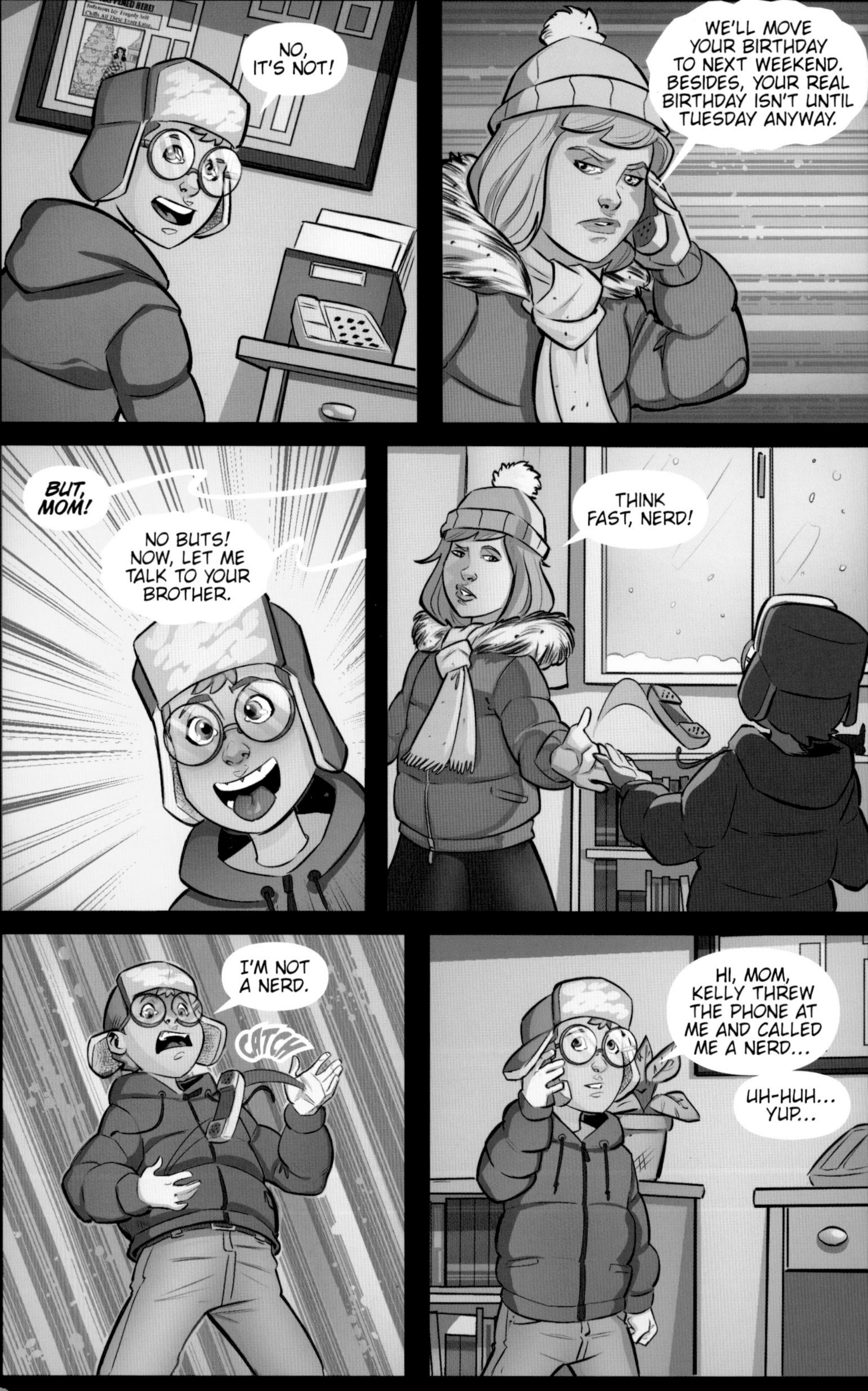
NO, IT'S NOT!
WE'LL MOVE YOUR BIRTHDAY TO NEXT WEEKEND. BESIDES, YOUR REAL BIRTHDAY ISN'T UNTIL TUESDAY ANYWAY.
BUT, MOM!
NO BUTS! NOW, LET ME TALK TO YOUR BROTHER.
THINK FAST, NERD!
I'M NOT A NERD.
CATCH
HI, MOM, KELLY THREW THE PHONE AT ME AND CALLED ME A NERD...
UH-HUH... YUP...

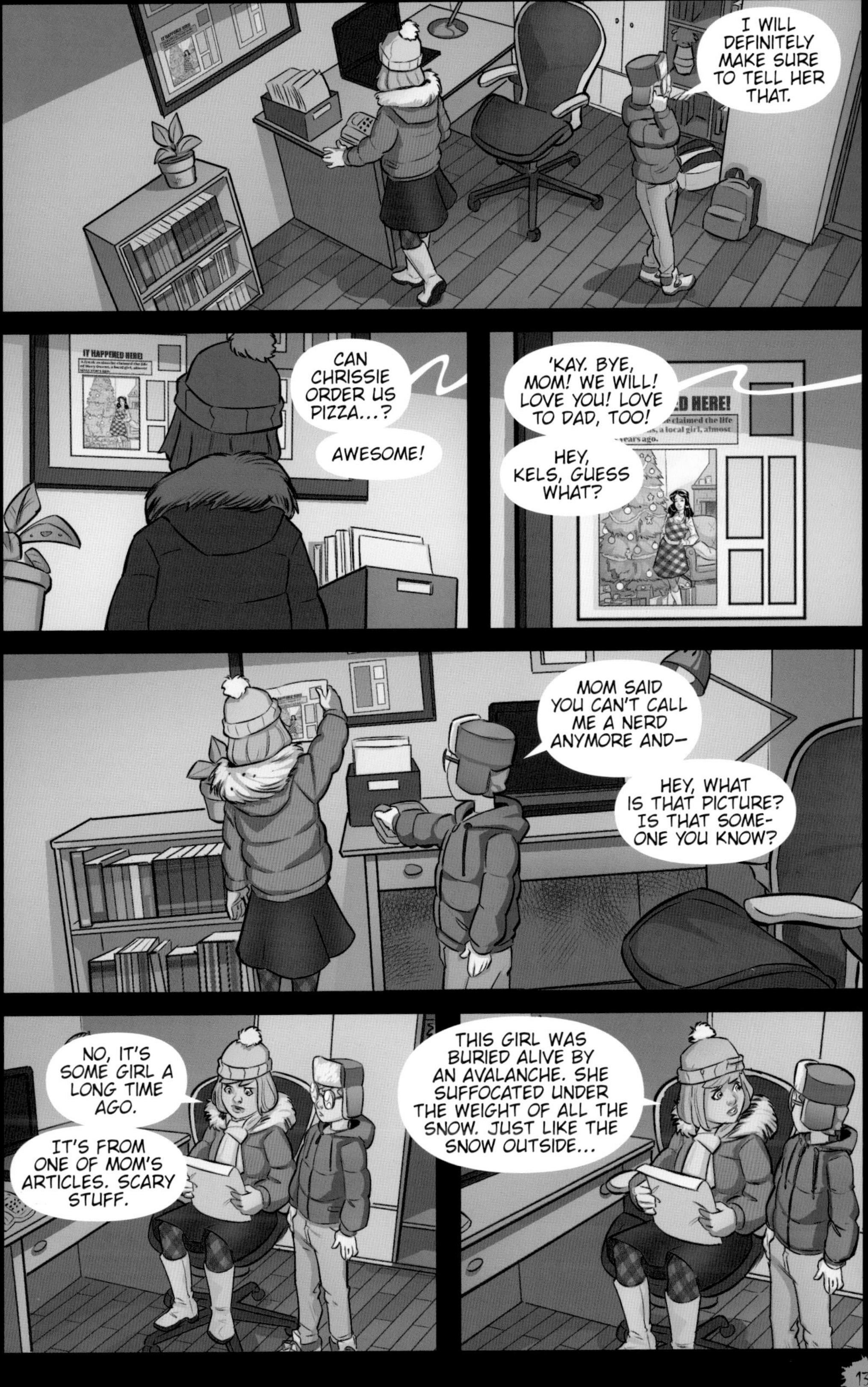
I WILL DEFINITELY MAKE SURE TO TELL HER THAT.
IT HAPPENED HERE!
CAN CHRISSIE ORDER US PIZZA...?
AWESOME!
'KAY. BYE, MOM! WE WILL! LOVE YOU! LOVE TO DAD, TOO!
HEY, KELS, GUESS WHAT?
MOM SAID YOU CAN'T CALL ME A NERD ANYMORE AND—
HEY, WHAT IS THAT PICTURE? IS THAT SOME-ONE YOU KNOW?
NO, IT'S SOME GIRL A LONG TIME AGO.
IT'S FROM ONE OF MOM'S ARTICLES. SCARY STUFF.
THIS GIRL WAS BURIED ALIVE BY AN AVALANCHE. SHE SUFFOCATED UNDER THE WEIGHT OF ALL THE SNOW. JUST LIKE THE SNOW OUTSIDE...

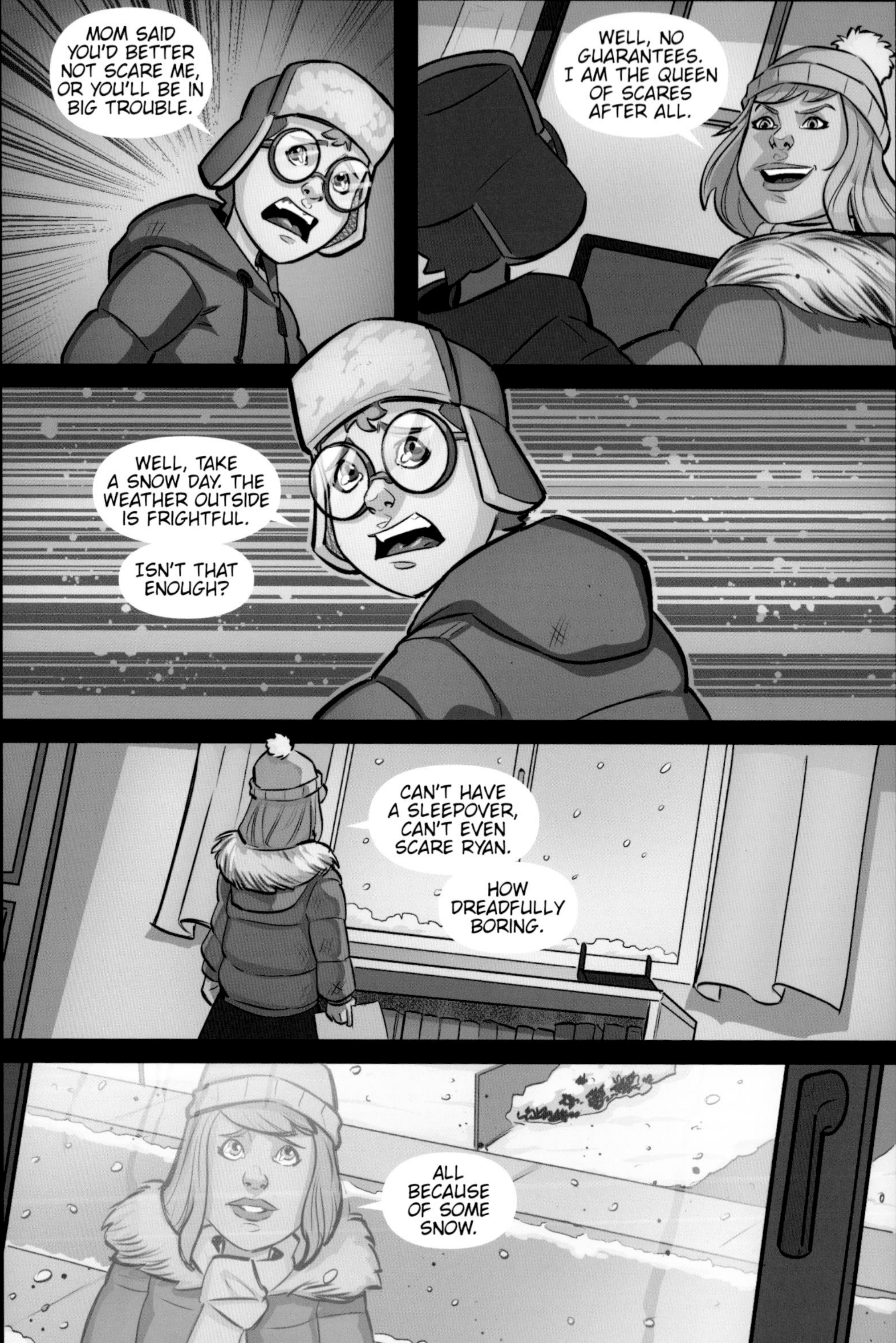
MOM SAID YOU'D BETTER NOT SCARE ME, OR YOU'LL BE IN BIG TROUBLE.
WELL, NO GUARANTEES. I AM THE QUEEN OF SCARES AFTER ALL.
WELL, TAKE A SNOW DAY. THE WEATHER OUTSIDE IS FRIGHTFUL.
ISN'T THAT ENOUGH?
CAN'T HAVE A SLEEPOVER, CAN'T EVEN SCARE RYAN.
HOW DREADFULLY BORING.
ALL BECAUSE OF SOME SNOW.

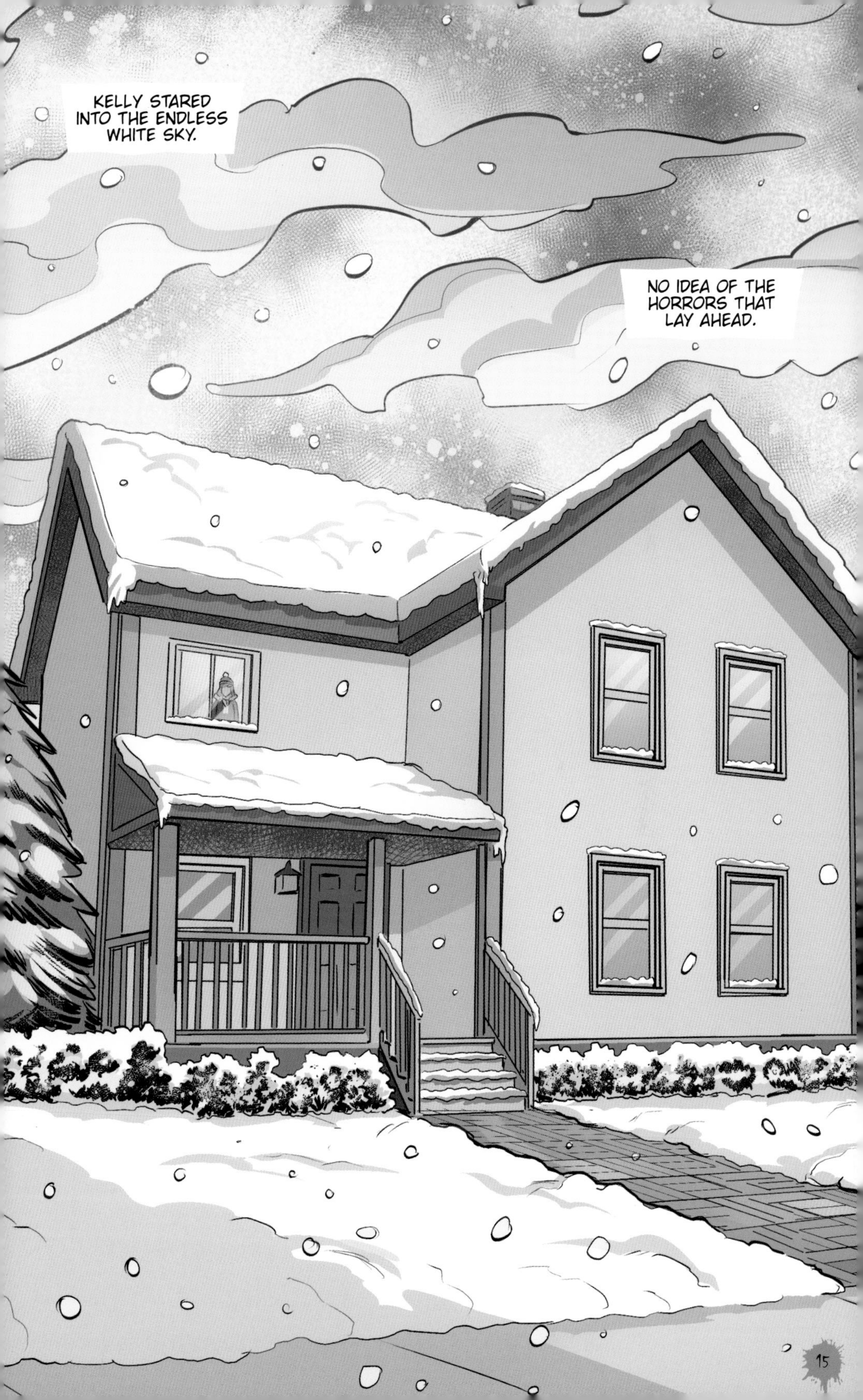
KELLY STARED INTO THE ENDLESS WHITE SKY.
NO IDEA OF THE HORRORS THAT LAY AHEAD.

# CHAPTER 2

MOMENTS LATER, IT WAS TIME FOR KELLY TO ACCEPT HER FATE...

...AND DELIVER THE BAD NEWS.

TAP TAP

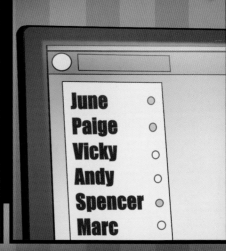

June
Paige
Vicky
Andy
Spencer
Marc

CLICK

June
Paige
Vicky
Andy
Spencer
Marc
Samantha
Martin
Jamal
Erica

# CHAT WITH JUNE AND PAIGE

**KELLY**

BAD NEWS.

**JUNE**

?

**KELLY**

No sleepover tonight.
Parents trapped in Philly
😣

**PAIGE**

I heard. Can't believe your
mom thinks Chrissie is gonna
keep u safe! LOL

**KELLY**

I KNOW.
So not my idea!

**JUNE**

Hold up. Chrissie is
babysitting???!!!!????

**KELLY**

NOT 👋
MY 👋
IDEA 👋

**PAIGE**

I mean, it is kinda scary
at night alone 👻

**JUNE**

Better watch out, Kels!

**KELLY**

Whatevs.
So NOT scared!

**JUNE**

Sad about your sleepover.
I have a present 4 u.

**PAIGE**

Yeah me 2.

**KELLY**

Thx! You guys r the best.
I have to move it to next weekend.
STINKS. Had so many great scares
planned for u tonight.

**PAIGE**

Maybe I'm safer at home, haha.

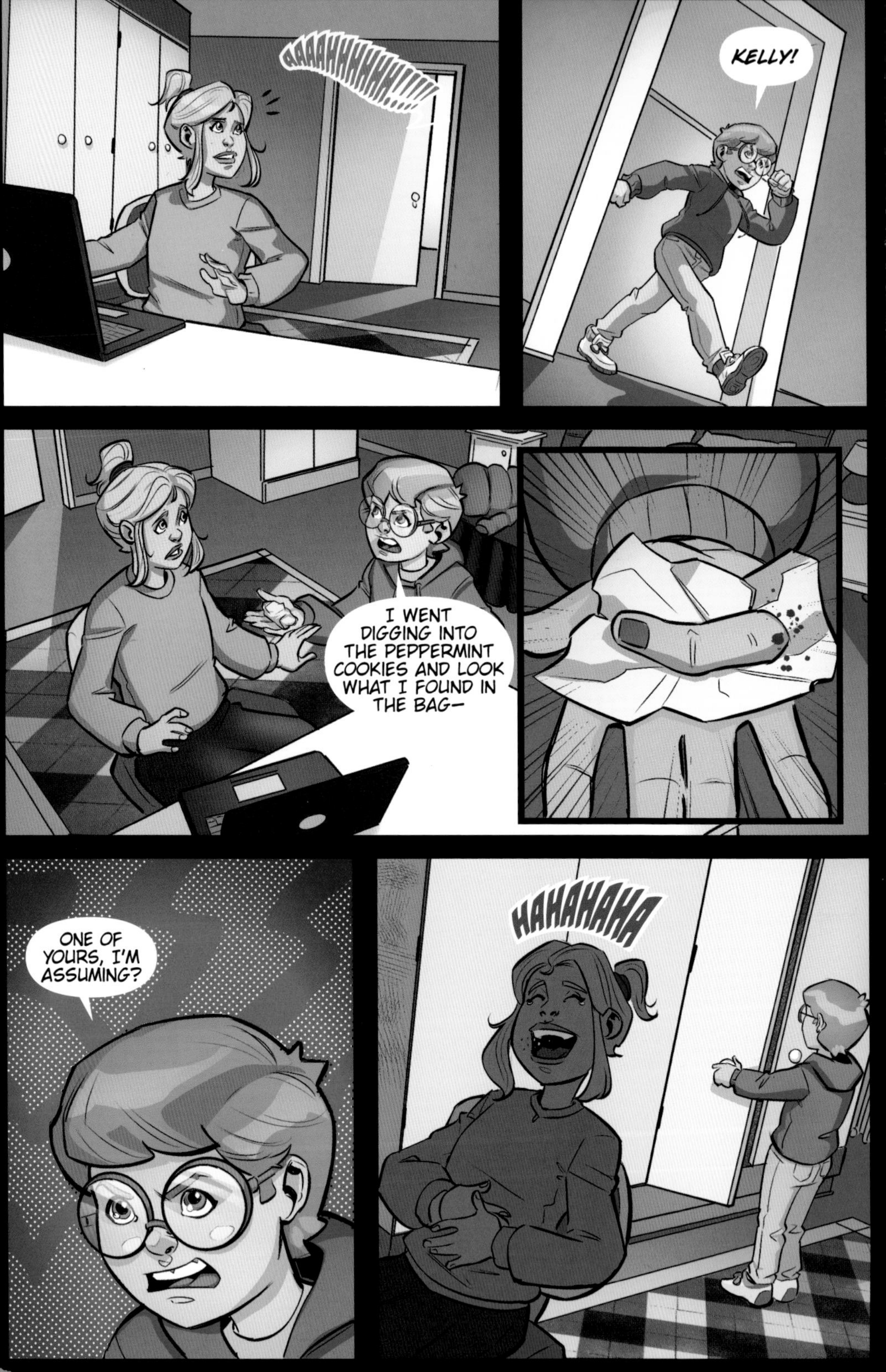
AAAAHHHHHH!!!!!!
KELLY!
I WENT DIGGING INTO THE PEPPERMINT COOKIES AND LOOK WHAT I FOUND IN THE BAG—
ONE OF YOURS, I'M ASSUMING?
HAHAHAHA

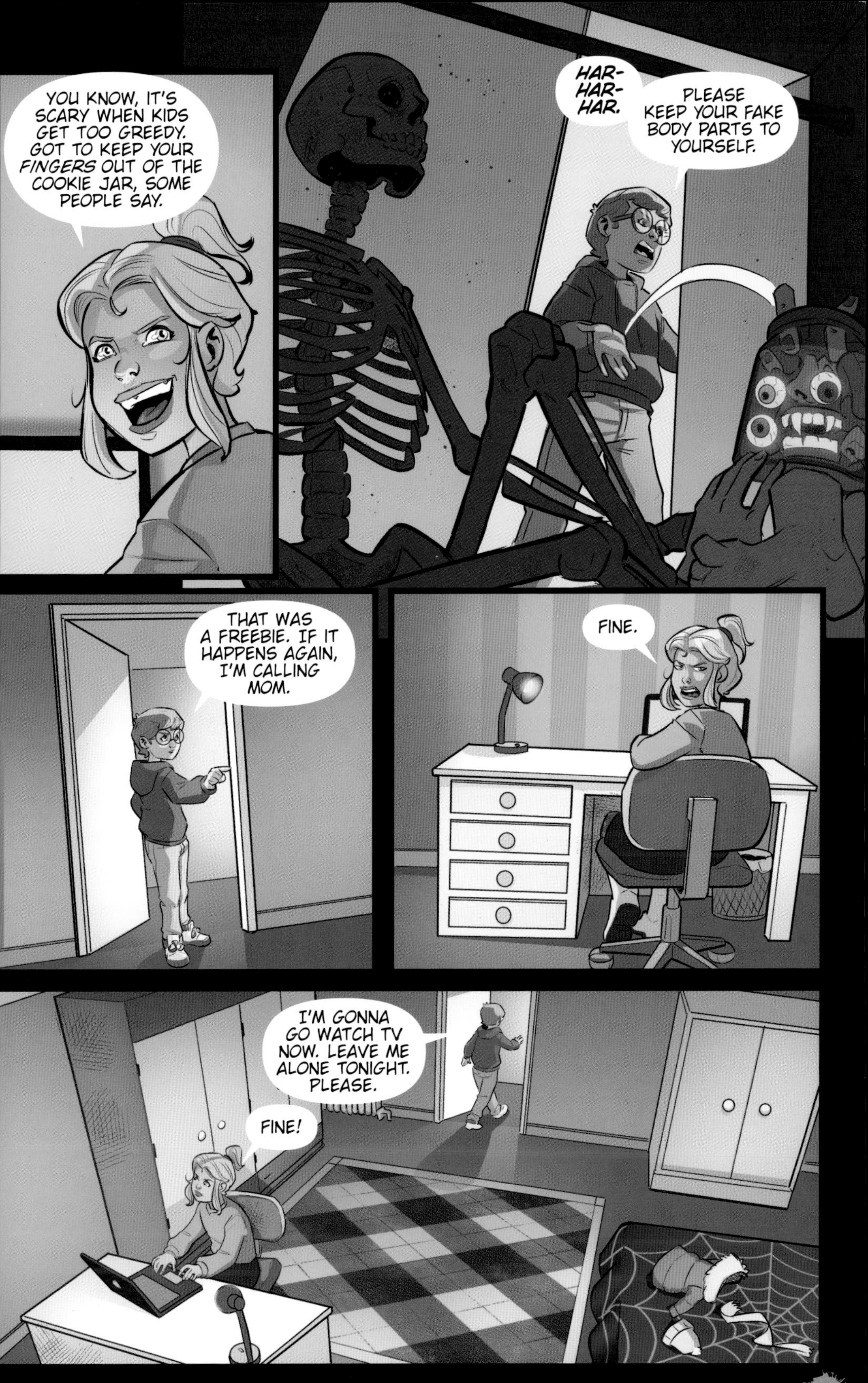
YOU KNOW, IT'S SCARY WHEN KIDS GET TOO GREEDY. GOT TO KEEP YOUR *FINGERS* OUT OF THE COOKIE JAR, SOME PEOPLE SAY.
HAR-HAR-HAR.
PLEASE KEEP YOUR FAKE BODY PARTS TO YOURSELF.
THAT WAS A FREEBIE. IF IT HAPPENS AGAIN, I'M CALLING MOM.
FINE.
I'M GONNA GO WATCH TV NOW. LEAVE ME ALONE TONIGHT. PLEASE.
FINE!

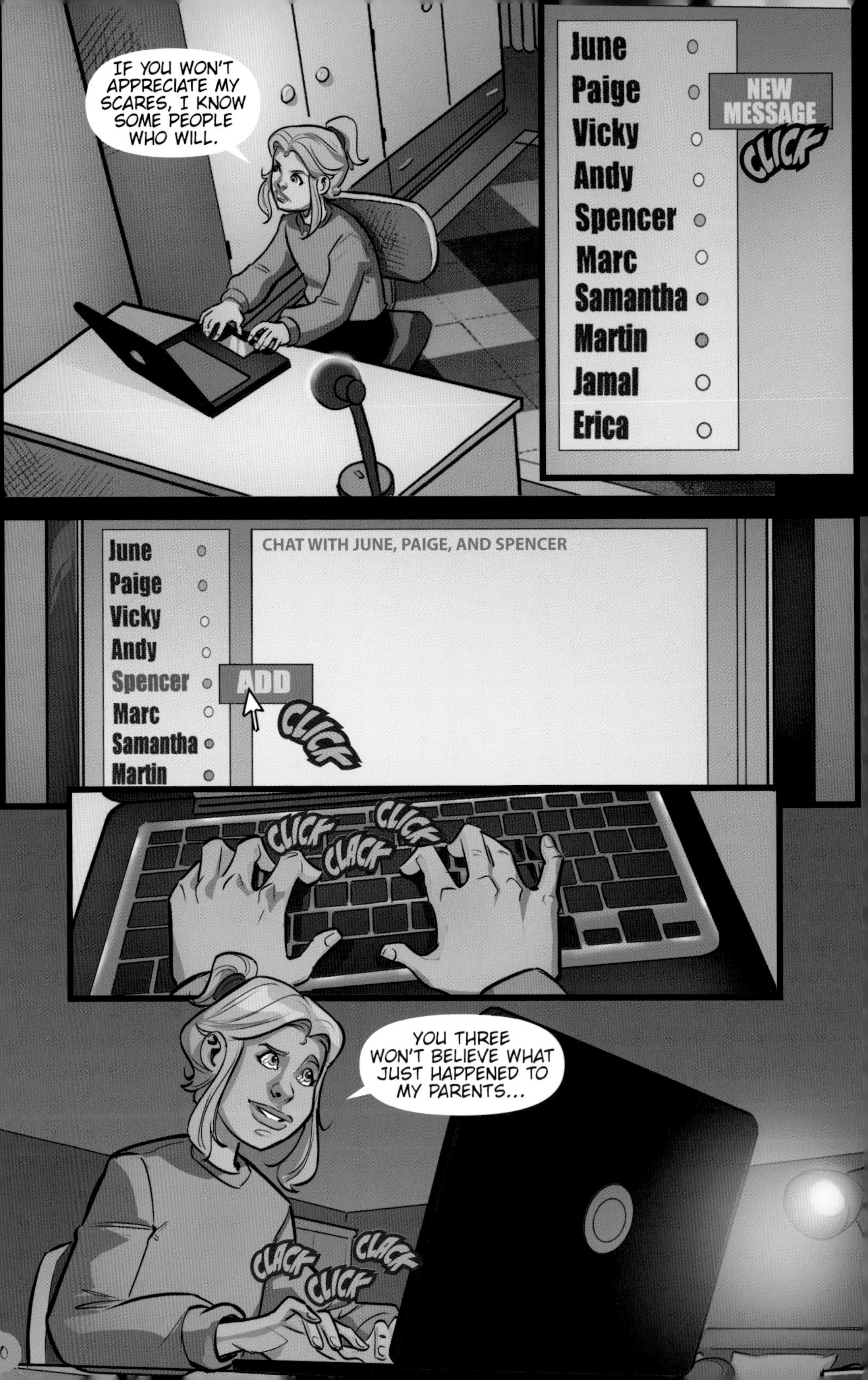
IF YOU WON'T APPRECIATE MY SCARES, I KNOW SOME PEOPLE WHO WILL.
June
Paige
Vicky
Andy
Spencer
Marc
Samantha
Martin
Jamal
Erica
NEW MESSAGE
CLICK
CHAT WITH JUNE, PAIGE, AND SPENCER
June
Paige
Vicky
Andy
Spencer
Marc
Samantha
Martin
ADD
CLICK
CLICK
CLACK
CLICK
YOU THREE WON'T BELIEVE WHAT JUST HAPPENED TO MY PARENTS...
CLACK
CLICK
CLACK

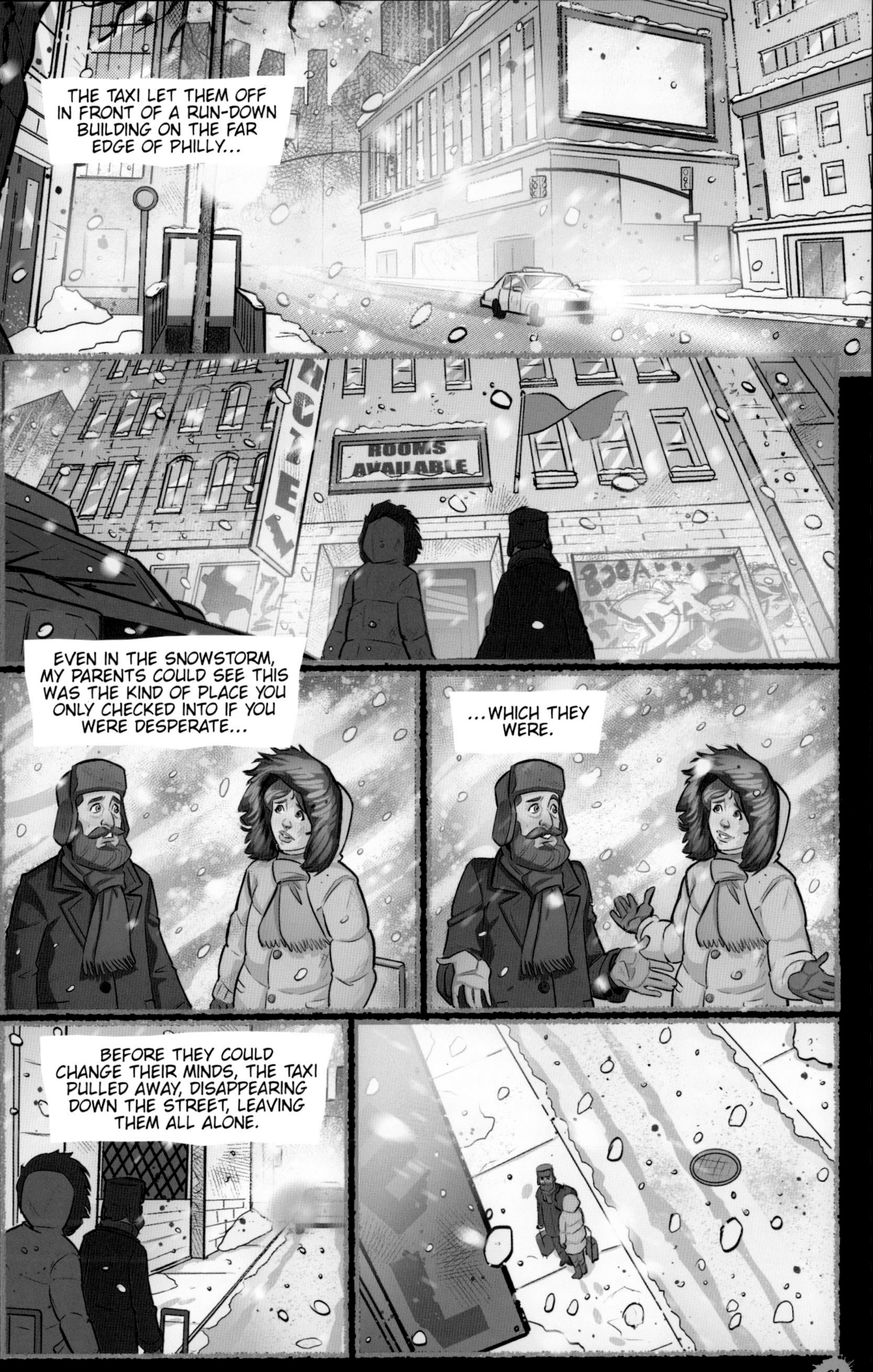
THE TAXI LET THEM OFF IN FRONT OF A RUN-DOWN BUILDING ON THE FAR EDGE OF PHILLY...
ROOMS AVAILABLE
EVEN IN THE SNOWSTORM, MY PARENTS COULD SEE THIS WAS THE KIND OF PLACE YOU ONLY CHECKED INTO IF YOU WERE DESPERATE...
...WHICH THEY WERE.
BEFORE THEY COULD CHANGE THEIR MINDS, THE TAXI PULLED AWAY, DISAPPEARING DOWN THE STREET, LEAVING THEM ALL ALONE.

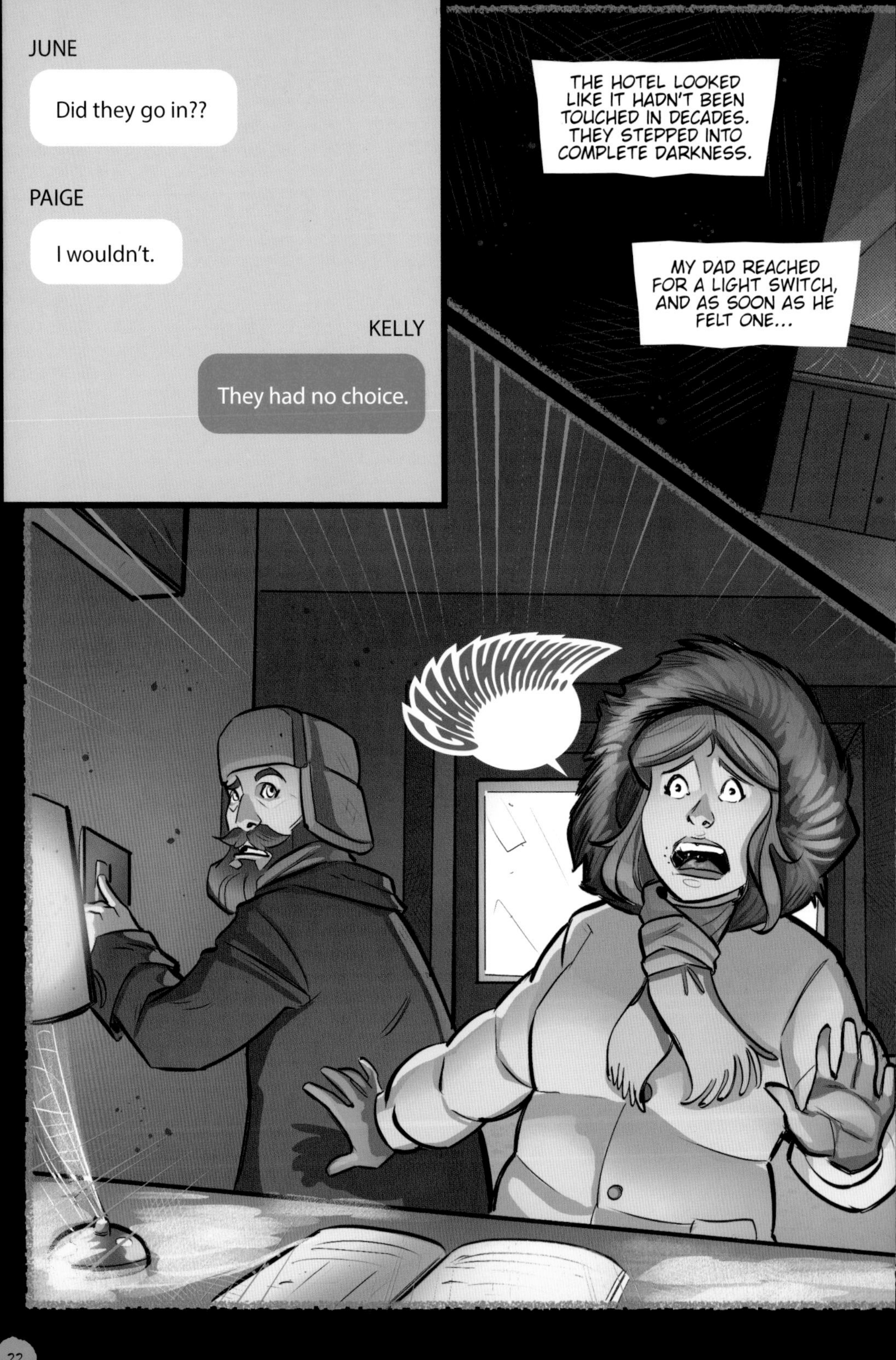
JUNE
Did they go in??
PAIGE
I wouldn't.
KELLY
They had no choice.
THE HOTEL LOOKED LIKE IT HADN'T BEEN TOUCHED IN DECADES. THEY STEPPED INTO COMPLETE DARKNESS.
MY DAD REACHED FOR A LIGHT SWITCH, AND AS SOON AS HE FELT ONE...

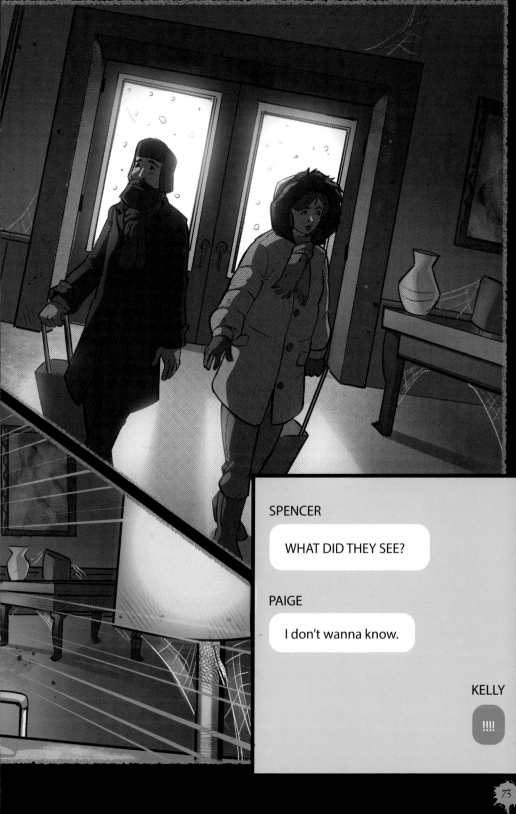

SPENCER

WHAT DID THEY SEE?

PAIGE

I don't wanna know.

KELLY

!!!!

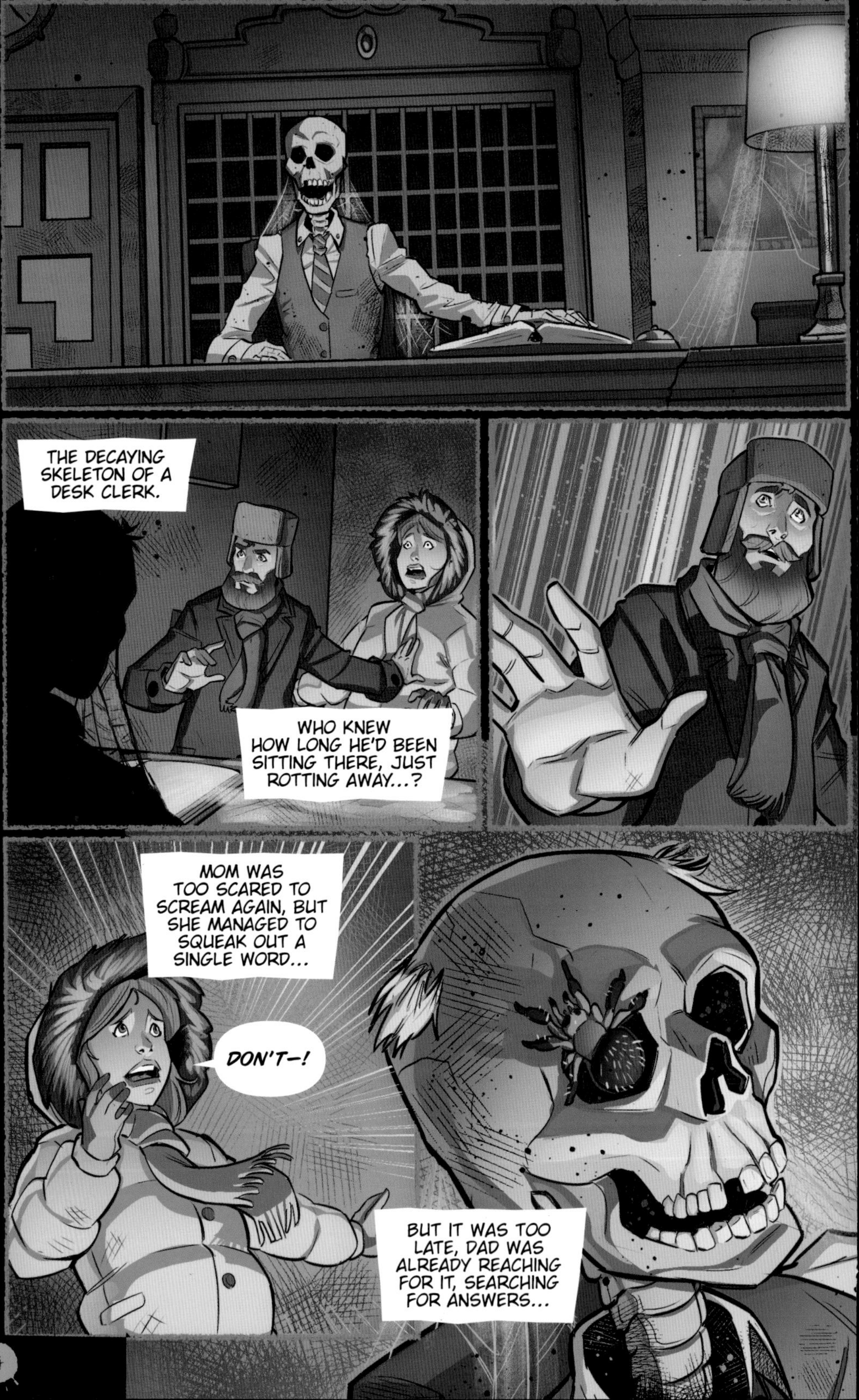
THE DECAYING SKELETON OF A DESK CLERK.
WHO KNEW HOW LONG HE'D BEEN SITTING THERE, JUST ROTTING AWAY...?
MOM WAS TOO SCARED TO SCREAM AGAIN, BUT SHE MANAGED TO SQUEAK OUT A SINGLE WORD...
DON'T-!
BUT IT WAS TOO LATE, DAD WAS ALREADY REACHING FOR IT, SEARCHING FOR ANSWERS...

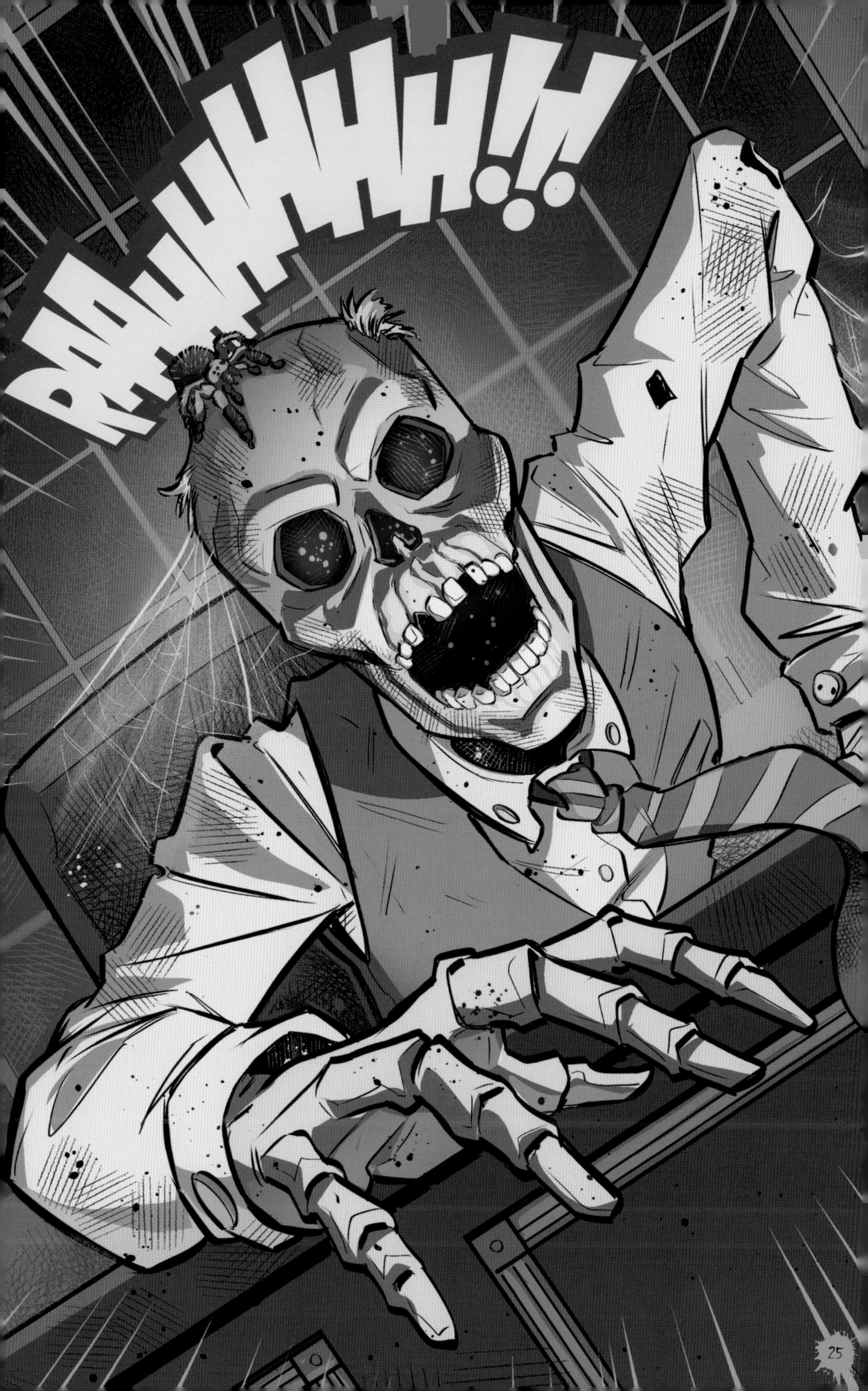

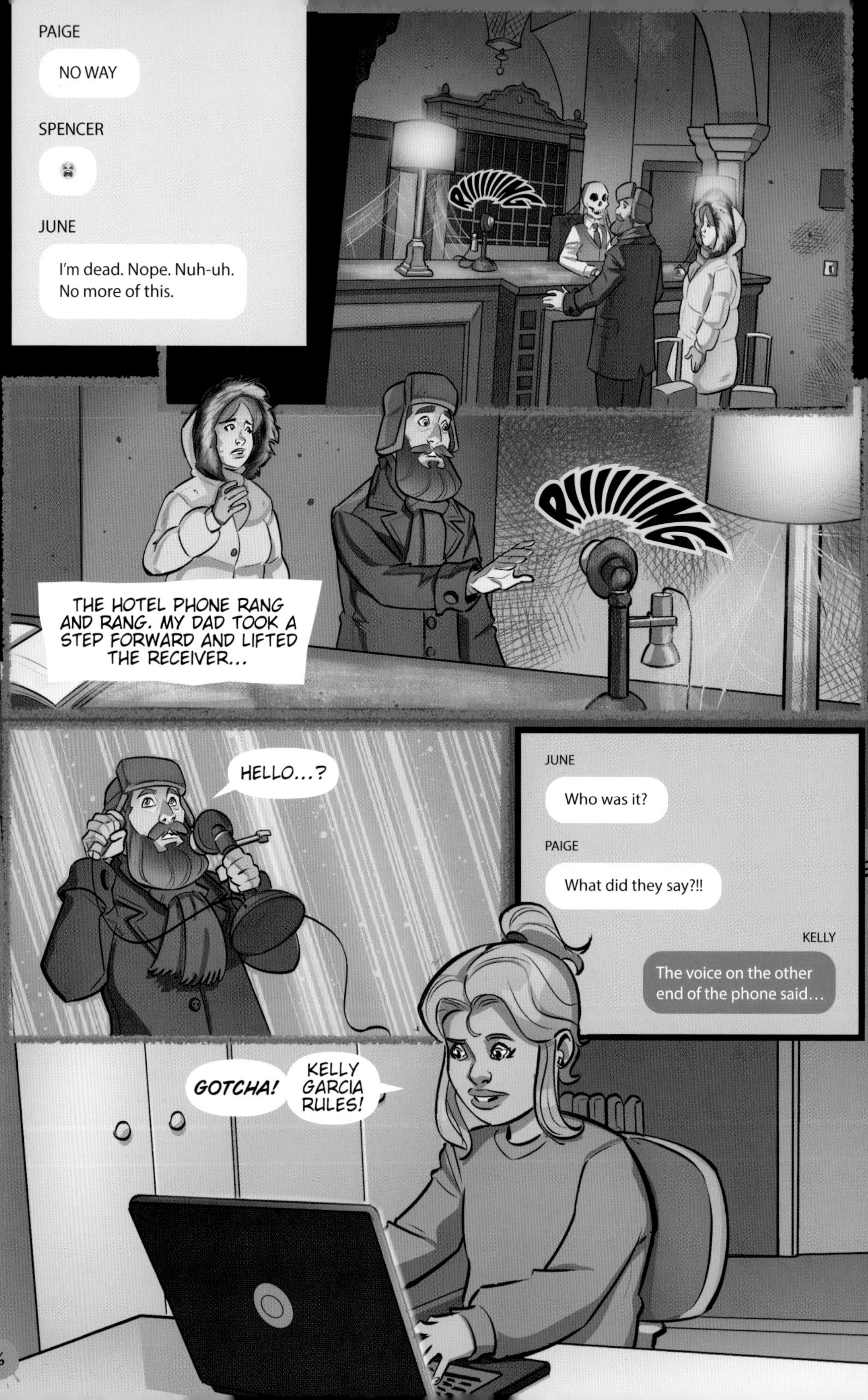
PAIGE
NO WAY
SPENCER
JUNE
I'm dead. Nope. Nuh-uh. No more of this.
RIIIING
RIIIING
THE HOTEL PHONE RANG AND RANG. MY DAD TOOK A STEP FORWARD AND LIFTED THE RECEIVER...
HELLO...?
JUNE
Who was it?
PAIGE
What did they say?!!
KELLY
The voice on the other end of the phone said...
GOTCHA!
KELLY GARCIA RULES!

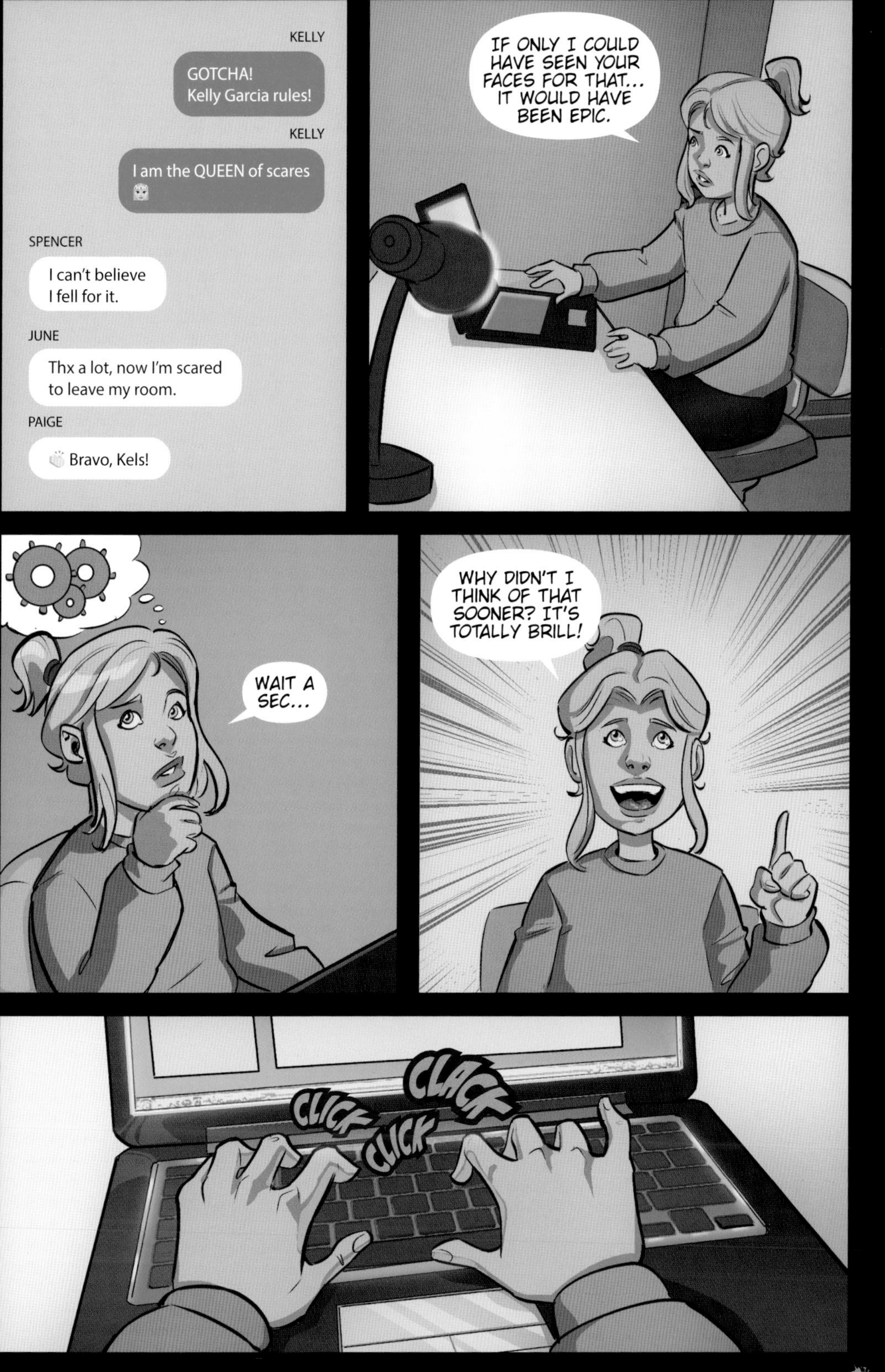
KELLY
GOTCHA! Kelly Garcia rules!
KELLY
I am the QUEEN of scares
SPENCER
I can't believe I fell for it.
JUNE
Thx a lot, now I'm scared to leave my room.
PAIGE
Bravo, Kels!
IF ONLY I COULD HAVE SEEN YOUR FACES FOR THAT... IT WOULD HAVE BEEN EPIC.
WAIT A SEC...
WHY DIDN'T I THINK OF THAT SOONER? IT'S TOTALLY BRILL!
CLICK
CLACK
CLICK

Let's have a VIRTUAL SLEEPOVER tonight! All of us.

PAIGE

How's that gonna work?

KELLY

Just like we did for classes at home! Go to your CAMERA TIME app, put on your camera, and then we can all see each other and hang out all night, like we would if we were together. Spencer can come too since it'll be virtual!

SPENCER

Woohoo!

KELLY

8 o'clock. Wear pj's.

PAIGE

Love this!

JUNE

C u then!

KELLY

Before then, I have to warn u about something…

PAIGE

Oh great, now what?

KELLY

It's SERIOUS!

SPENCER

Spit it out!

KELLY

Get ready to be SCARED! VERY SCARED!

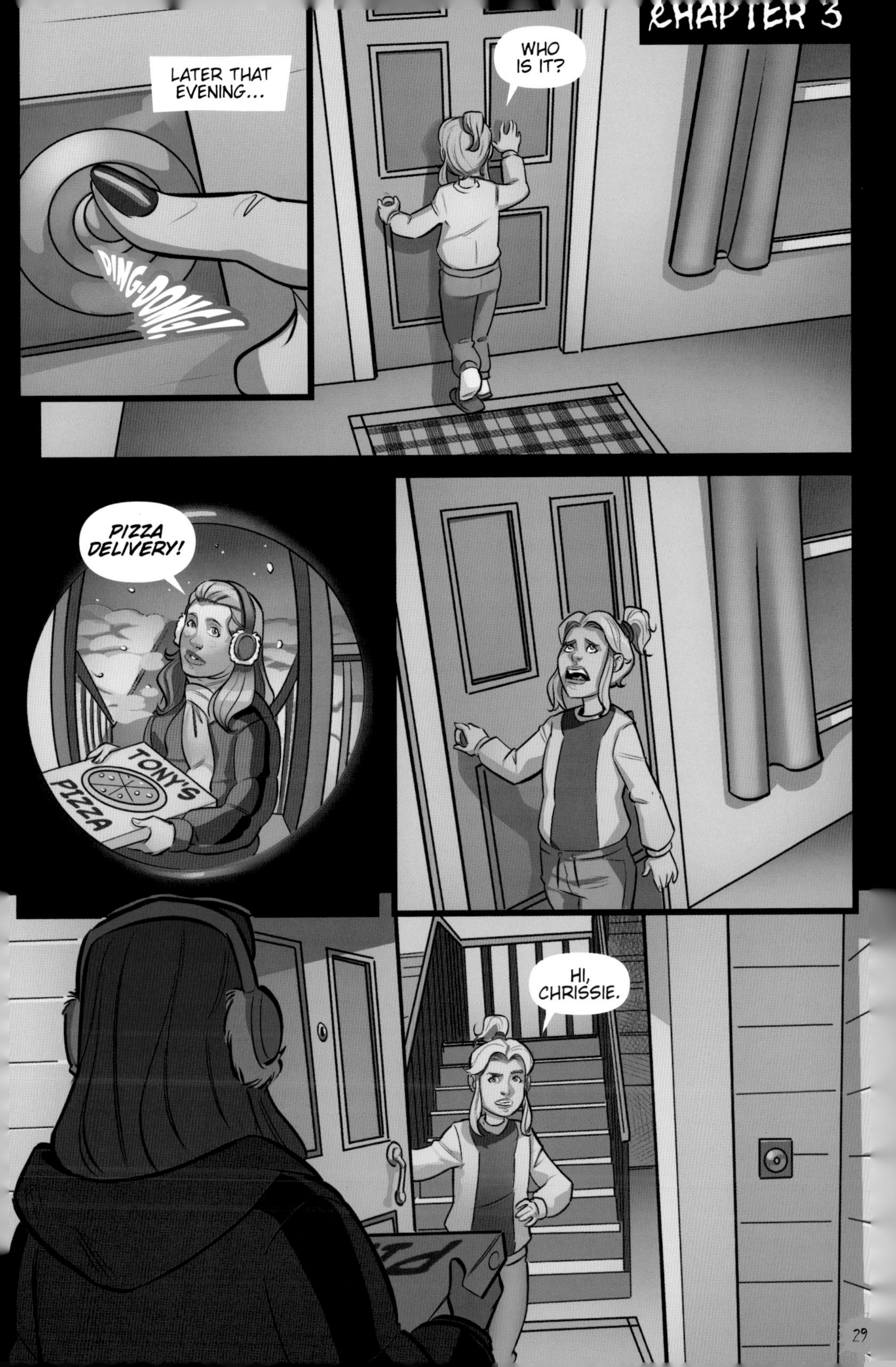
CHAPTER 3
LATER THAT EVENING...
DING-DONG!
WHO IS IT?
PIZZA DELIVERY!
TONY'S PIZZA
HI, CHRISSIE.

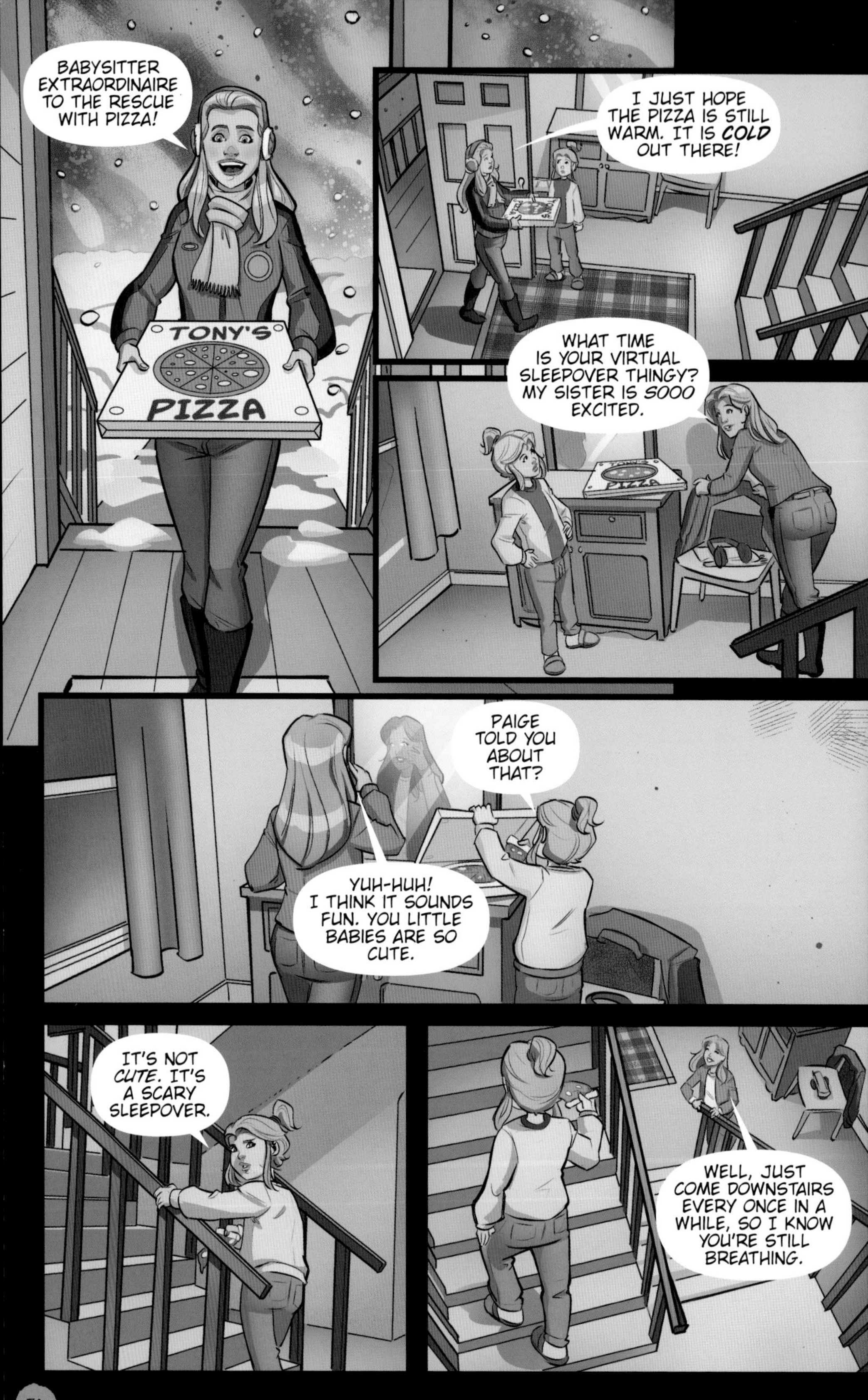
BABYSITTER EXTRAORDINAIRE TO THE RESCUE WITH PIZZA!
TONY'S PIZZA
I JUST HOPE THE PIZZA IS STILL WARM. IT IS ***COLD*** OUT THERE!
WHAT TIME IS YOUR VIRTUAL SLEEPOVER THINGY? MY SISTER IS *SOOO* EXCITED.
PAIGE TOLD YOU ABOUT THAT?
YUH-HUH! I THINK IT SOUNDS FUN. YOU LITTLE BABIES ARE SO CUTE.
IT'S NOT *CUTE*. IT'S A SCARY SLEEPOVER.
WELL, JUST COME DOWNSTAIRS EVERY ONCE IN A WHILE, SO I KNOW YOU'RE STILL BREATHING.

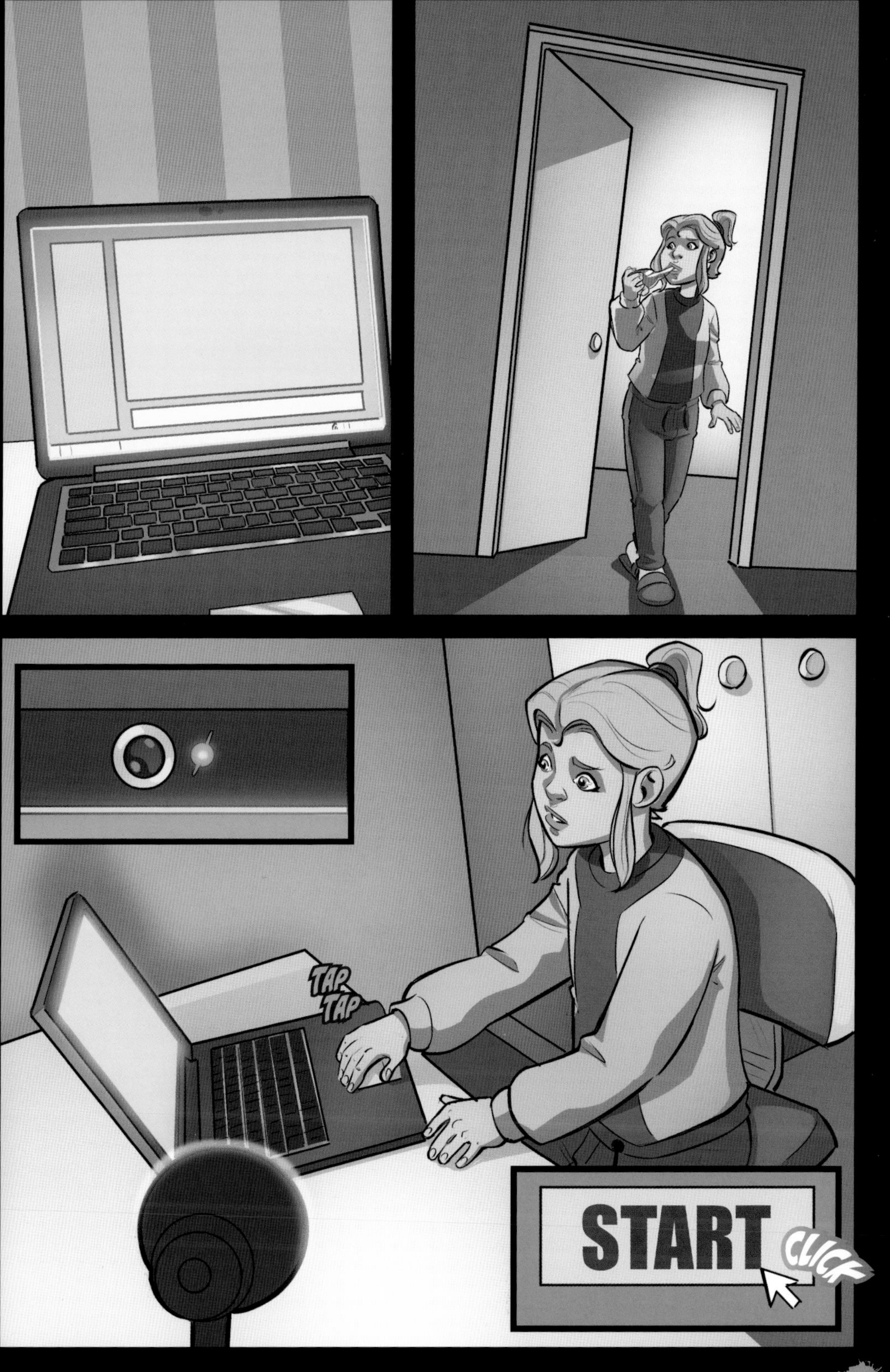
TAP
TAP
START
CLICK

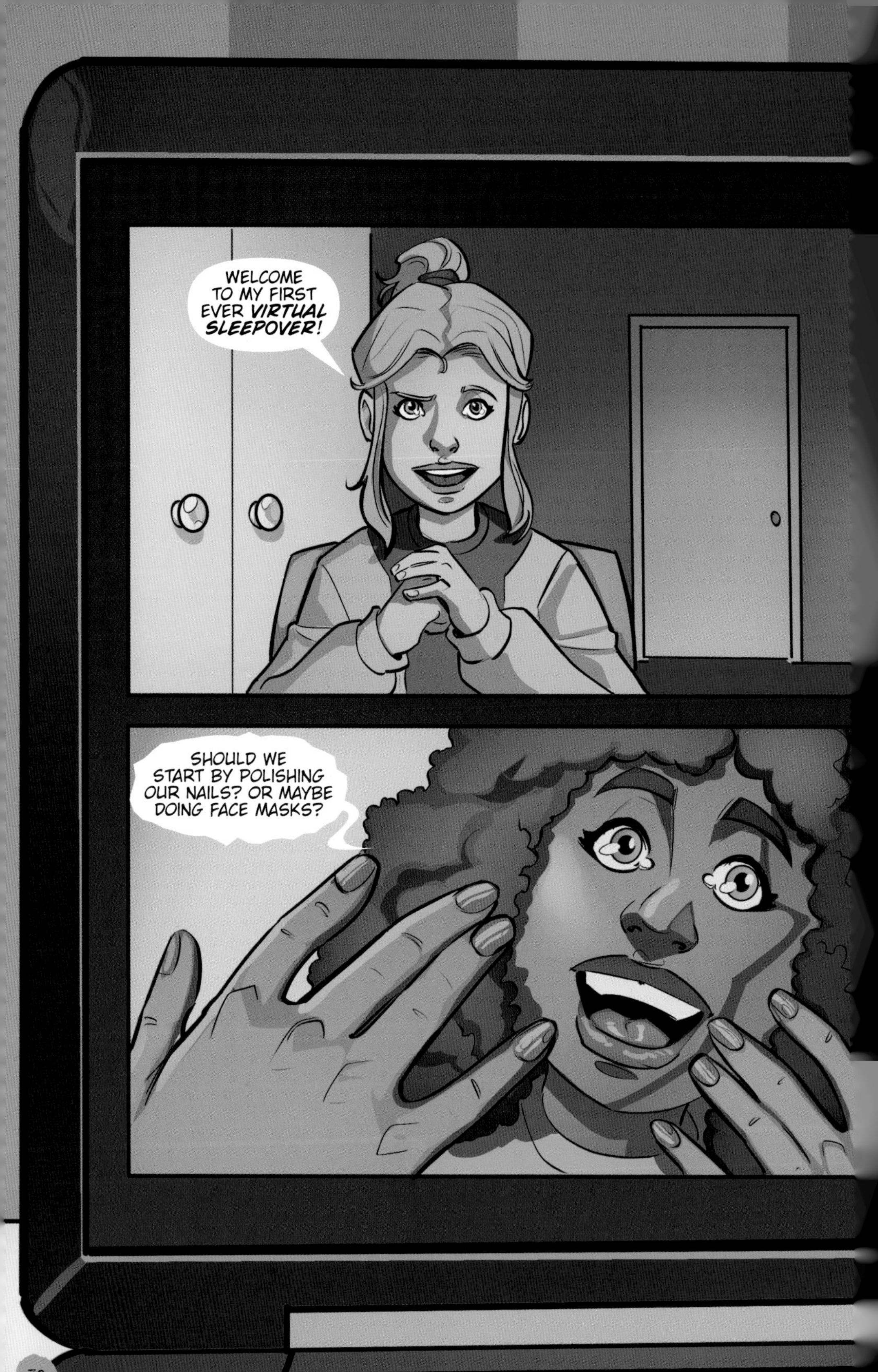
WELCOME TO MY FIRST EVER VIRTUAL SLEEPOVER!
SHOULD WE START BY POLISHING OUR NAILS? OR MAYBE DOING FACE MASKS?

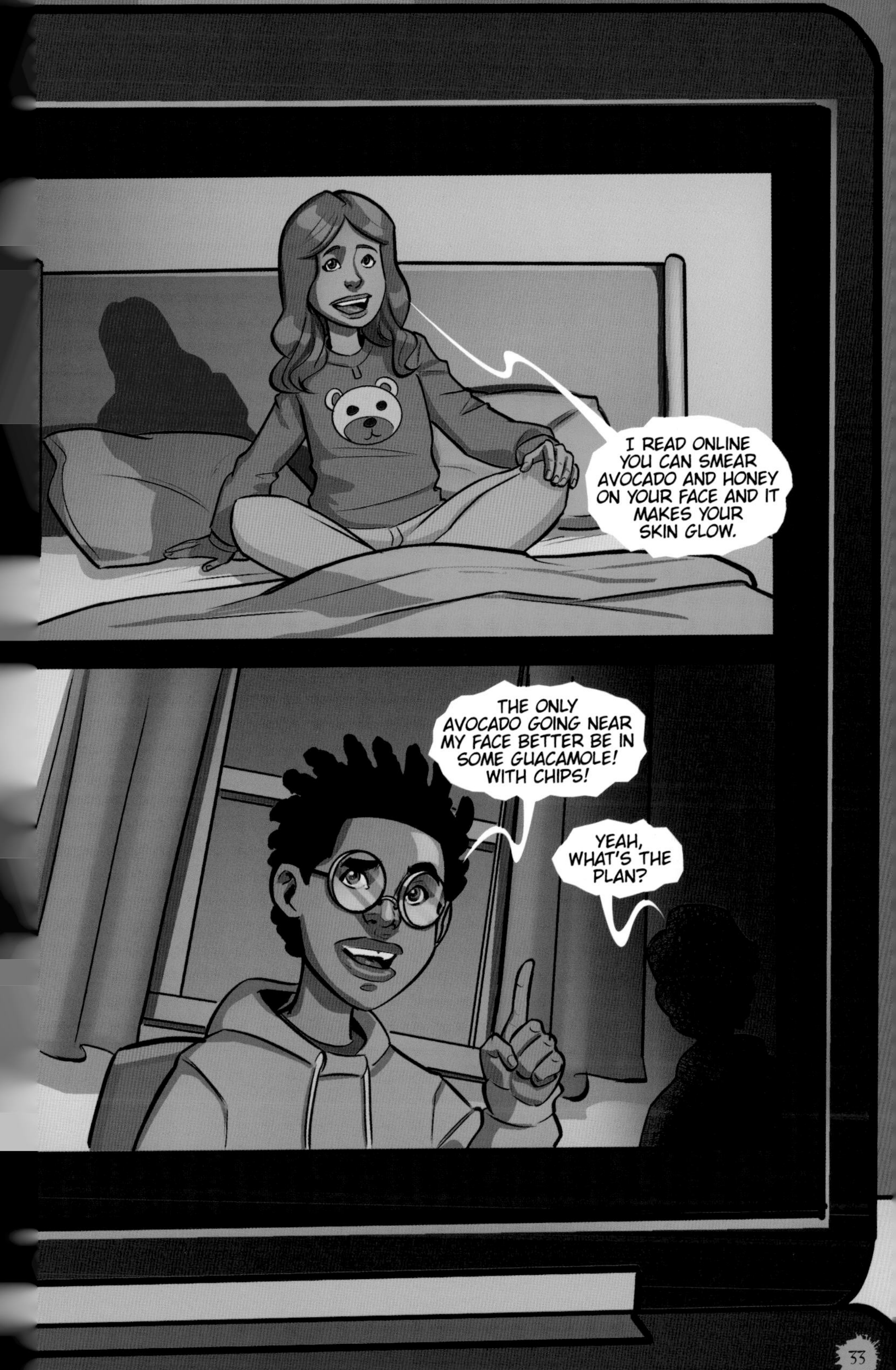
I READ ONLINE YOU CAN SMEAR AVOCADO AND HONEY ON YOUR FACE AND IT MAKES YOUR SKIN GLOW.
THE ONLY AVOCADO GOING NEAR MY FACE BETTER BE IN SOME GUACAMOLE! WITH CHIPS!
YEAH, WHAT'S THE PLAN?

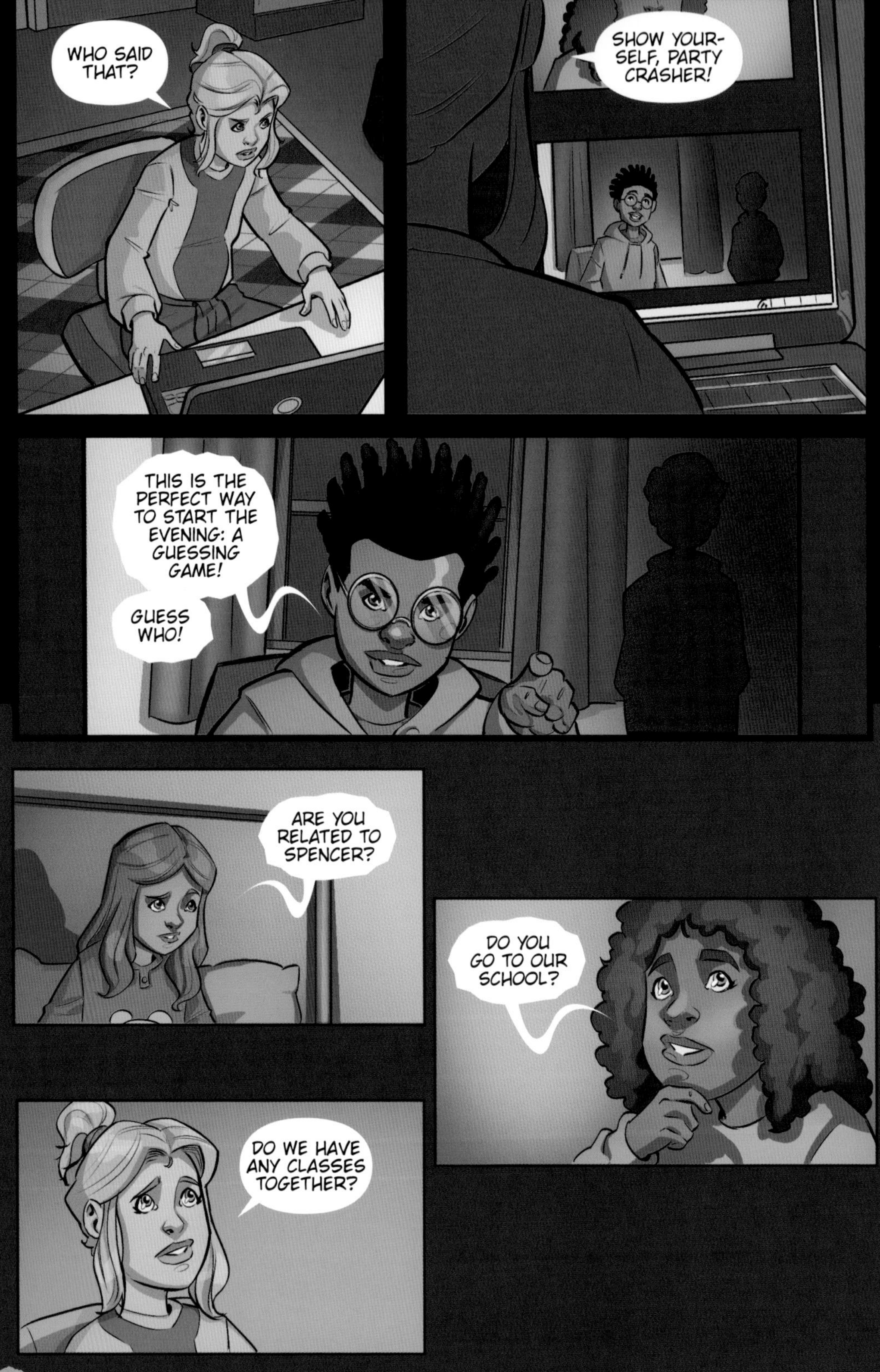
WHO SAID THAT?
SHOW YOURSELF, PARTY CRASHER!
THIS IS THE PERFECT WAY TO START THE EVENING: A GUESSING GAME!
GUESS WHO!
ARE YOU RELATED TO SPENCER?
DO YOU GO TO OUR SCHOOL?
DO WE HAVE ANY CLASSES TOGETHER?

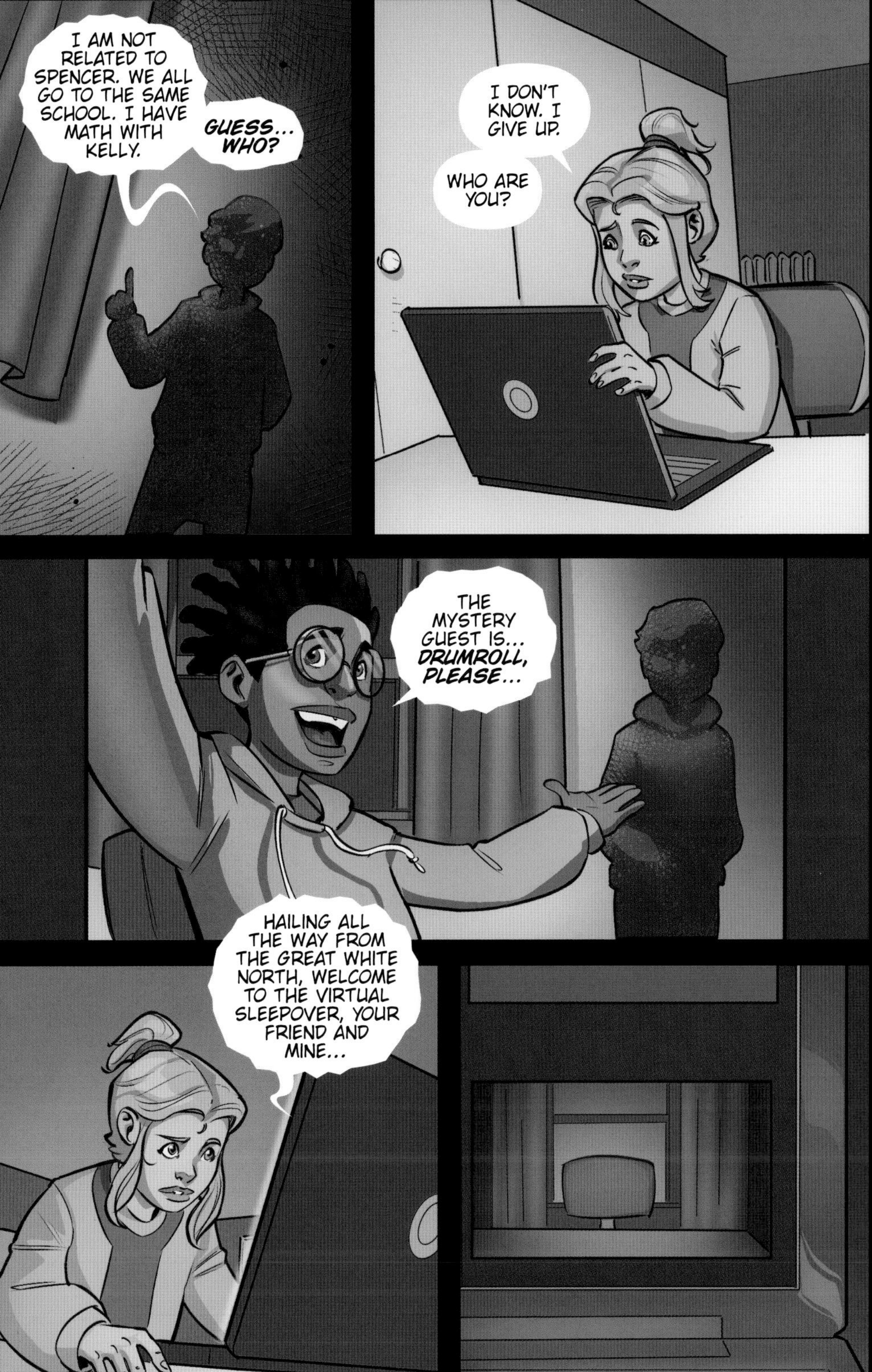
I AM NOT RELATED TO SPENCER. WE ALL GO TO THE SAME SCHOOL. I HAVE MATH WITH KELLY.
GUESS... WHO?
I DON'T KNOW. I GIVE UP.
WHO ARE YOU?
THE MYSTERY GUEST IS... DRUMROLL, PLEASE...
HAILING ALL THE WAY FROM THE GREAT WHITE NORTH, WELCOME TO THE VIRTUAL SLEEPOVER, YOUR FRIEND AND MINE...

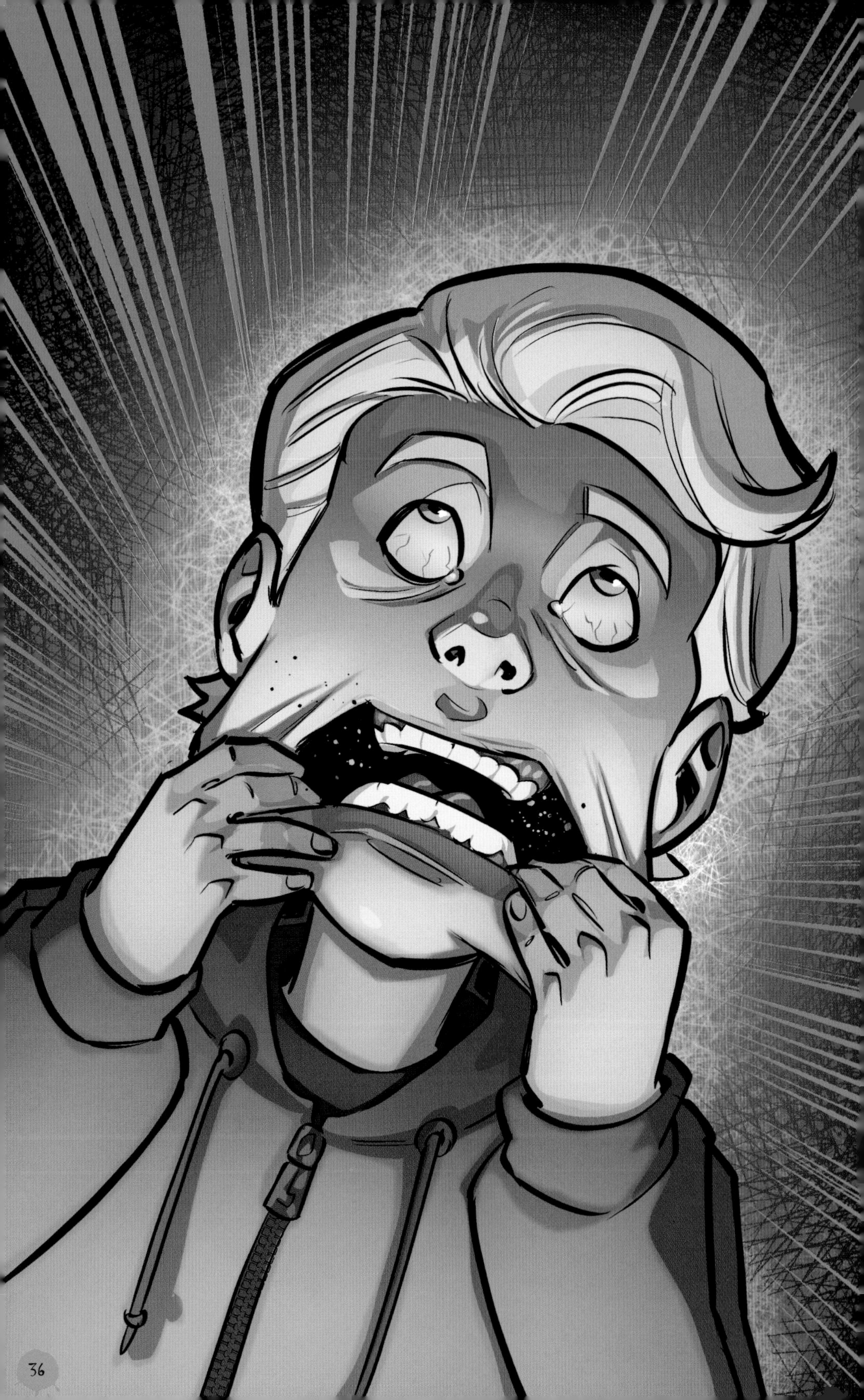

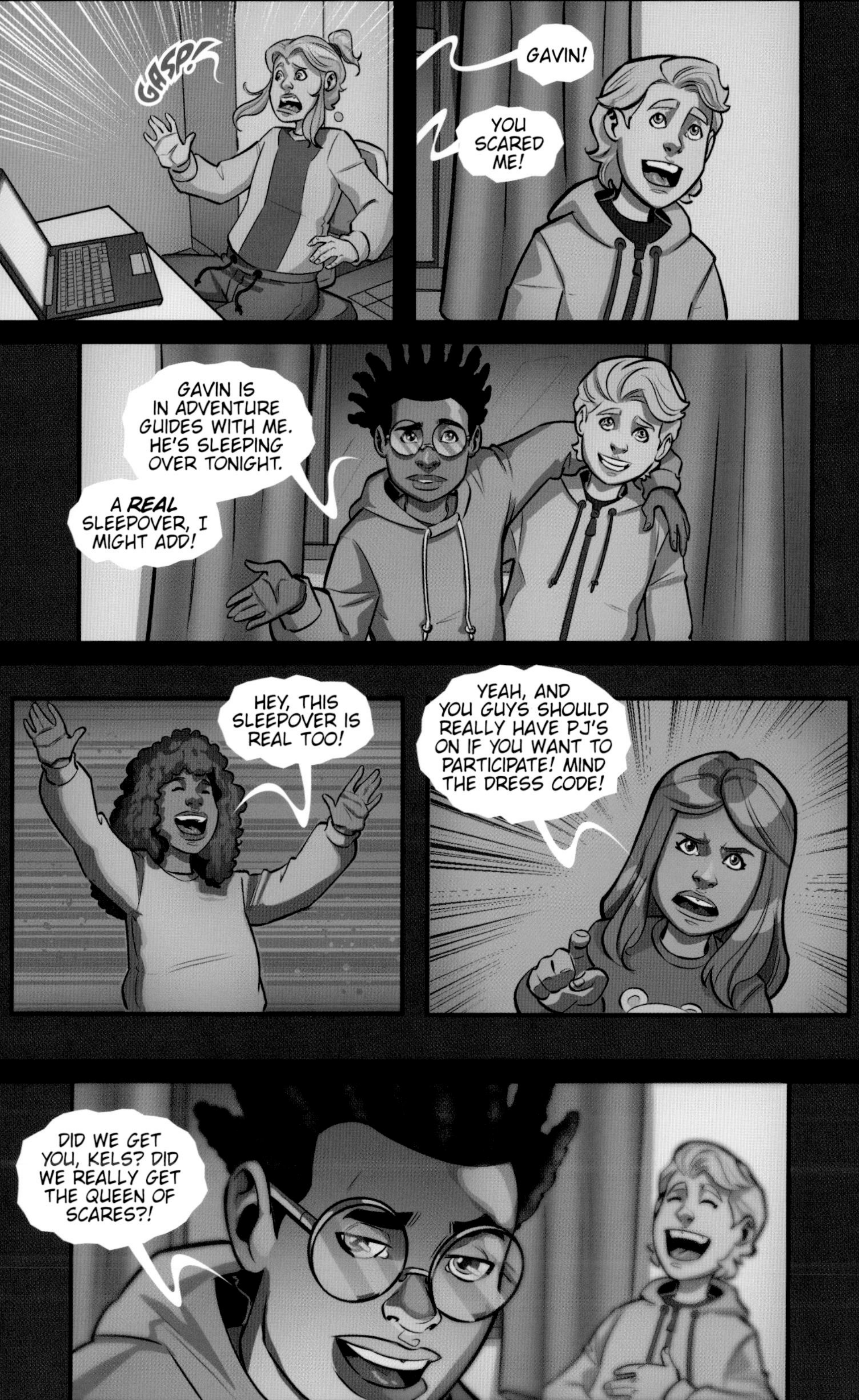
GASP!
GAVIN!
YOU SCARED ME!
GAVIN IS IN ADVENTURE GUIDES WITH ME. HE'S SLEEPING OVER TONIGHT.
A REAL SLEEPOVER, I MIGHT ADD!
HEY, THIS SLEEPOVER IS REAL TOO!
YEAH, AND YOU GUYS SHOULD REALLY HAVE PJ'S ON IF YOU WANT TO PARTICIPATE! MIND THE DRESS CODE!
DID WE GET YOU, KELS? DID WE REALLY GET THE QUEEN OF SCARES?!

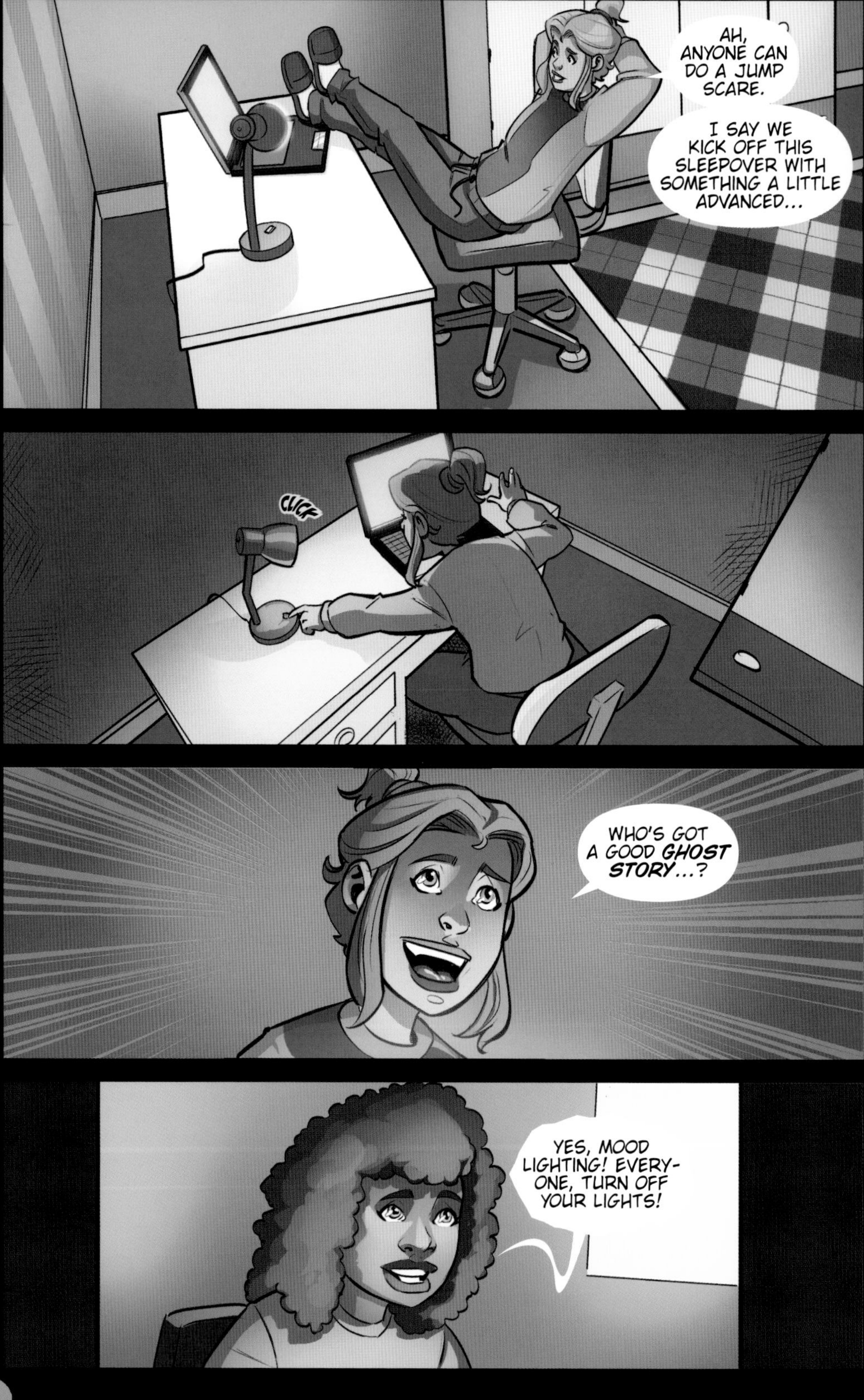
AH, ANYONE CAN DO A JUMP SCARE.
I SAY WE KICK OFF THIS SLEEPOVER WITH SOMETHING A LITTLE ADVANCED...
CLICK
WHO'S GOT A GOOD **GHOST STORY**...?
YES, MOOD LIGHTING! EVERY-ONE, TURN OFF YOUR LIGHTS!

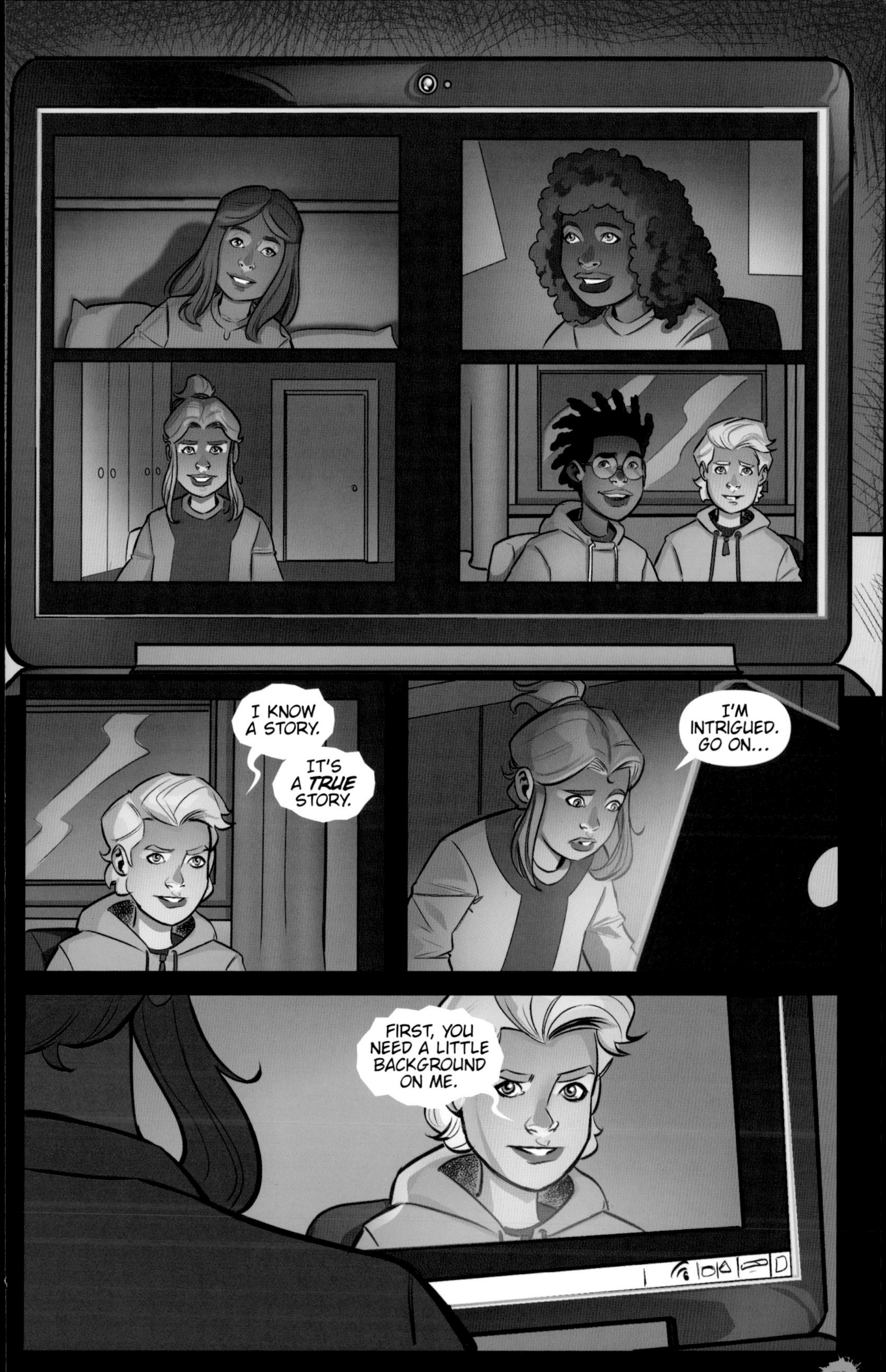
I KNOW A STORY.
IT'S A ***TRUE*** STORY.
I'M INTRIGUED. GO ON...
FIRST, YOU NEED A LITTLE BACKGROUND ON ME.

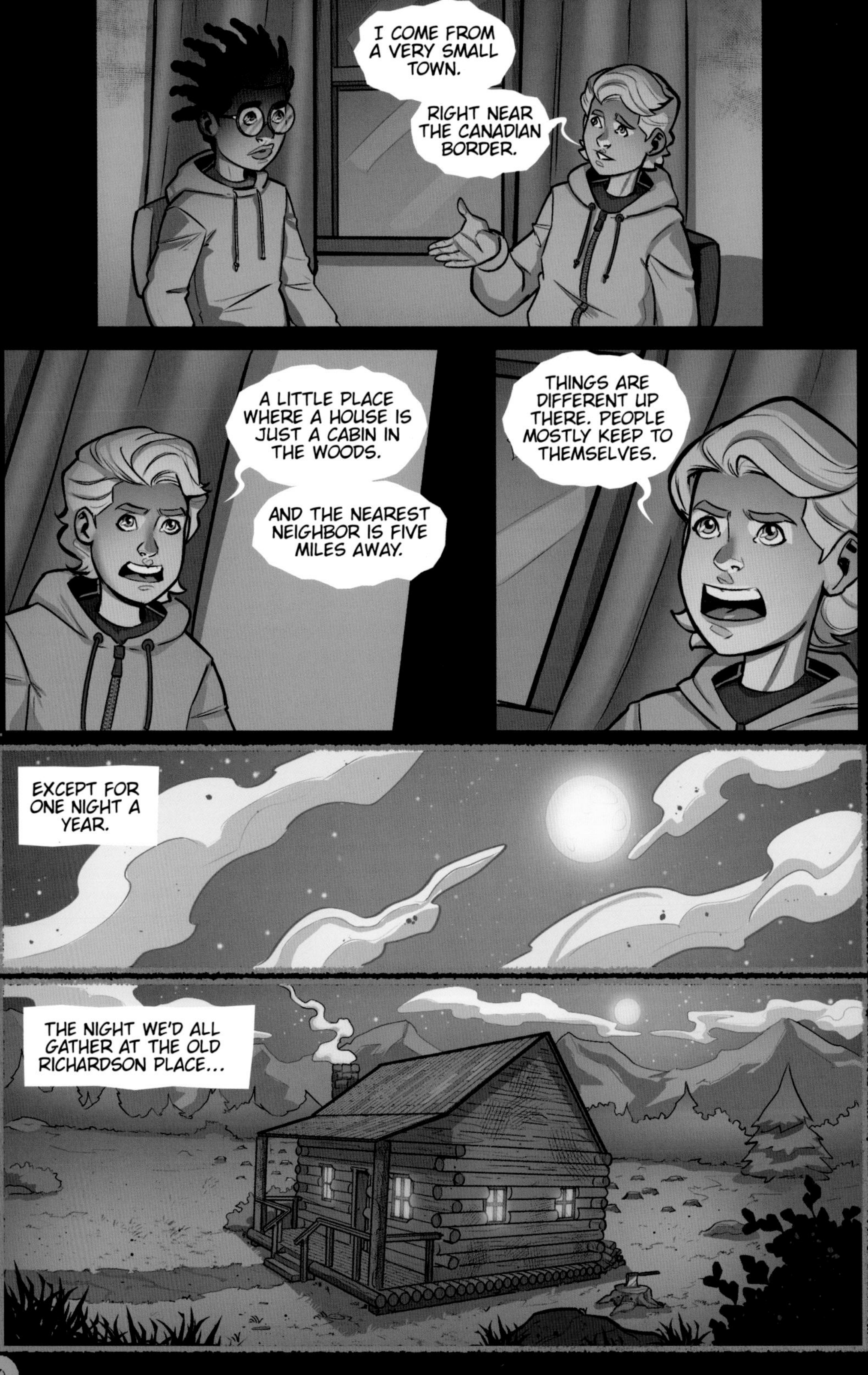
I COME FROM A VERY SMALL TOWN.
RIGHT NEAR THE CANADIAN BORDER.
A LITTLE PLACE WHERE A HOUSE IS JUST A CABIN IN THE WOODS.
AND THE NEAREST NEIGHBOR IS FIVE MILES AWAY.
THINGS ARE DIFFERENT UP THERE. PEOPLE MOSTLY KEEP TO THEMSELVES.
EXCEPT FOR ONE NIGHT A YEAR.
THE NIGHT WE'D ALL GATHER AT THE OLD RICHARDSON PLACE...

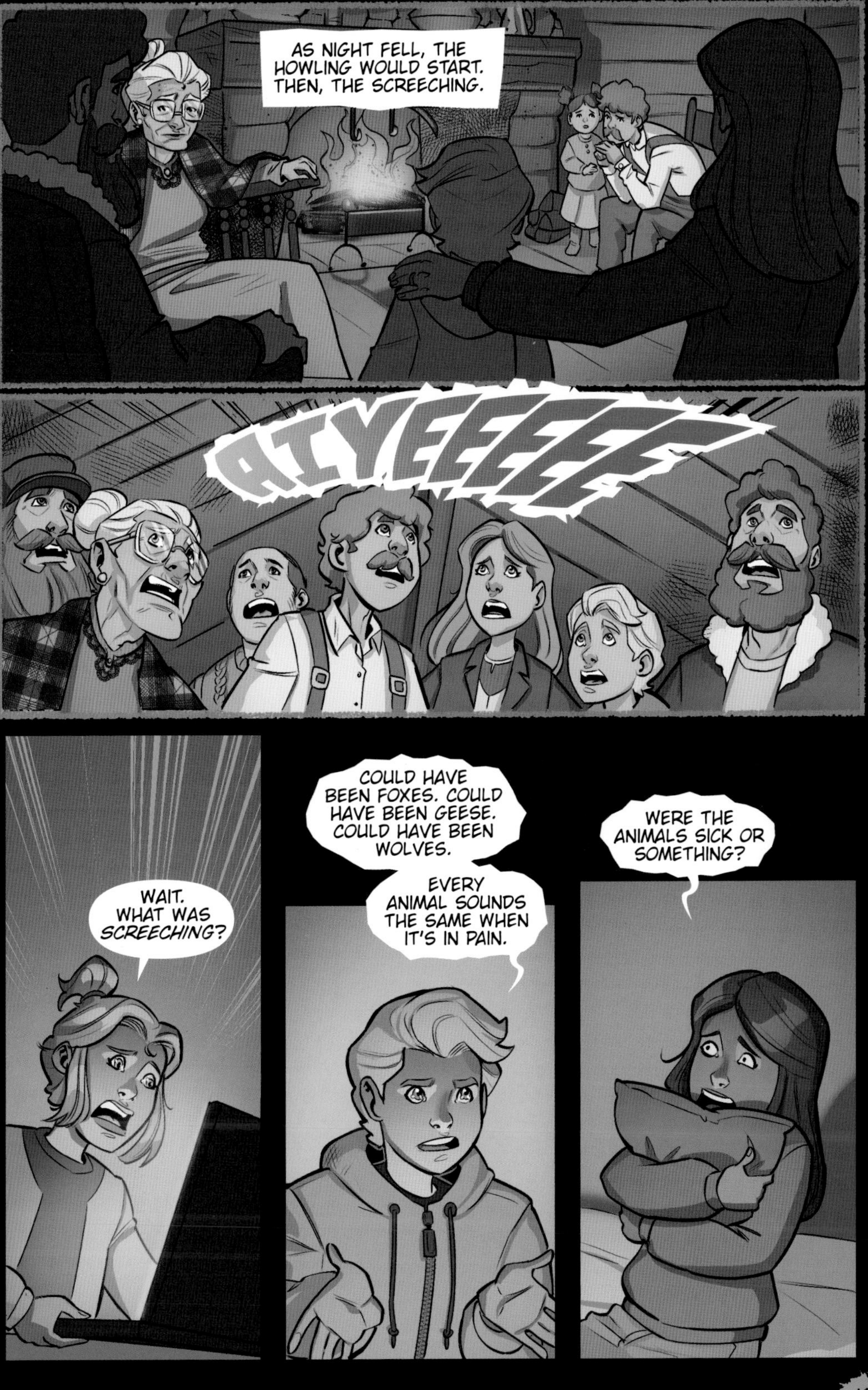
AS NIGHT FELL, THE HOWLING WOULD START. THEN, THE SCREECHING.
AIYEEEEE
WAIT. WHAT WAS SCREECHING?
COULD HAVE BEEN FOXES. COULD HAVE BEEN GEESE. COULD HAVE BEEN WOLVES.
EVERY ANIMAL SOUNDS THE SAME WHEN IT'S IN PAIN.
WERE THE ANIMALS SICK OR SOMETHING?

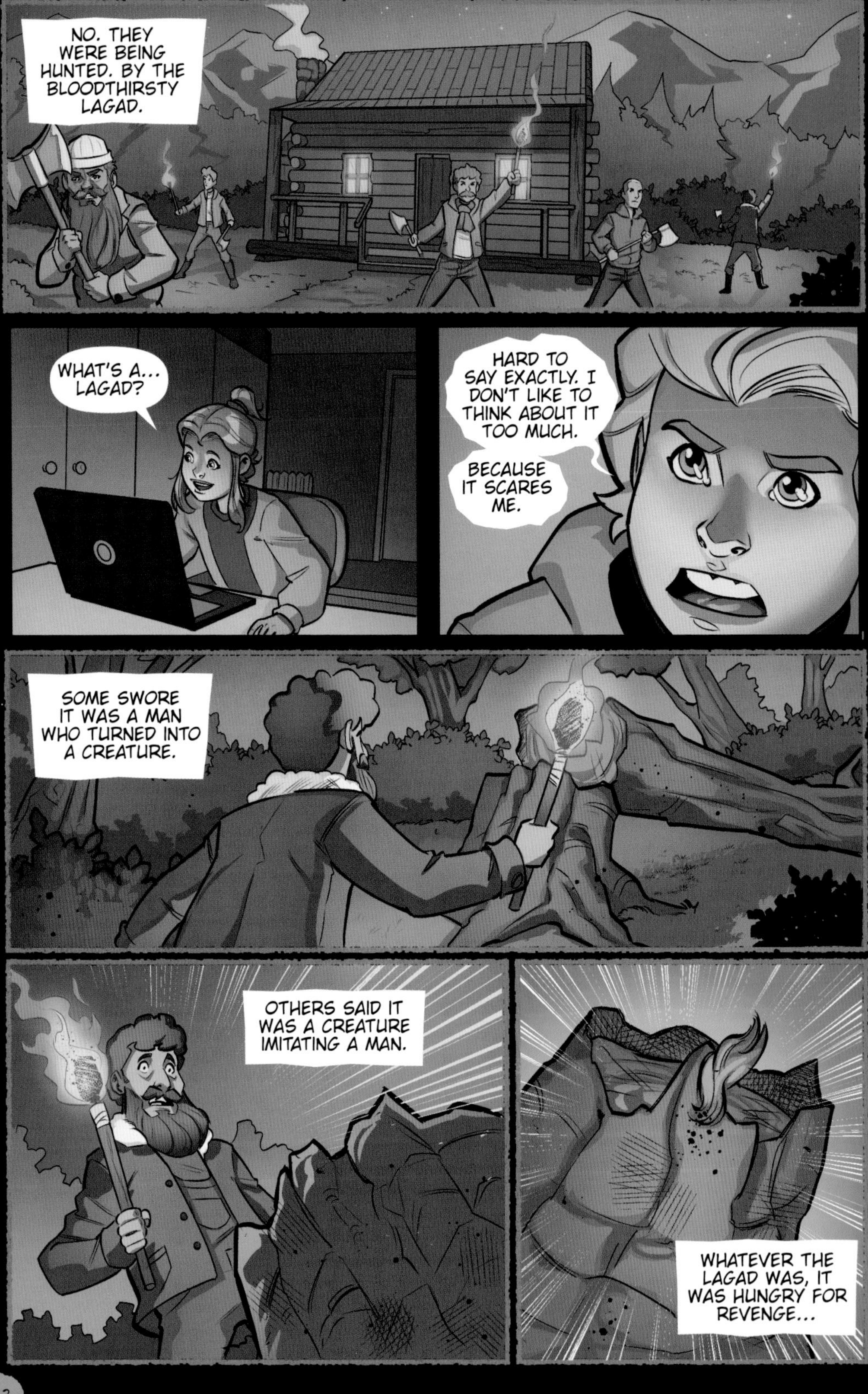
NO. THEY WERE BEING HUNTED. BY THE BLOODTHIRSTY LAGAD.
WHAT'S A... LAGAD?
HARD TO SAY EXACTLY. I DON'T LIKE TO THINK ABOUT IT TOO MUCH.
BECAUSE IT SCARES ME.
SOME SWORE IT WAS A MAN WHO TURNED INTO A CREATURE.
OTHERS SAID IT WAS A CREATURE IMITATING A MAN.
WHATEVER THE LAGAD WAS, IT WAS HUNGRY FOR REVENGE...

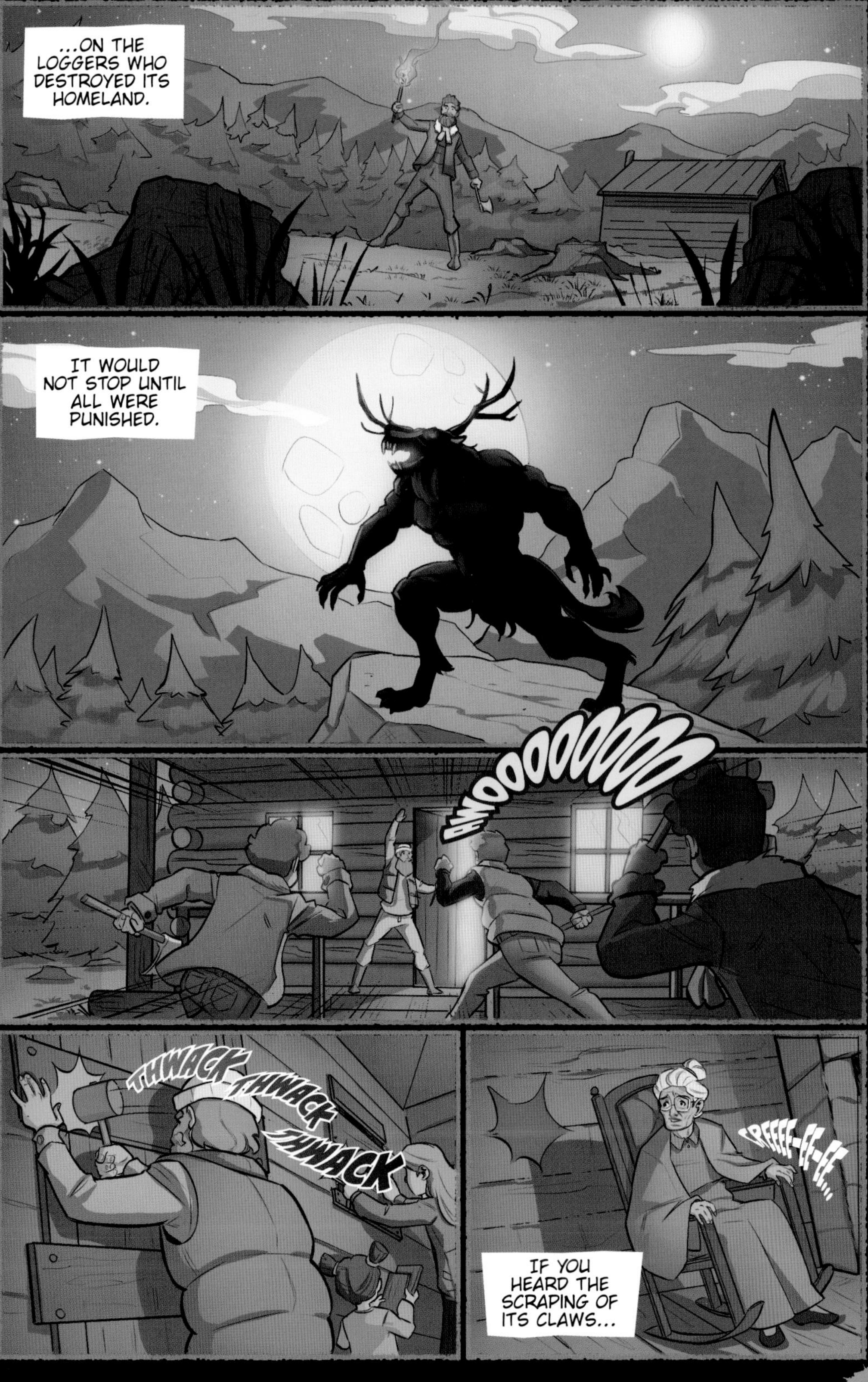
...ON THE LOGGERS WHO DESTROYED ITS HOMELAND.
IT WOULD NOT STOP UNTIL ALL WERE PUNISHED.
AWOOOOOOOO
THWACK
THWACK
THWACK
CREEEE-EE-EE...
IF YOU HEARD THE SCRAPING OF ITS CLAWS...

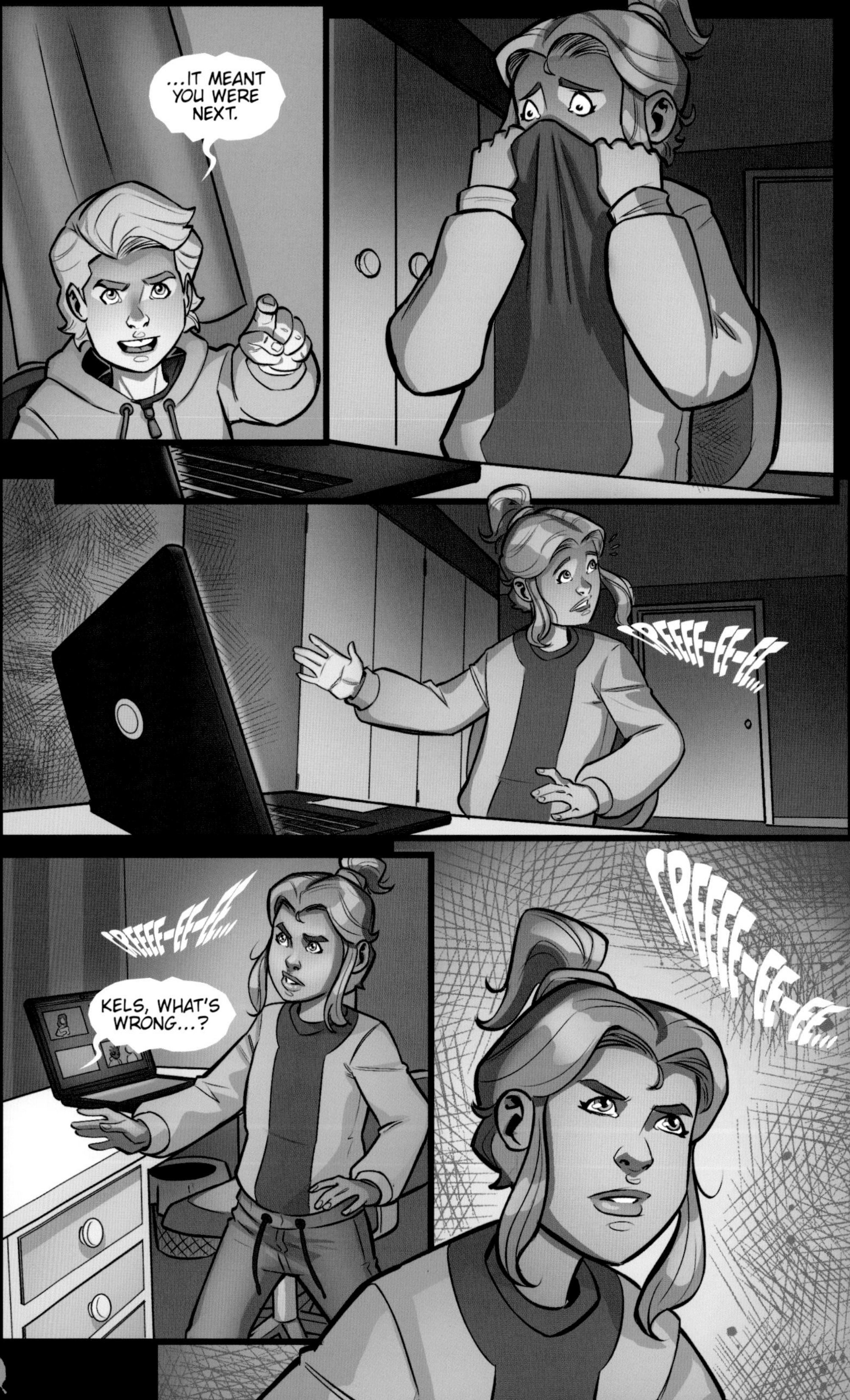
...IT MEANT YOU WERE NEXT.
CREEEE-EE-EE...
CREEEE-EE-EE...
KELS, WHAT'S WRONG...?
CREEEE-EE-EE...

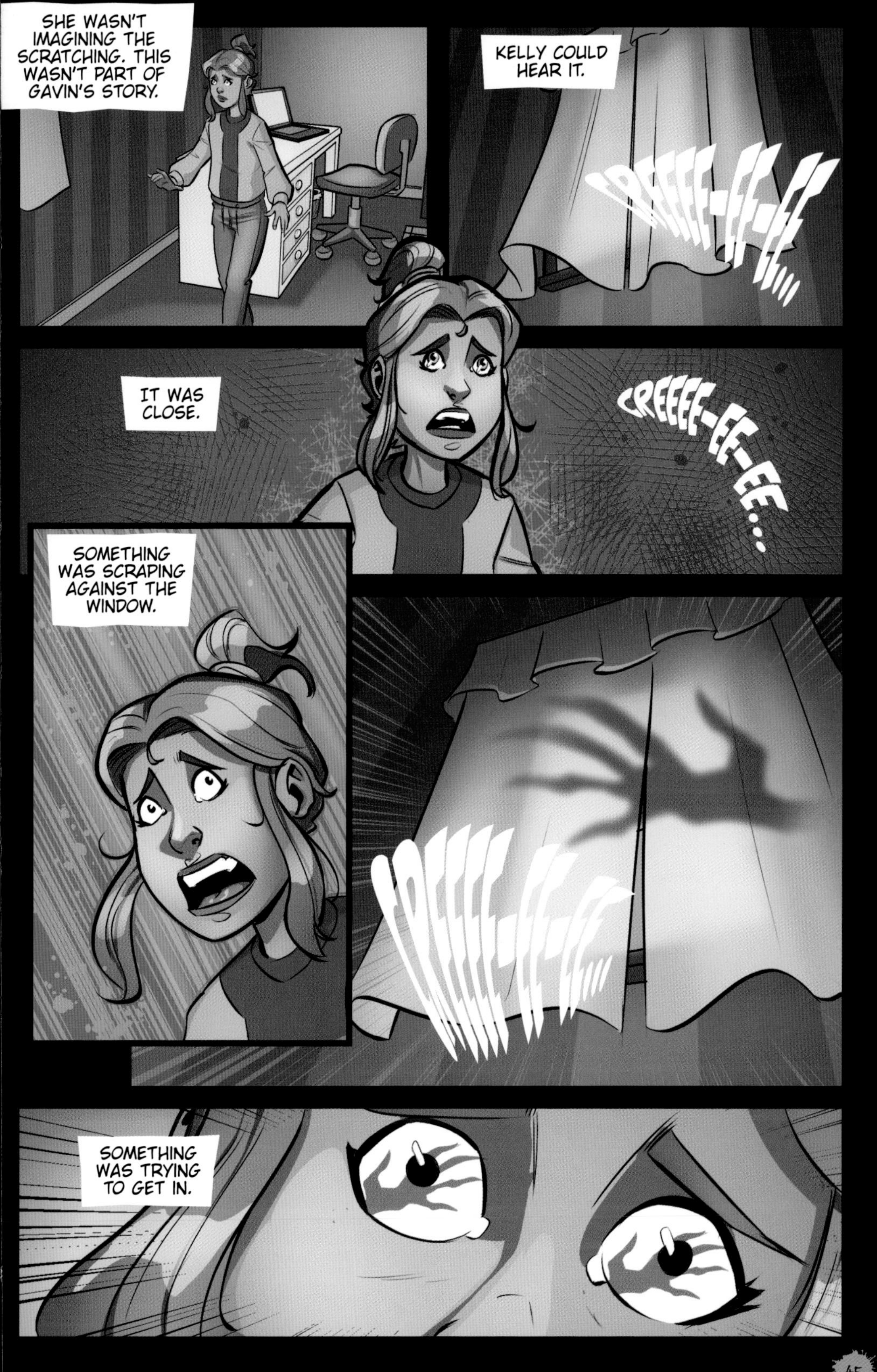
SHE WASN'T IMAGINING THE SCRATCHING. THIS WASN'T PART OF GAVIN'S STORY.
KELLY COULD HEAR IT.
CREEEE-EE-EE...
IT WAS CLOSE.
CREEEE-EE-EE...
SOMETHING WAS SCRAPING AGAINST THE WINDOW.
CREEEE-EE-EE...
SOMETHING WAS TRYING TO GET IN.

# CHAPTER 4

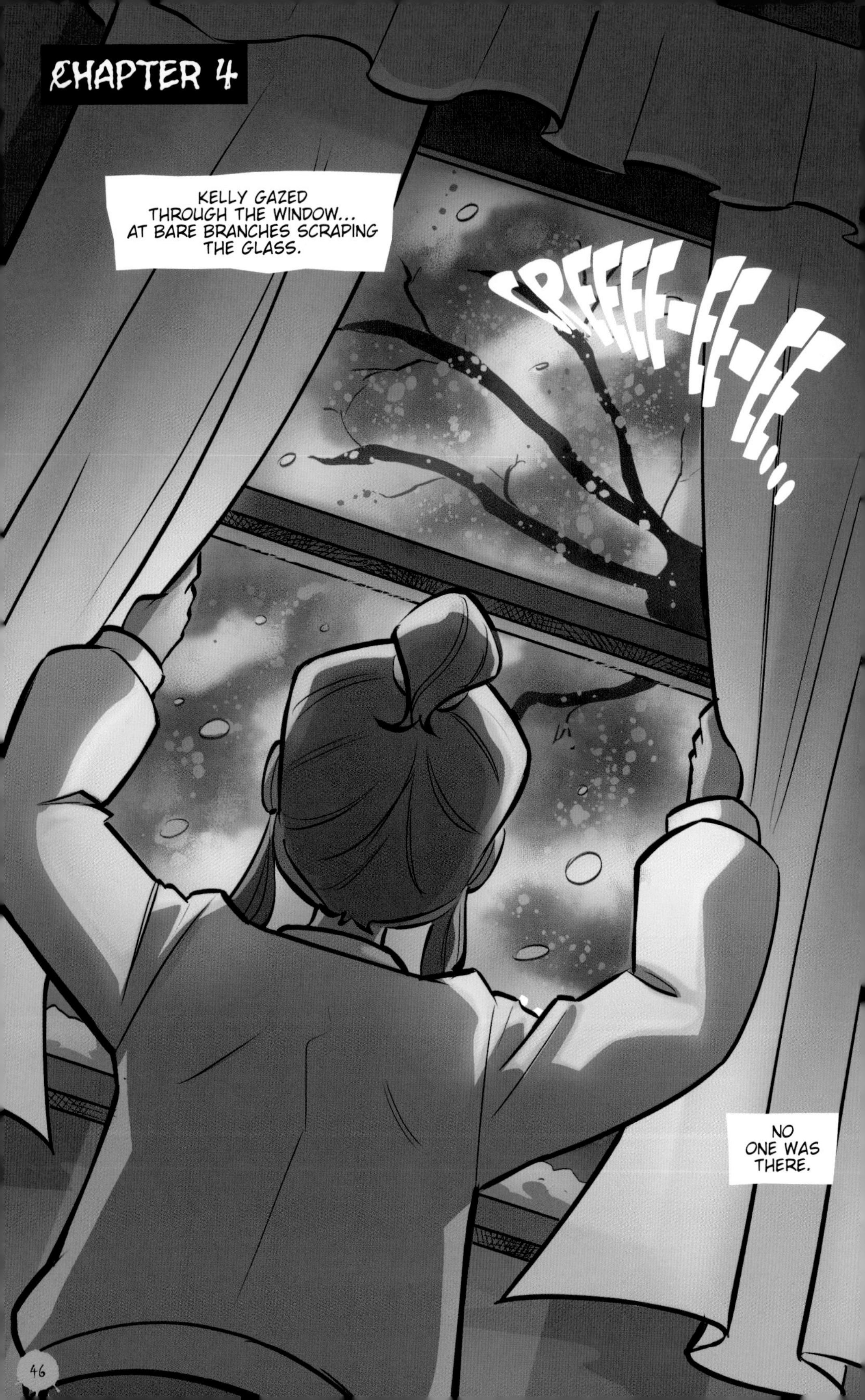
KELLY GAZED THROUGH THE WINDOW... AT BARE BRANCHES SCRAPING THE GLASS.
CREEEEE-EE-EE...
NO ONE WAS THERE.

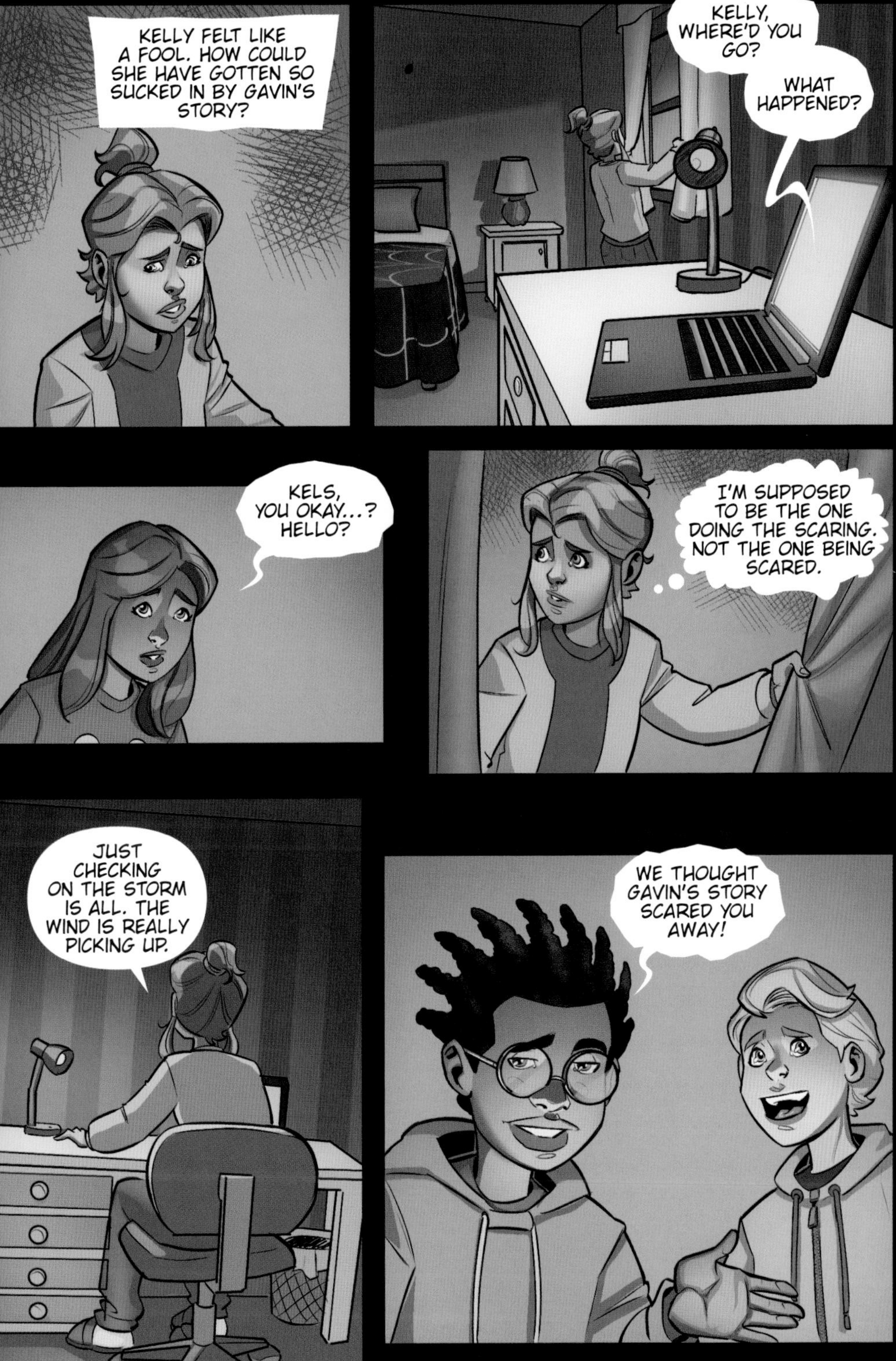
KELLY FELT LIKE A FOOL. HOW COULD SHE HAVE GOTTEN SO SUCKED IN BY GAVIN'S STORY?
KELLY, WHERE'D YOU GO?
WHAT HAPPENED?
KELS, YOU OKAY...? HELLO?
I'M SUPPOSED TO BE THE ONE DOING THE SCARING. NOT THE ONE BEING SCARED.
JUST CHECKING ON THE STORM IS ALL. THE WIND IS REALLY PICKING UP.
WE THOUGHT GAVIN'S STORY SCARED YOU AWAY!

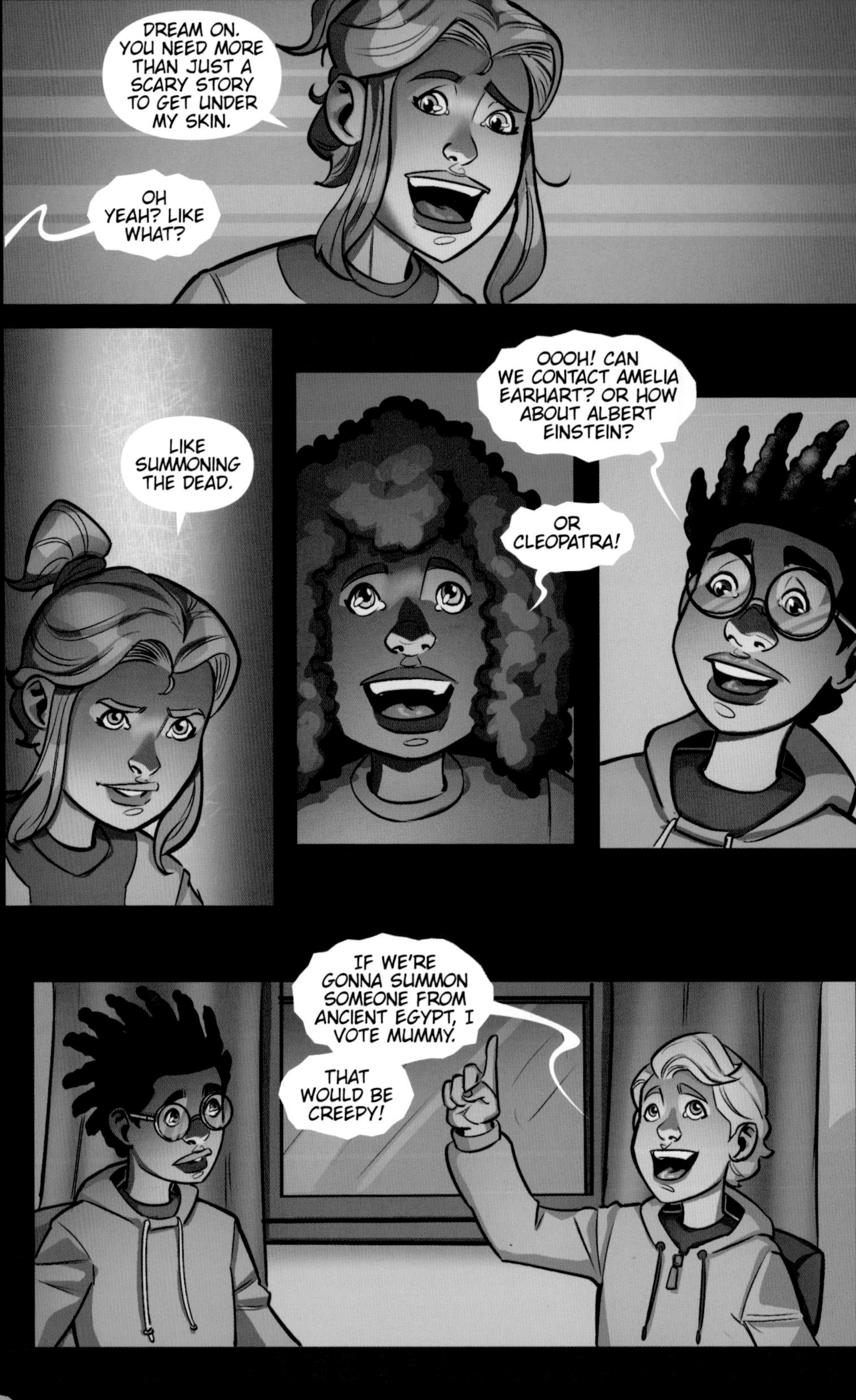
DREAM ON. YOU NEED MORE THAN JUST A SCARY STORY TO GET UNDER MY SKIN.
OH YEAH? LIKE WHAT?
LIKE SUMMONING THE DEAD.
OOOH! CAN WE CONTACT AMELIA EARHART? OR HOW ABOUT ALBERT EINSTEIN?
OR CLEOPATRA!
IF WE'RE GONNA SUMMON SOMEONE FROM ANCIENT EGYPT, I VOTE MUMMY.
THAT WOULD BE CREEPY!

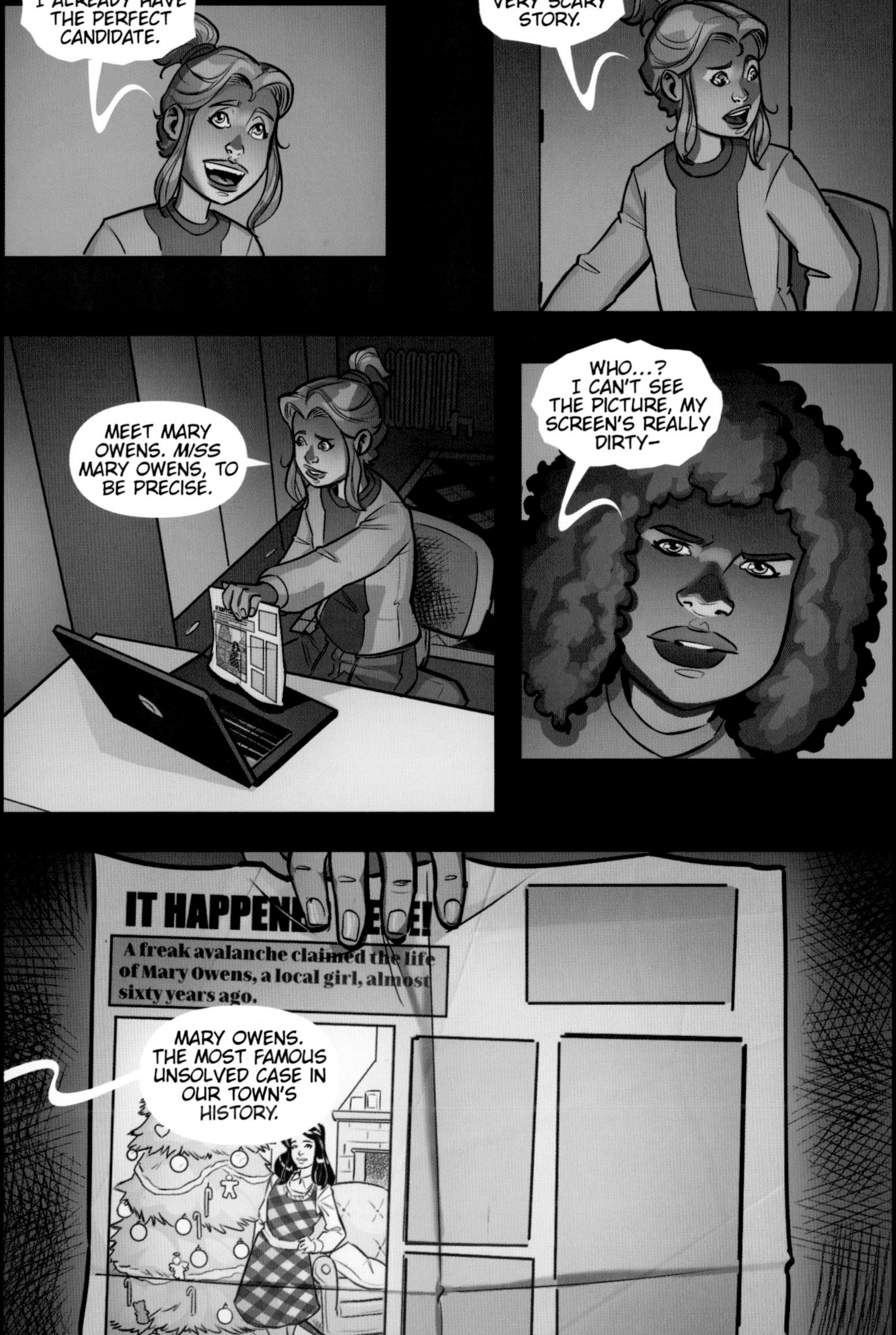
EVERYONE! I ALREADY HAVE THE PERFECT CANDIDATE.
WITH A VERY SCARY STORY.
MEET MARY OWENS. *MISS* MARY OWENS, TO BE PRECISE.
WHO...? I CAN'T SEE THE PICTURE, MY SCREEN'S REALLY DIRTY–
IT HAPPEN
A freak avalanche claimed the life of Mary Owens, a local girl, almost sixty years ago.
MARY OWENS. THE MOST FAMOUS UNSOLVED CASE IN OUR TOWN'S HISTORY.

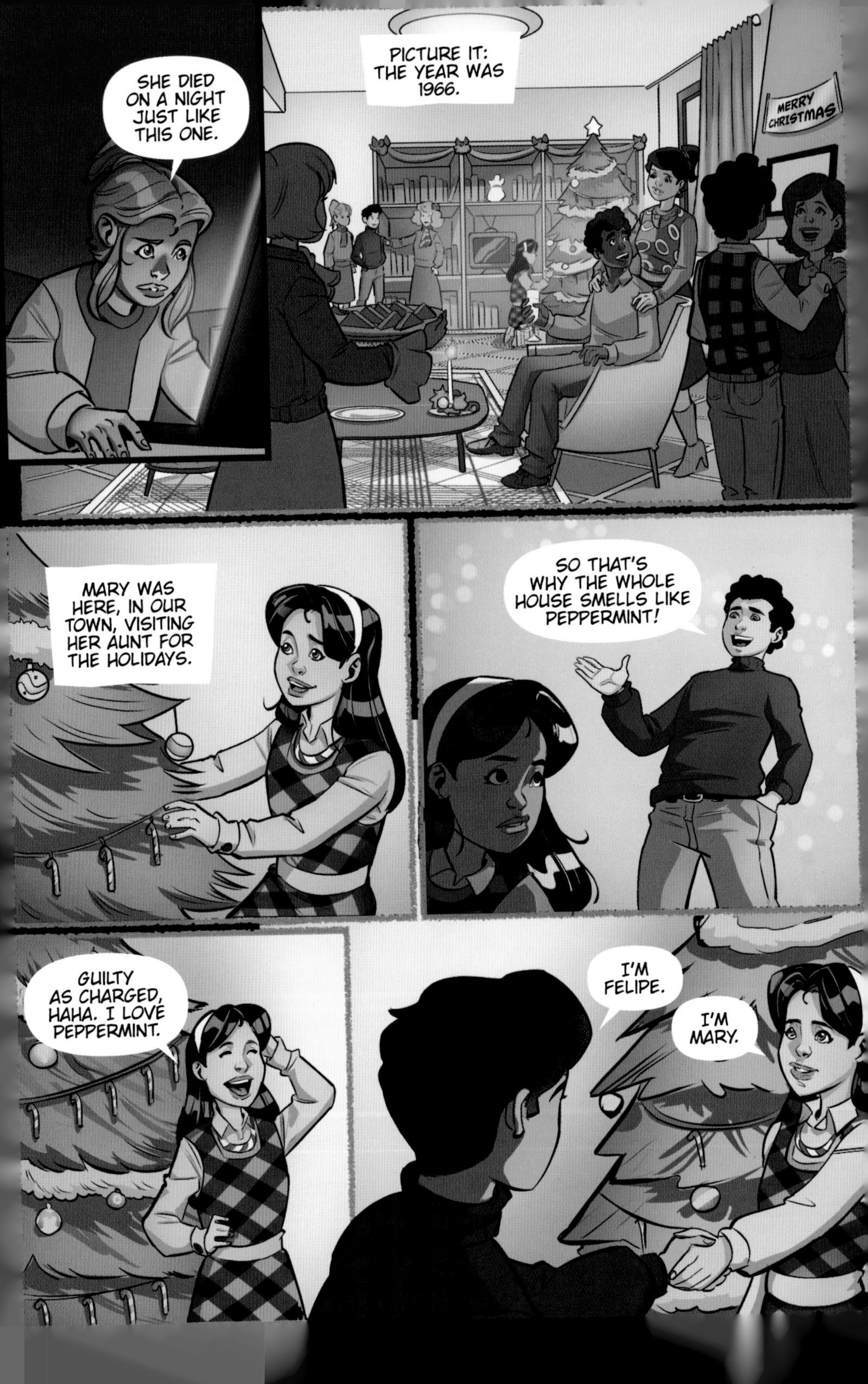
SHE DIED ON A NIGHT JUST LIKE THIS ONE.
PICTURE IT: THE YEAR WAS 1966.
MERRY CHRISTMAS
MARY WAS HERE, IN OUR TOWN, VISITING HER AUNT FOR THE HOLIDAYS.
SO THAT'S WHY THE WHOLE HOUSE SMELLS LIKE PEPPERMINT!
GUILTY AS CHARGED, HAHA. I LOVE PEPPERMINT.
I'M FELIPE.
I'M MARY.

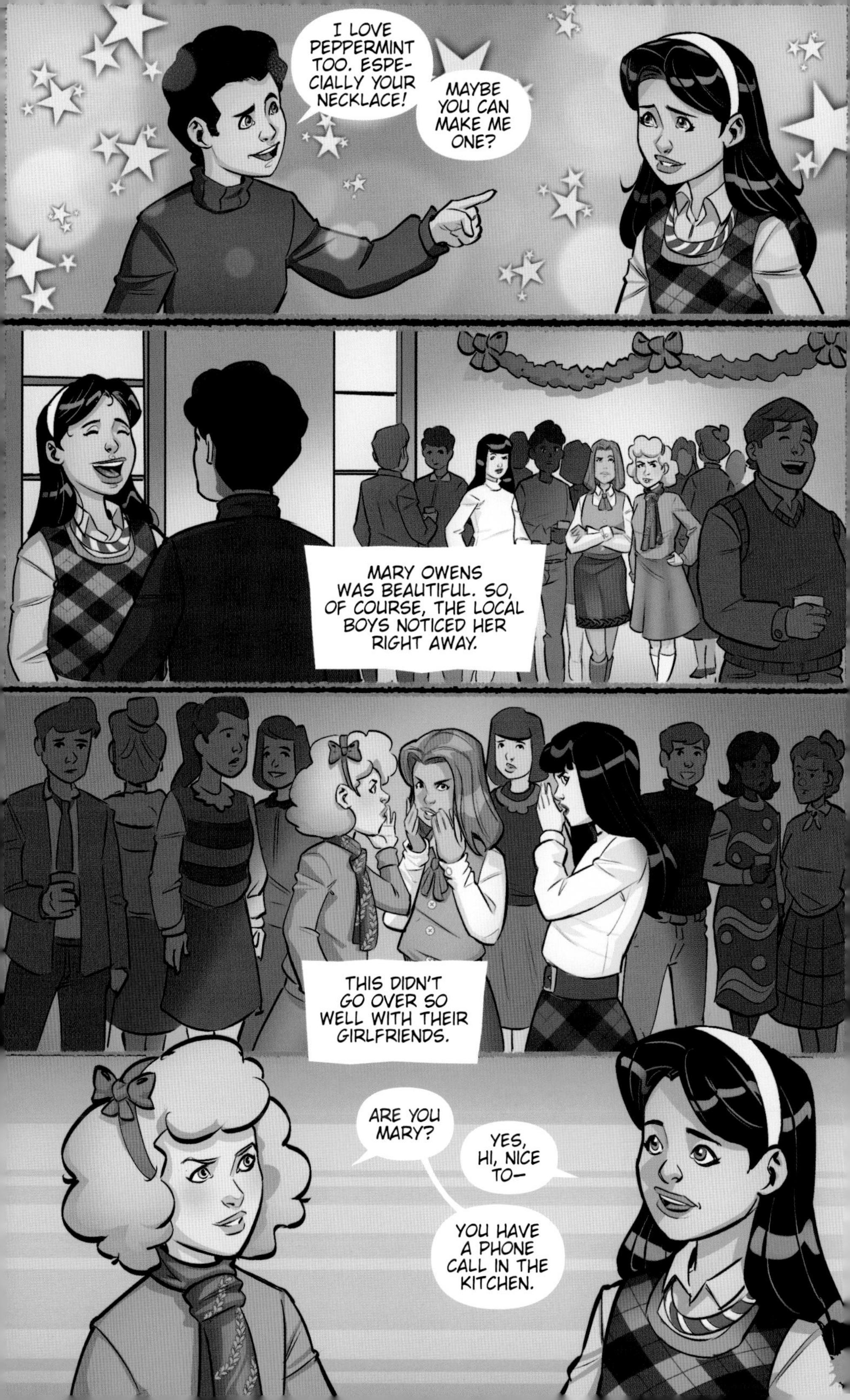
I LOVE PEPPERMINT TOO. ESPE-CIALLY YOUR NECKLACE!
MAYBE YOU CAN MAKE ME ONE?
MARY OWENS WAS BEAUTIFUL. SO, OF COURSE, THE LOCAL BOYS NOTICED HER RIGHT AWAY.
THIS DIDN'T GO OVER SO WELL WITH THEIR GIRLFRIENDS.
ARE YOU MARY?
YES, HI, NICE TO—
YOU HAVE A PHONE CALL IN THE KITCHEN.

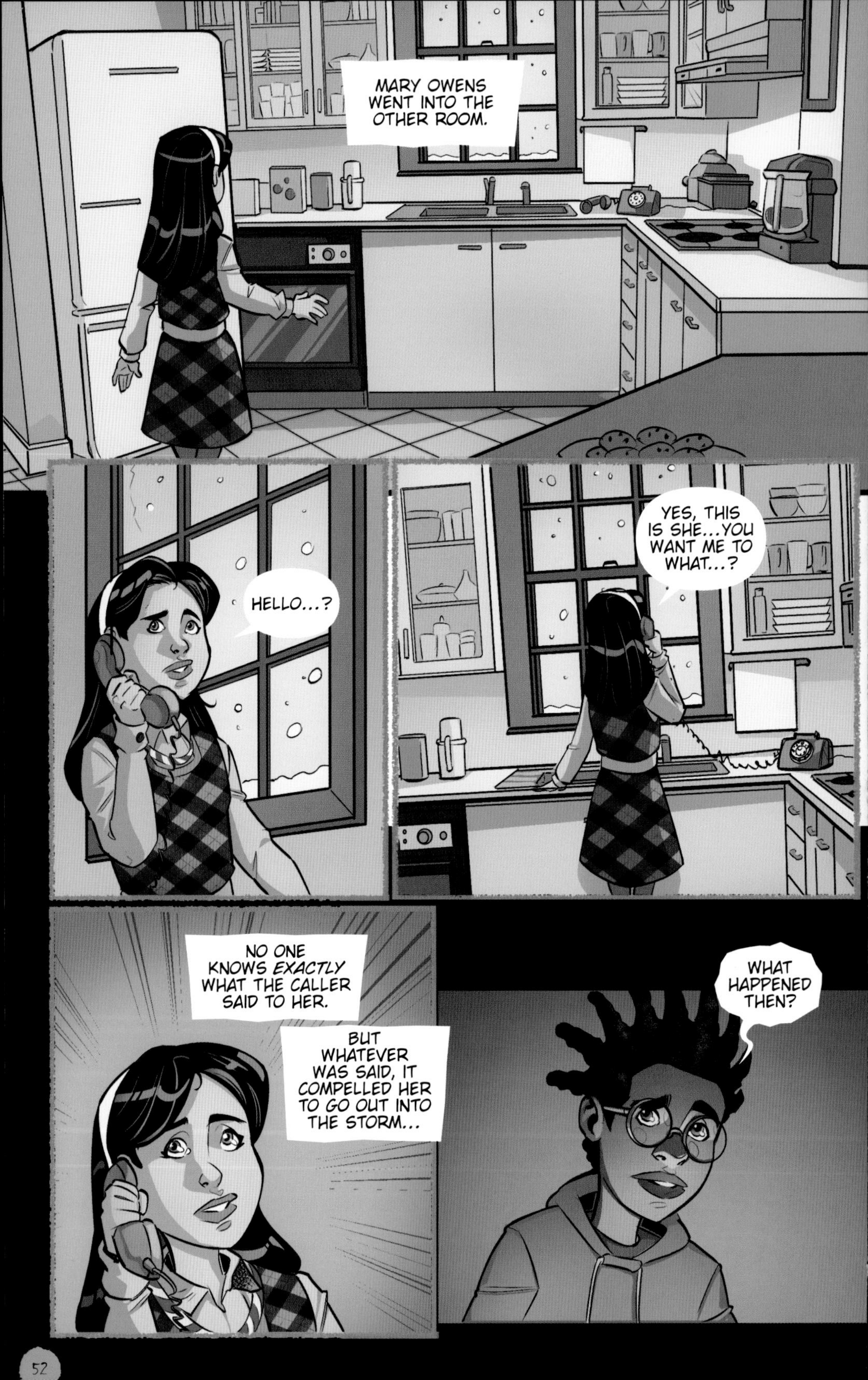
MARY OWENS WENT INTO THE OTHER ROOM.
HELLO...?
YES, THIS IS SHE...YOU WANT ME TO WHAT...?
NO ONE KNOWS *EXACTLY* WHAT THE CALLER SAID TO HER.
BUT WHATEVER WAS SAID, IT COMPELLED HER TO GO OUT INTO THE STORM...
WHAT HAPPENED THEN?

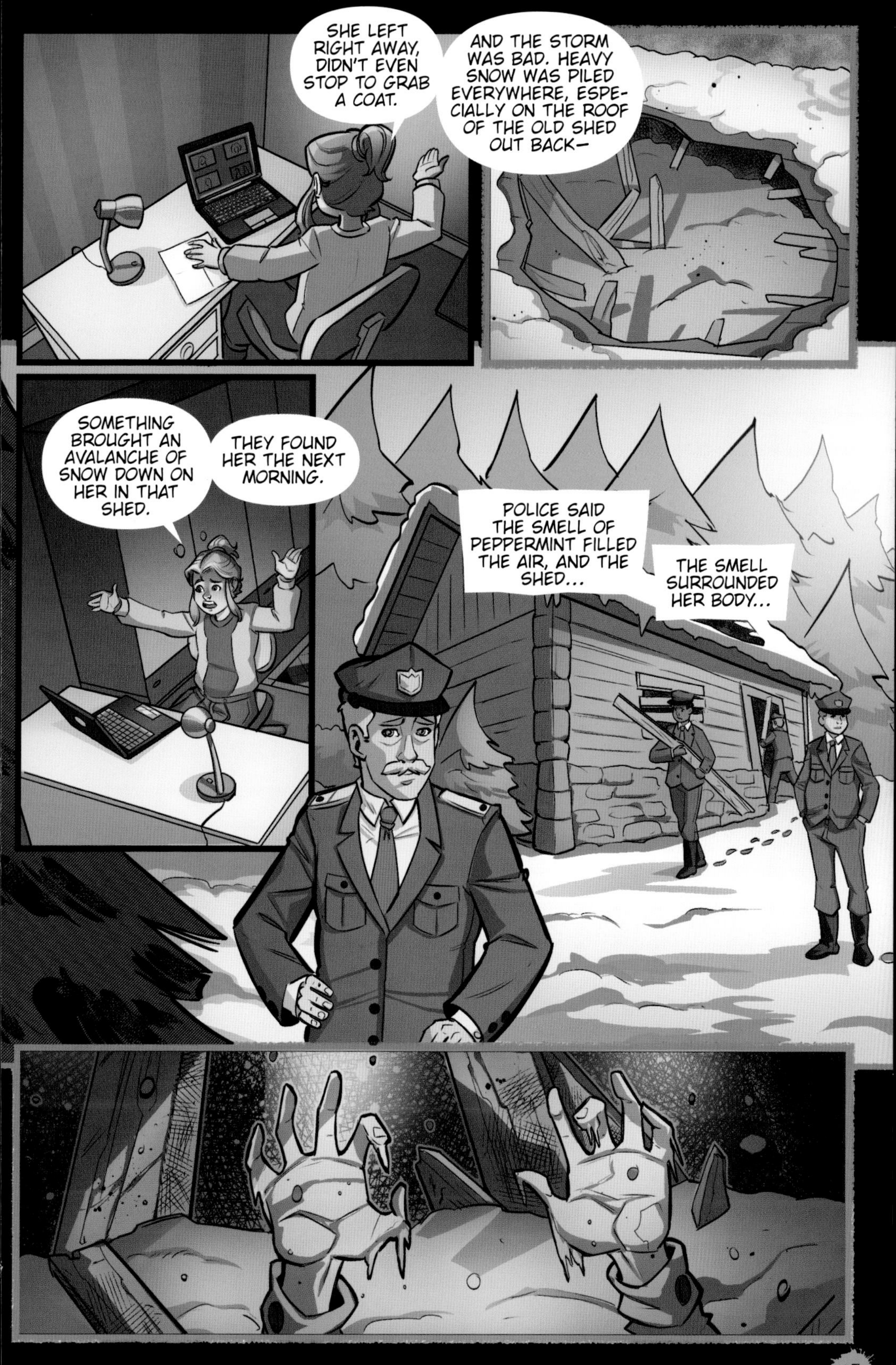
SHE LEFT RIGHT AWAY, DIDN'T EVEN STOP TO GRAB A COAT.
AND THE STORM WAS BAD. HEAVY SNOW WAS PILED EVERYWHERE, ESPE-CIALLY ON THE ROOF OF THE OLD SHED OUT BACK—
SOMETHING BROUGHT AN AVALANCHE OF SNOW DOWN ON HER IN THAT SHED.
THEY FOUND HER THE NEXT MORNING.
POLICE SAID THE SMELL OF PEPPERMINT FILLED THE AIR, AND THE SHED...
THE SMELL SURROUNDED HER BODY...

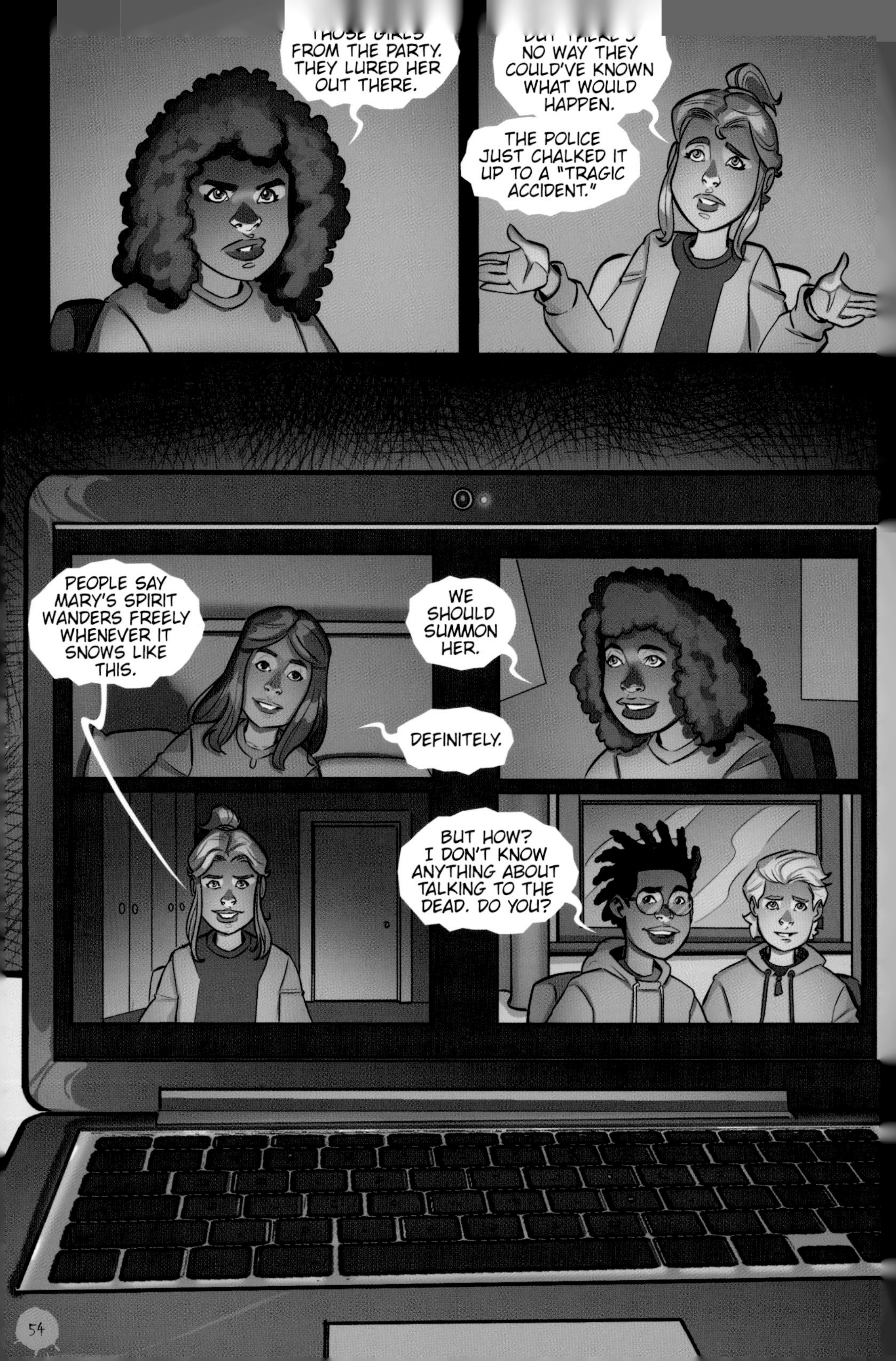
FROM THE PARTY. THEY LURED HER OUT THERE.
NO WAY THEY COULD'VE KNOWN WHAT WOULD HAPPEN.
THE POLICE JUST CHALKED IT UP TO A "TRAGIC ACCIDENT."
PEOPLE SAY MARY'S SPIRIT WANDERS FREELY WHENEVER IT SNOWS LIKE THIS.
WE SHOULD SUMMON HER.
DEFINITELY.
BUT HOW? I DON'T KNOW ANYTHING ABOUT TALKING TO THE DEAD. DO YOU?

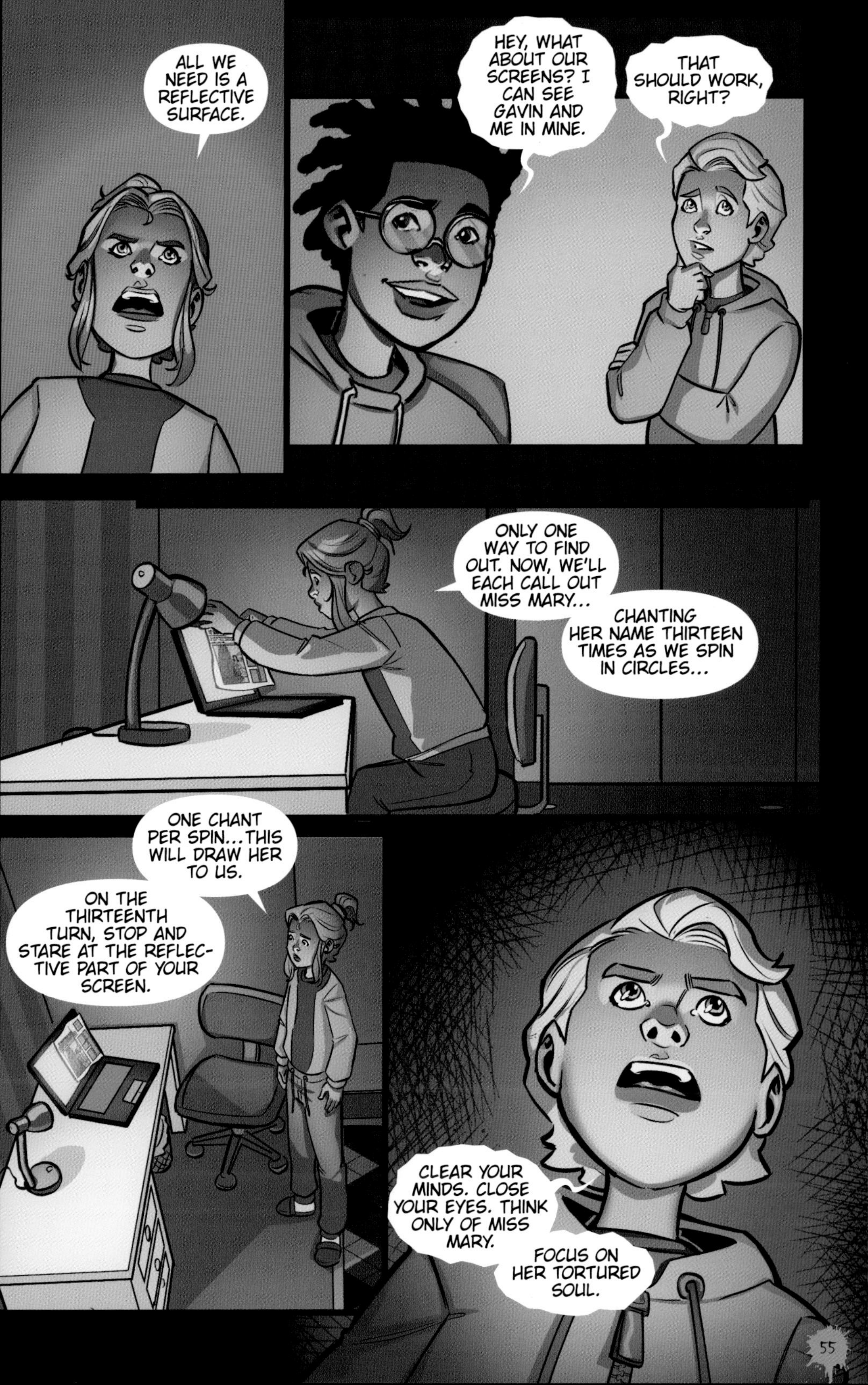
ALL WE NEED IS A REFLECTIVE SURFACE.
HEY, WHAT ABOUT OUR SCREENS? I CAN SEE GAVIN AND ME IN MINE.
THAT SHOULD WORK, RIGHT?
ONLY ONE WAY TO FIND OUT. NOW, WE'LL EACH CALL OUT MISS MARY...
CHANTING HER NAME THIRTEEN TIMES AS WE SPIN IN CIRCLES...
ONE CHANT PER SPIN...THIS WILL DRAW HER TO US.
ON THE THIRTEENTH TURN, STOP AND STARE AT THE REFLEC-TIVE PART OF YOUR SCREEN.
CLEAR YOUR MINDS. CLOSE YOUR EYES. THINK ONLY OF MISS MARY.
FOCUS ON HER TORTURED SOUL.

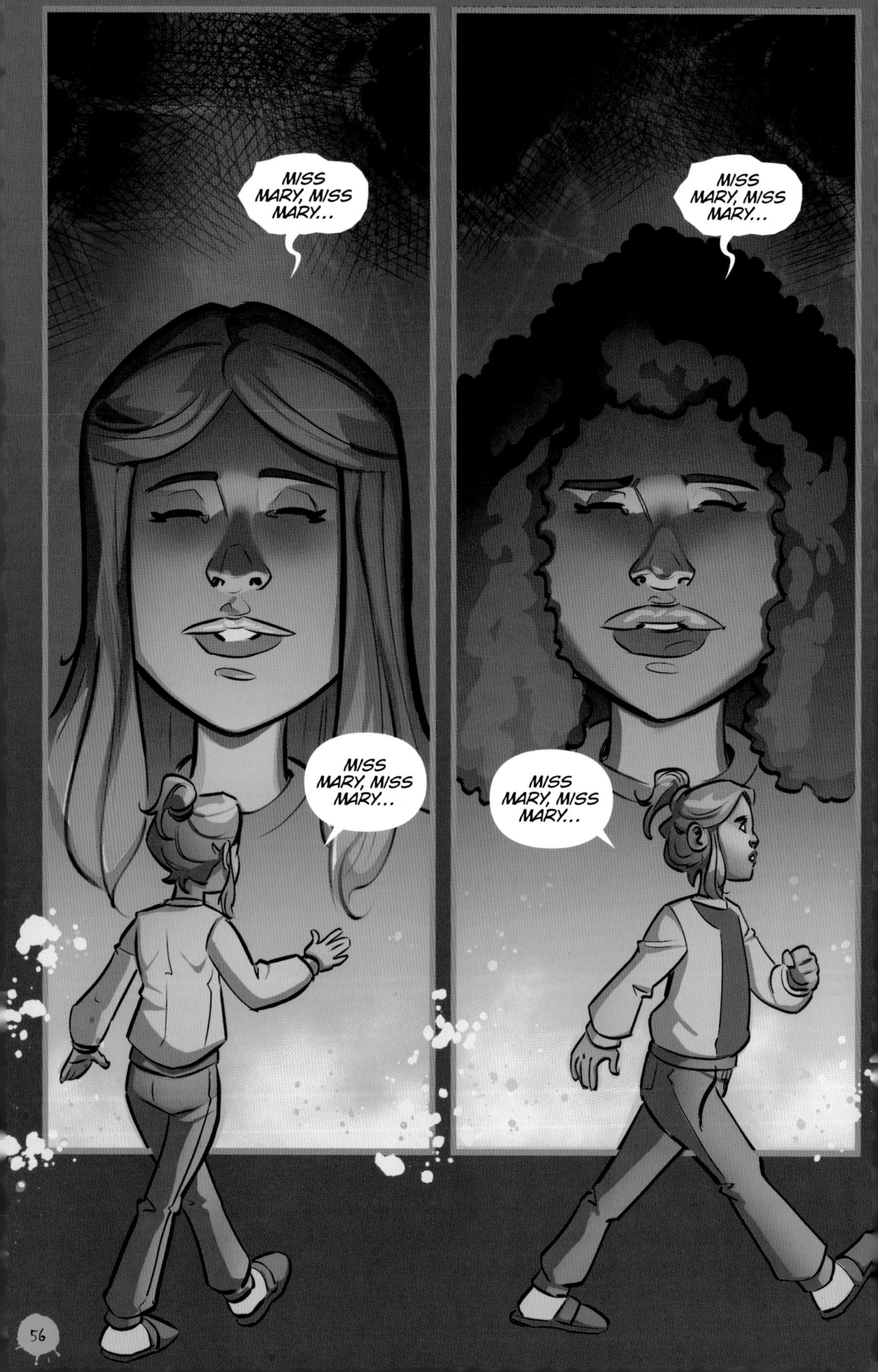
MISS MARY, MISS MARY...
MISS MARY, MISS MARY...
MISS MARY, MISS MARY...
MISS MARY, MISS MARY...

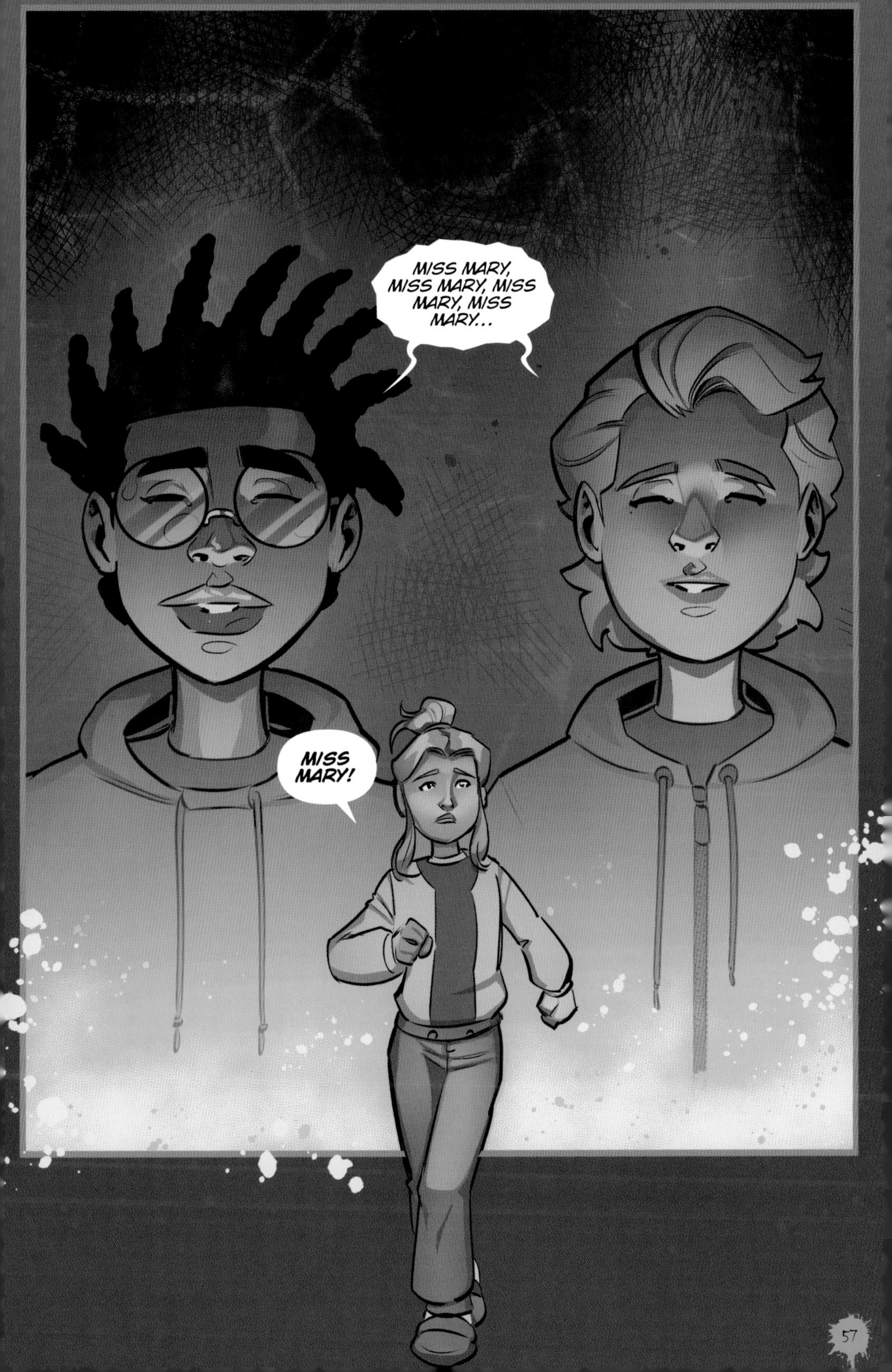
MISS MARY, MISS MARY, MISS MARY, MISS MARY...
MISS MARY!

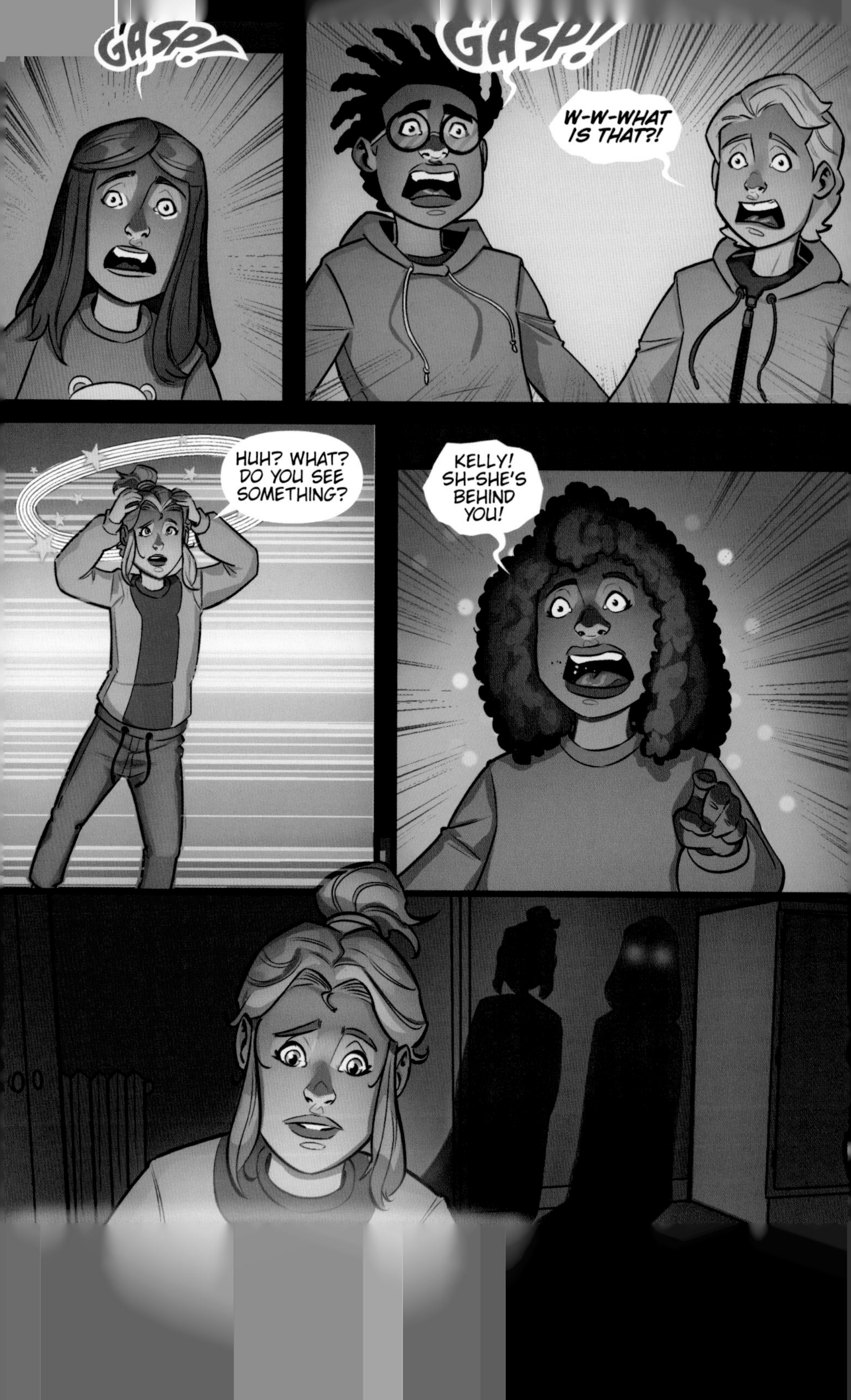
GASP!
GASP!
W-W-WHAT IS THAT?!
HUH? WHAT? DO YOU SEE SOMETHING?
KELLY! SH-SHE'S BEHIND YOU!

# CHAPTER 5

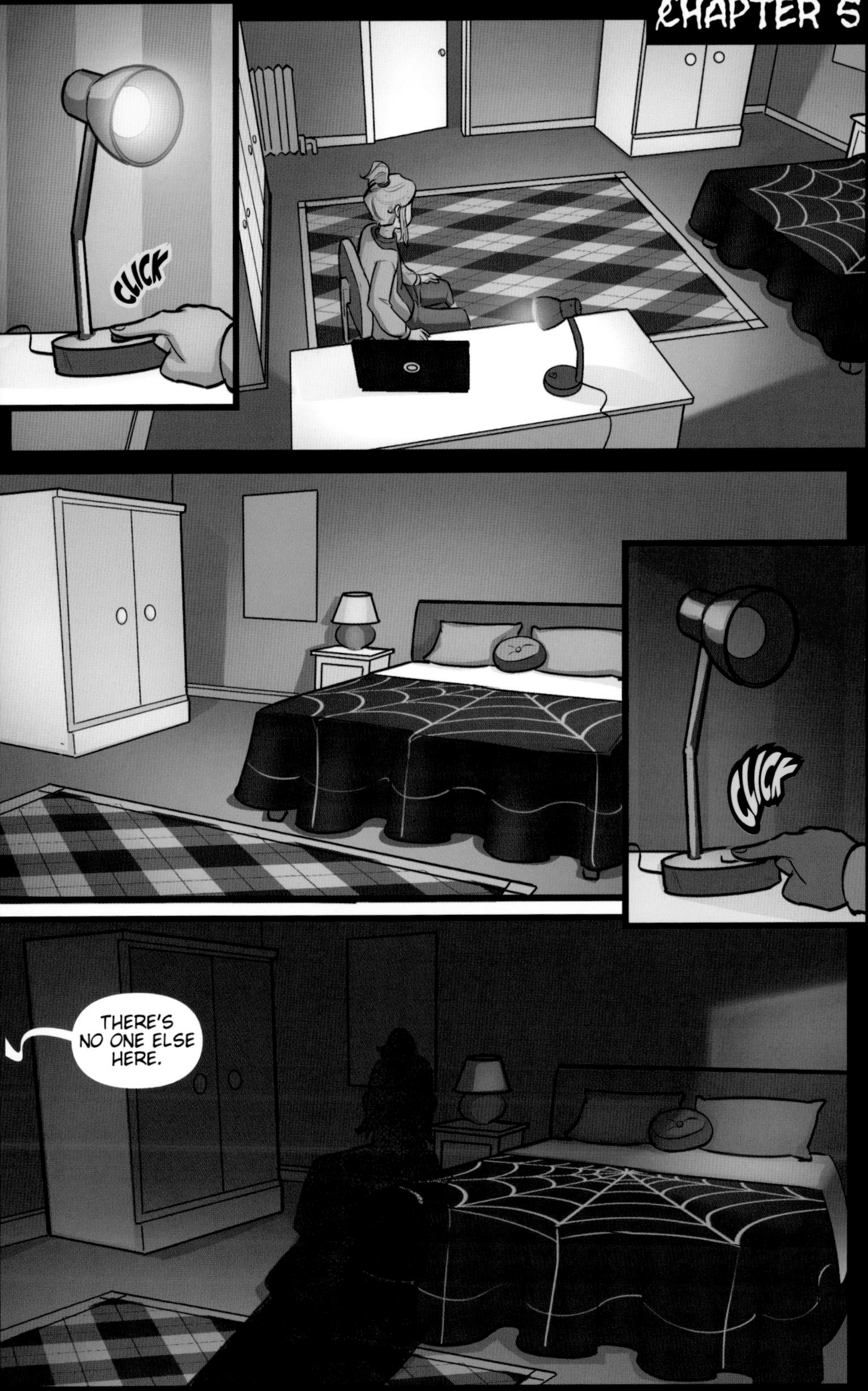
CLICK
CLICK
THERE'S NO ONE ELSE HERE.

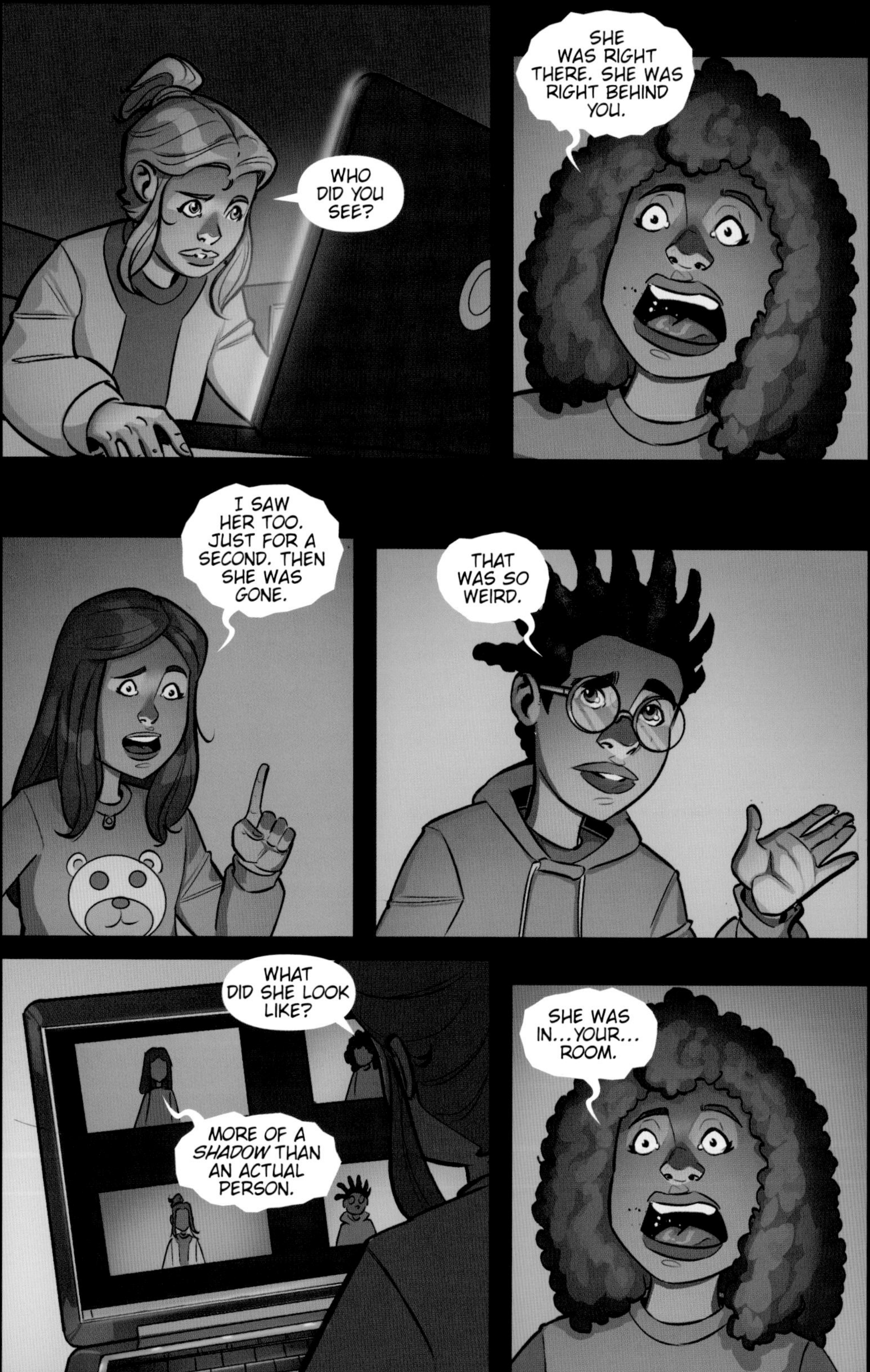
WHO DID YOU SEE?
SHE WAS RIGHT THERE. SHE WAS RIGHT BEHIND YOU.
I SAW HER TOO. JUST FOR A SECOND. THEN SHE WAS GONE.
THAT WAS SO WEIRD.
WHAT DID SHE LOOK LIKE?
MORE OF A *SHADOW* THAN AN ACTUAL PERSON.
SHE WAS IN... YOUR... ROOM.

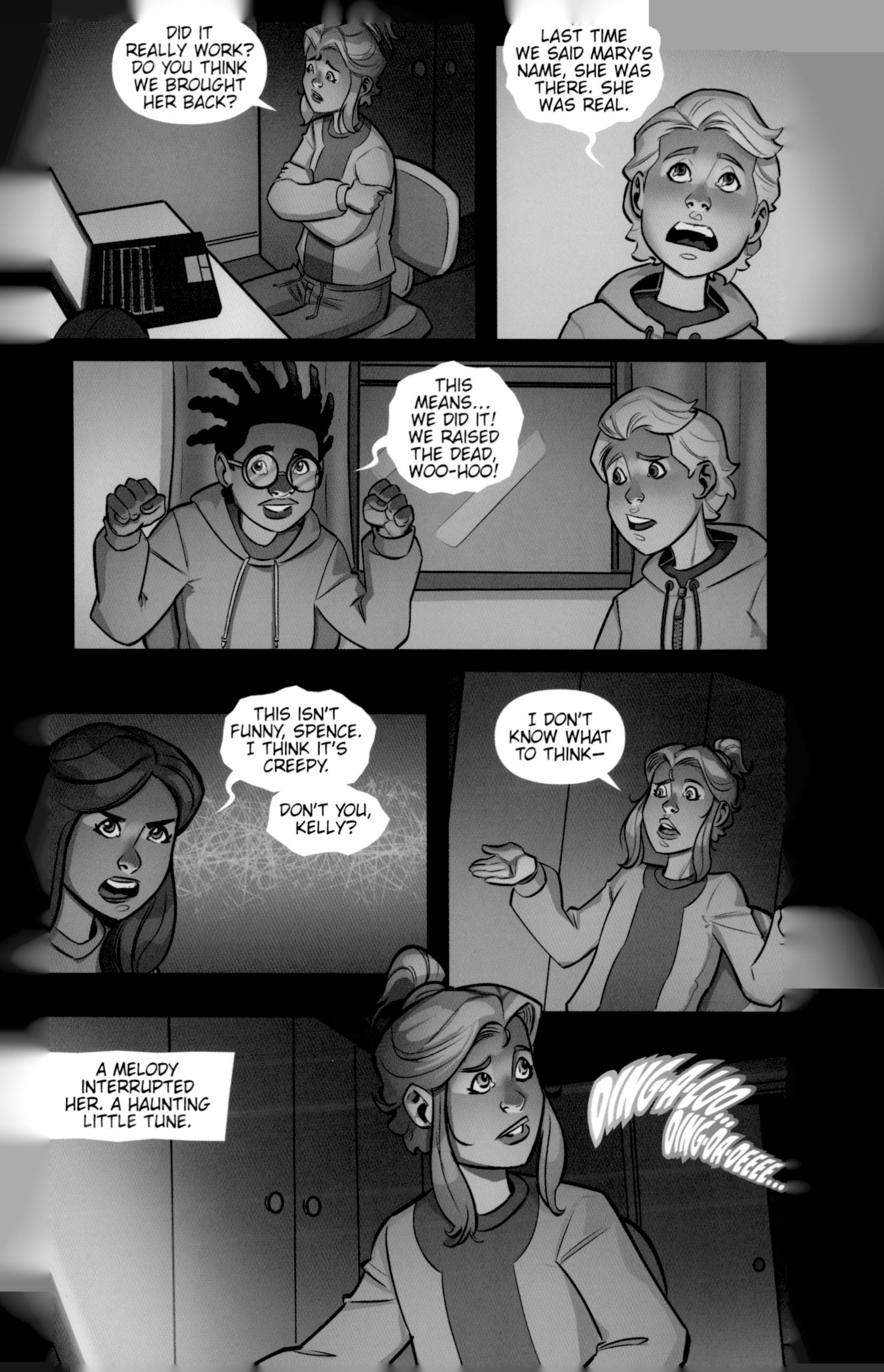
DID IT REALLY WORK? DO YOU THINK WE BROUGHT HER BACK?
LAST TIME WE SAID MARY'S NAME, SHE WAS THERE. SHE WAS REAL.
THIS MEANS... WE DID IT! WE RAISED THE DEAD, WOO-HOO!
THIS ISN'T FUNNY, SPENCE. I THINK IT'S CREEPY.
DON'T YOU, KELLY?
I DON'T KNOW WHAT TO THINK—
A MELODY INTERRUPTED HER. A HAUNTING LITTLE TUNE.
DING-A-LOO... DING-DA-DEEEE...

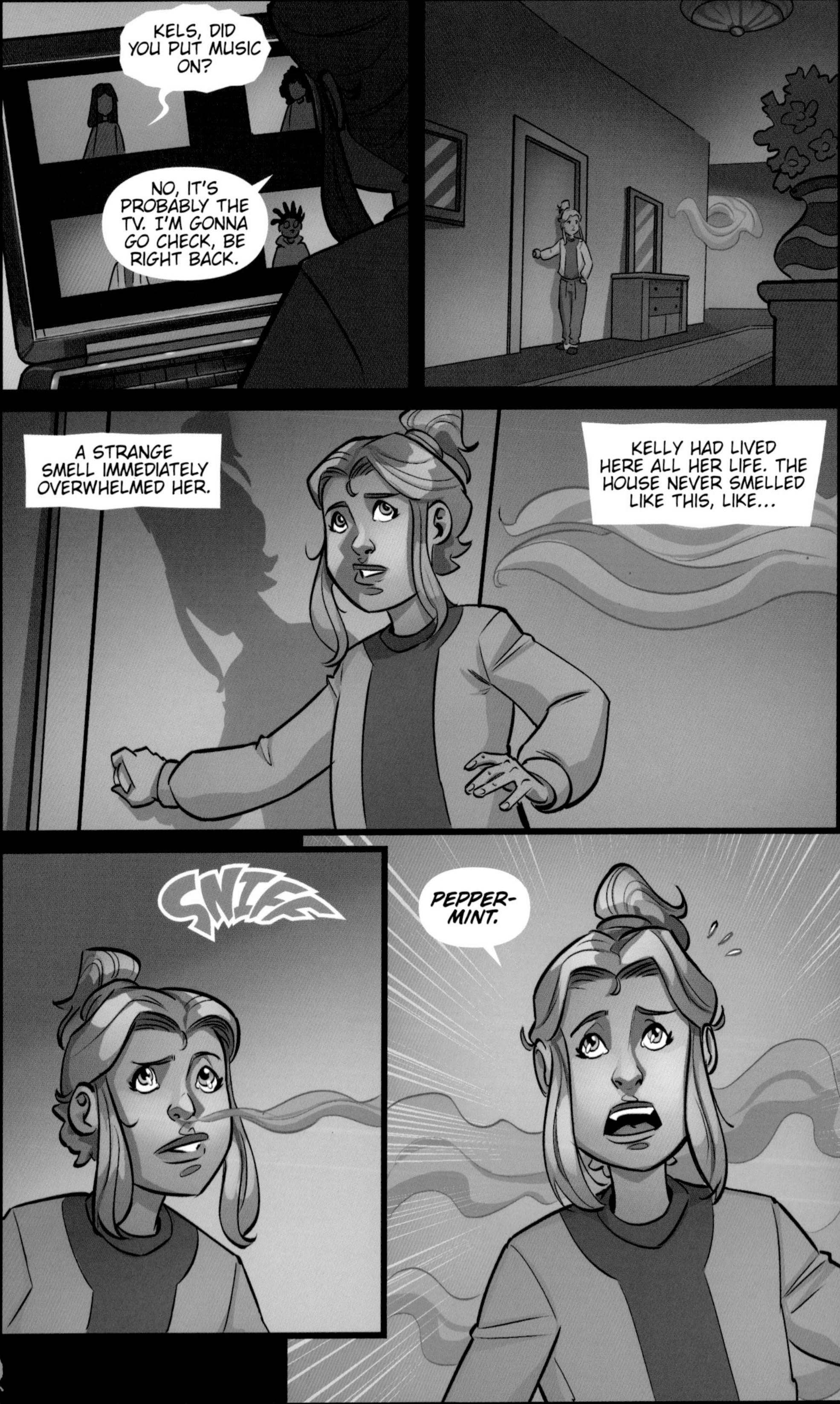

KELS, DID YOU PUT MUSIC ON?
NO, IT'S PROBABLY THE TV. I'M GONNA GO CHECK, BE RIGHT BACK.
A STRANGE SMELL IMMEDIATELY OVERWHELMED HER.
KELLY HAD LIVED HERE ALL HER LIFE. THE HOUSE NEVER SMELLED LIKE THIS, LIKE...
SNIFF
PEPPER-MINT.

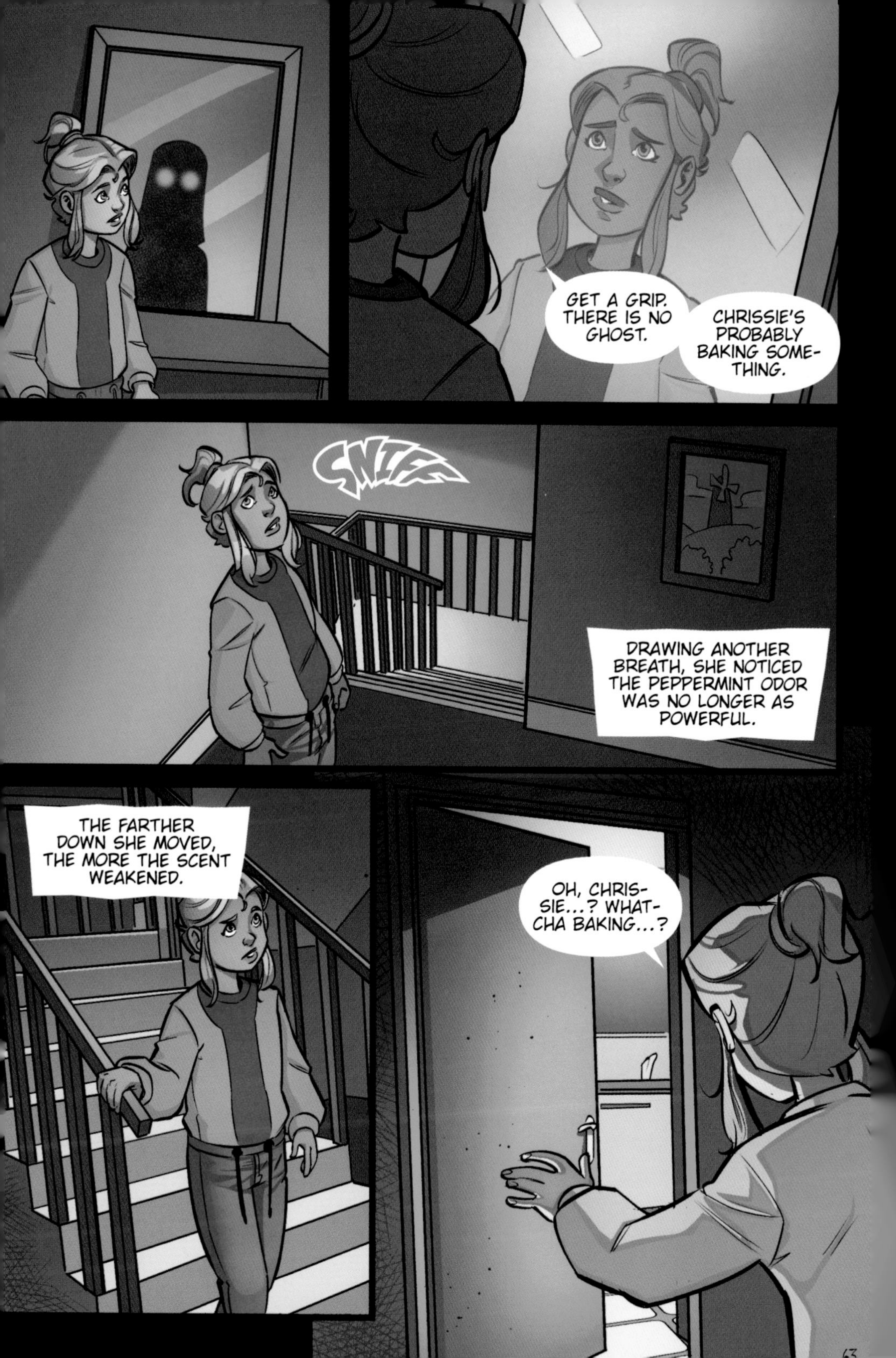
GET A GRIP. THERE IS NO GHOST.
CHRISSIE'S PROBABLY BAKING SOMETHING.
SNIFF
DRAWING ANOTHER BREATH, SHE NOTICED THE PEPPERMINT ODOR WAS NO LONGER AS POWERFUL.
THE FARTHER DOWN SHE MOVED, THE MORE THE SCENT WEAKENED.
OH, CHRISSIE...? WHATCHA BAKING...?

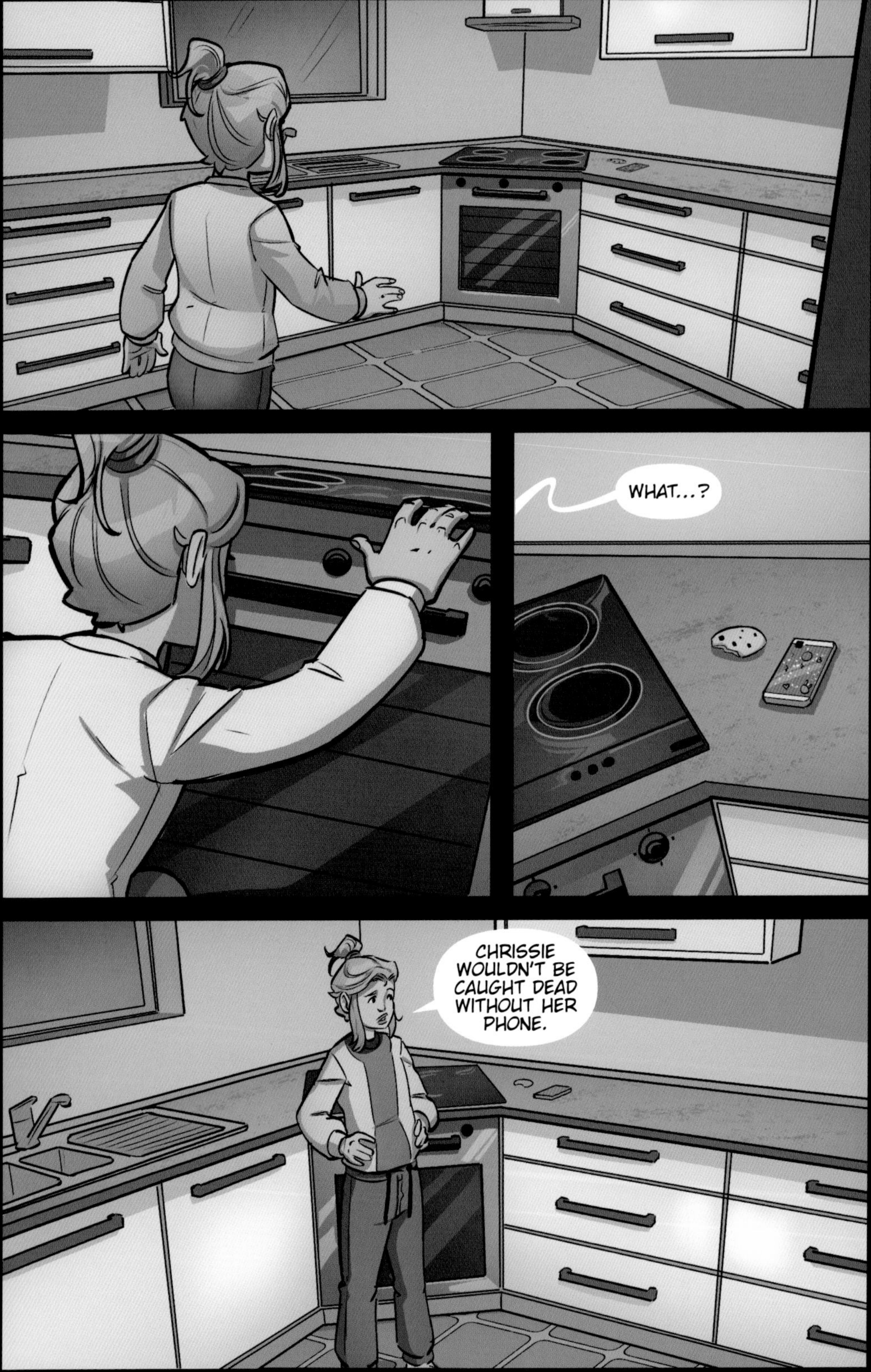
WHAT...?
CHRISSIE WOULDN'T BE CAUGHT DEAD WITHOUT HER PHONE.

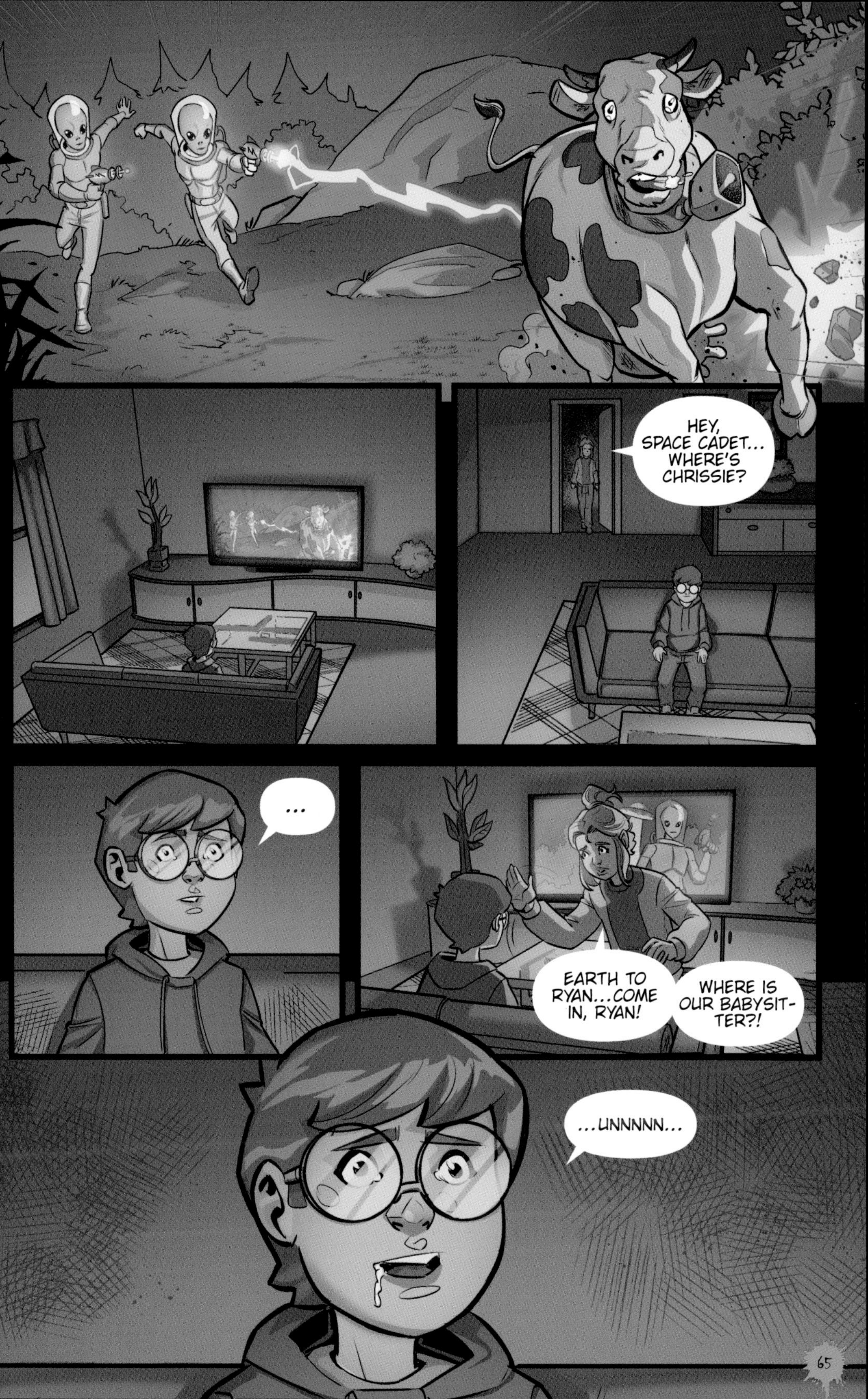
HEY, SPACE CADET... WHERE'S CHRISSIE?
...
EARTH TO RYAN...COME IN, RYAN!
WHERE IS OUR BABYSIT-TER?!
...UNNNNN...

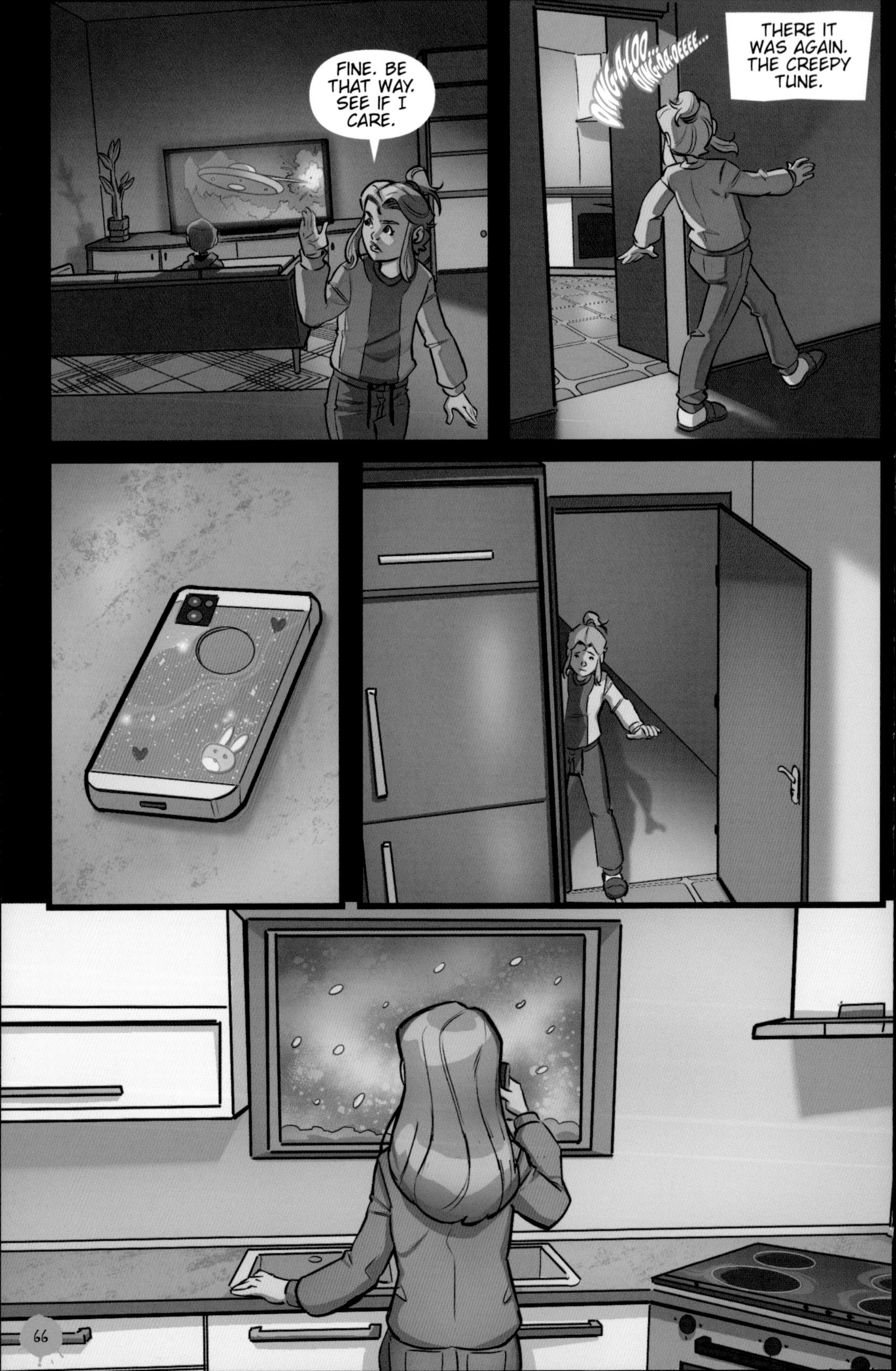
FINE. BE THAT WAY. SEE IF I CARE.
DING-A-LOO... DING-DA-DEEEE...
THERE IT WAS AGAIN. THE CREEPY TUNE.

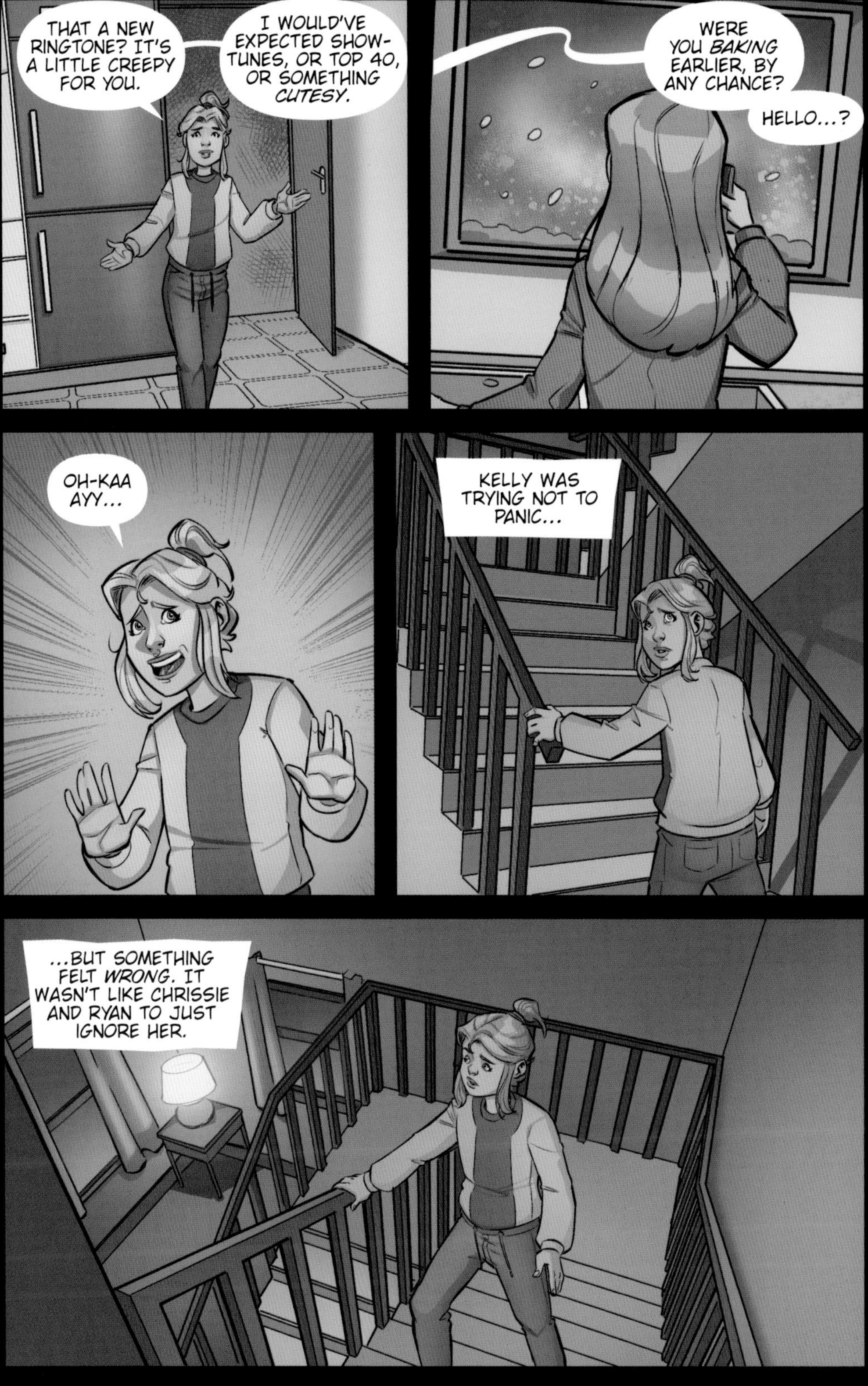
THAT A NEW RINGTONE? IT'S A LITTLE CREEPY FOR YOU.
I WOULD'VE EXPECTED SHOW-TUNES, OR TOP 40, OR SOMETHING *CUTESY*.
WERE YOU *BAKING* EARLIER, BY ANY CHANCE?
HELLO...?
OH-KAA AYY...
KELLY WAS TRYING NOT TO PANIC...
...BUT SOMETHING FELT *WRONG*. IT WASN'T LIKE CHRISSIE AND RYAN TO JUST IGNORE HER.

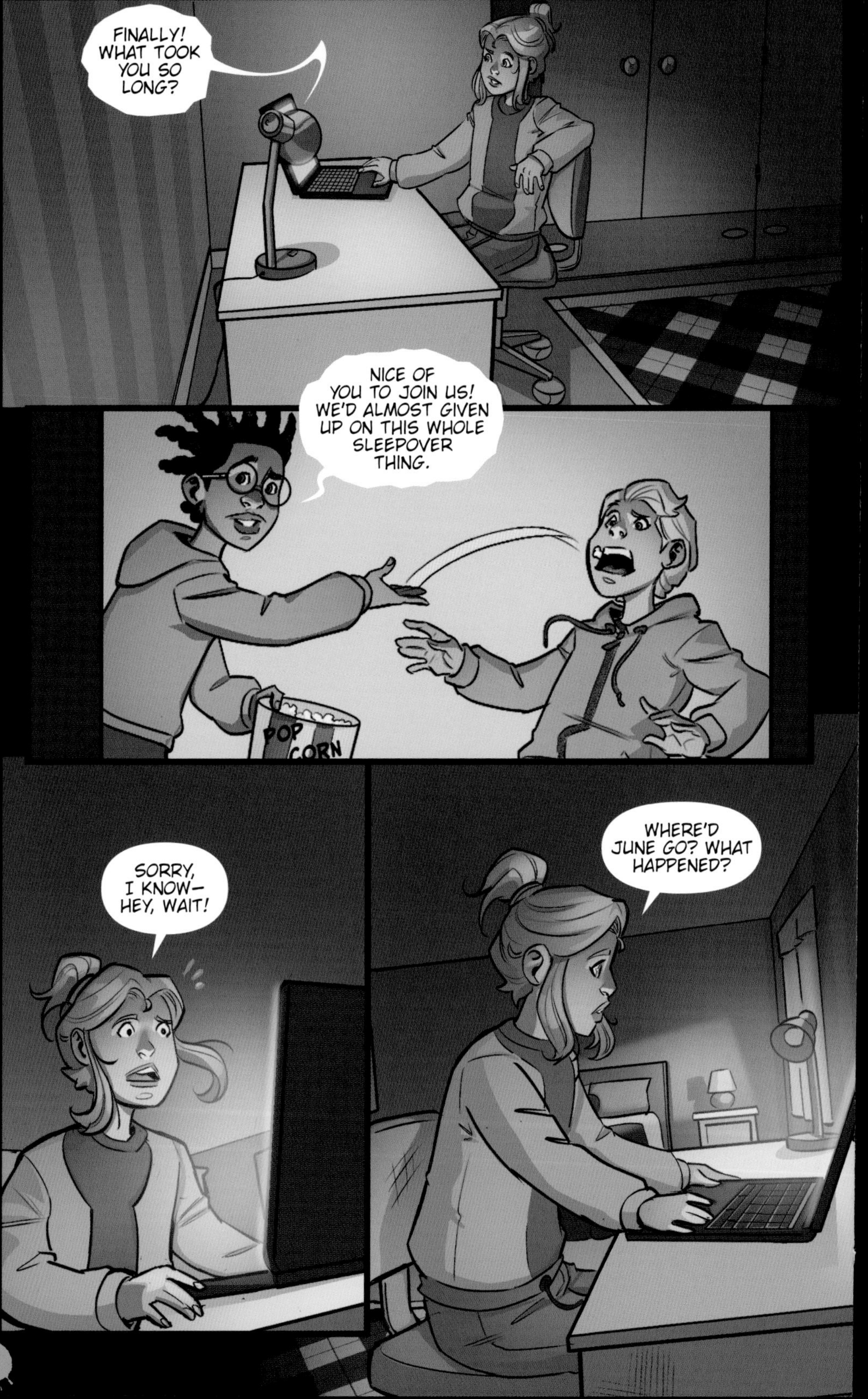
FINALLY! WHAT TOOK YOU SO LONG?
NICE OF YOU TO JOIN US! WE'D ALMOST GIVEN UP ON THIS WHOLE SLEEPOVER THING.
POP CORN
SORRY, I KNOW— HEY, WAIT!
WHERE'D JUNE GO? WHAT HAPPENED?

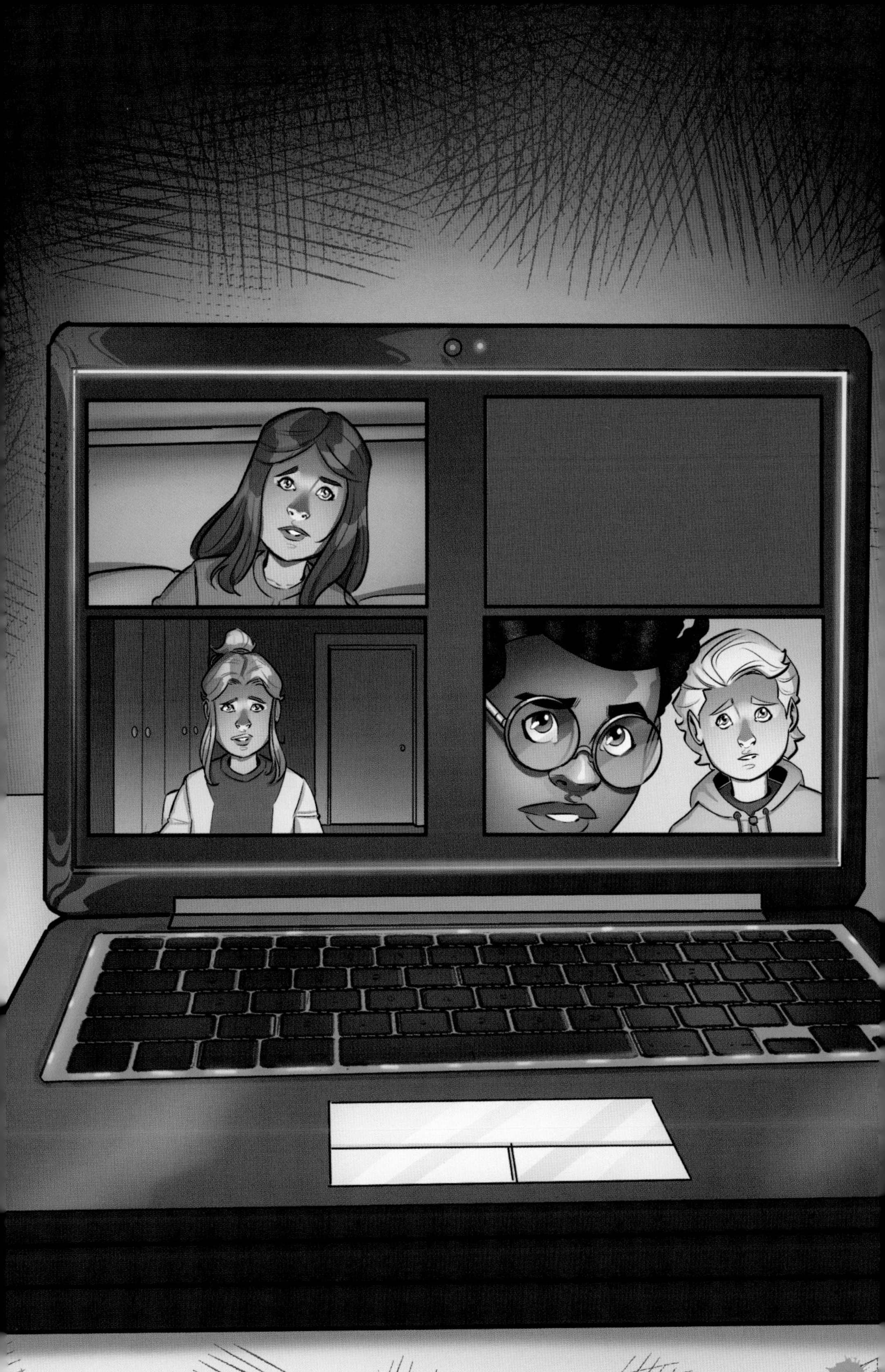

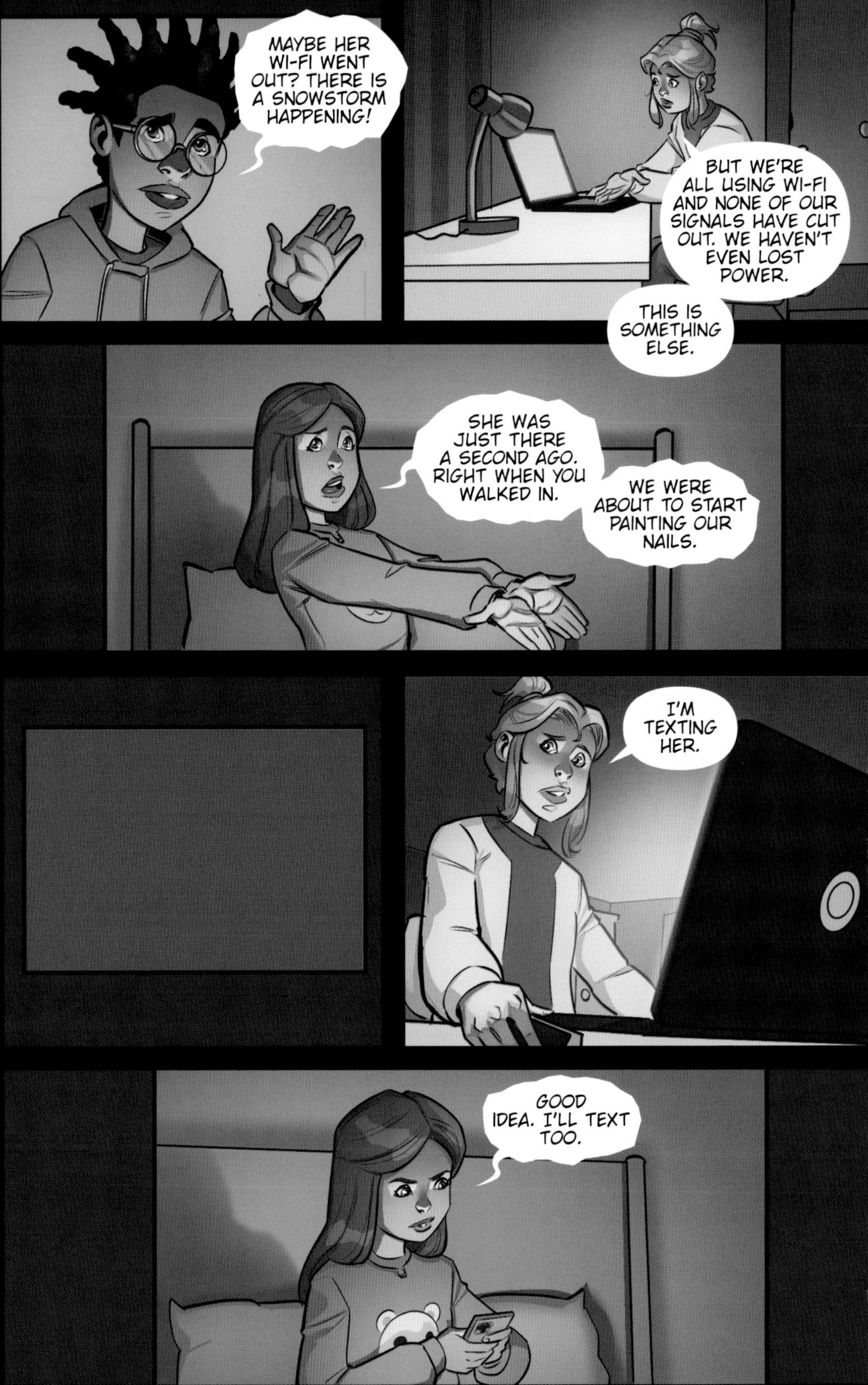
MAYBE HER WI-FI WENT OUT? THERE IS A SNOWSTORM HAPPENING!
BUT WE'RE ALL USING WI-FI AND NONE OF OUR SIGNALS HAVE CUT OUT. WE HAVEN'T EVEN LOST POWER.
THIS IS SOMETHING ELSE.
SHE WAS JUST THERE A SECOND AGO. RIGHT WHEN YOU WALKED IN.
WE WERE ABOUT TO START PAINTING OUR NAILS.
I'M TEXTING HER.
GOOD IDEA. I'LL TEXT TOO.

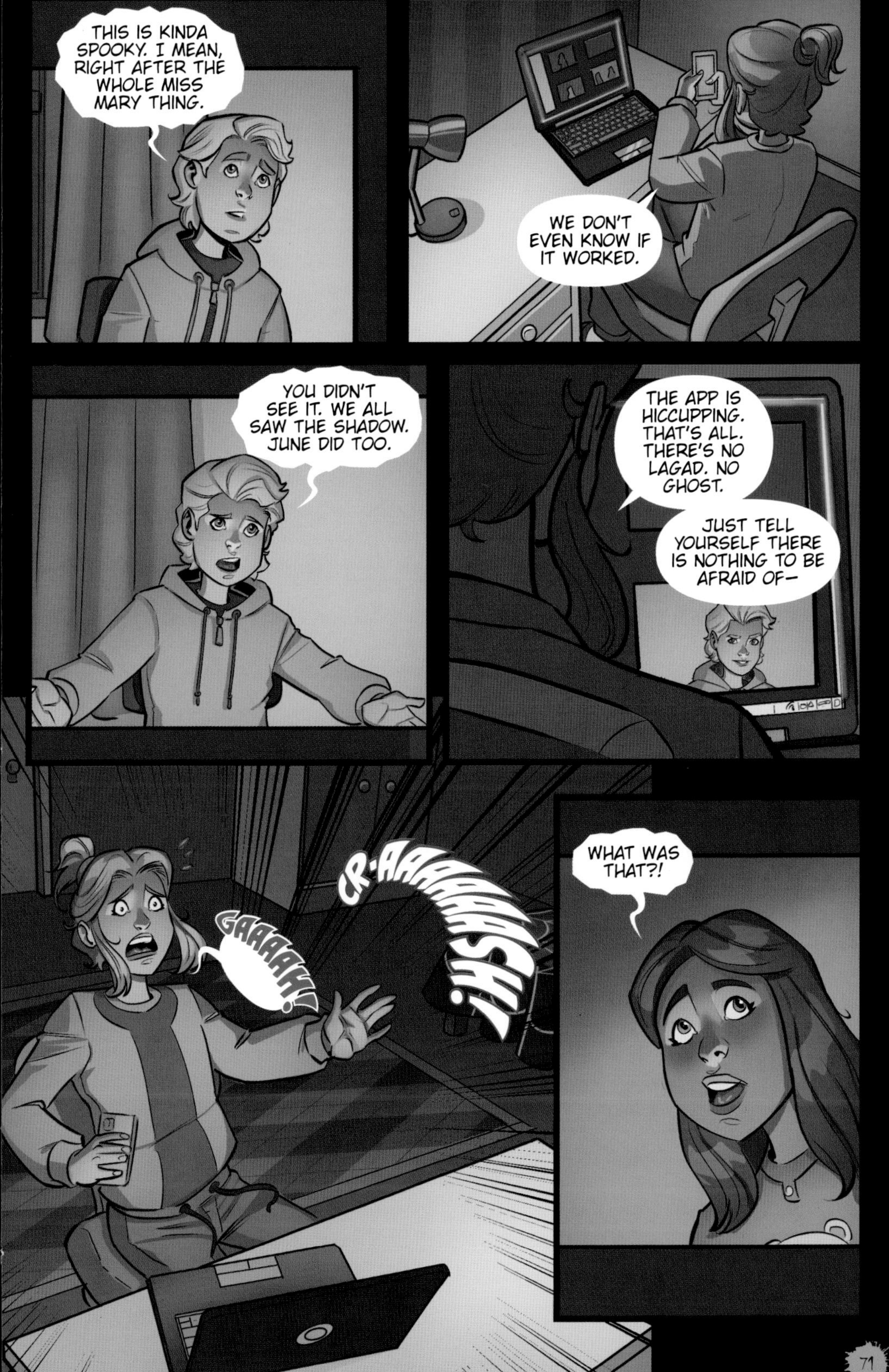
THIS IS KINDA SPOOKY. I MEAN, RIGHT AFTER THE WHOLE MISS MARY THING.
WE DON'T EVEN KNOW IF IT WORKED.
YOU DIDN'T SEE IT. WE ALL SAW THE SHADOW. JUNE DID TOO.
THE APP IS HICCUPPING. THAT'S ALL. THERE'S NO LAGAD. NO GHOST.
JUST TELL YOURSELF THERE IS NOTHING TO BE AFRAID OF—
CR-AAAAAASH!
GAAAAH!
WHAT WAS THAT?!

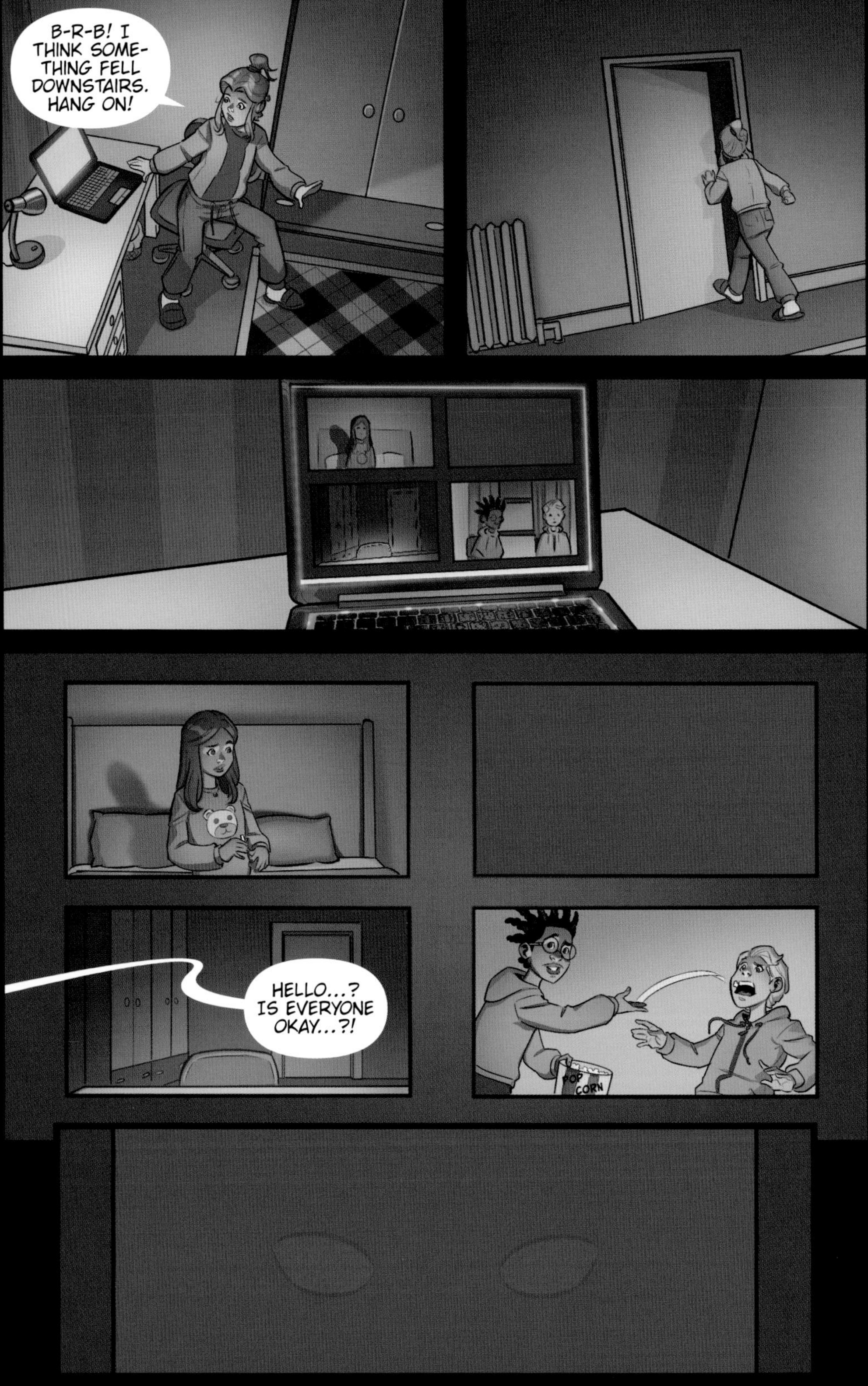
B-R-B! I THINK SOMETHING FELL DOWNSTAIRS. HANG ON!
HELLO...? IS EVERYONE OKAY...?!
POP CORN

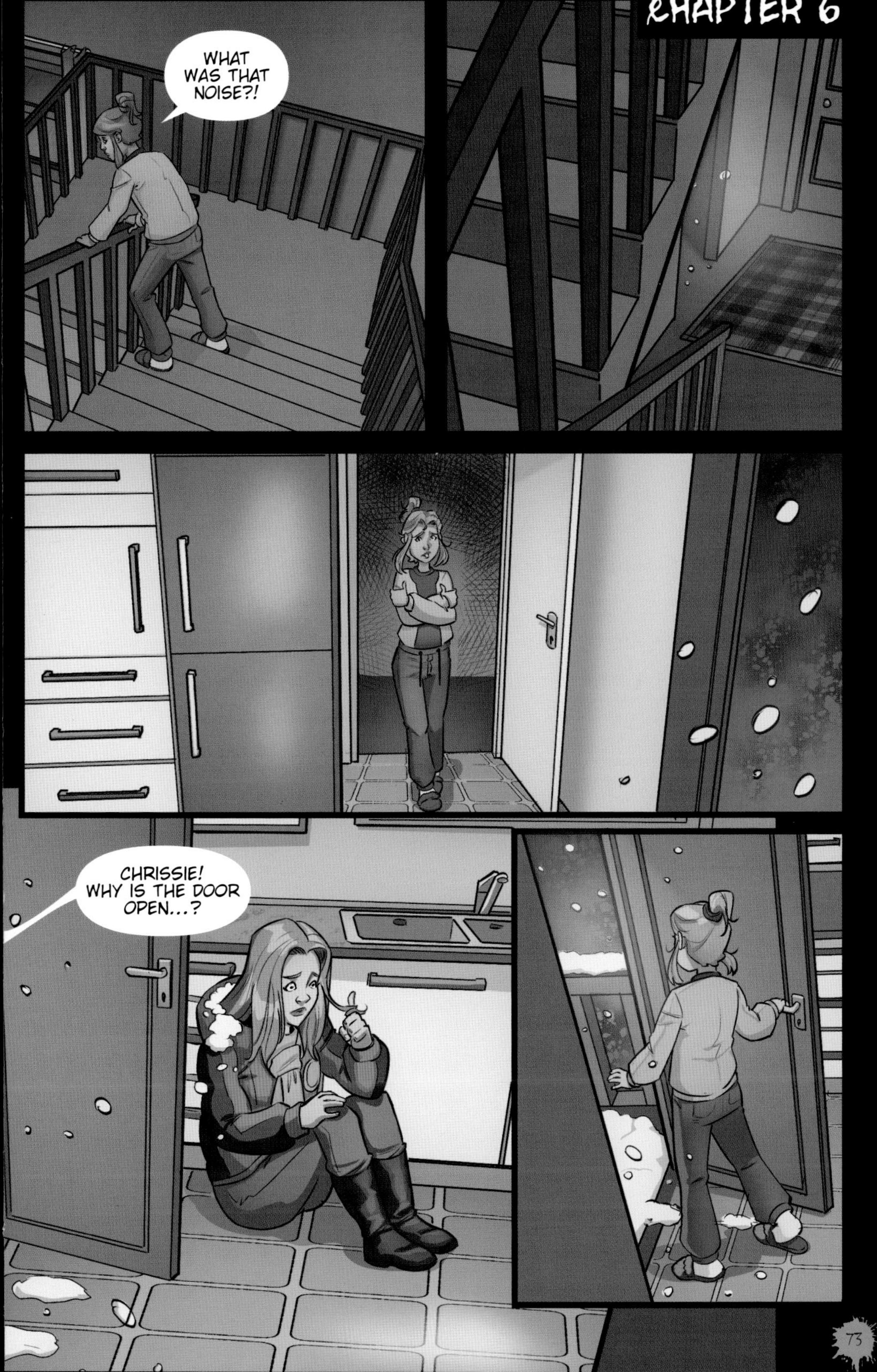
CHAPTER 6
WHAT WAS THAT NOISE?!
CHRISSIE! WHY IS THE DOOR OPEN...?

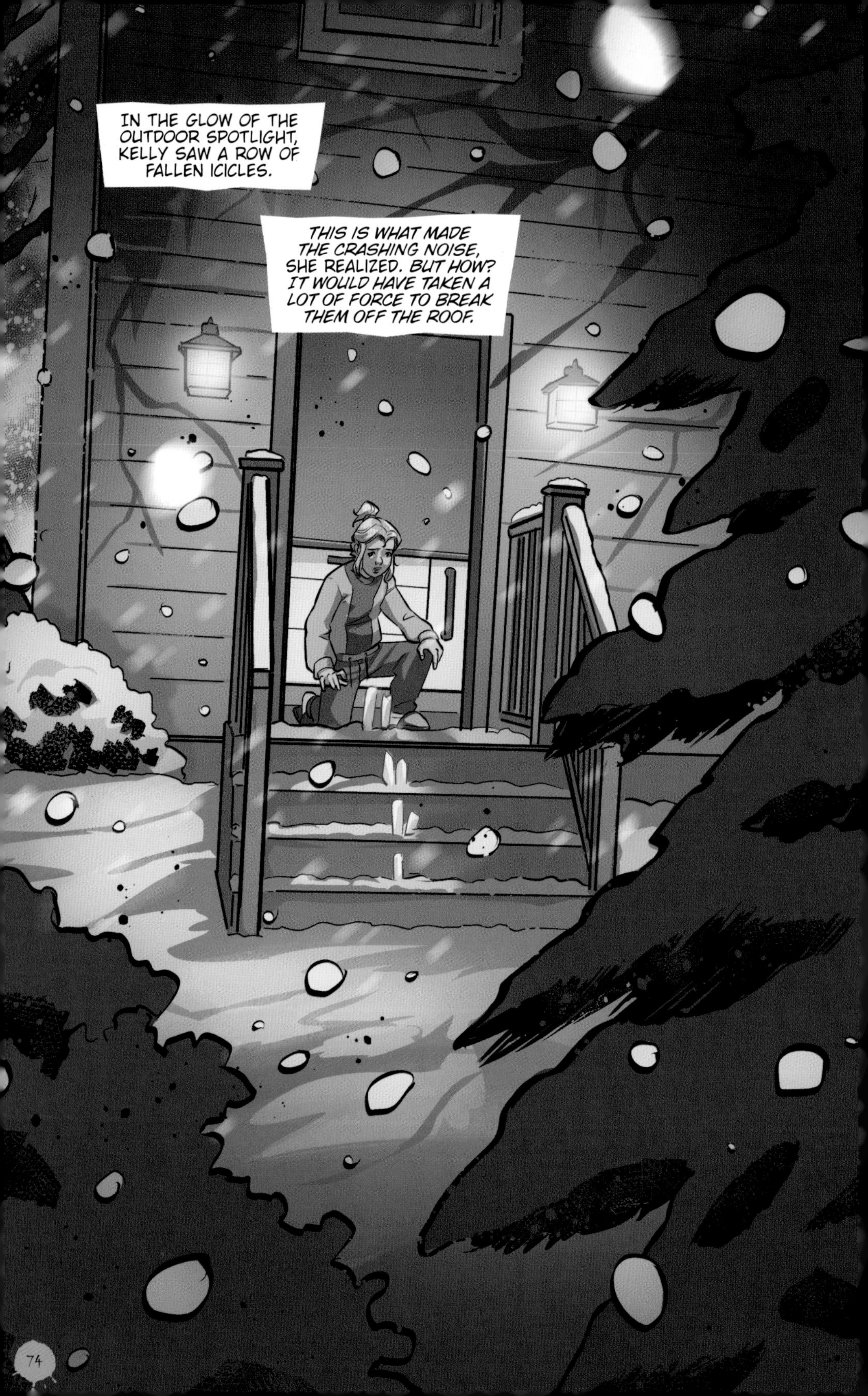
IN THE GLOW OF THE OUTDOOR SPOTLIGHT, KELLY SAW A ROW OF FALLEN ICICLES.
THIS IS WHAT MADE THE CRASHING NOISE, SHE REALIZED. BUT HOW? IT WOULD HAVE TAKEN A LOT OF FORCE TO BREAK THEM OFF THE ROOF.

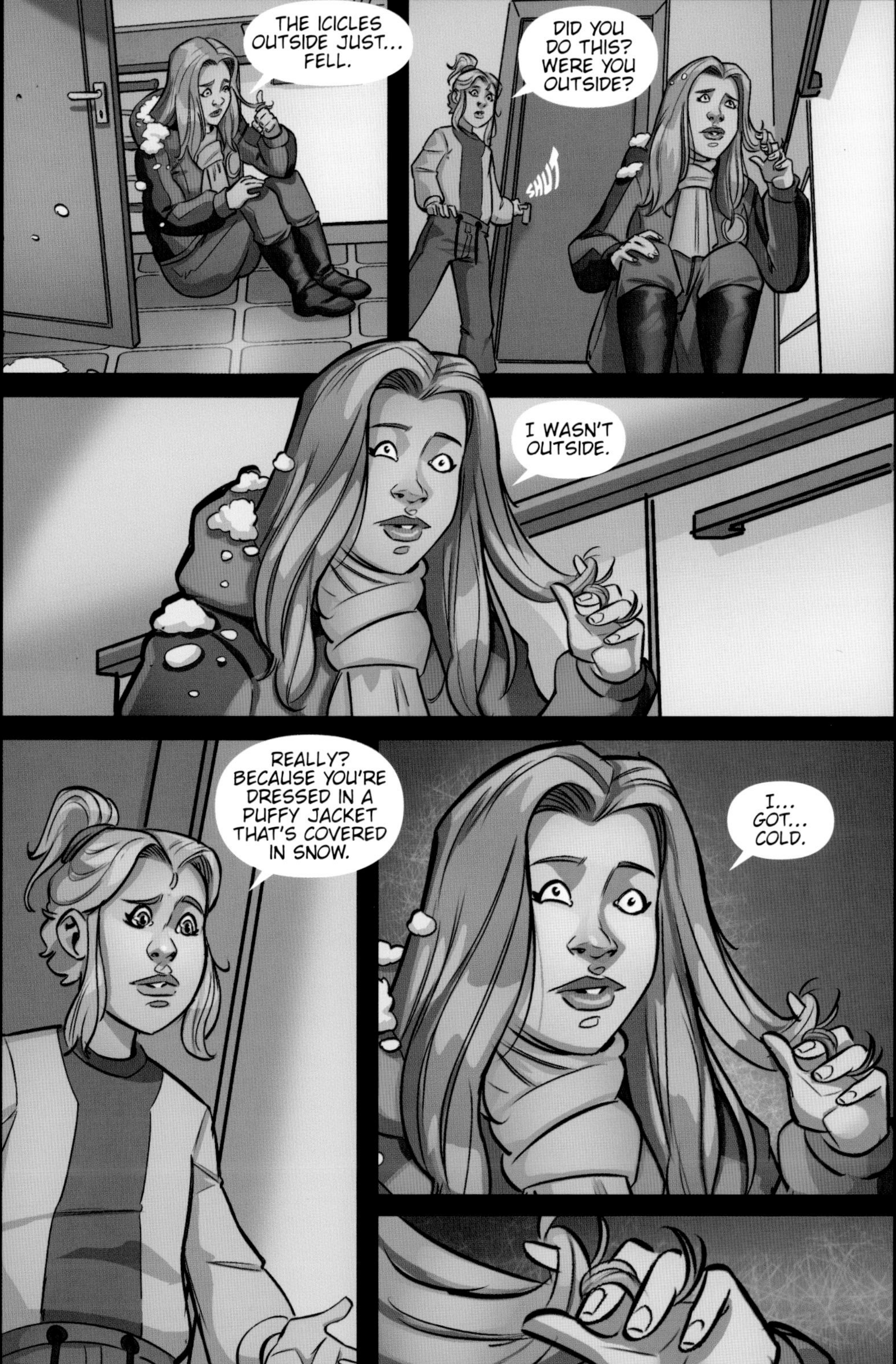
THE ICICLES OUTSIDE JUST... FELL.
DID YOU DO THIS? WERE YOU OUTSIDE?
SHUT
I WASN'T OUTSIDE.
REALLY? BECAUSE YOU'RE DRESSED IN A PUFFY JACKET THAT'S COVERED IN SNOW.
I... GOT... COLD.

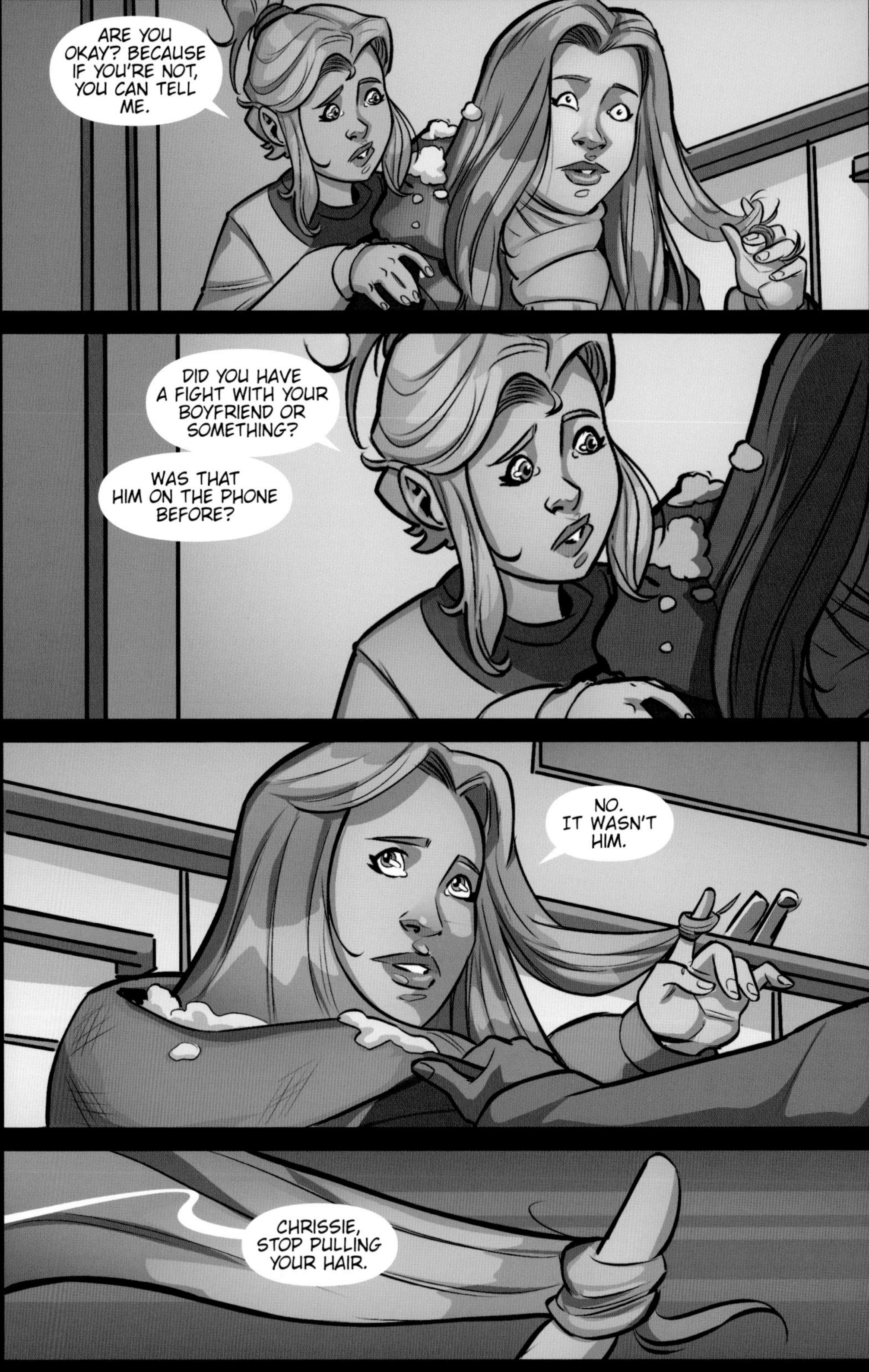
ARE YOU OKAY? BECAUSE IF YOU'RE NOT, YOU CAN TELL ME.
DID YOU HAVE A FIGHT WITH YOUR BOYFRIEND OR SOMETHING?
WAS THAT HIM ON THE PHONE BEFORE?
NO. IT WASN'T HIM.
CHRISSIE, STOP PULLING YOUR HAIR.

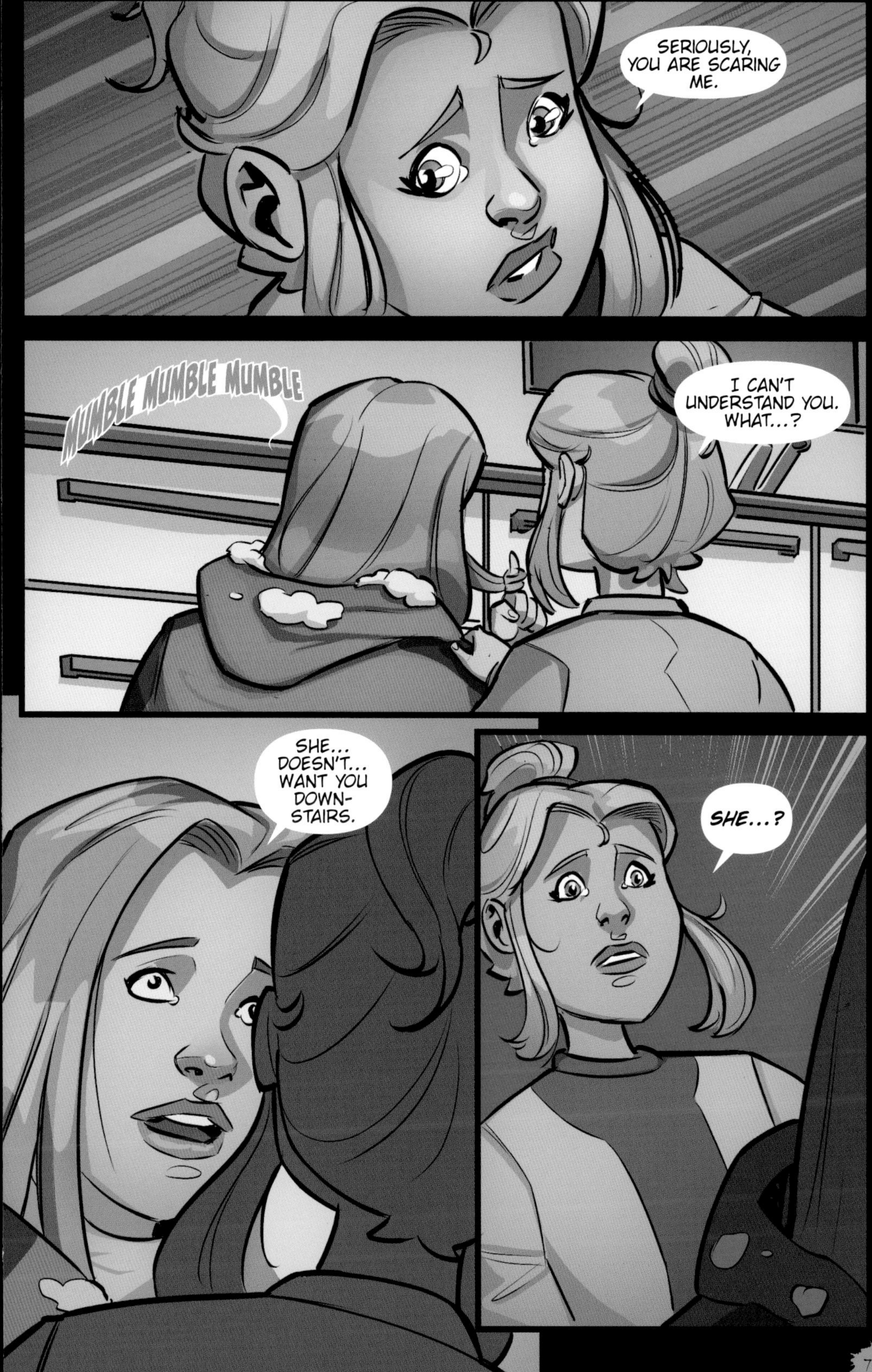
SERIOUSLY, YOU ARE SCARING ME.
MUMBLE MUMBLE MUMBLE
I CAN'T UNDERSTAND YOU. WHAT...?
SHE... DOESN'T... WANT YOU DOWN-STAIRS.
SHE...?

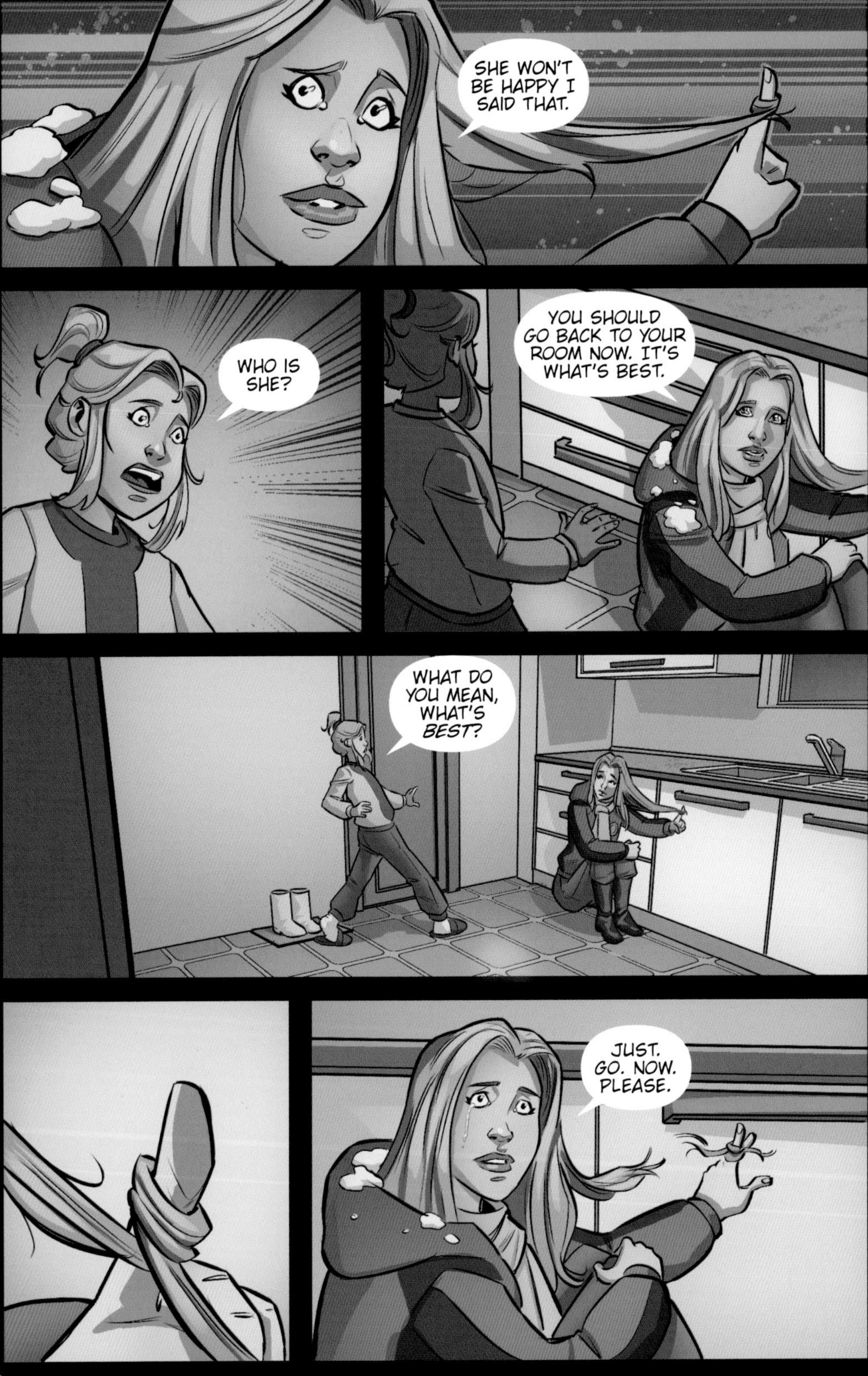
SHE WON'T BE HAPPY I SAID THAT.
WHO IS SHE?
YOU SHOULD GO BACK TO YOUR ROOM NOW. IT'S WHAT'S BEST.
WHAT DO YOU MEAN, WHAT'S *BEST*?
JUST. GO. NOW. PLEASE.

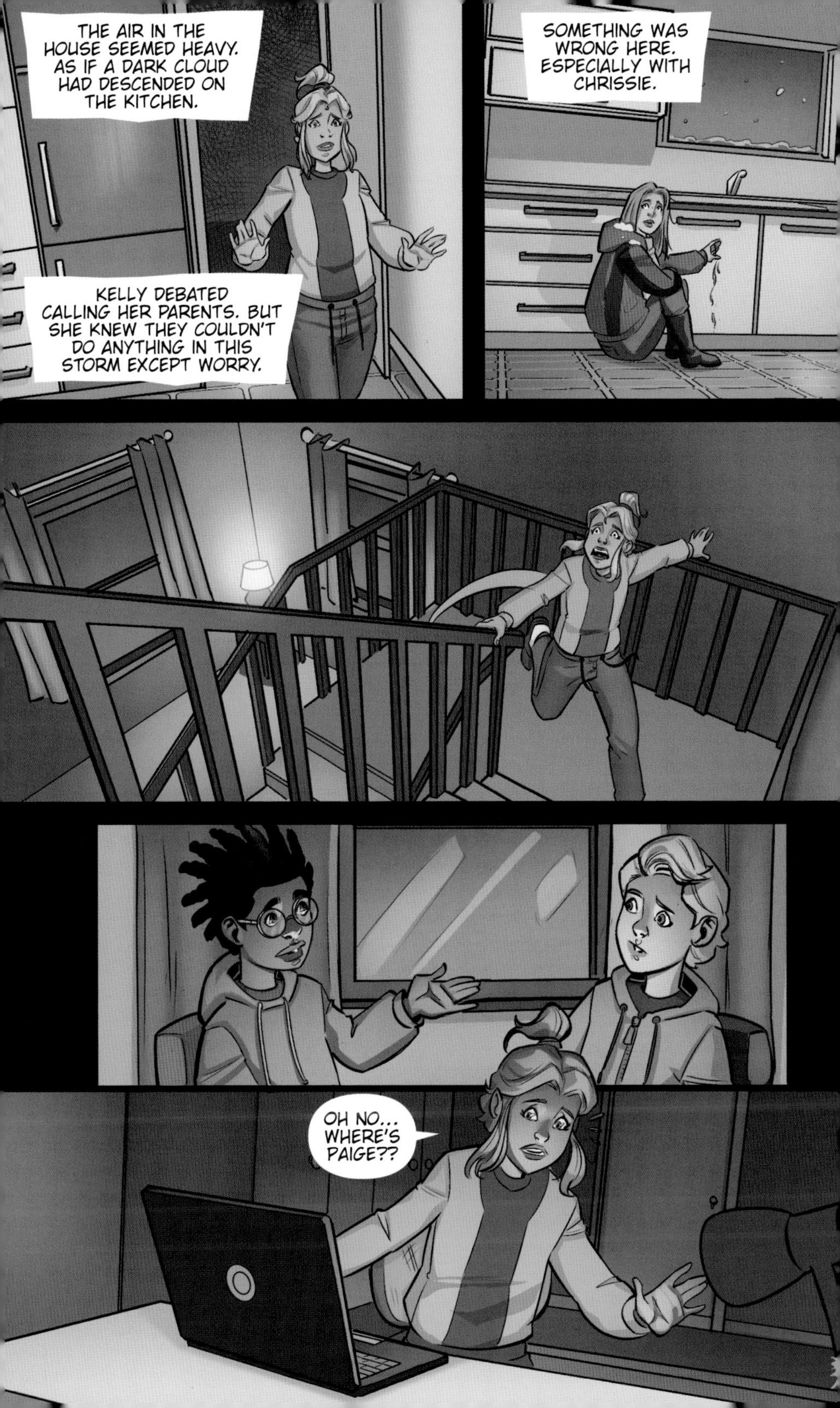
THE AIR IN THE HOUSE SEEMED HEAVY. AS IF A DARK CLOUD HAD DESCENDED ON THE KITCHEN.
KELLY DEBATED CALLING HER PARENTS. BUT SHE KNEW THEY COULDN'T DO ANYTHING IN THIS STORM EXCEPT WORRY.
SOMETHING WAS WRONG HERE. ESPECIALLY WITH CHRISSIE.
OH NO... WHERE'S PAIGE??

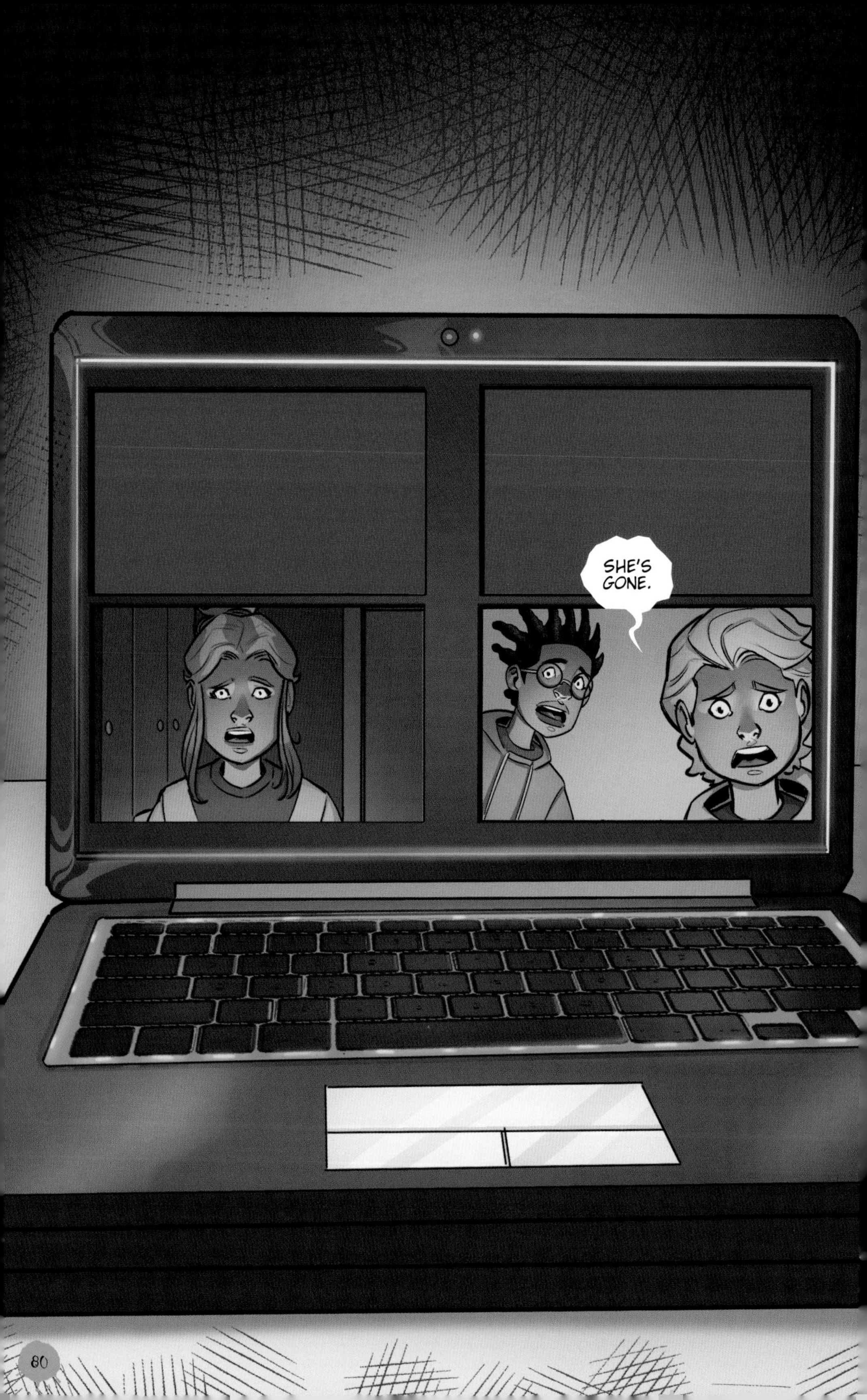
SHE'S GONE.

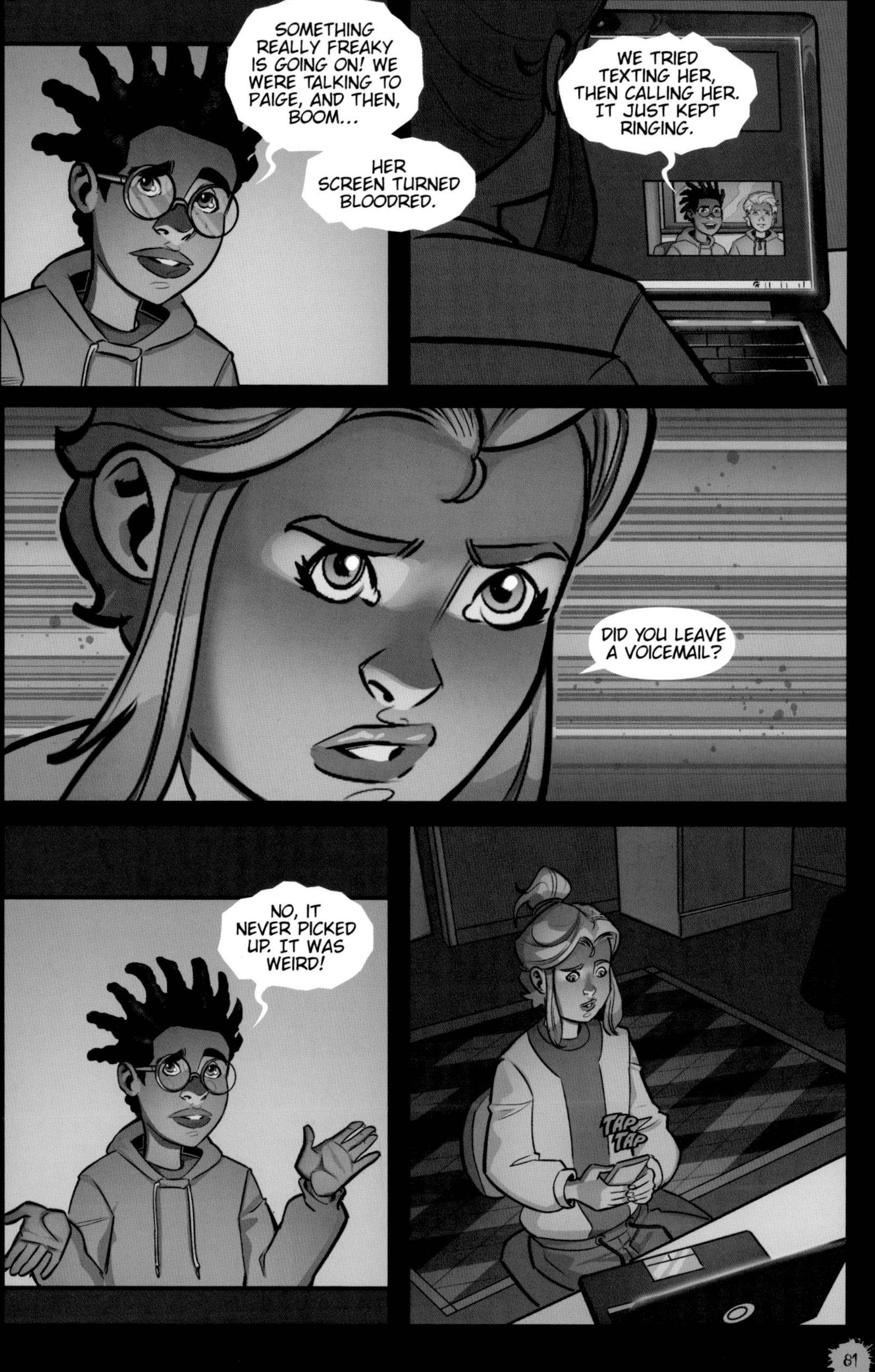
SOMETHING REALLY FREAKY IS GOING ON! WE WERE TALKING TO PAIGE, AND THEN, BOOM...
HER SCREEN TURNED BLOODRED.
WE TRIED TEXTING HER, THEN CALLING HER. IT JUST KEPT RINGING.
DID YOU LEAVE A VOICEMAIL?
NO, IT NEVER PICKED UP. IT WAS WEIRD!
TAP TAP

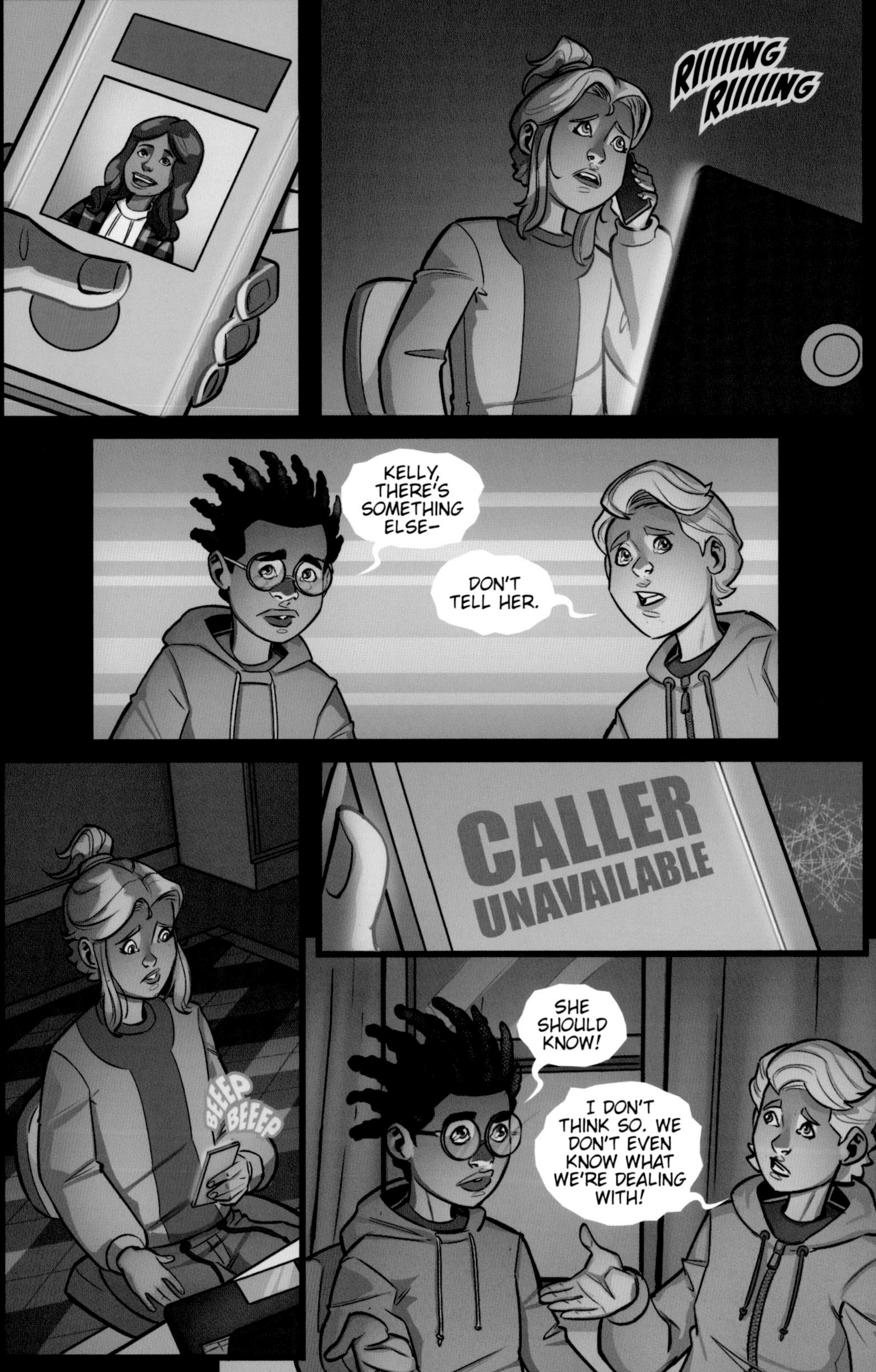
RIIIIING
RIIIIING
KELLY, THERE'S SOMETHING ELSE–
DON'T TELL HER.
CALLER UNAVAILABLE
BEEEP BEEEP
SHE SHOULD KNOW!
I DON'T THINK SO. WE DON'T EVEN KNOW WHAT WE'RE DEALING WITH!

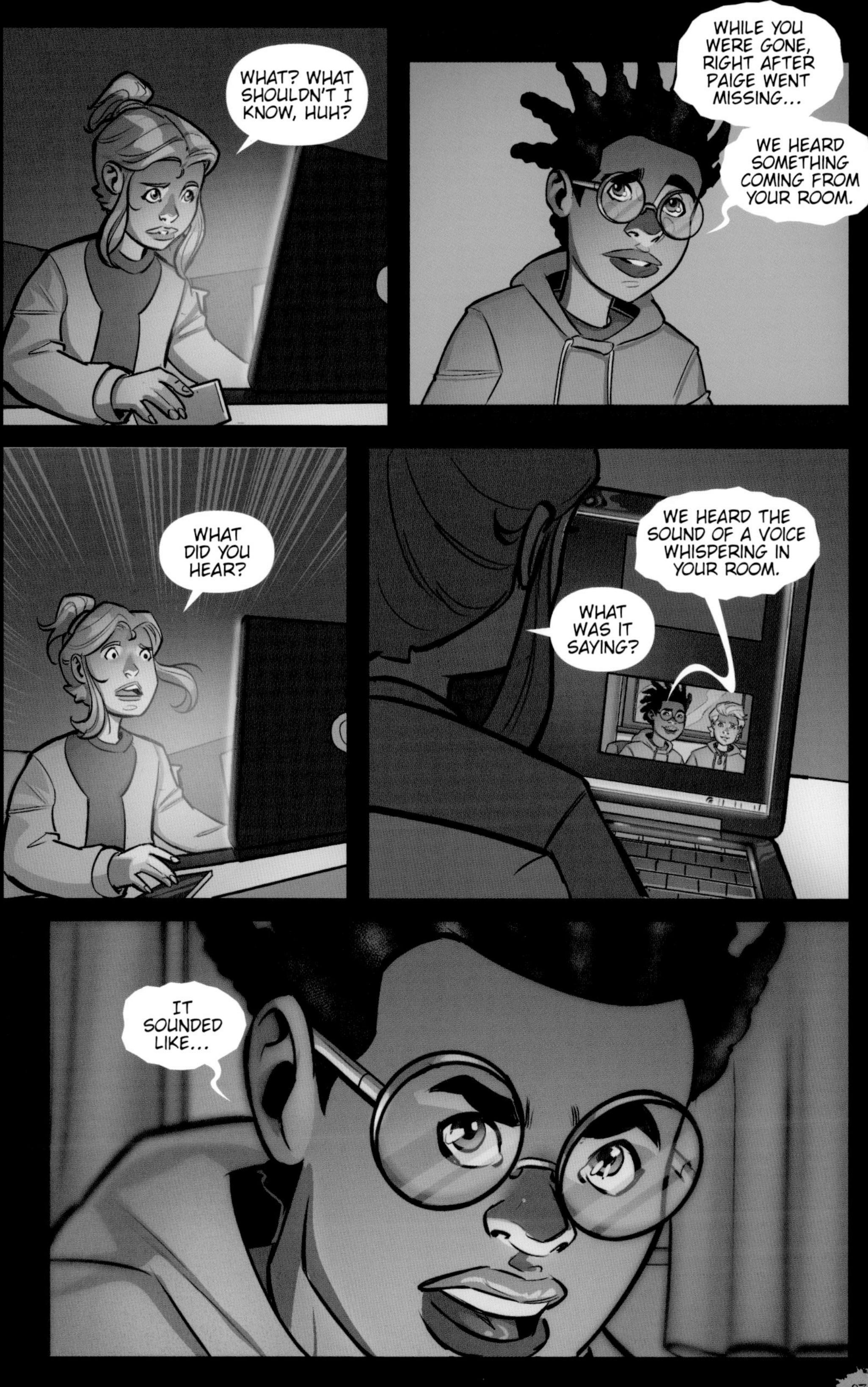
WHAT? WHAT SHOULDN'T I KNOW, HUH?
WHILE YOU WERE GONE, RIGHT AFTER PAIGE WENT MISSING...
WE HEARD SOMETHING COMING FROM YOUR ROOM.
WHAT DID YOU HEAR?
WE HEARD THE SOUND OF A VOICE WHISPERING IN YOUR ROOM.
WHAT WAS IT SAYING?
IT SOUNDED LIKE...

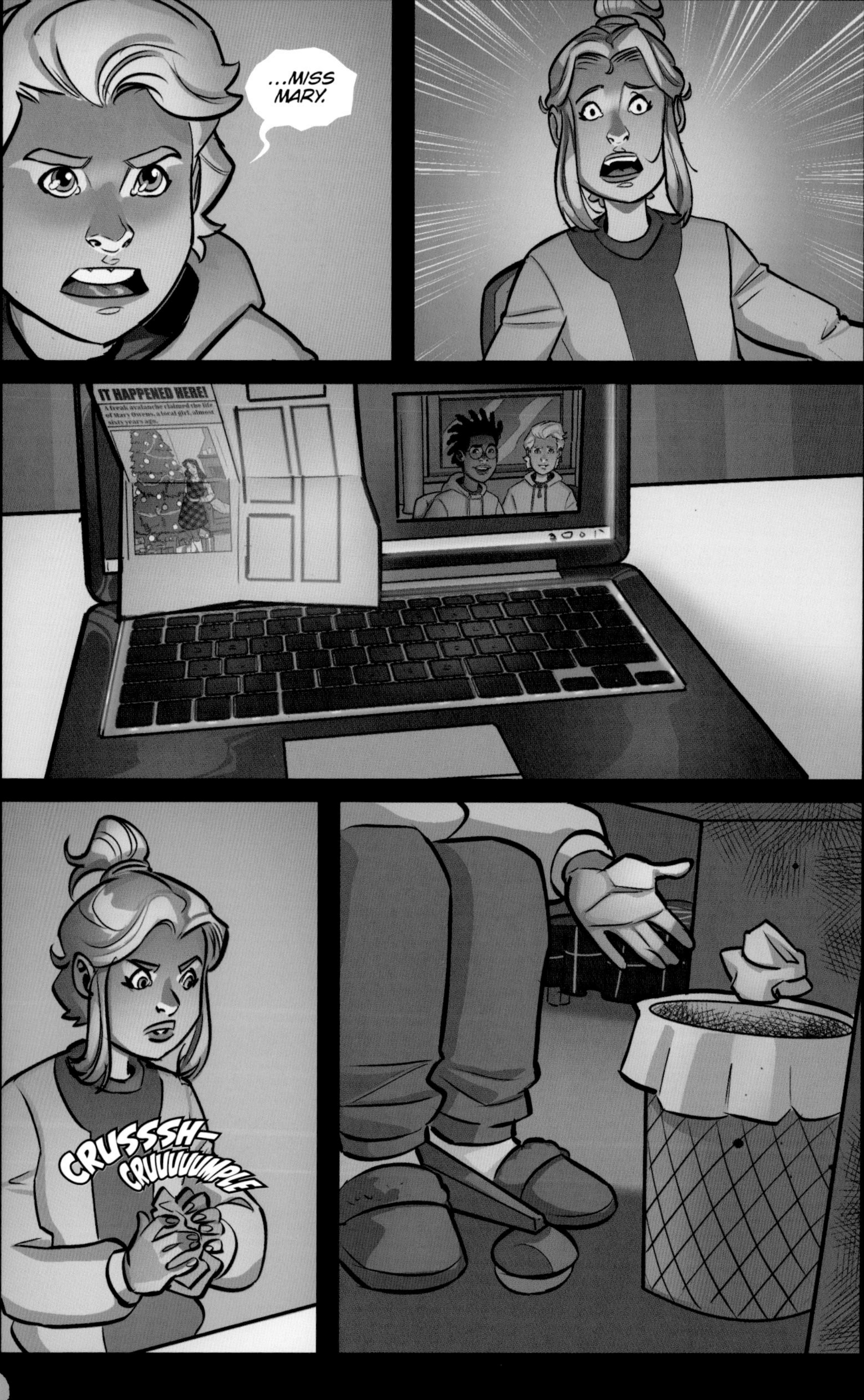
...MISS MARY.
IT HAPPENED HERE!
A freak avalanche claimed the life of Mary Owens, a local girl, almost sixty years ago.
CRUSSSH-
CRUUUUUMPLE

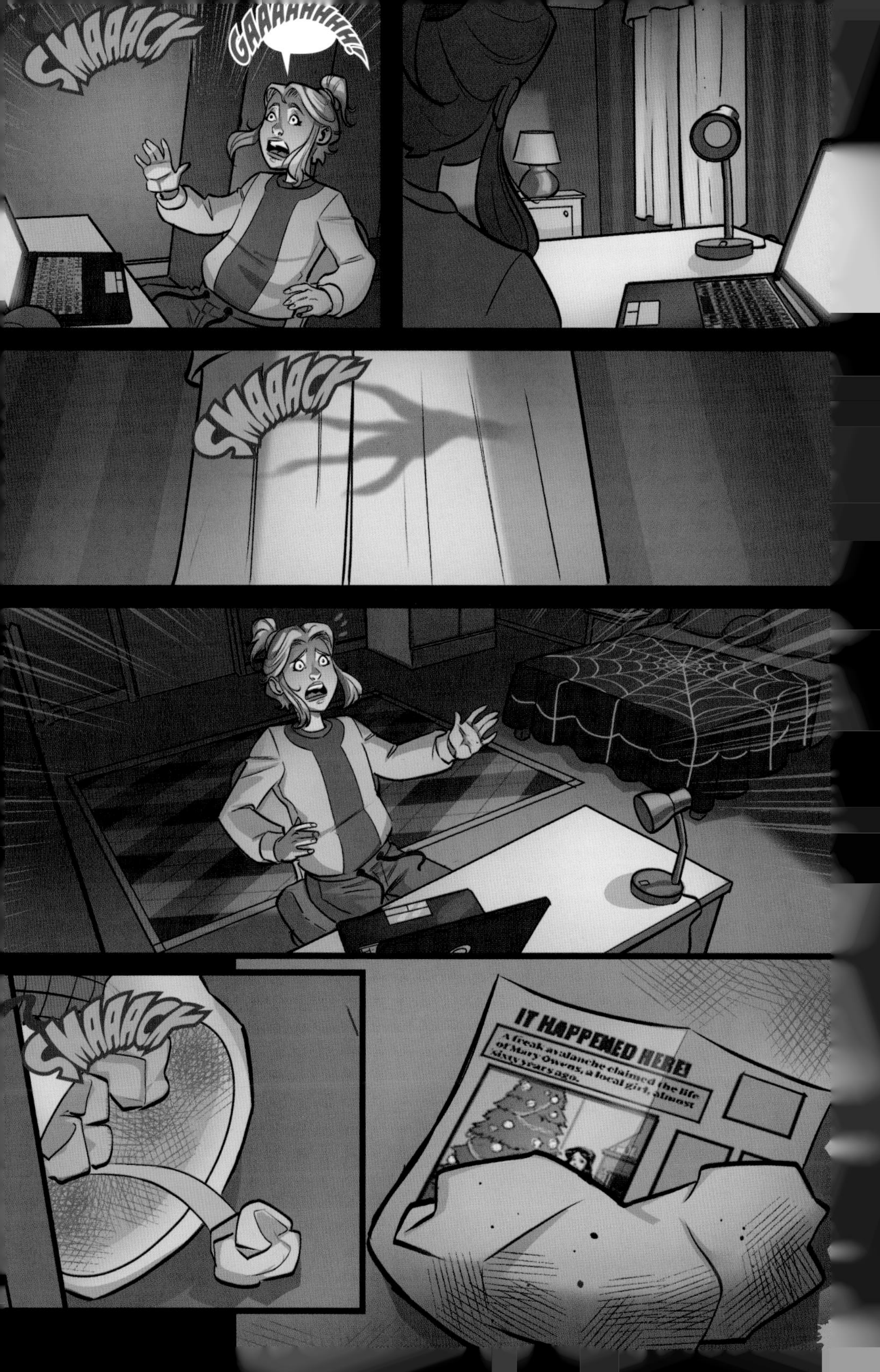
SMAAACK
GAAAHHHH!
SMAAACK
SMAAACK
IT HAPPENED HERE!
A freak avalanche claimed the life of Mary Owens, a local girl, almost sixty years ago.

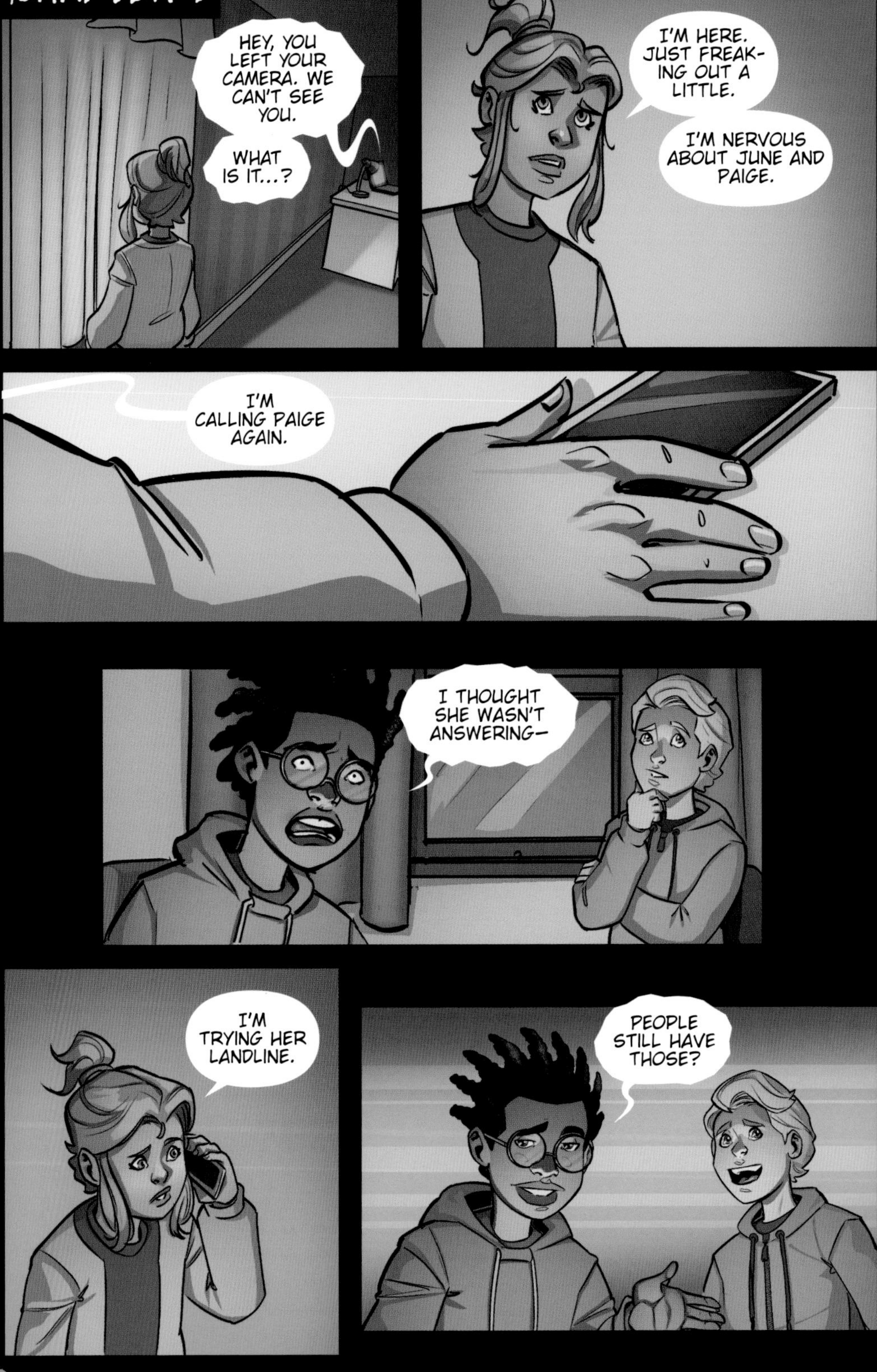
HEY, YOU LEFT YOUR CAMERA. WE CAN'T SEE YOU.
WHAT IS IT...?
I'M HERE. JUST FREAK-ING OUT A LITTLE.
I'M NERVOUS ABOUT JUNE AND PAIGE.
I'M CALLING PAIGE AGAIN.
I THOUGHT SHE WASN'T ANSWERING—
I'M TRYING HER LANDLINE.
PEOPLE STILL HAVE THOSE?

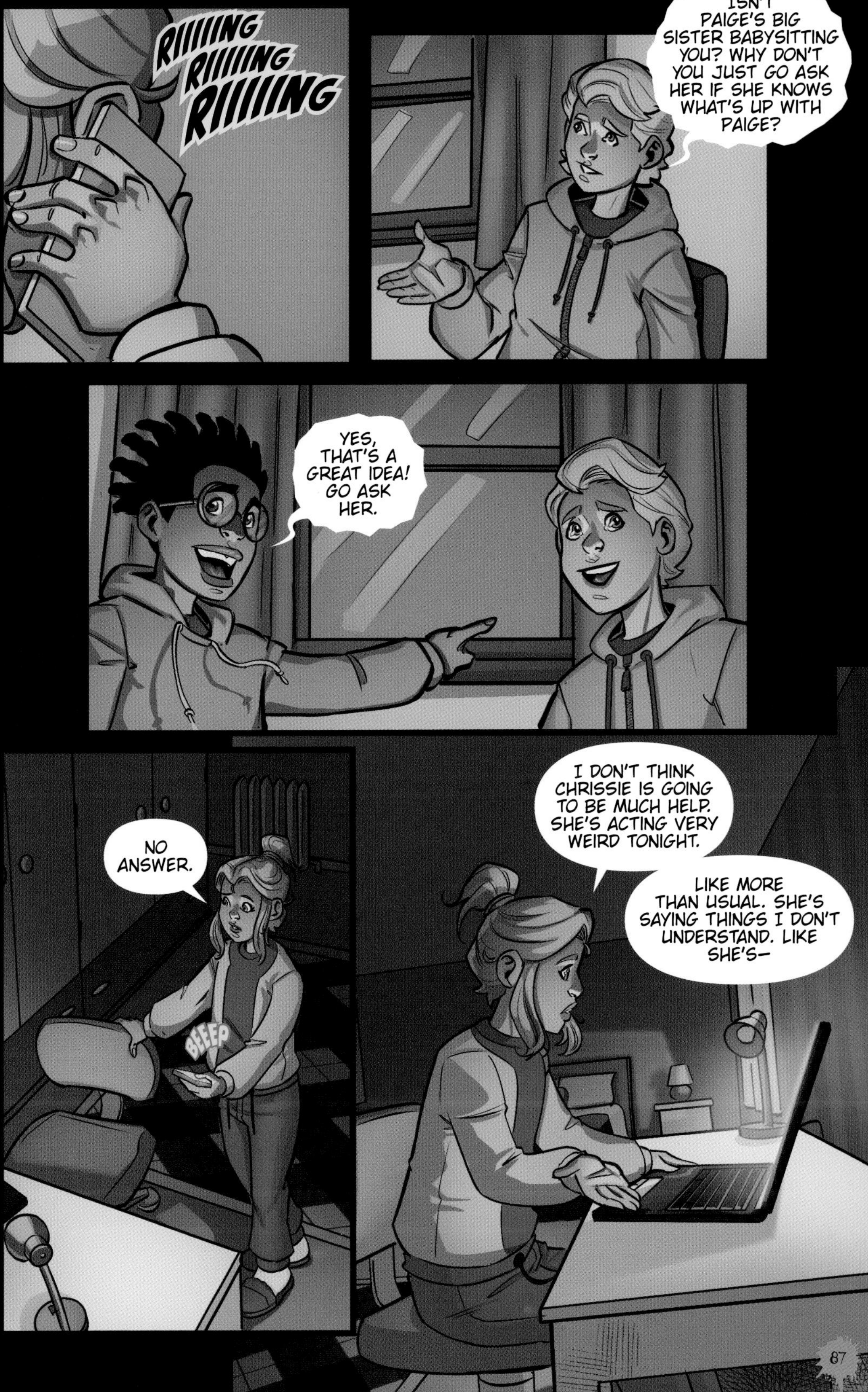
RIIIIING RIIIIING RIIIIING
ISN'T PAIGE'S BIG SISTER BABYSITTING YOU? WHY DON'T YOU JUST GO ASK HER IF SHE KNOWS WHAT'S UP WITH PAIGE?
YES, THAT'S A GREAT IDEA! GO ASK HER.
NO ANSWER.
BEEEP
I DON'T THINK CHRISSIE IS GOING TO BE MUCH HELP. SHE'S ACTING VERY WEIRD TONIGHT.
LIKE MORE THAN USUAL. SHE'S SAYING THINGS I DON'T UNDERSTAND. LIKE SHE'S—

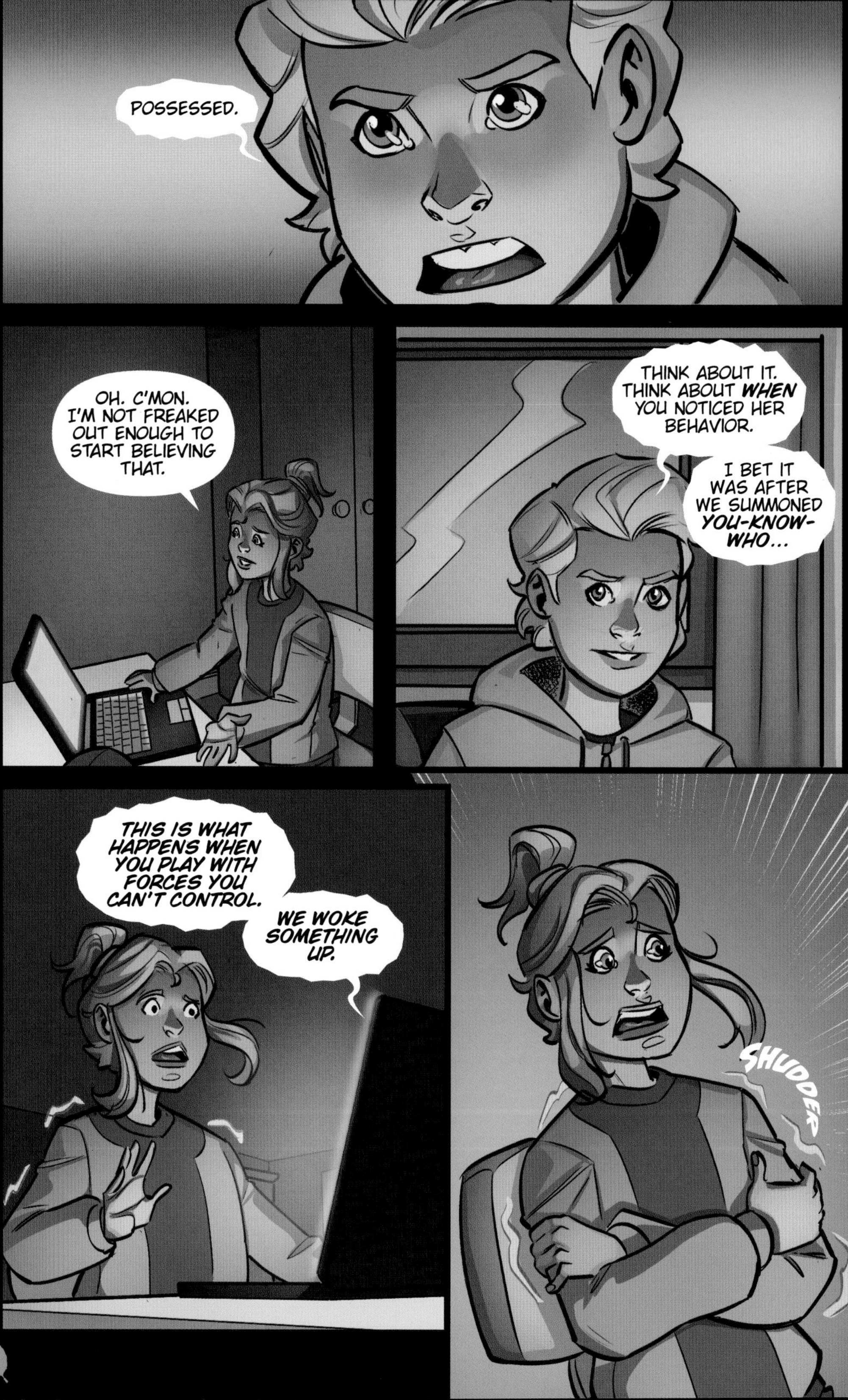
POSSESSED.
OH. C'MON. I'M NOT FREAKED OUT ENOUGH TO START BELIEVING THAT.
THINK ABOUT IT. THINK ABOUT WHEN YOU NOTICED HER BEHAVIOR.
I BET IT WAS AFTER WE SUMMONED YOU-KNOW-WHO...
THIS IS WHAT HAPPENS WHEN YOU PLAY WITH FORCES YOU CAN'T CONTROL.
WE WOKE SOMETHING UP.
SHUDDER

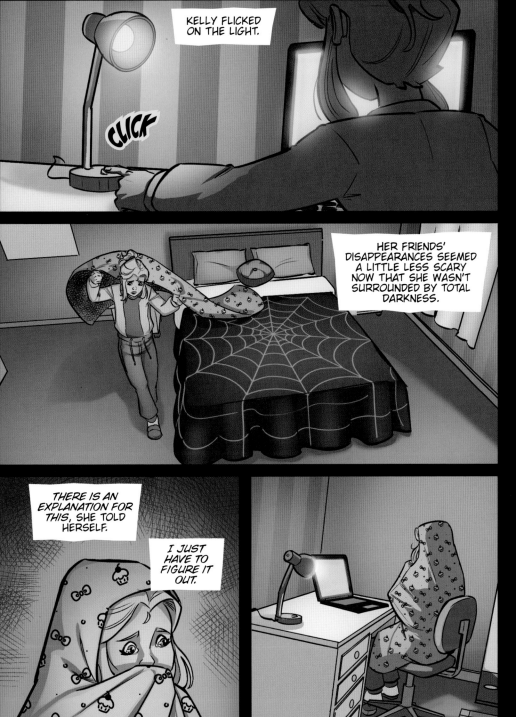

KELLY FLICKED ON THE LIGHT.

CLICK

HER FRIENDS' DISAPPEARANCES SEEMED A LITTLE LESS SCARY NOW THAT SHE WASN'T SURROUNDED BY TOTAL DARKNESS.

THERE IS AN EXPLANATION FOR THIS, SHE TOLD HERSELF.

I JUST HAVE TO FIGURE IT OUT.

UH-OH, DID WE LOSE GAVIN, TOO?

I NEED TO TALK TO YOU! TURN OFF YOUR MIC...

DM ME.

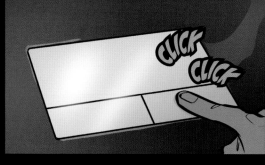

CLICK CLICK

CLICK TO MUTE

# CHAT WITH SPENCER

**KELLY**

What's wrong?

**SPENCER**

Gavin is what's wrong.

**KELLY**

???

**SPENCER**

Don't have much time. I am freaking out over here.

**KELLY**

About Miss Mary?

**SPENCER**

Yes, but about Gavin too.

**KELLY**

Y?

**SPENCER**

He's been acting strange all night. Twitchy. Nervous. It started with the Miss Mary thing. He keeps mumbling stuff under his breath too. You can't hear it on your end, but I can.

**KELLY**

What is he saying?

**SPENCER**

Stuff that makes no sense. COLDNESS IS COMING and LAGAD IS LIFE and YOU CANNOT BE HERE.

He is NOT in control, IMO.

**KELLY**

That sounds EXACTLY like Chrissie!!!!

WAIT. Is it possible he's playing you?

**SPENCER**

Maybe? I barely know him. I don't want him to stay over anymore. I don't trust him.

I don't feel safe.

What do I do?

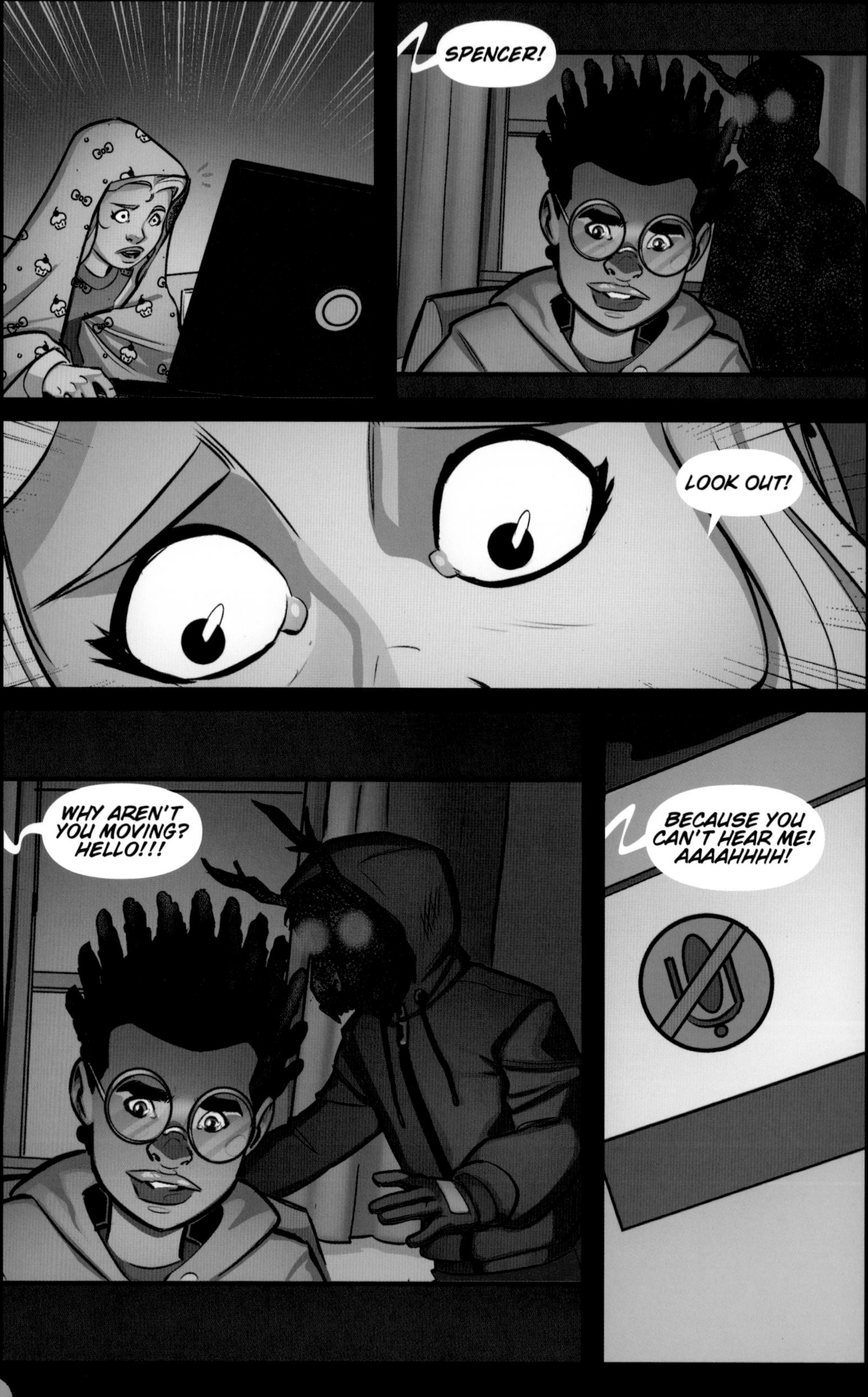
SPENCER!
LOOK OUT!
WHY AREN'T YOU MOVING? HELLO!!!
BECAUSE YOU CAN'T HEAR ME! AAAAHHHH!

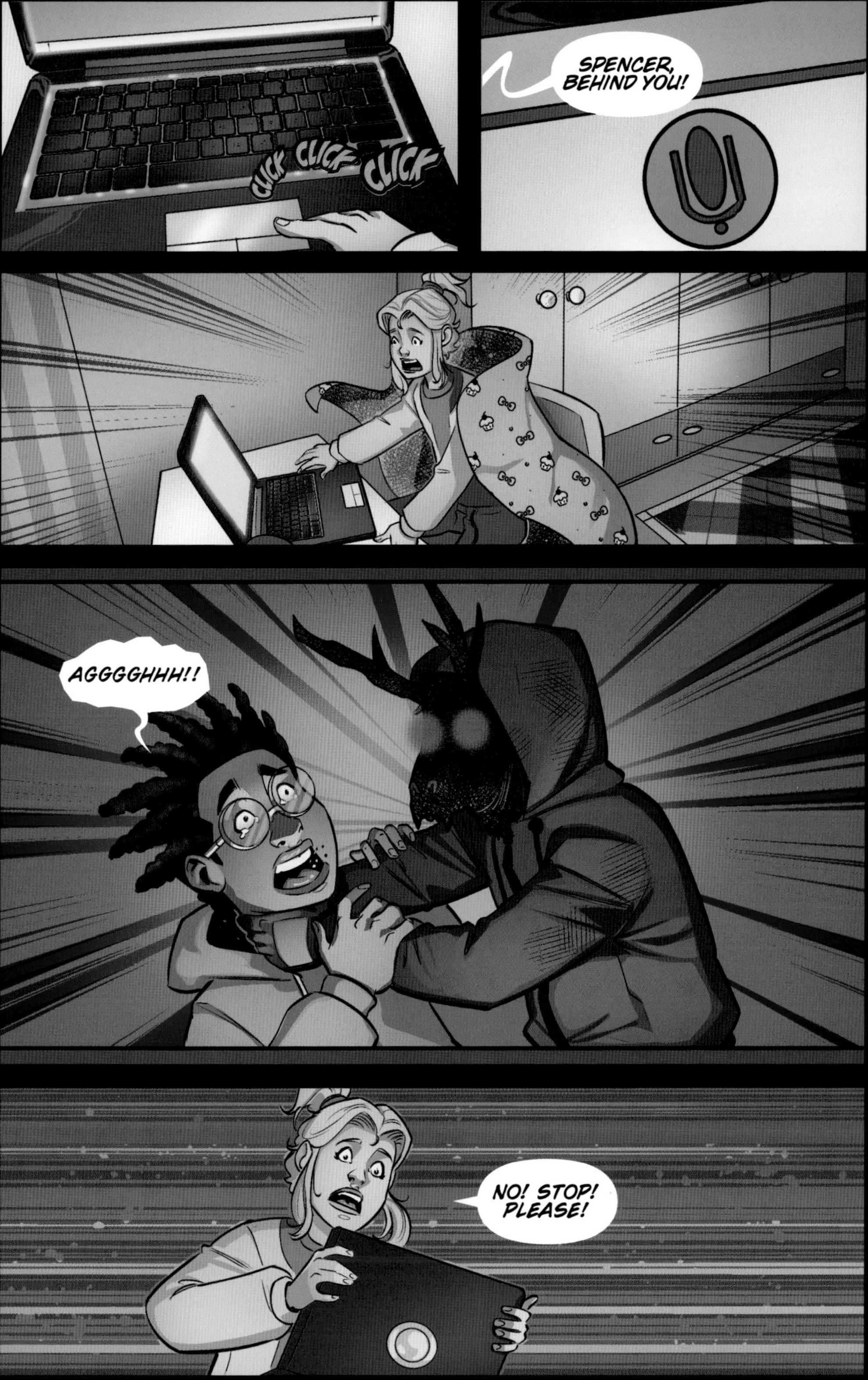
CLICK CLICK CLICK
SPENCER, BEHIND YOU!
AGGGGHHH!!
NO! STOP! PLEASE!

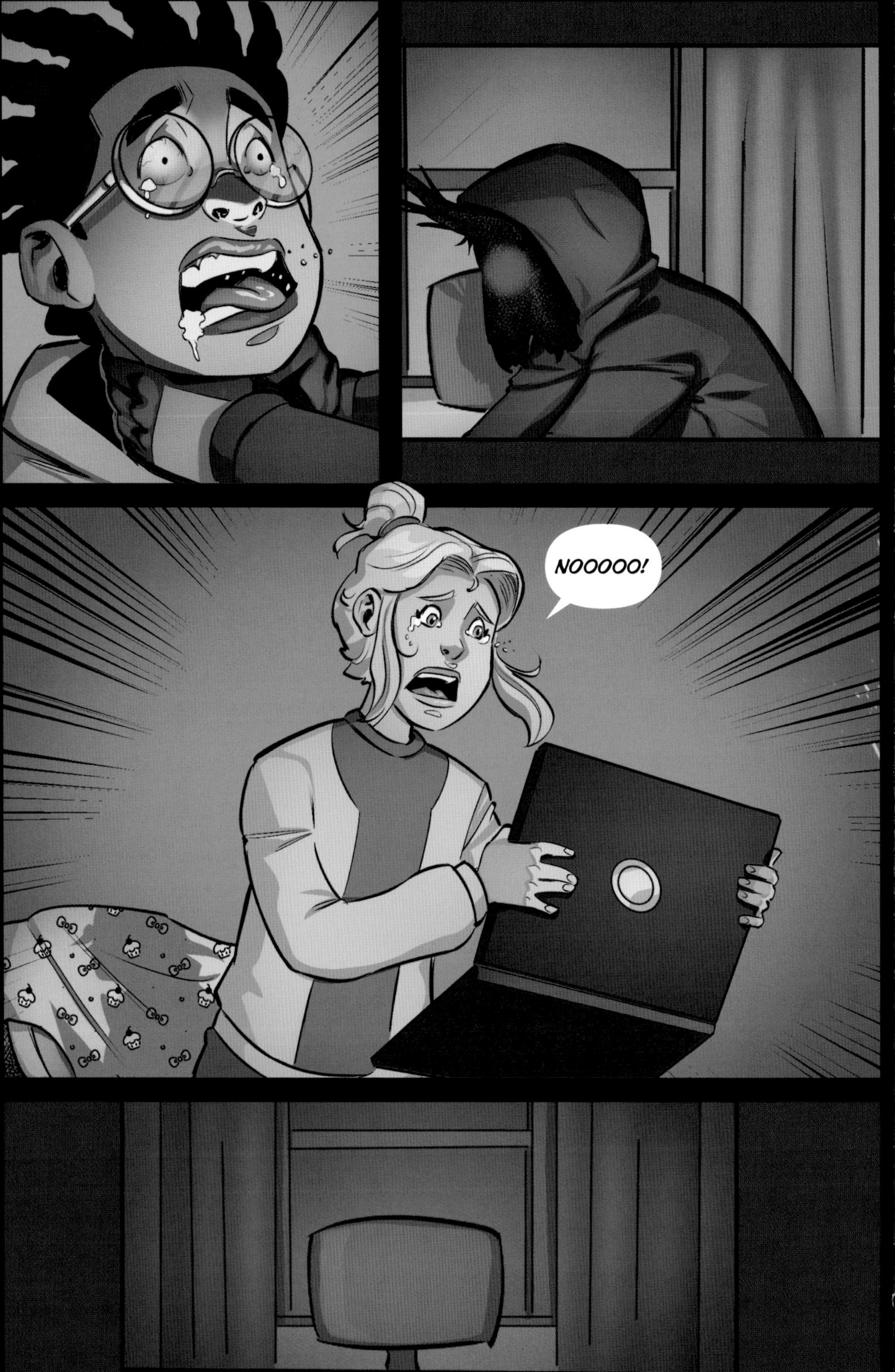
NOOOOO!

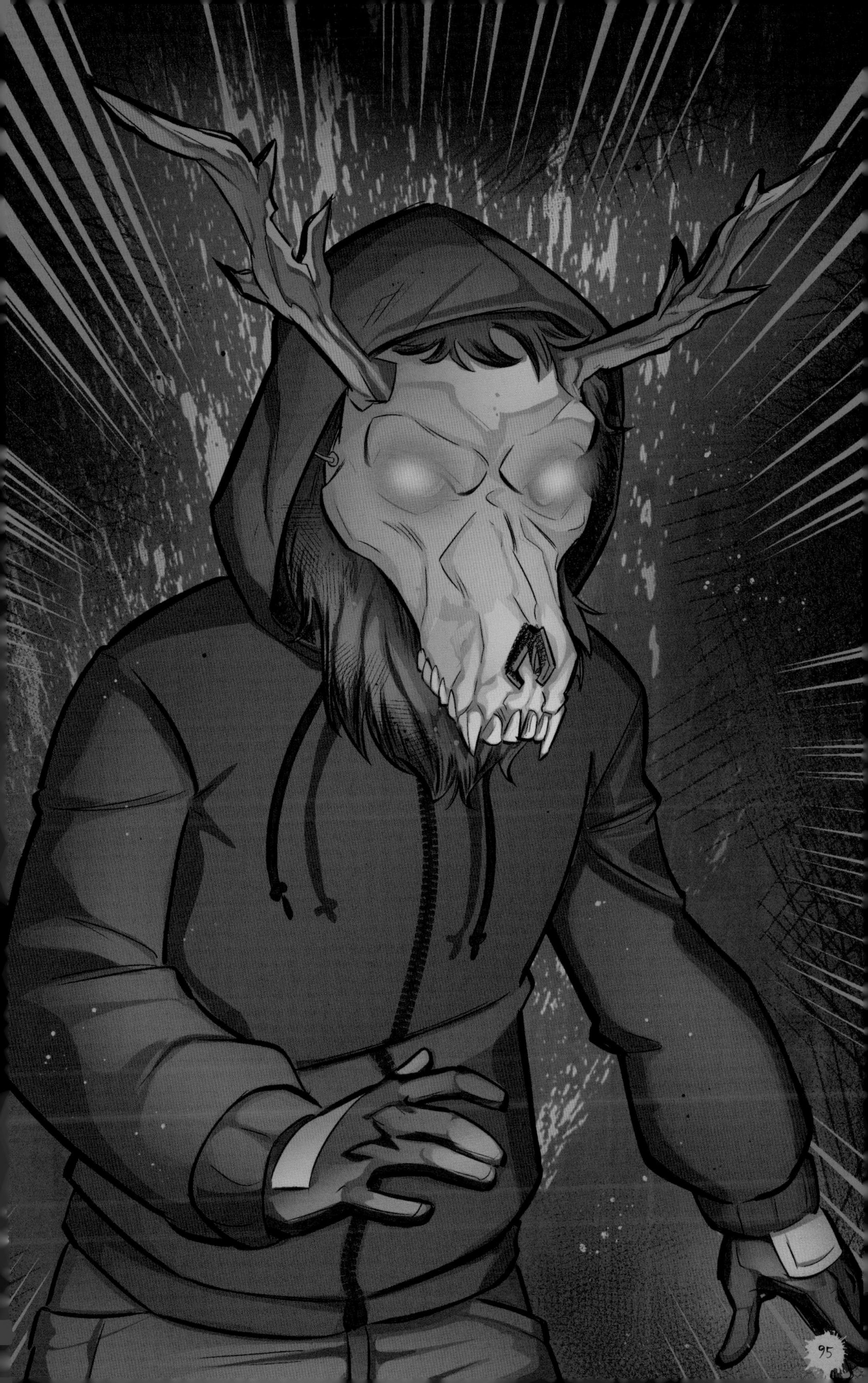

# CHAPTER 8

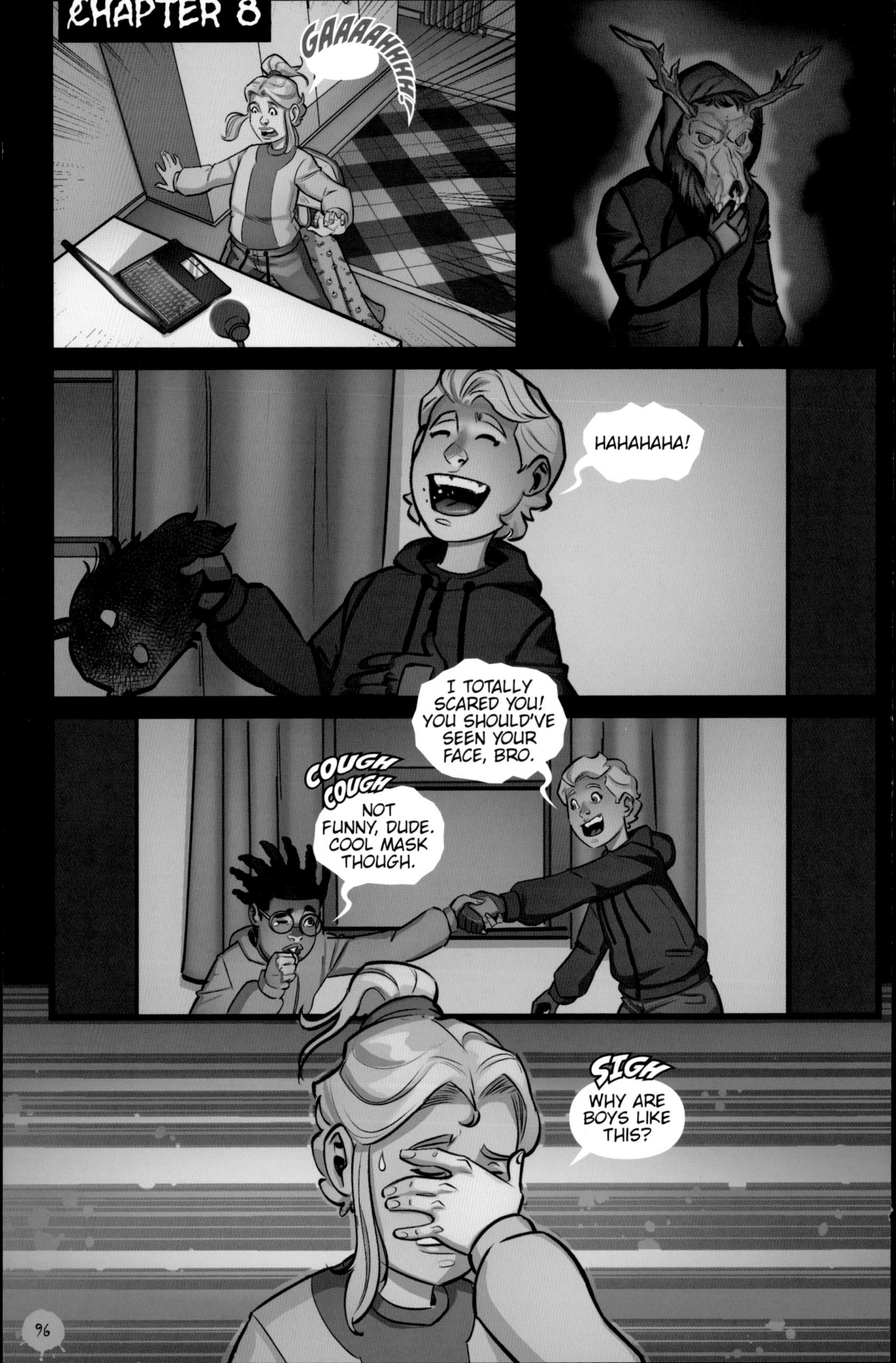
GAAAAHHHHH!
HAHAHAHA!
I TOTALLY SCARED YOU! YOU SHOULD'VE SEEN YOUR FACE, BRO.
COUGH COUGH
NOT FUNNY, DUDE. COOL MASK THOUGH.
SIGH
WHY ARE BOYS LIKE THIS?

SPENCER...?

HEY, YOUR VIDEO'S FROZEN.

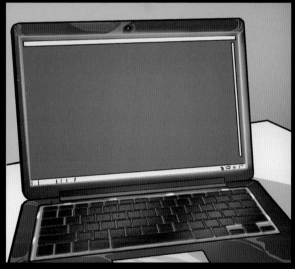

MAYBE THIS NIGHT REALLY IS *CURSED.*

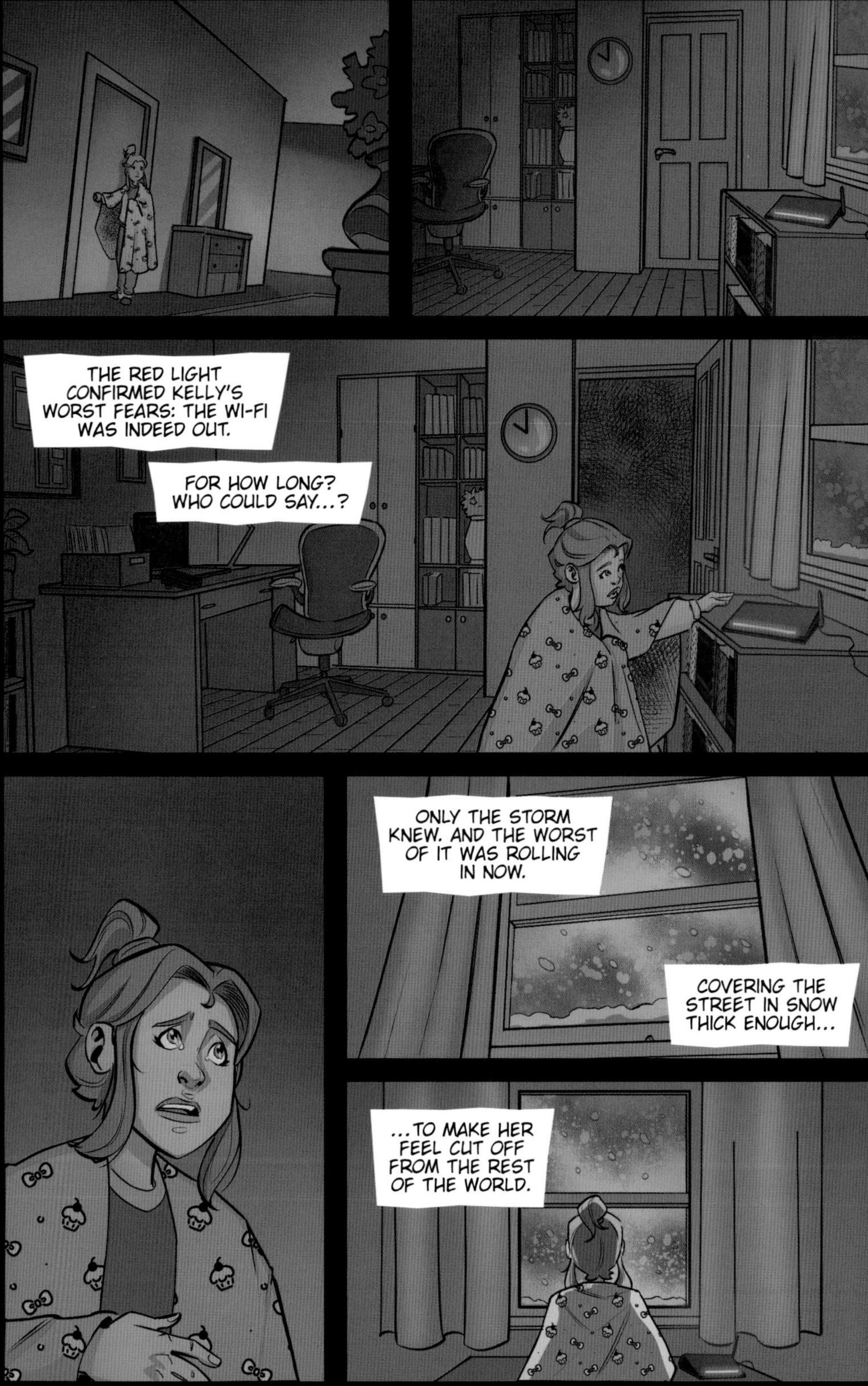
THE RED LIGHT CONFIRMED KELLY'S WORST FEARS: THE WI-FI WAS INDEED OUT.
FOR HOW LONG? WHO COULD SAY...?
ONLY THE STORM KNEW. AND THE WORST OF IT WAS ROLLING IN NOW.
COVERING THE STREET IN SNOW THICK ENOUGH...
...TO MAKE HER FEEL CUT OFF FROM THE REST OF THE WORLD.

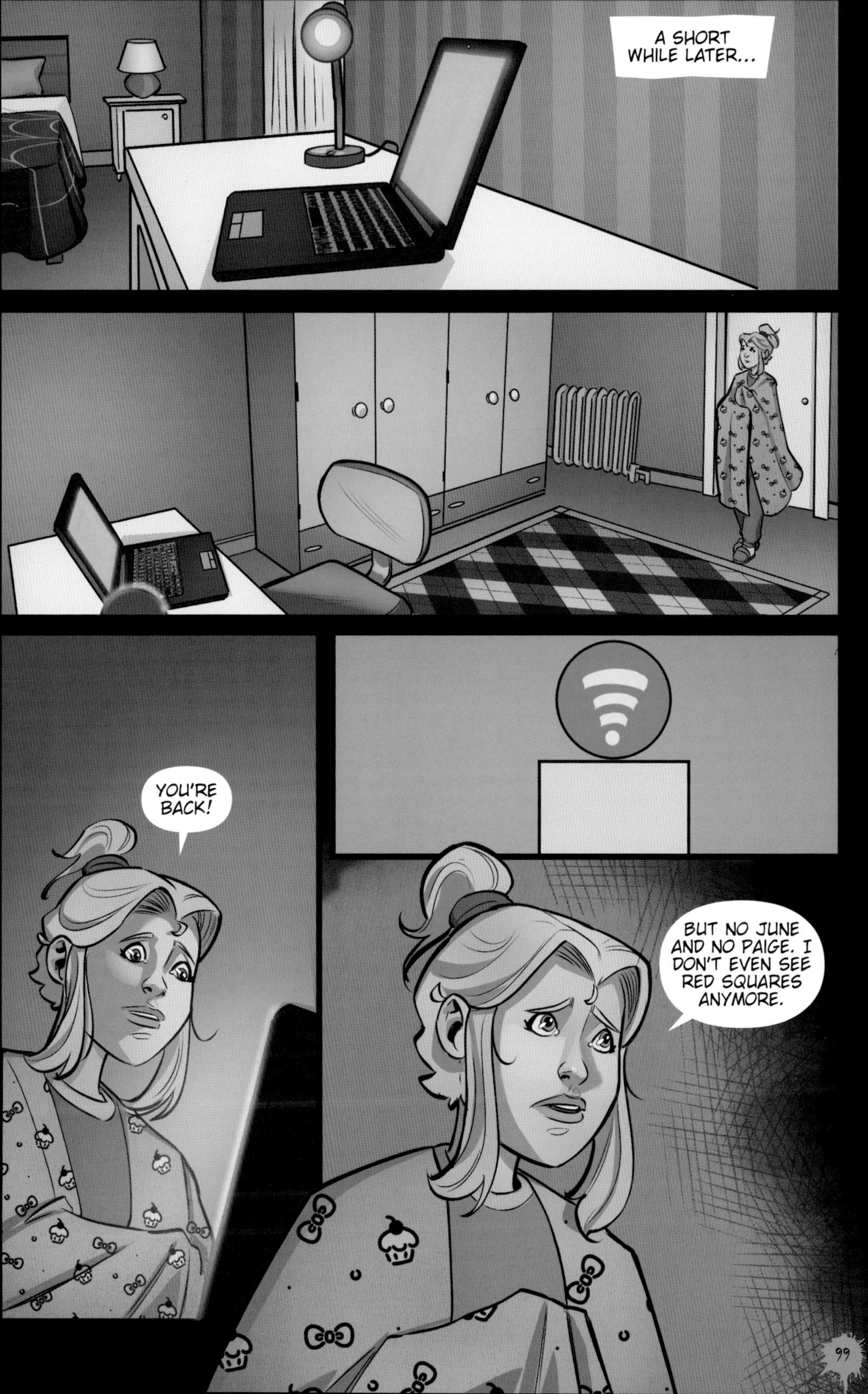
A SHORT WHILE LATER...
YOU'RE BACK!
BUT NO JUNE AND NO PAIGE. I DON'T EVEN SEE RED SQUARES ANYMORE.

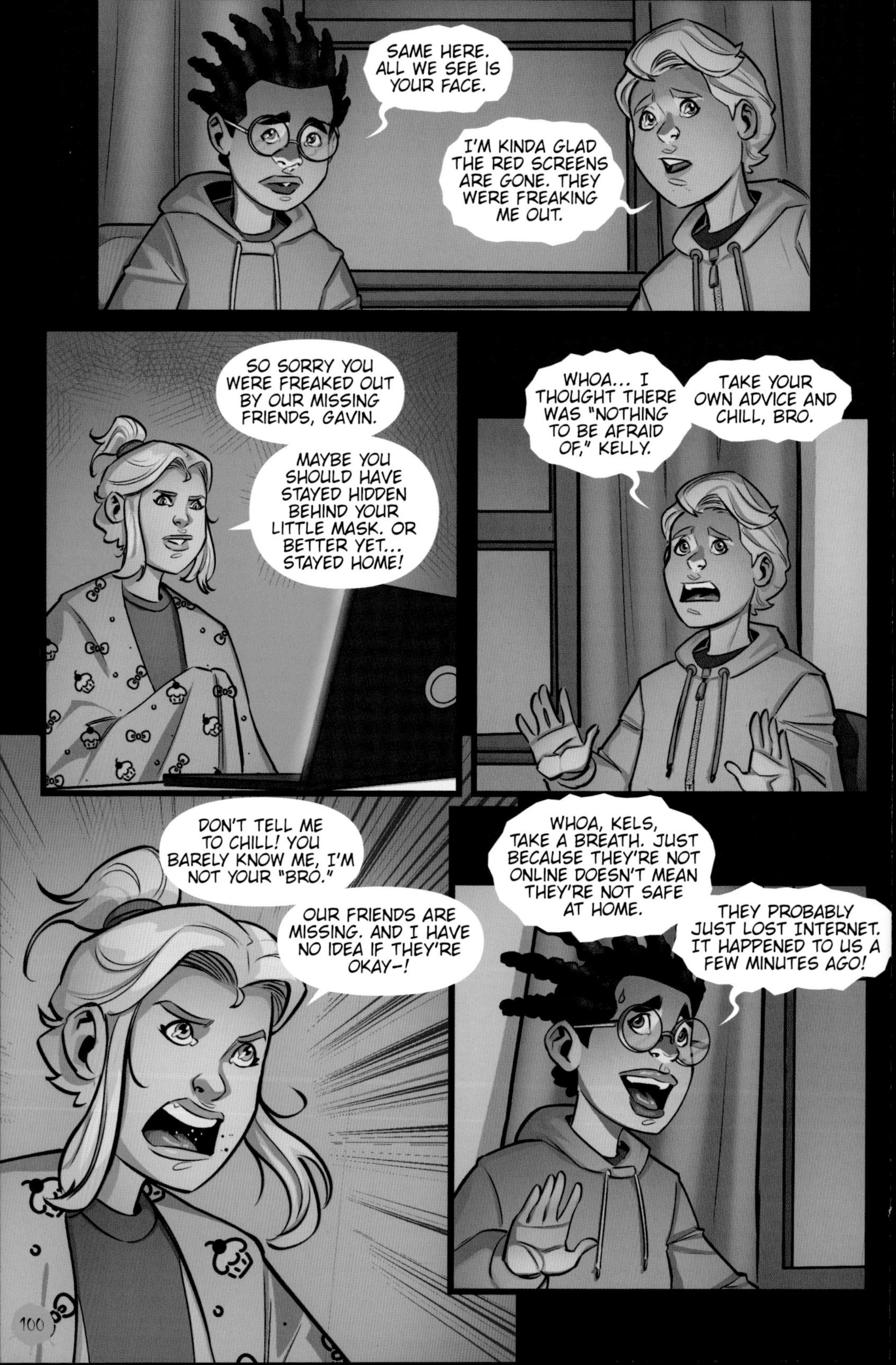
SAME HERE. ALL WE SEE IS YOUR FACE.
I'M KINDA GLAD THE RED SCREENS ARE GONE. THEY WERE FREAKING ME OUT.
SO SORRY YOU WERE FREAKED OUT BY OUR MISSING FRIENDS, GAVIN.
MAYBE YOU SHOULD HAVE STAYED HIDDEN BEHIND YOUR LITTLE MASK. OR BETTER YET... STAYED HOME!
WHOA... I THOUGHT THERE WAS "NOTHING TO BE AFRAID OF," KELLY.
TAKE YOUR OWN ADVICE AND CHILL, BRO.
DON'T TELL ME TO CHILL! YOU BARELY KNOW ME, I'M NOT YOUR "BRO."
OUR FRIENDS ARE MISSING. AND I HAVE NO IDEA IF THEY'RE OKAY–!
WHOA, KELS, TAKE A BREATH. JUST BECAUSE THEY'RE NOT ONLINE DOESN'T MEAN THEY'RE NOT SAFE AT HOME.
THEY PROBABLY JUST LOST INTERNET. IT HAPPENED TO US A FEW MINUTES AGO!

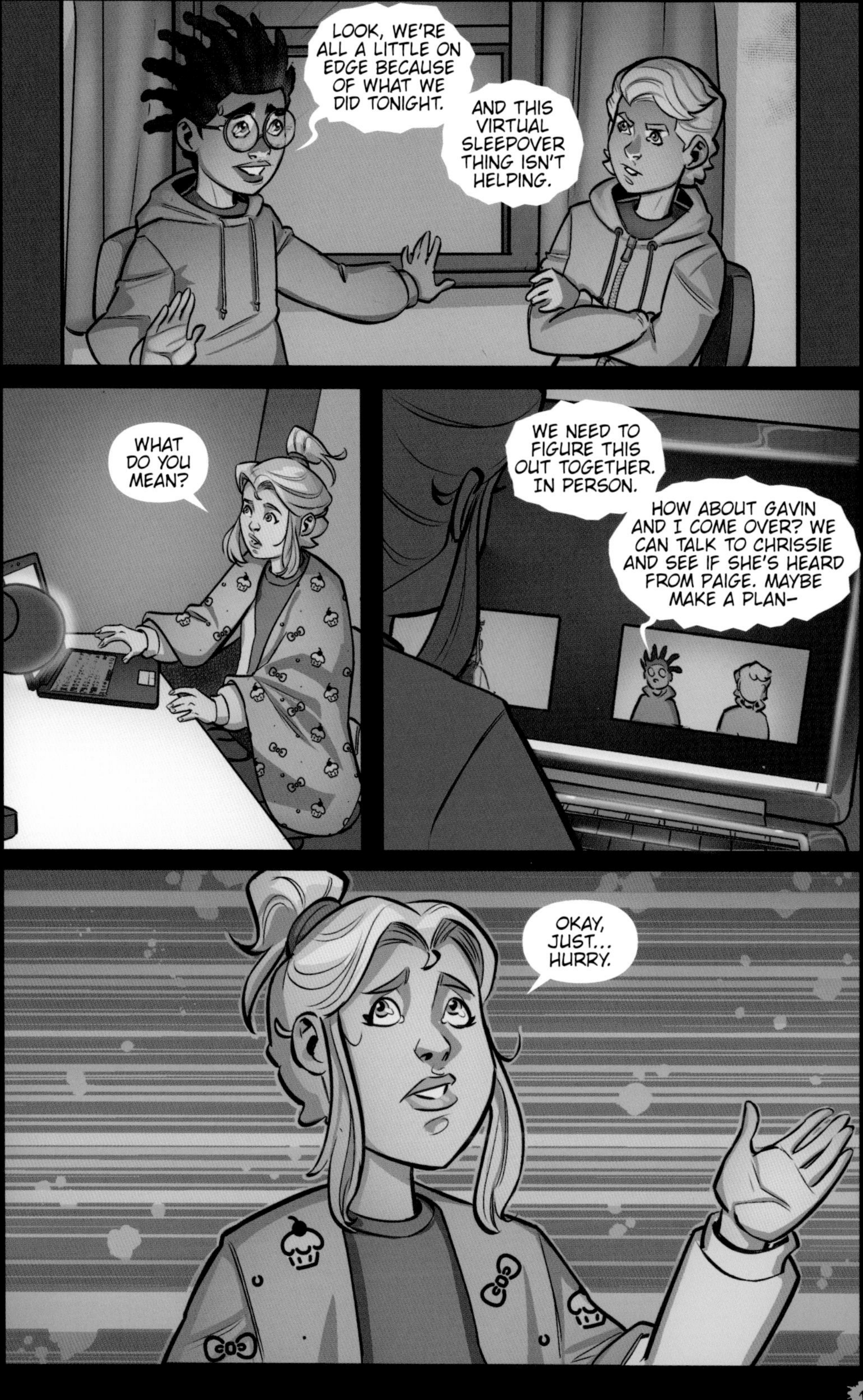
LOOK, WE'RE ALL A LITTLE ON EDGE BECAUSE OF WHAT WE DID TONIGHT.
AND THIS VIRTUAL SLEEPOVER THING ISN'T HELPING.
WHAT DO YOU MEAN?
WE NEED TO FIGURE THIS OUT TOGETHER. IN PERSON.
HOW ABOUT GAVIN AND I COME OVER? WE CAN TALK TO CHRISSIE AND SEE IF SHE'S HEARD FROM PAIGE. MAYBE MAKE A PLAN–
OKAY, JUST... HURRY.

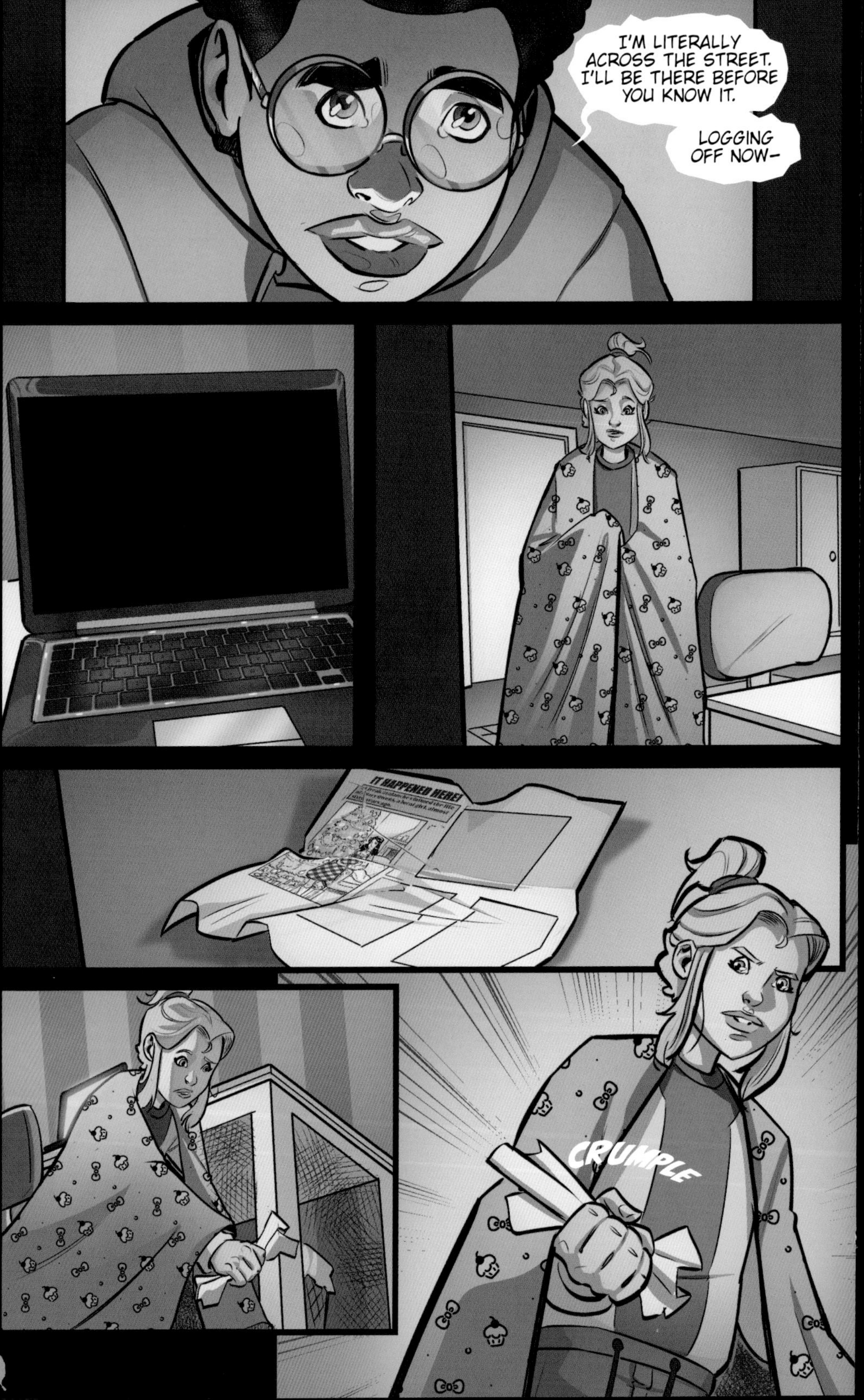
I'M LITERALLY ACROSS THE STREET. I'LL BE THERE BEFORE YOU KNOW IT.
LOGGING OFF NOW–
IT HAPPENED HERE!
CRUMPLE

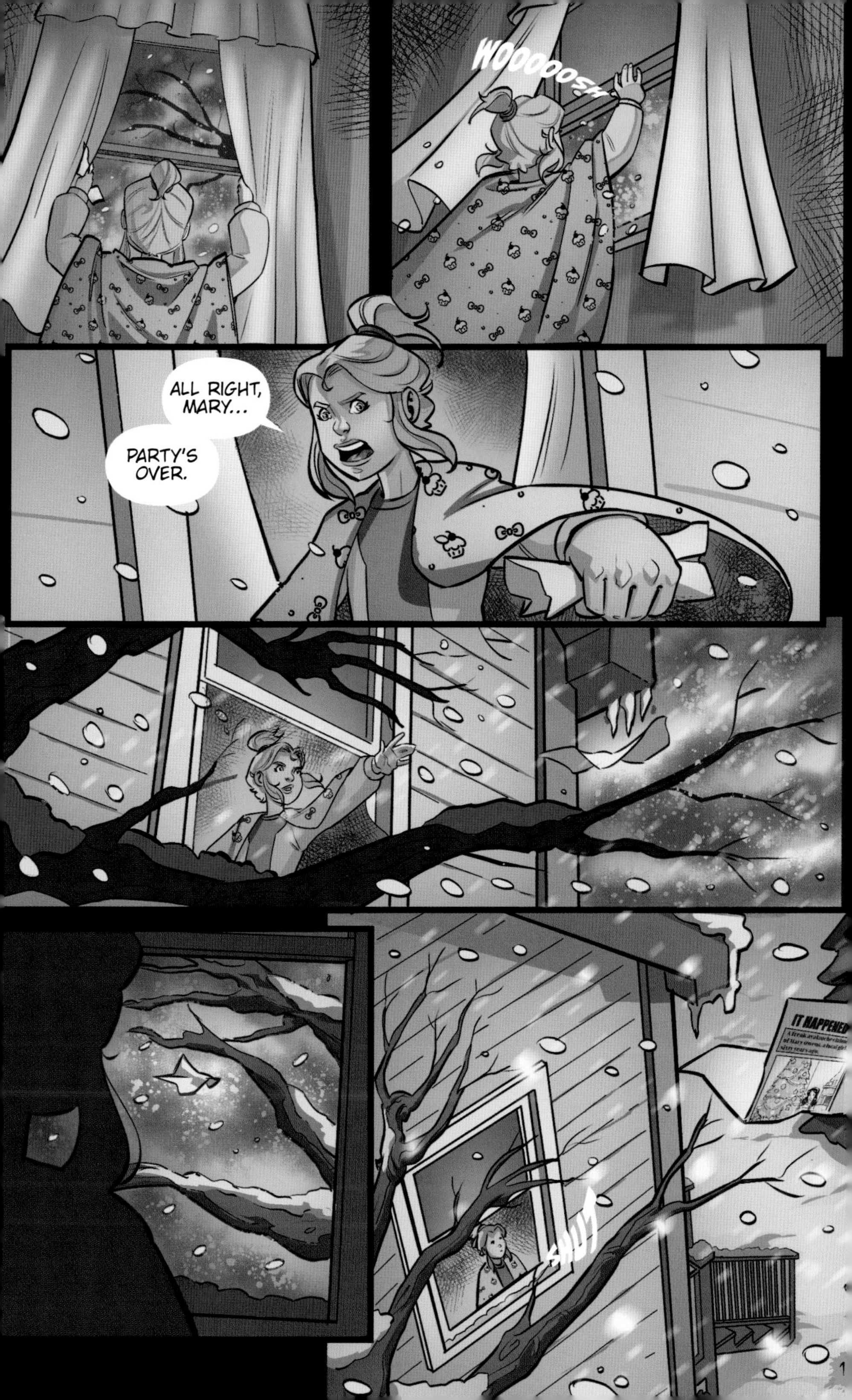
WOOOOOOSH
ALL RIGHT, MARY...
PARTY'S OVER.
IT HAPPENED
SHUT

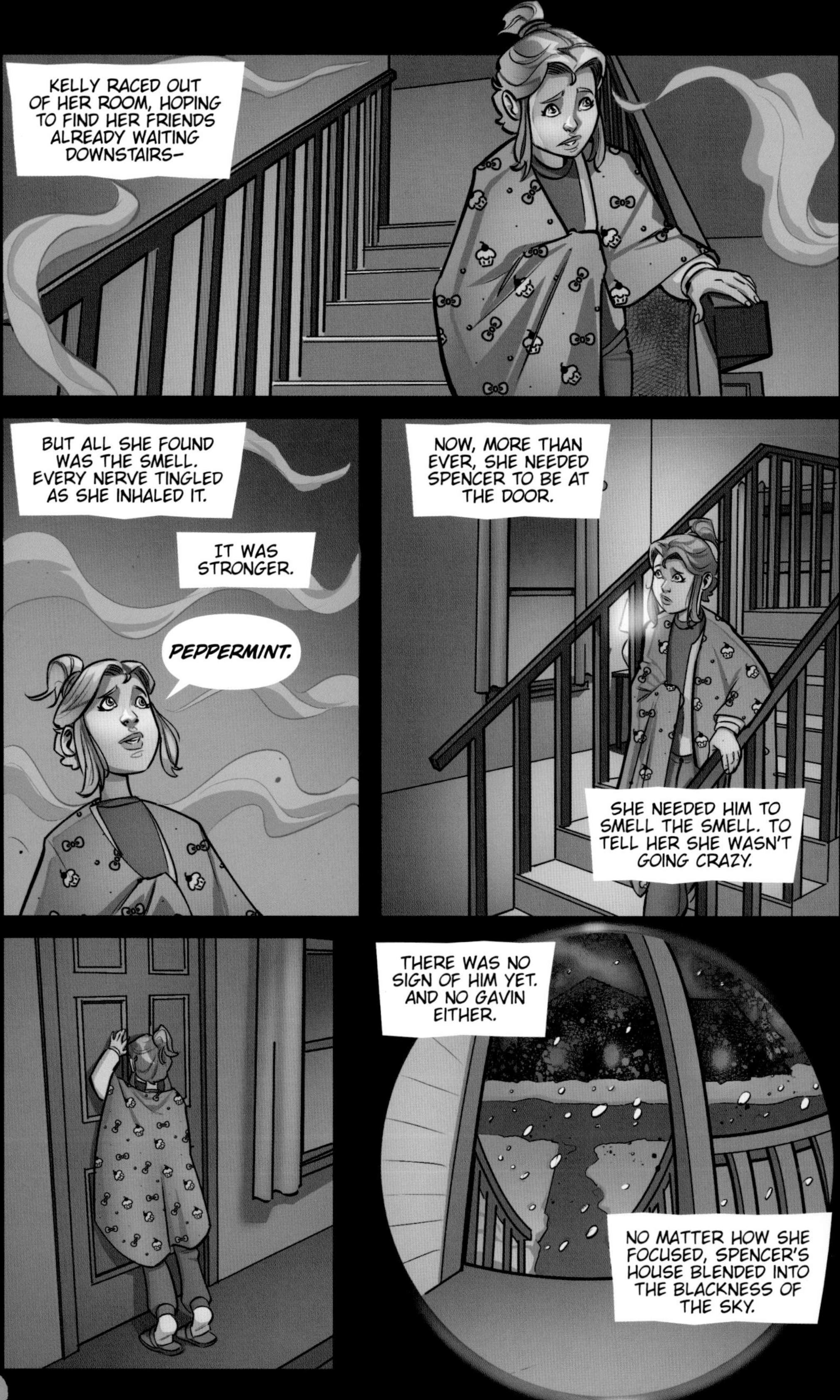
KELLY RACED OUT OF HER ROOM, HOPING TO FIND HER FRIENDS ALREADY WAITING DOWNSTAIRS—
BUT ALL SHE FOUND WAS THE SMELL. EVERY NERVE TINGLED AS SHE INHALED IT.
IT WAS STRONGER.
PEPPERMINT.
NOW, MORE THAN EVER, SHE NEEDED SPENCER TO BE AT THE DOOR.
SHE NEEDED HIM TO SMELL THE SMELL. TO TELL HER SHE WASN'T GOING CRAZY.
THERE WAS NO SIGN OF HIM YET. AND NO GAVIN EITHER.
NO MATTER HOW SHE FOCUSED, SPENCER'S HOUSE BLENDED INTO THE BLACKNESS OF THE SKY.

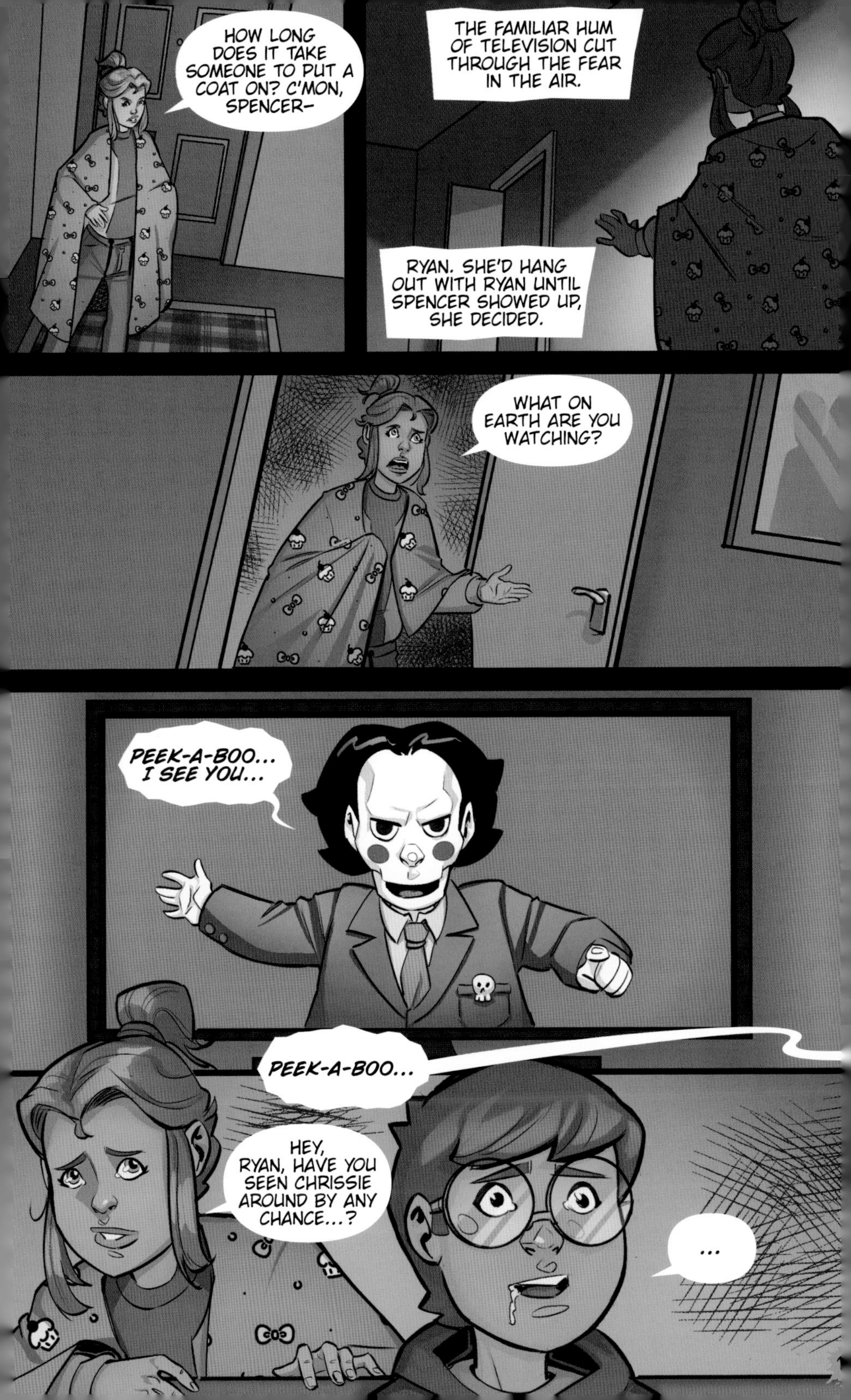
HOW LONG DOES IT TAKE SOMEONE TO PUT A COAT ON? C'MON, SPENCER–
THE FAMILIAR HUM OF TELEVISION CUT THROUGH THE FEAR IN THE AIR.
RYAN. SHE'D HANG OUT WITH RYAN UNTIL SPENCER SHOWED UP, SHE DECIDED.
WHAT ON EARTH ARE YOU WATCHING?
PEEK-A-BOO... I SEE YOU...
PEEK-A-BOO...
HEY, RYAN, HAVE YOU SEEN CHRISSIE AROUND BY ANY CHANCE...?
...

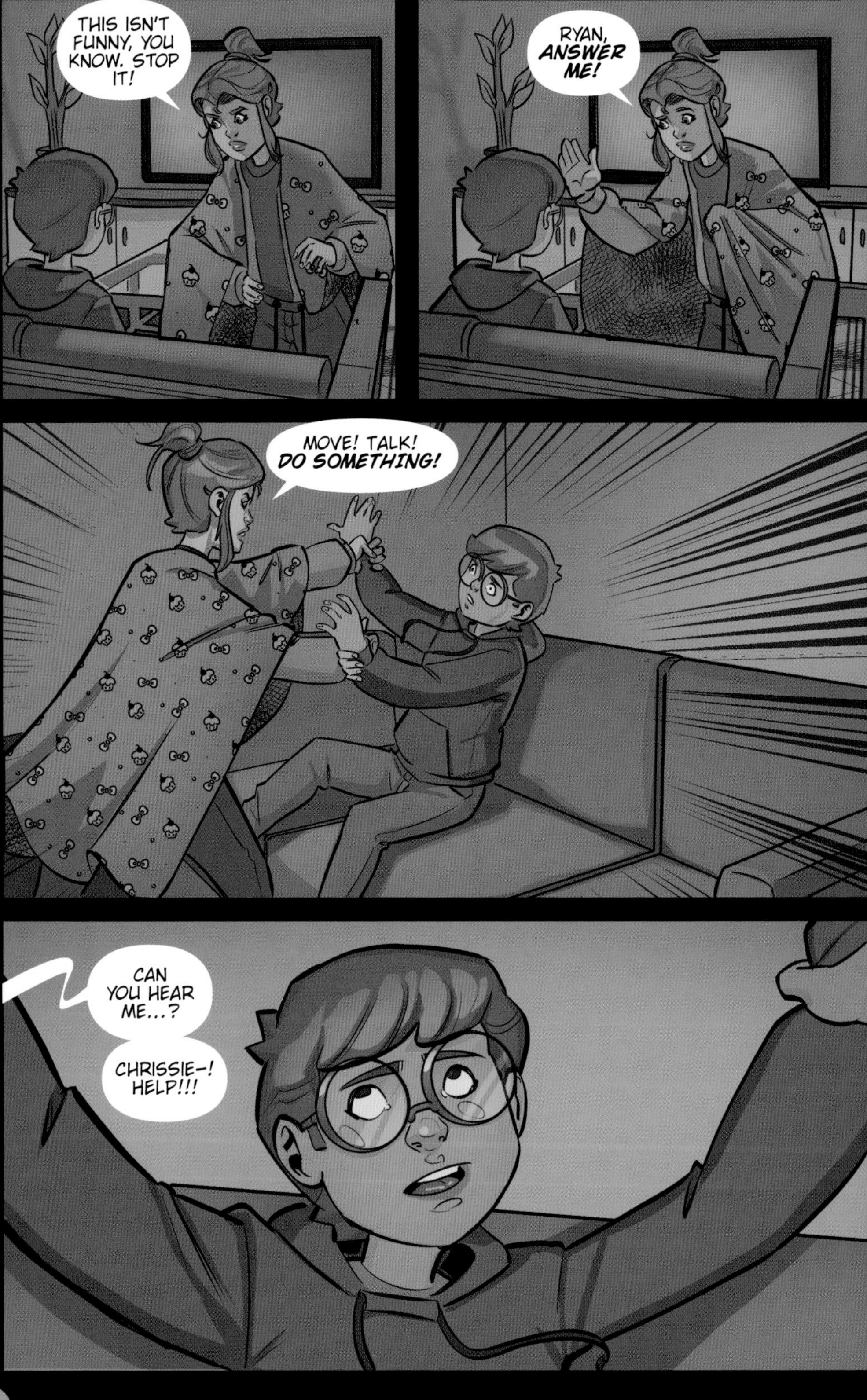
THIS ISN'T FUNNY, YOU KNOW. STOP IT!
RYAN, **ANSWER ME!**
MOVE! TALK! **DO SOMETHING!**
CAN YOU HEAR ME...?
CHRISSIE-! HELP!!!

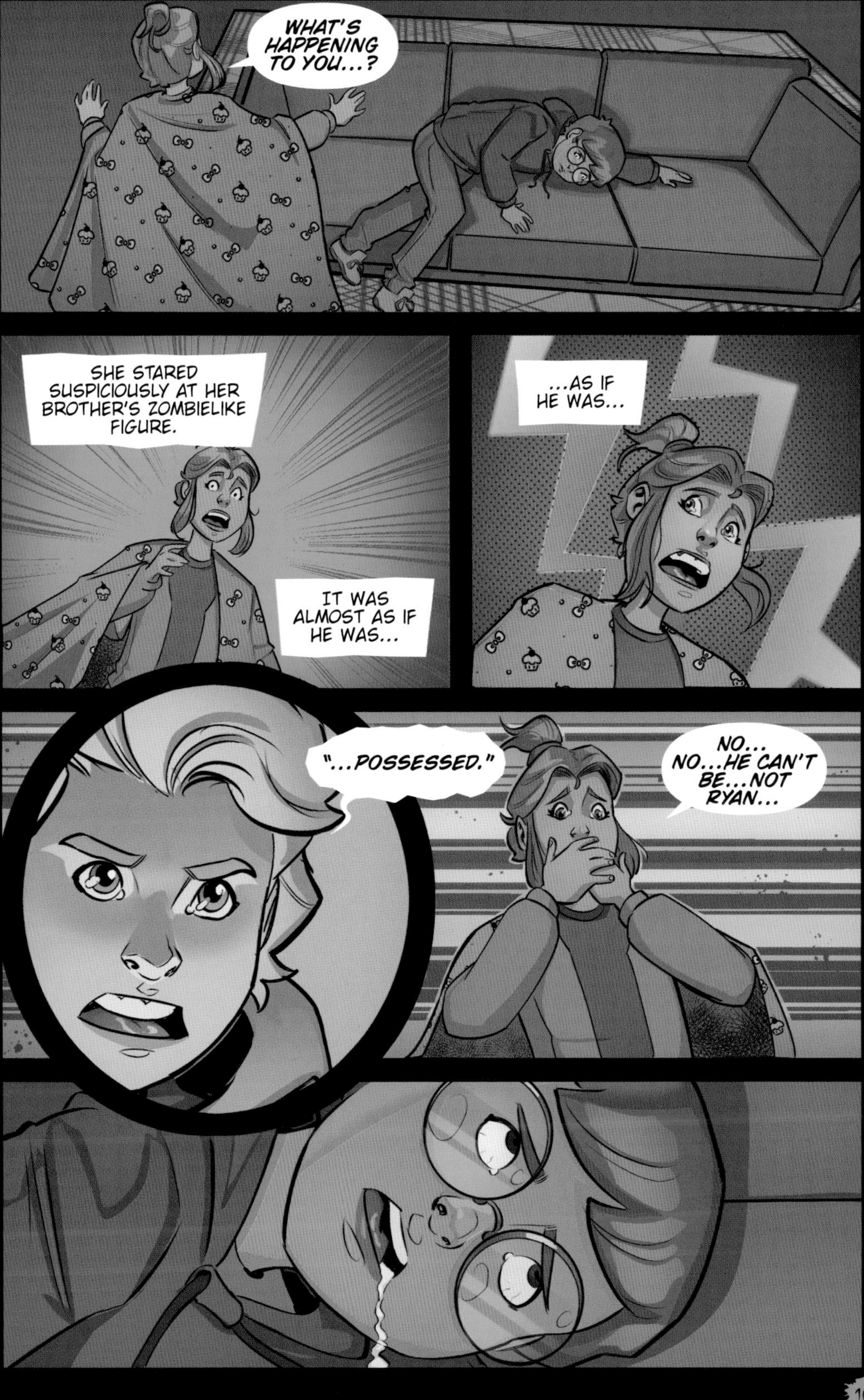
WHAT'S HAPPENING TO YOU...?
SHE STARED SUSPICIOUSLY AT HER BROTHER'S ZOMBIELIKE FIGURE.
IT WAS ALMOST AS IF HE WAS...
...AS IF HE WAS...
"...POSSESSED."
NO... NO...HE CAN'T BE...NOT RYAN...

CHAPTER 9

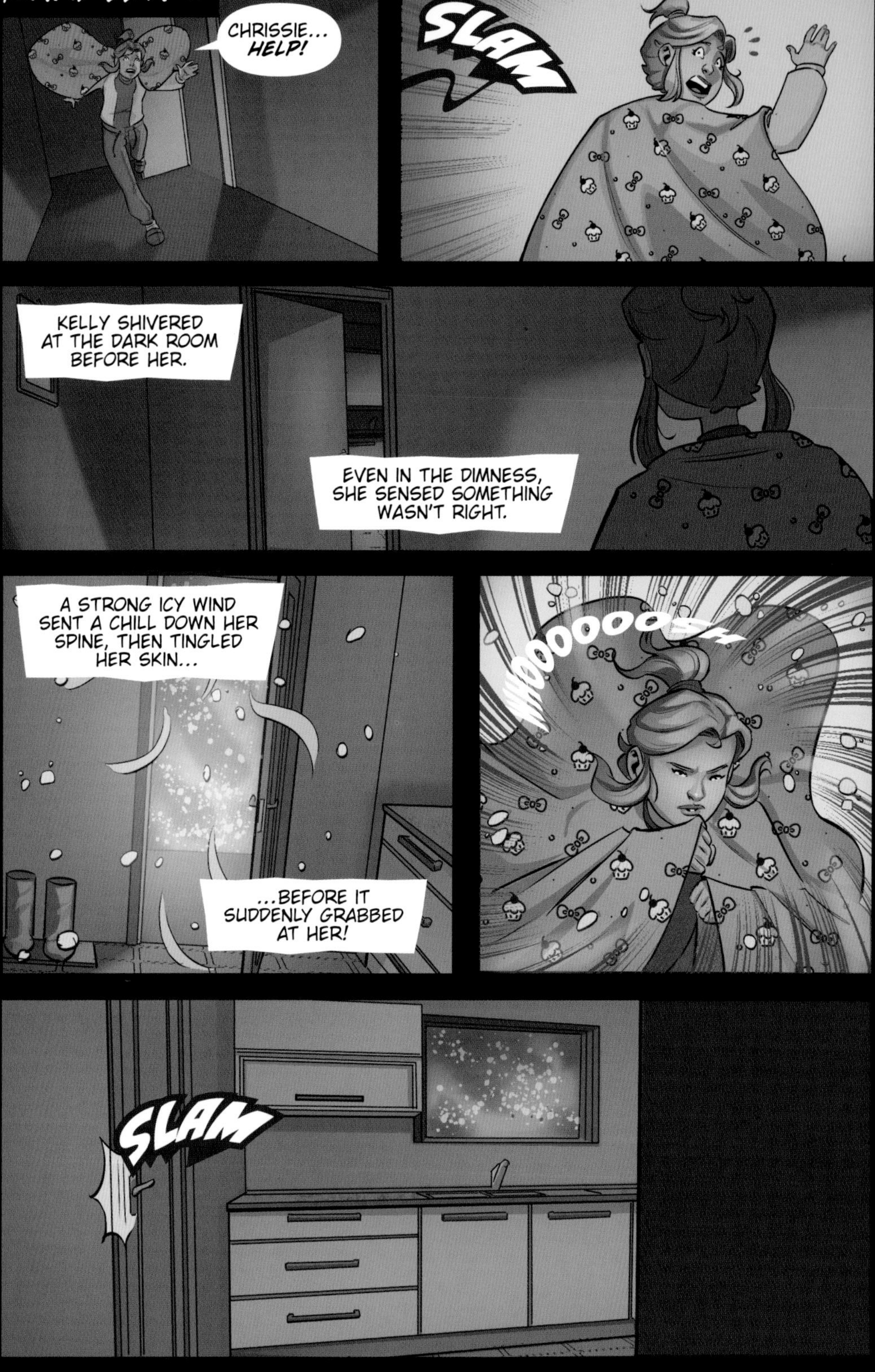

CHRISSIE... HELP!
SLAM
KELLY SHIVERED AT THE DARK ROOM BEFORE HER.
EVEN IN THE DIMNESS, SHE SENSED SOMETHING WASN'T RIGHT.
A STRONG ICY WIND SENT A CHILL DOWN HER SPINE, THEN TINGLED HER SKIN...
...BEFORE IT SUDDENLY GRABBED AT HER!
WHOOOOOOSH
SLAM

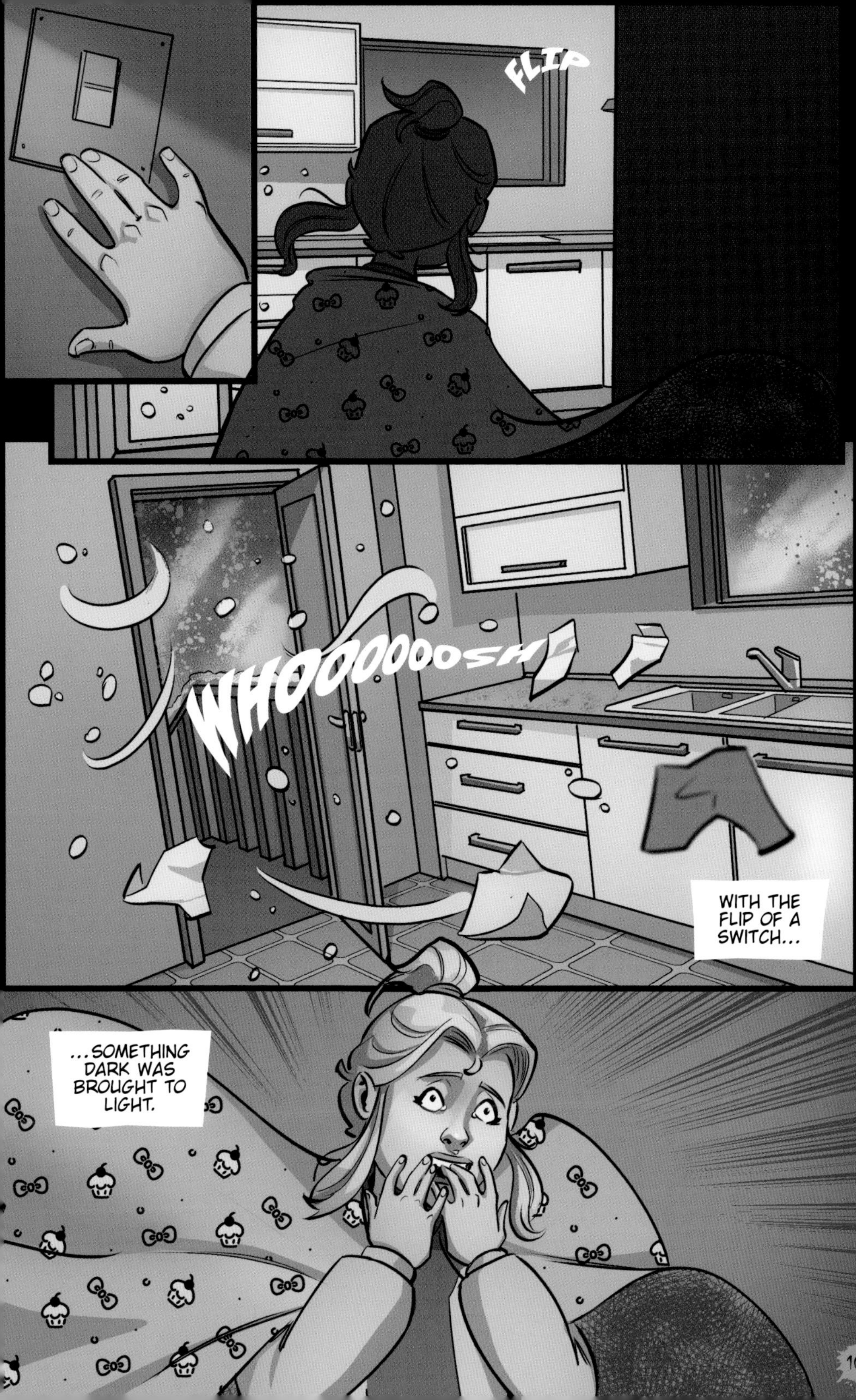
FLIP
WHOOOOOOOSH
WITH THE FLIP OF A SWITCH...
...SOMETHING DARK WAS BROUGHT TO LIGHT.

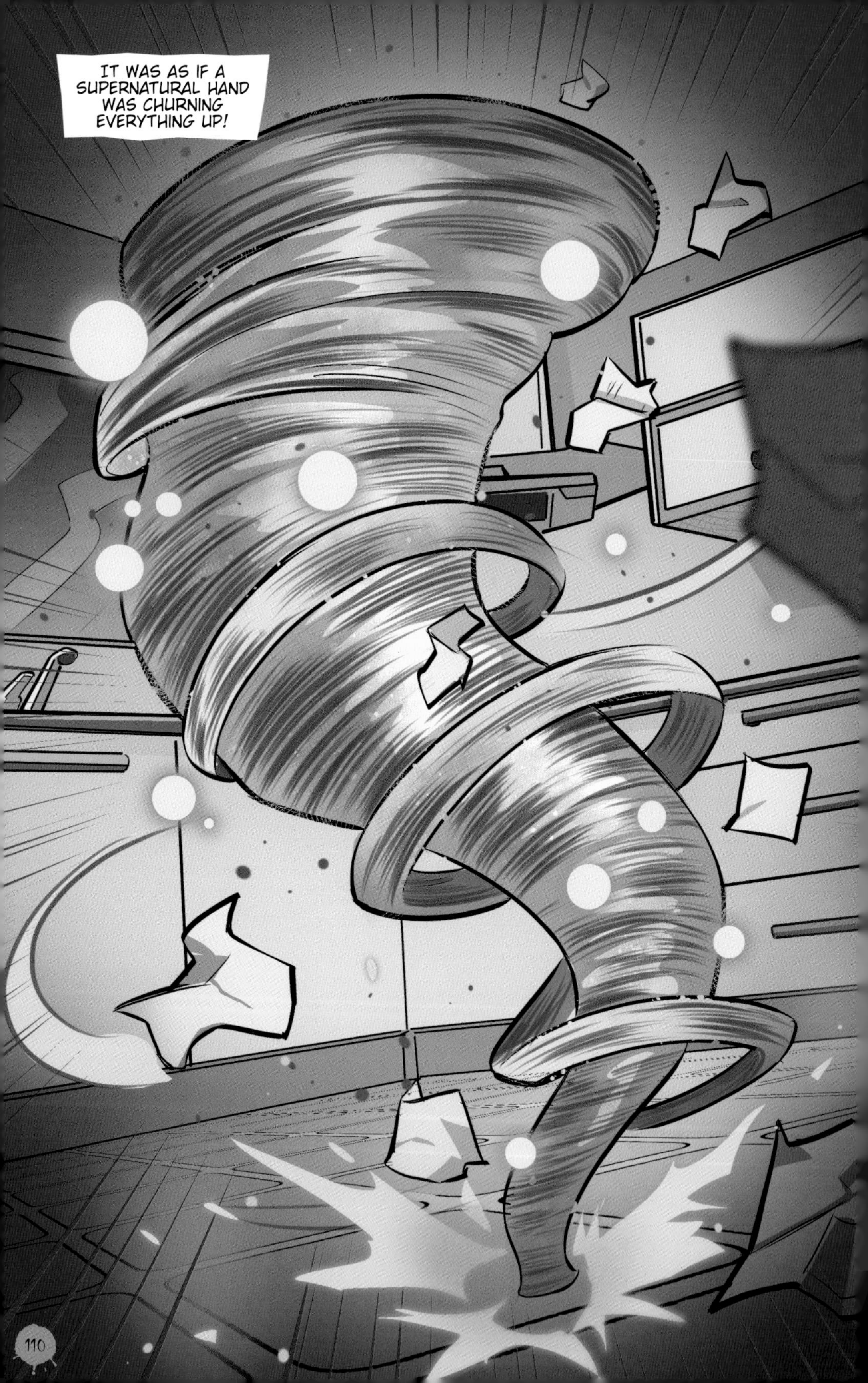
IT WAS AS IF A SUPERNATURAL HAND WAS CHURNING EVERYTHING UP!

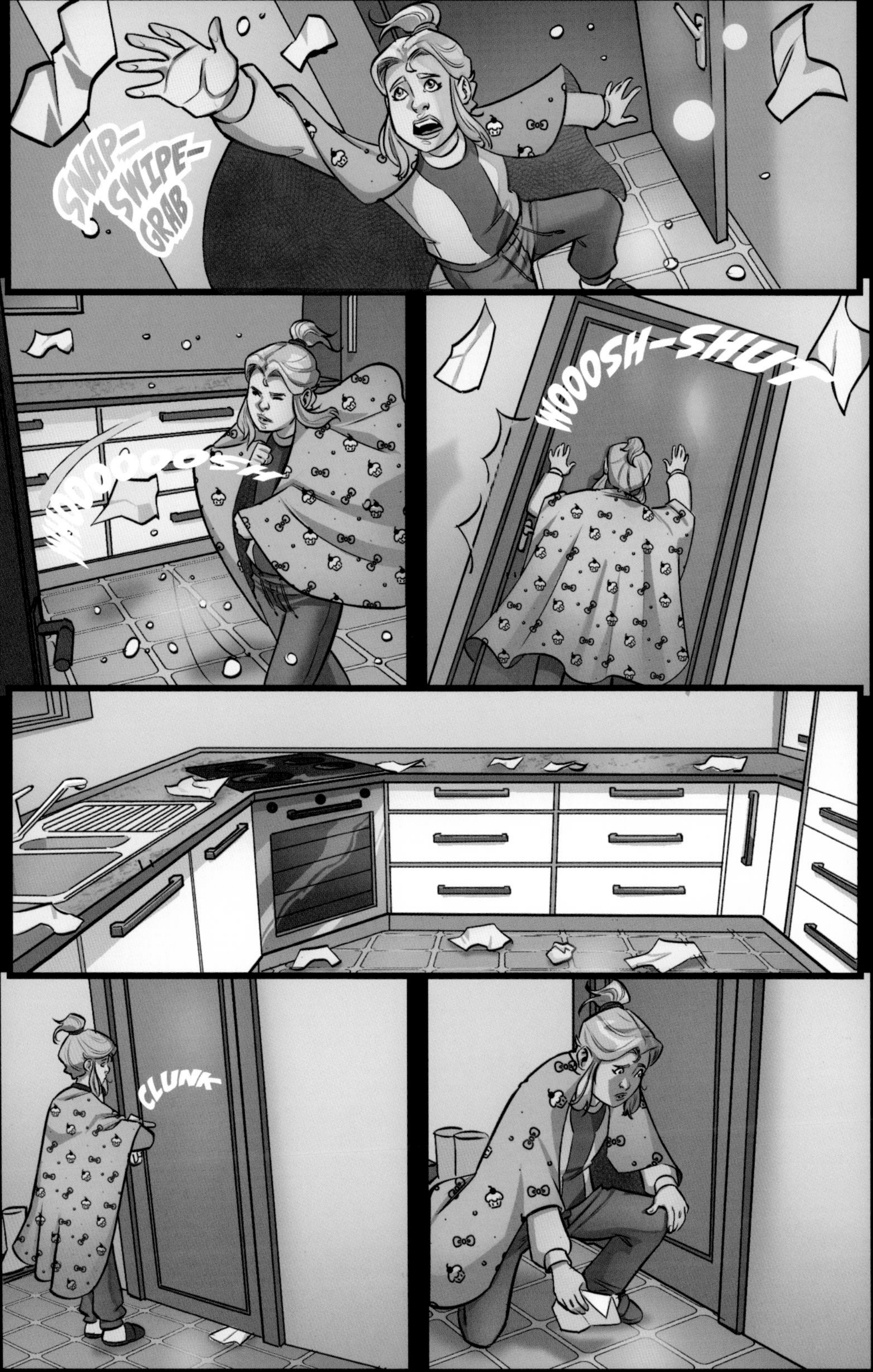

SNAP-
SWIPE-
GRAB
WHOOOOOOSH
WOOOSH-SHUT
CLUNK

KELLY STARED AT THE FAMILIAR FACE ON THE PAGE ONCE MORE.

SHE AND THE GIRL WERE REUNITED. ONE. A BOND UNBREAKABLE.

HELLO AGAIN, MARY.

DESPITE TWIRLING IN THE SNOW, MARY'S PICTURE WAS SOMEHOW BONE DRY...

IT HAPPENED HERE!

...claimed the life ...al girl, almost

...SAVE FOR A WET PATTERN ON THE TOP CORNER. *ALMOST LIKE A BOOT PRINT,* KELLY THOUGHT.

SHE HAD SEEN *CHRISSIE* WEARING SNOW BOOTS INSIDE EARLIER.

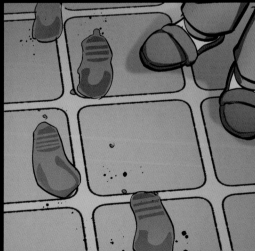

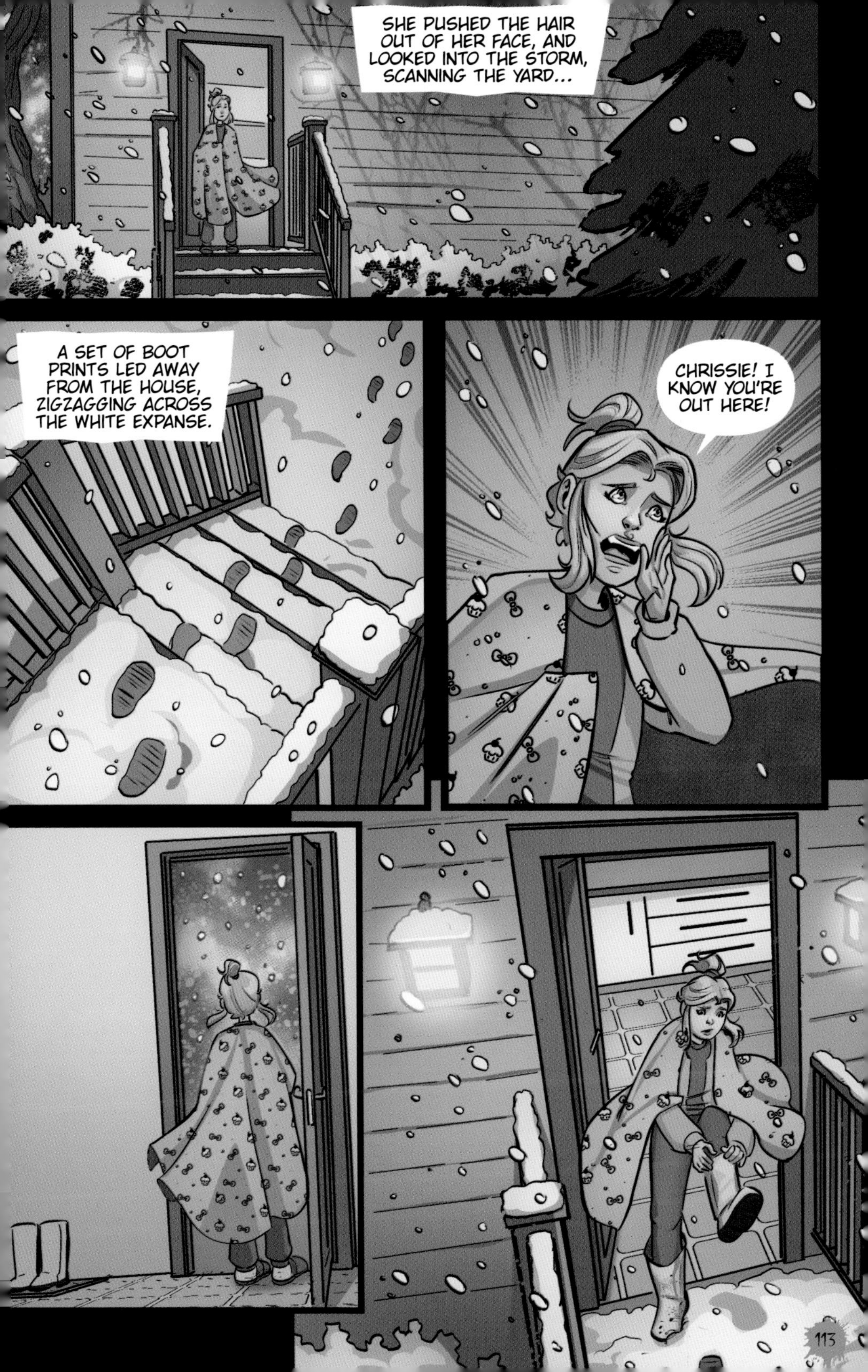
SHE PUSHED THE HAIR OUT OF HER FACE, AND LOOKED INTO THE STORM, SCANNING THE YARD...
A SET OF BOOT PRINTS LED AWAY FROM THE HOUSE, ZIGZAGGING ACROSS THE WHITE EXPANSE.
CHRISSIE! I KNOW YOU'RE OUT HERE!

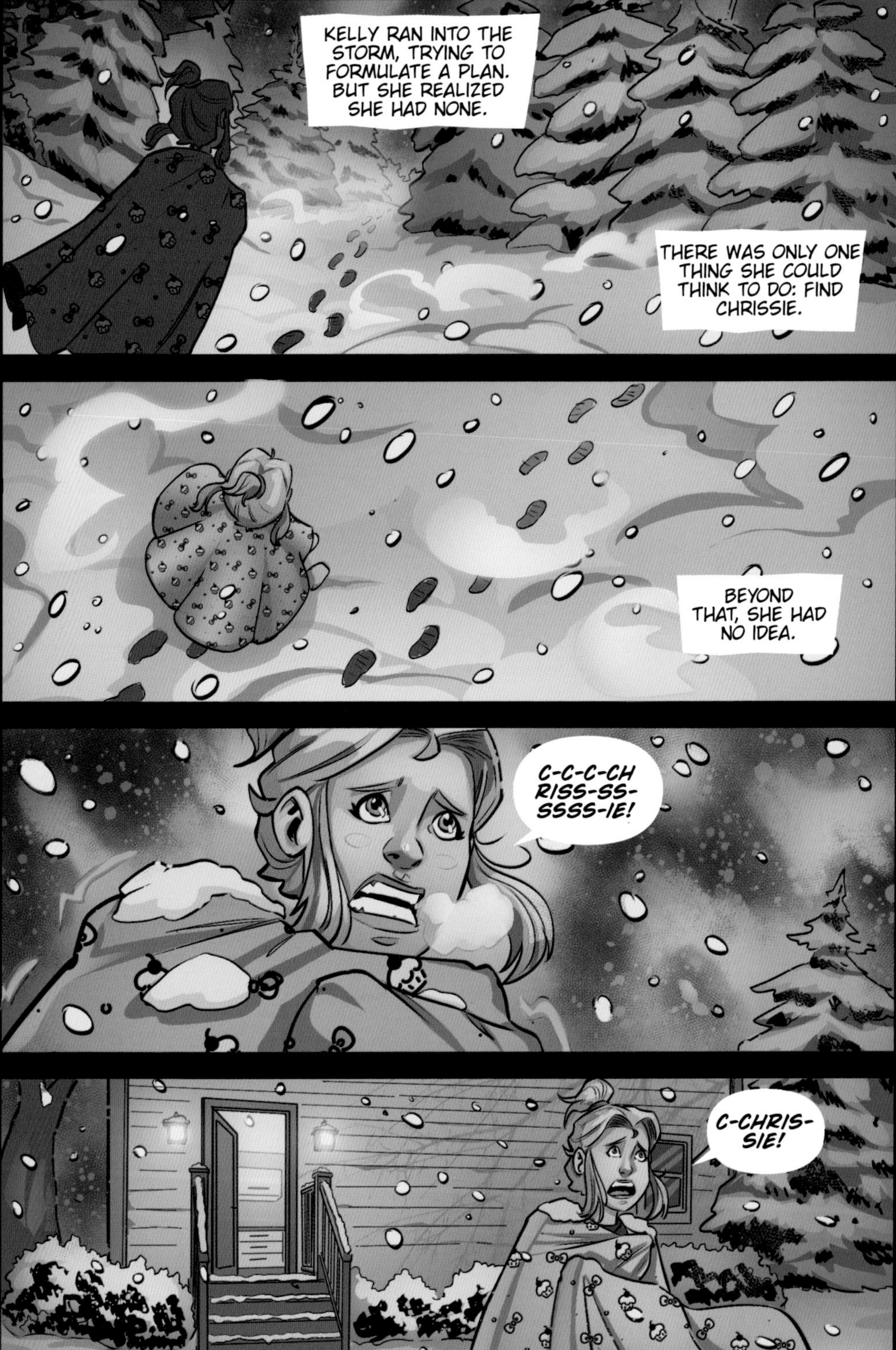
KELLY RAN INTO THE STORM, TRYING TO FORMULATE A PLAN. BUT SHE REALIZED SHE HAD NONE.
THERE WAS ONLY ONE THING SHE COULD THINK TO DO: FIND CHRISSIE.
BEYOND THAT, SHE HAD NO IDEA.
C-C-C-CH RISS-SS-SSSS-IE!
C-CHRIS-SIE!

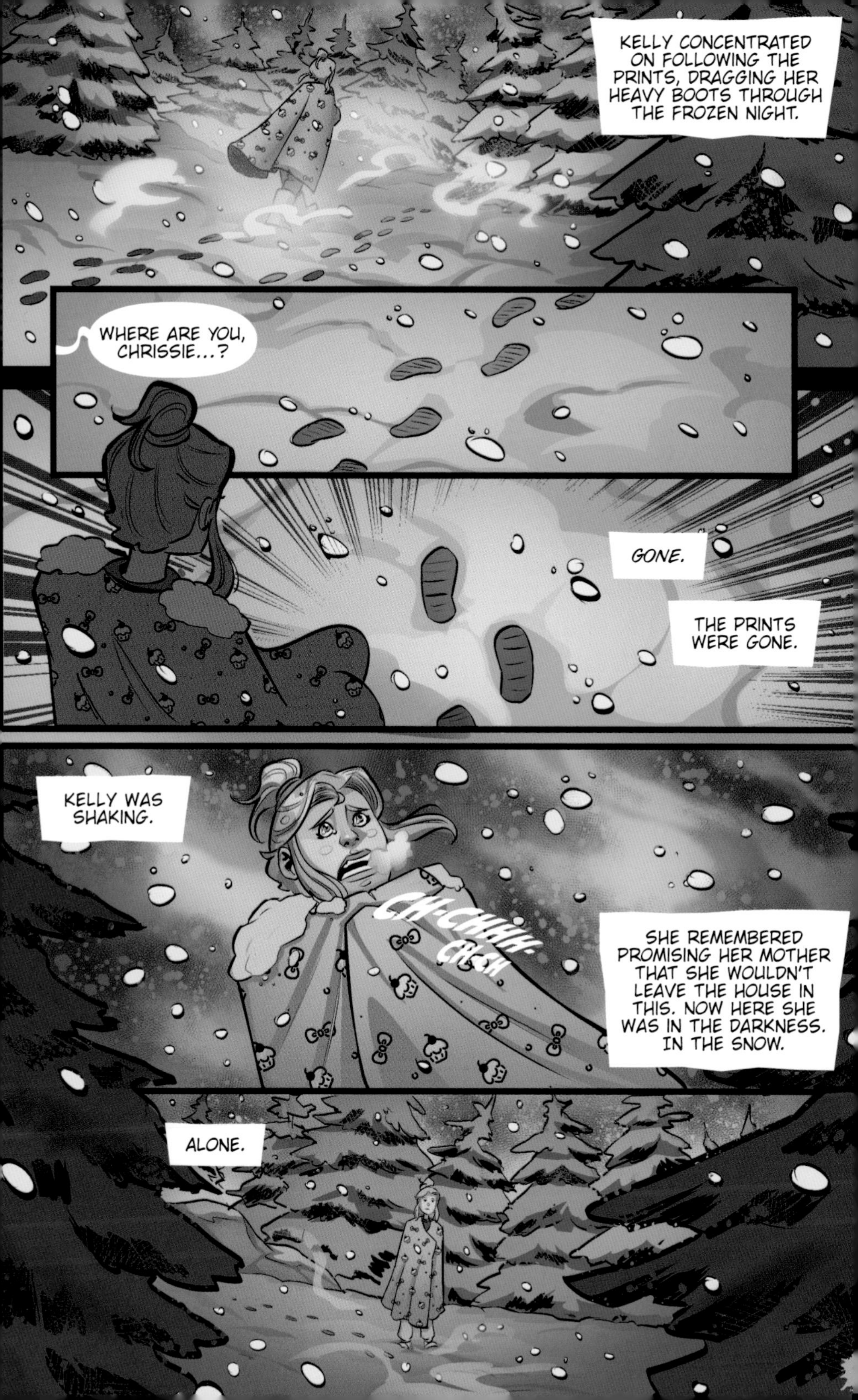
KELLY CONCENTRATED ON FOLLOWING THE PRINTS, DRAGGING HER HEAVY BOOTS THROUGH THE FROZEN NIGHT.
WHERE ARE YOU, CHRISSIE...?
GONE.
THE PRINTS WERE GONE.
KELLY WAS SHAKING.
CH-CHHH-CH-CH
SHE REMEMBERED PROMISING HER MOTHER THAT SHE WOULDN'T LEAVE THE HOUSE IN THIS. NOW HERE SHE WAS IN THE DARKNESS. IN THE SNOW.
ALONE.

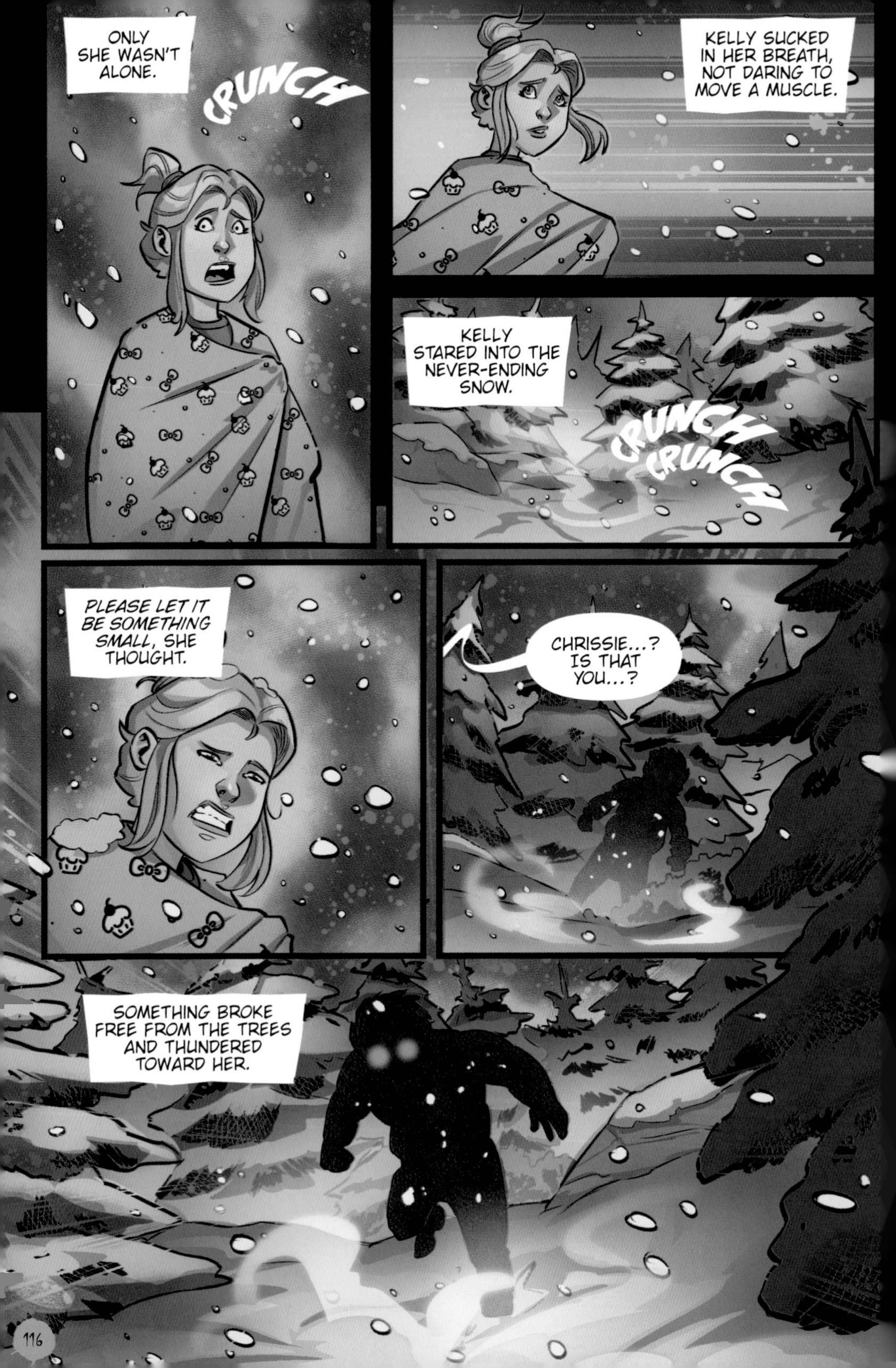
ONLY SHE WASN'T ALONE.
CRUNCH
KELLY SUCKED IN HER BREATH, NOT DARING TO MOVE A MUSCLE.
KELLY STARED INTO THE NEVER-ENDING SNOW.
CRUNCH
CRUNCH
PLEASE LET IT BE SOMETHING SMALL, SHE THOUGHT.
CHRISSIE...? IS THAT YOU...?
SOMETHING BROKE FREE FROM THE TREES AND THUNDERED TOWARD HER.

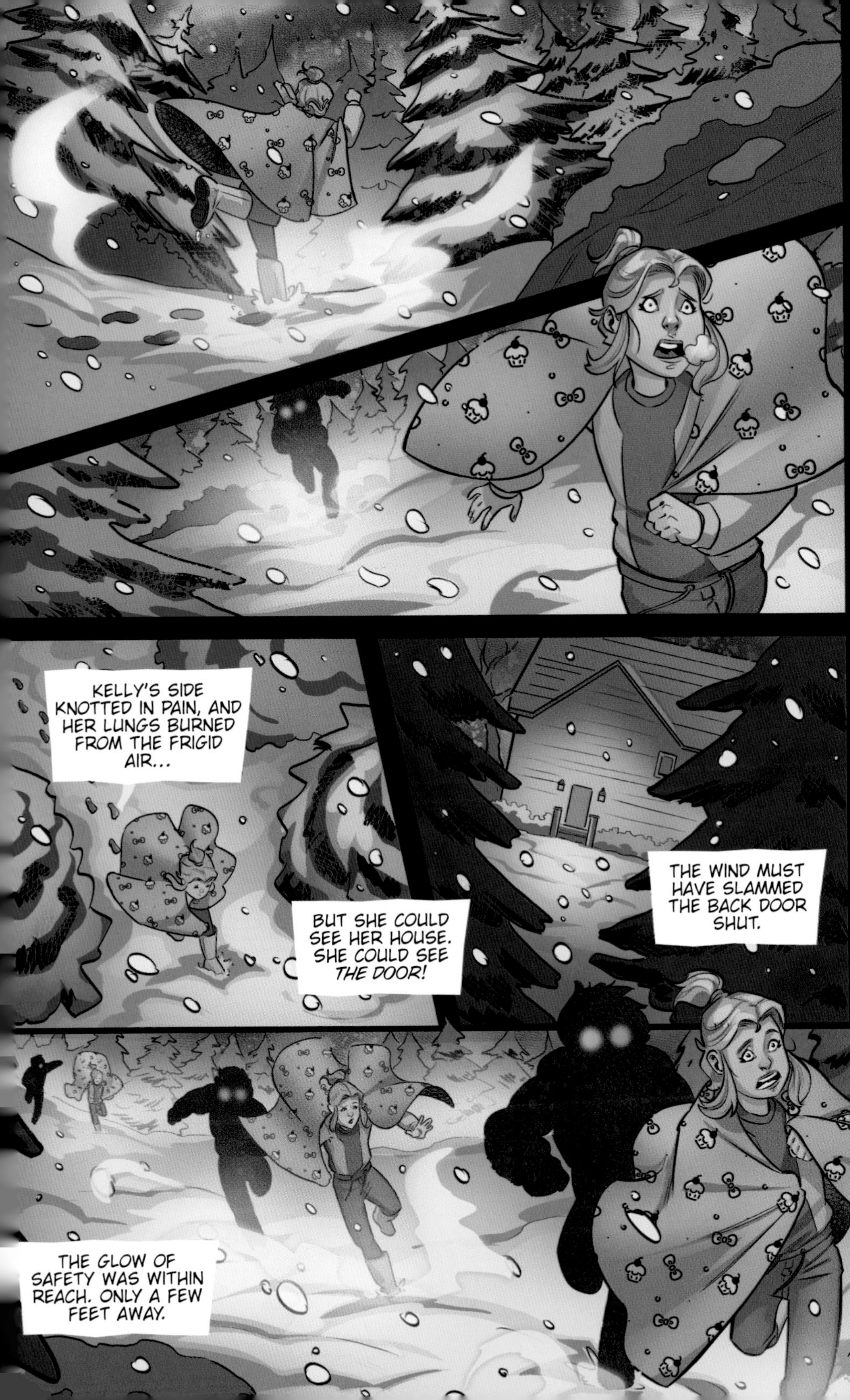
KELLY'S SIDE KNOTTED IN PAIN, AND HER LUNGS BURNED FROM THE FRIGID AIR...
BUT SHE COULD SEE HER HOUSE. SHE COULD SEE *THE DOOR!*
THE WIND MUST HAVE SLAMMED THE BACK DOOR SHUT.
THE GLOW OF SAFETY WAS WITHIN REACH. ONLY A FEW FEET AWAY.

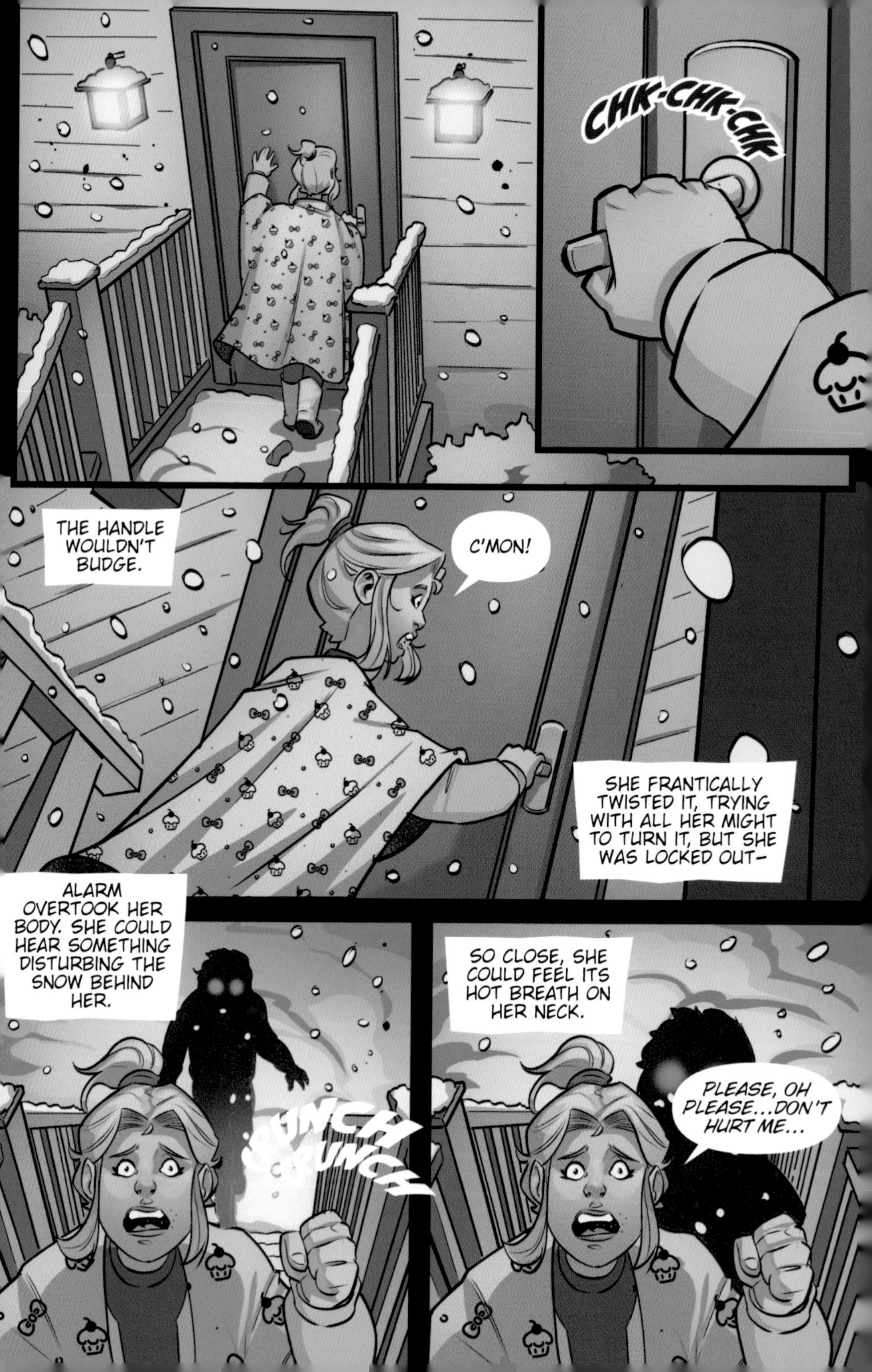
CHK-CHK-CHK
THE HANDLE WOULDN'T BUDGE.
C'MON!
SHE FRANTICALLY TWISTED IT, TRYING WITH ALL HER MIGHT TO TURN IT, BUT SHE WAS LOCKED OUT–
ALARM OVERTOOK HER BODY. SHE COULD HEAR SOMETHING DISTURBING THE SNOW BEHIND HER.
SO CLOSE, SHE COULD FEEL ITS HOT BREATH ON HER NECK.
PLEASE, OH PLEASE...DON'T HURT ME...

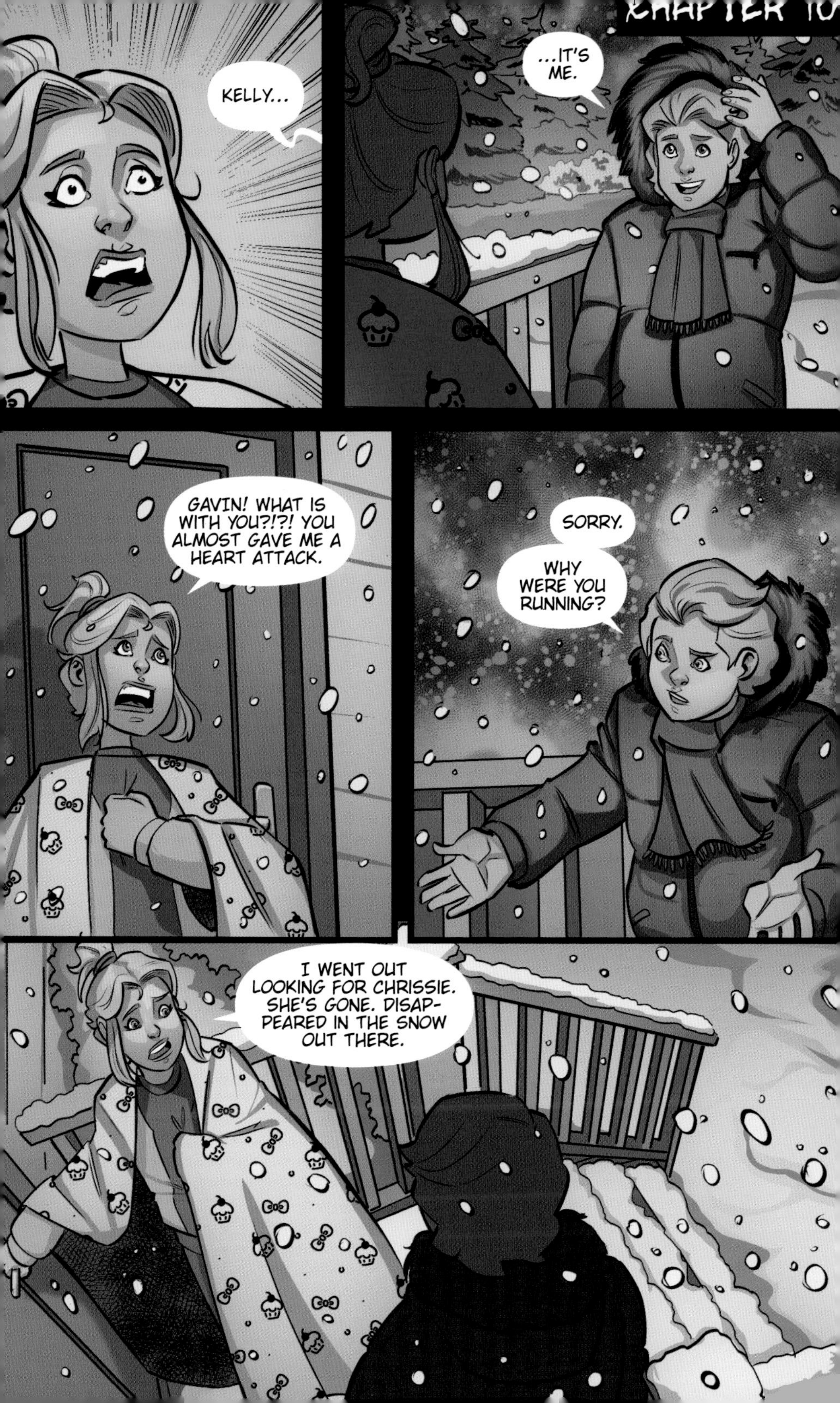
KELLY...
...IT'S ME.
GAVIN! WHAT IS WITH YOU?!?! YOU ALMOST GAVE ME A HEART ATTACK.
SORRY.
WHY WERE YOU RUNNING?
I WENT OUT LOOKING FOR CHRISSIE. SHE'S GONE. DISAP-PEARED IN THE SNOW OUT THERE.

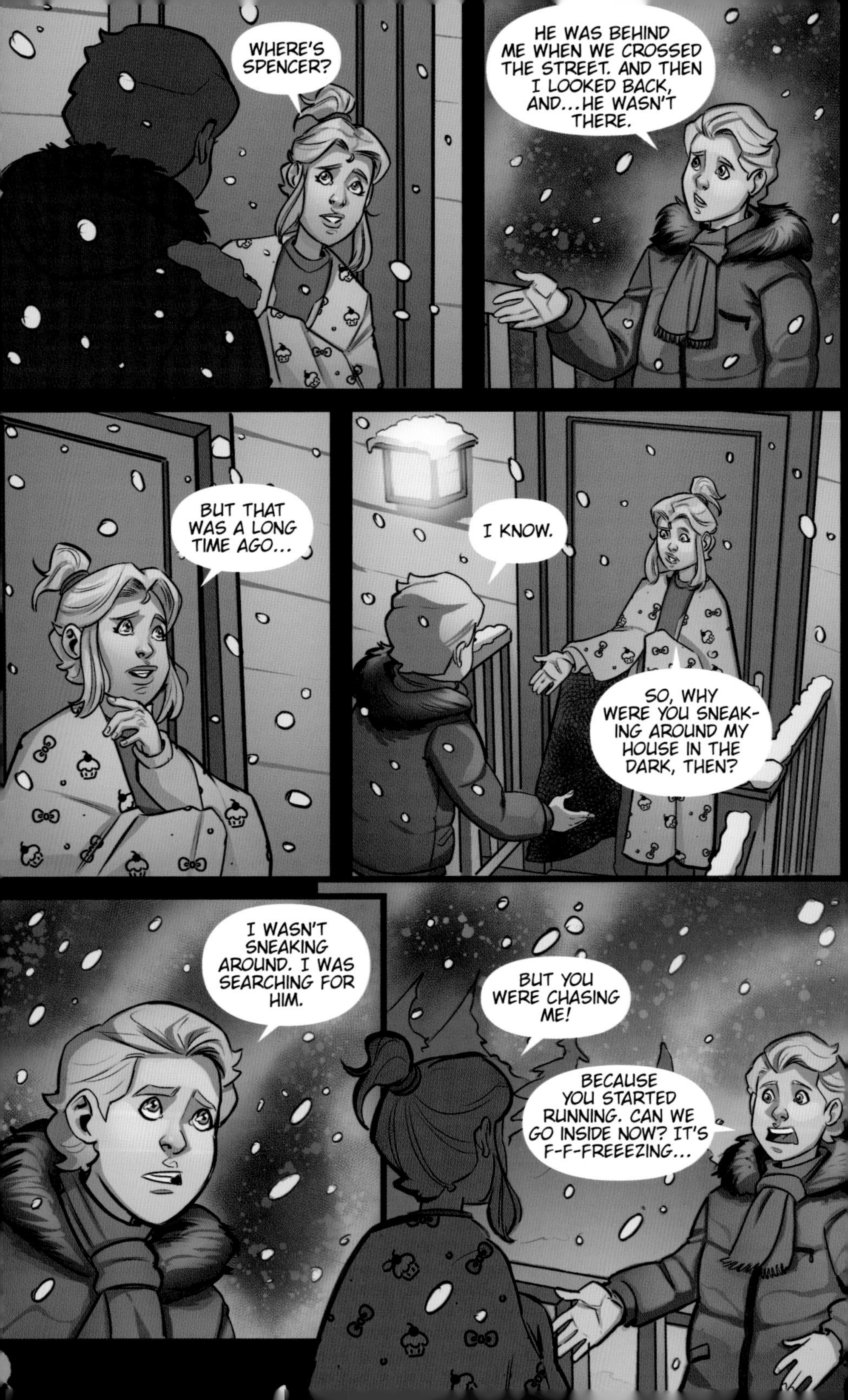
WHERE'S SPENCER?
HE WAS BEHIND ME WHEN WE CROSSED THE STREET. AND THEN I LOOKED BACK, AND...HE WASN'T THERE.
BUT THAT WAS A LONG TIME AGO...
I KNOW.
SO, WHY WERE YOU SNEAK-ING AROUND MY HOUSE IN THE DARK, THEN?
I WASN'T SNEAKING AROUND. I WAS SEARCHING FOR HIM.
BUT YOU WERE CHASING ME!
BECAUSE YOU STARTED RUNNING. CAN WE GO INSIDE NOW? IT'S F-F-FREEZING...

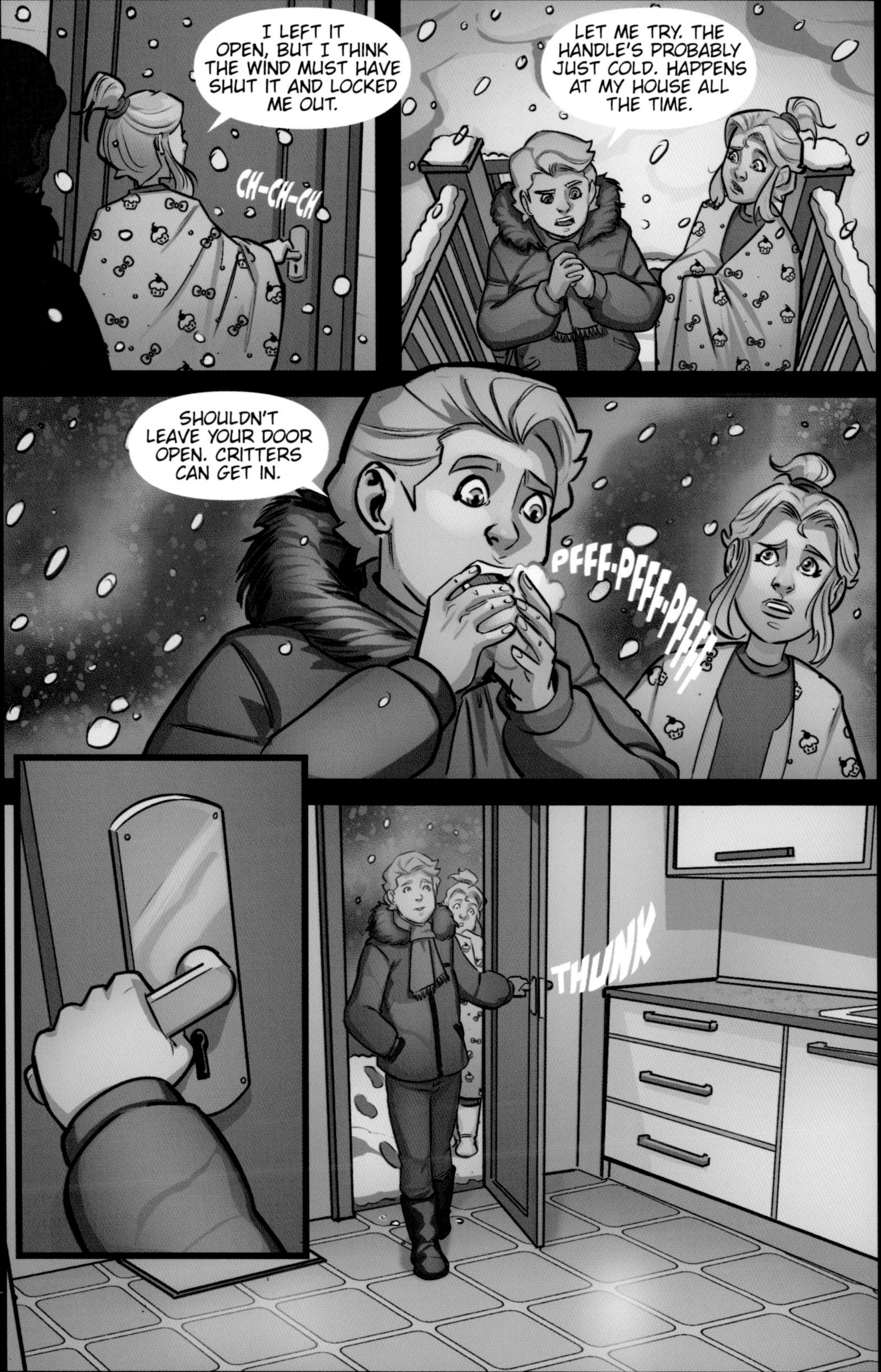

I LEFT IT OPEN, BUT I THINK THE WIND MUST HAVE SHUT IT AND LOCKED ME OUT.
CH-CH-CH
LET ME TRY. THE HANDLE'S PROBABLY JUST COLD. HAPPENS AT MY HOUSE ALL THE TIME.
SHOULDN'T LEAVE YOUR DOOR OPEN. CRITTERS CAN GET IN.
PFFF-PFFF-PFFF
THUNK

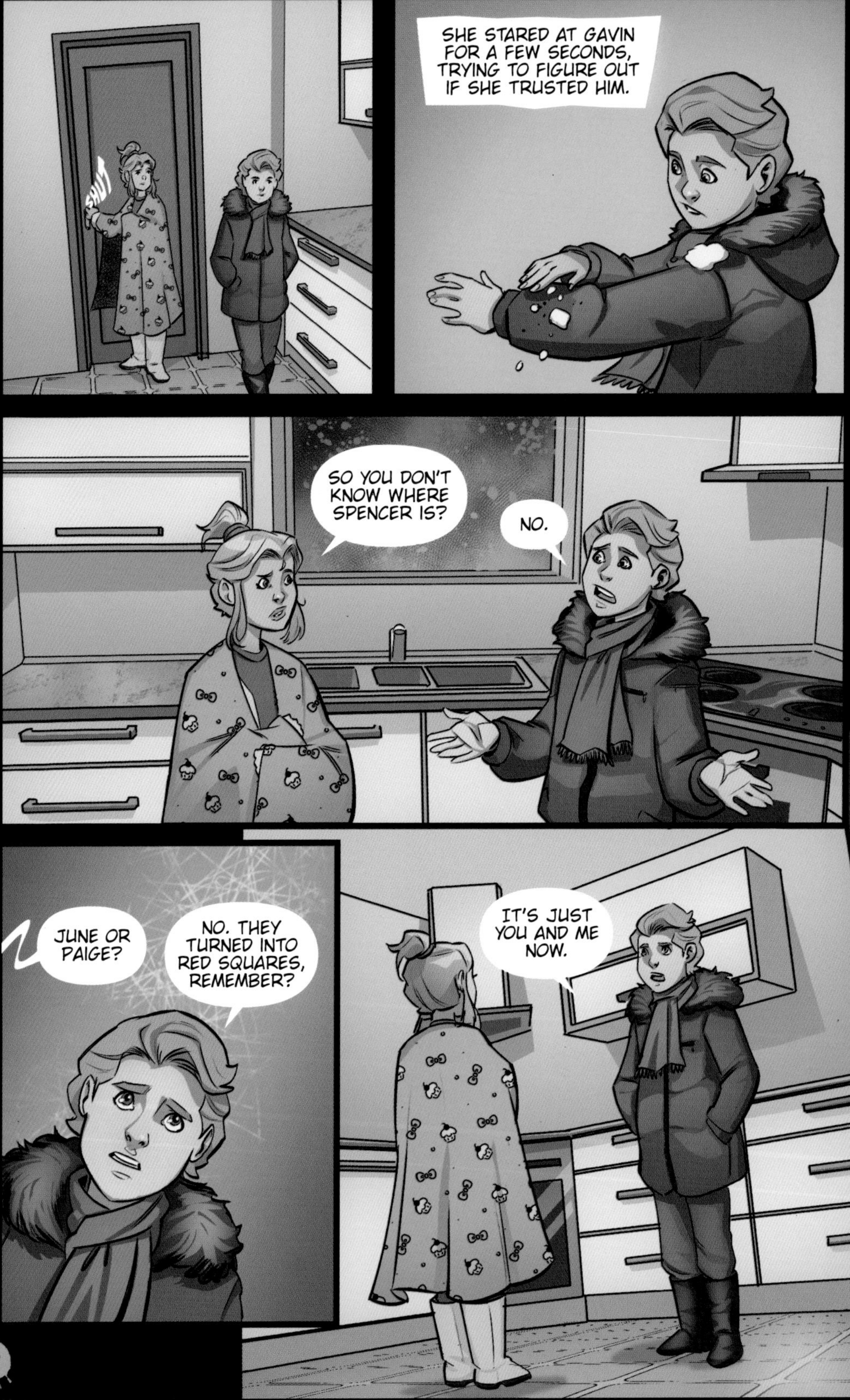
SHUT
SHE STARED AT GAVIN FOR A FEW SECONDS, TRYING TO FIGURE OUT IF SHE TRUSTED HIM.
SO YOU DON'T KNOW WHERE SPENCER IS?
NO.
JUNE OR PAIGE?
NO. THEY TURNED INTO RED SQUARES, REMEMBER?
IT'S JUST YOU AND ME NOW.

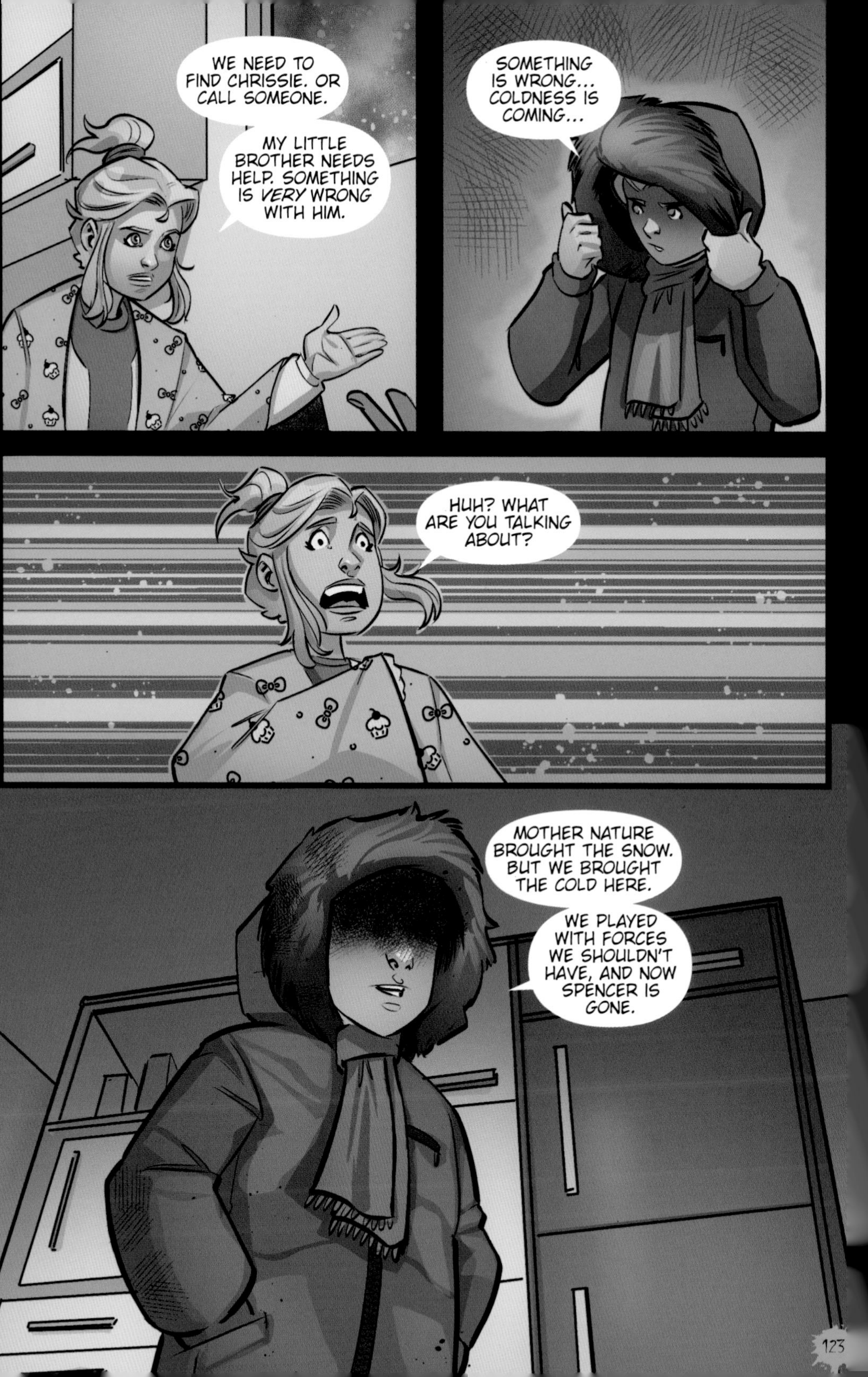
WE NEED TO FIND CHRISSIE. OR CALL SOMEONE.
MY LITTLE BROTHER NEEDS HELP. SOMETHING IS *VERY* WRONG WITH HIM.
SOMETHING IS WRONG... COLDNESS IS COMING...
HUH? WHAT ARE YOU TALKING ABOUT?
MOTHER NATURE BROUGHT THE SNOW. BUT WE BROUGHT THE COLD HERE.
WE PLAYED WITH FORCES WE SHOULDN'T HAVE, AND NOW SPENCER IS GONE.

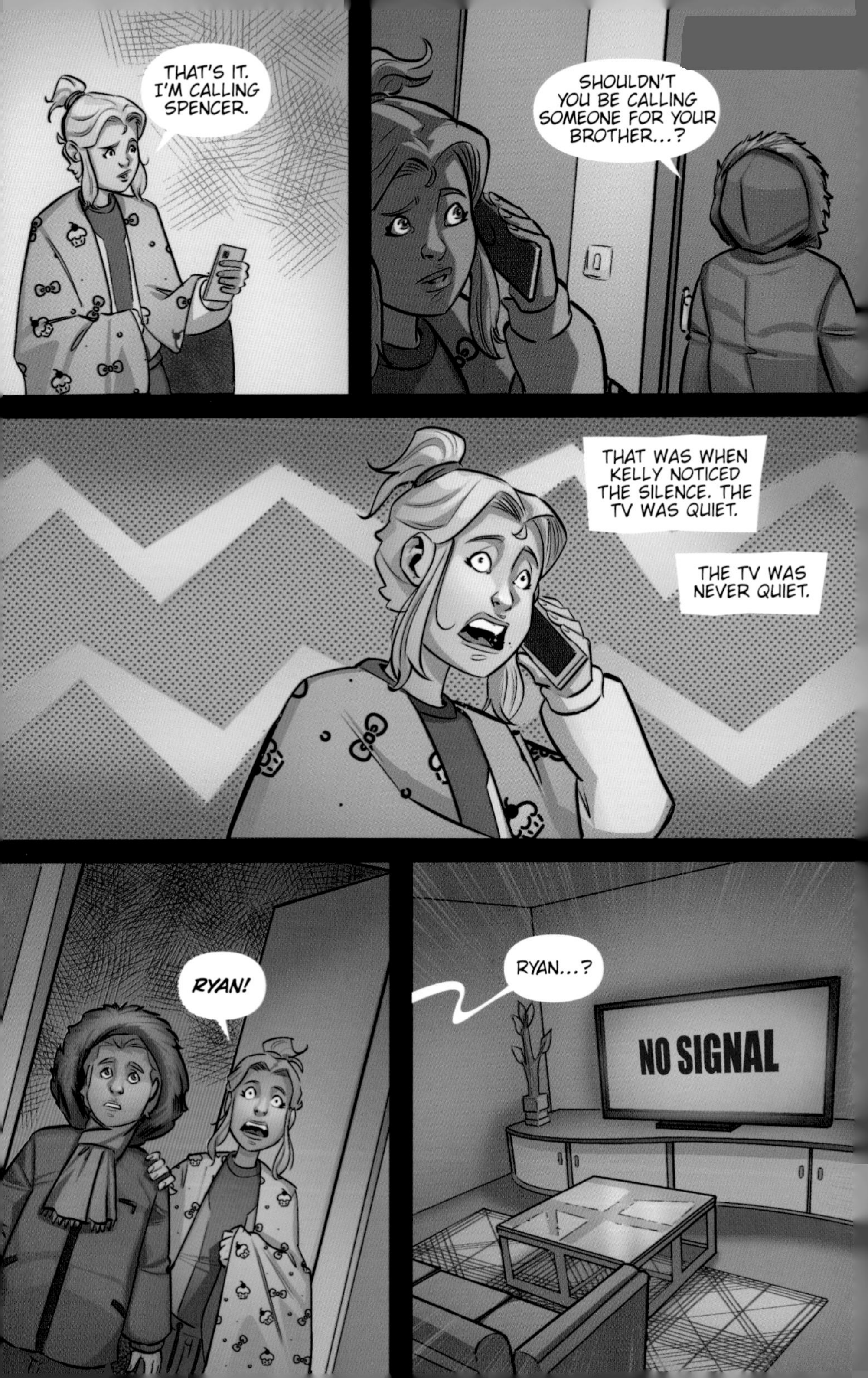
THAT'S IT. I'M CALLING SPENCER.
SHOULDN'T YOU BE CALLING SOMEONE FOR YOUR BROTHER...?
THAT WAS WHEN KELLY NOTICED THE SILENCE. THE TV WAS QUIET.
THE TV WAS NEVER QUIET.
RYAN!
RYAN...?
NO SIGNAL

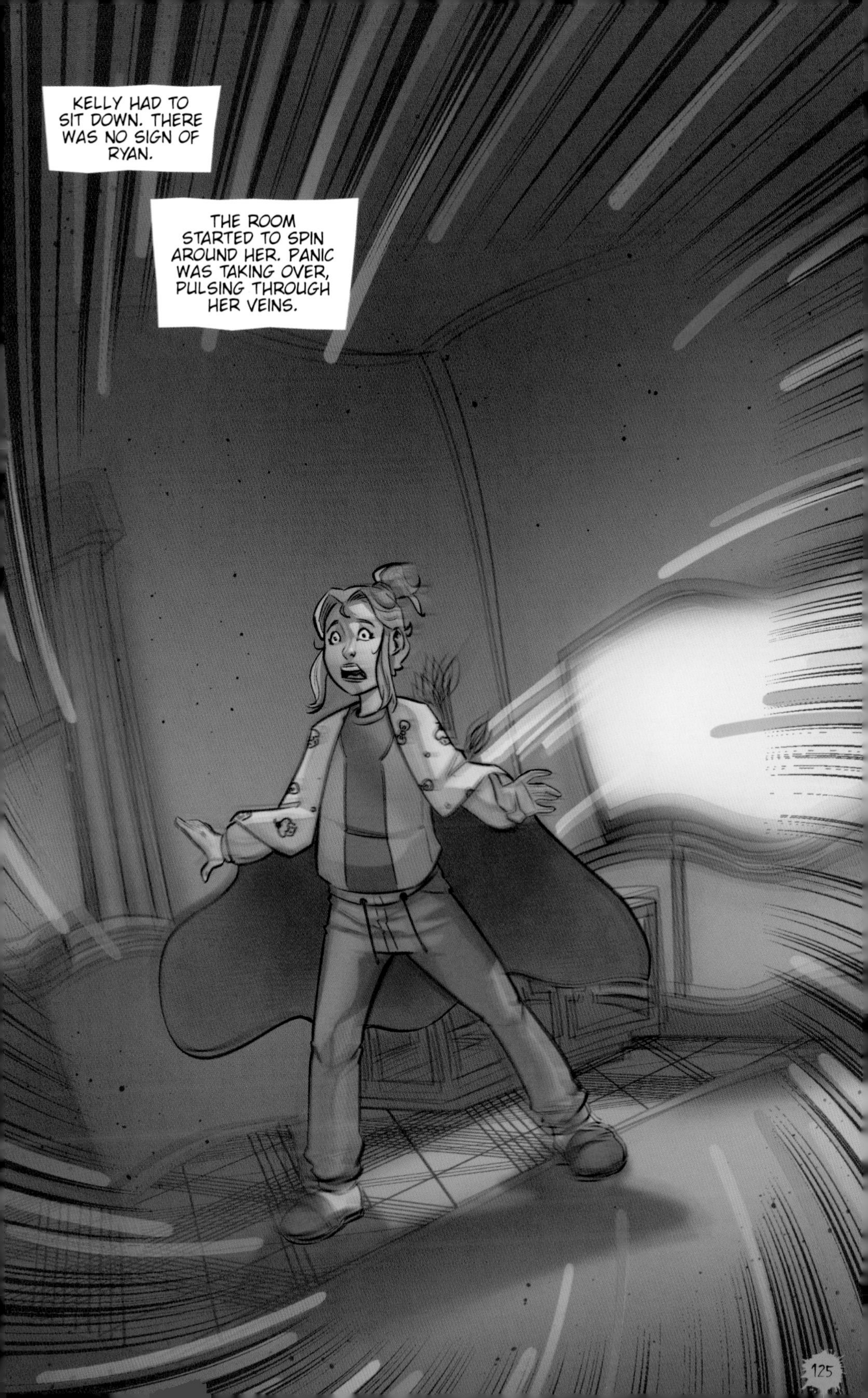
KELLY HAD TO SIT DOWN. THERE WAS NO SIGN OF RYAN.
THE ROOM STARTED TO SPIN AROUND HER. PANIC WAS TAKING OVER, PULSING THROUGH HER VEINS.

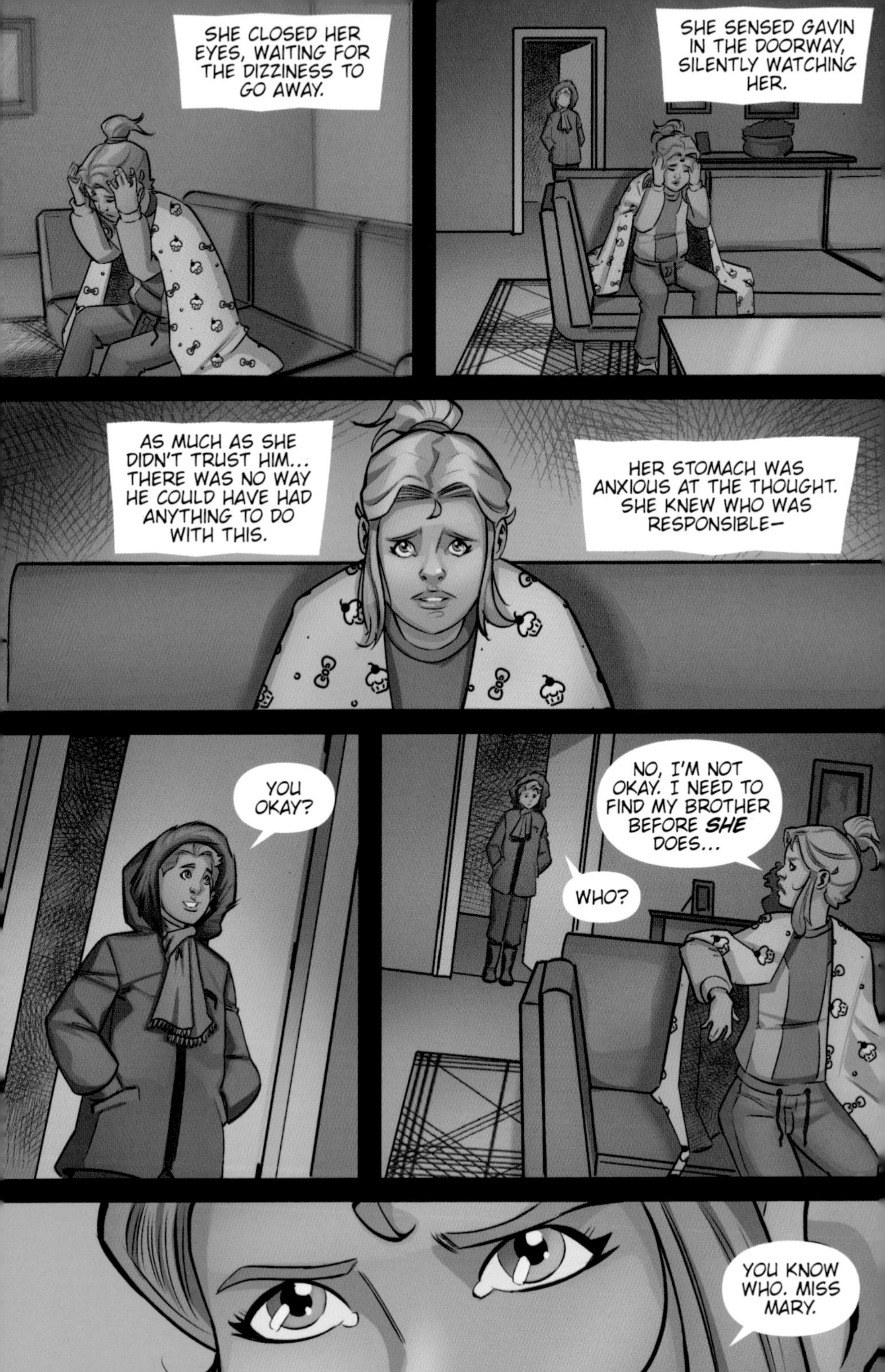
SHE CLOSED HER EYES, WAITING FOR THE DIZZINESS TO GO AWAY.
SHE SENSED GAVIN IN THE DOORWAY, SILENTLY WATCHING HER.
AS MUCH AS SHE DIDN'T TRUST HIM... THERE WAS NO WAY HE COULD HAVE HAD ANYTHING TO DO WITH THIS.
HER STOMACH WAS ANXIOUS AT THE THOUGHT. SHE KNEW WHO WAS RESPONSIBLE—
YOU OKAY?
NO, I'M NOT OKAY. I NEED TO FIND MY BROTHER BEFORE ***SHE*** DOES...
WHO?
YOU KNOW WHO. MISS MARY.

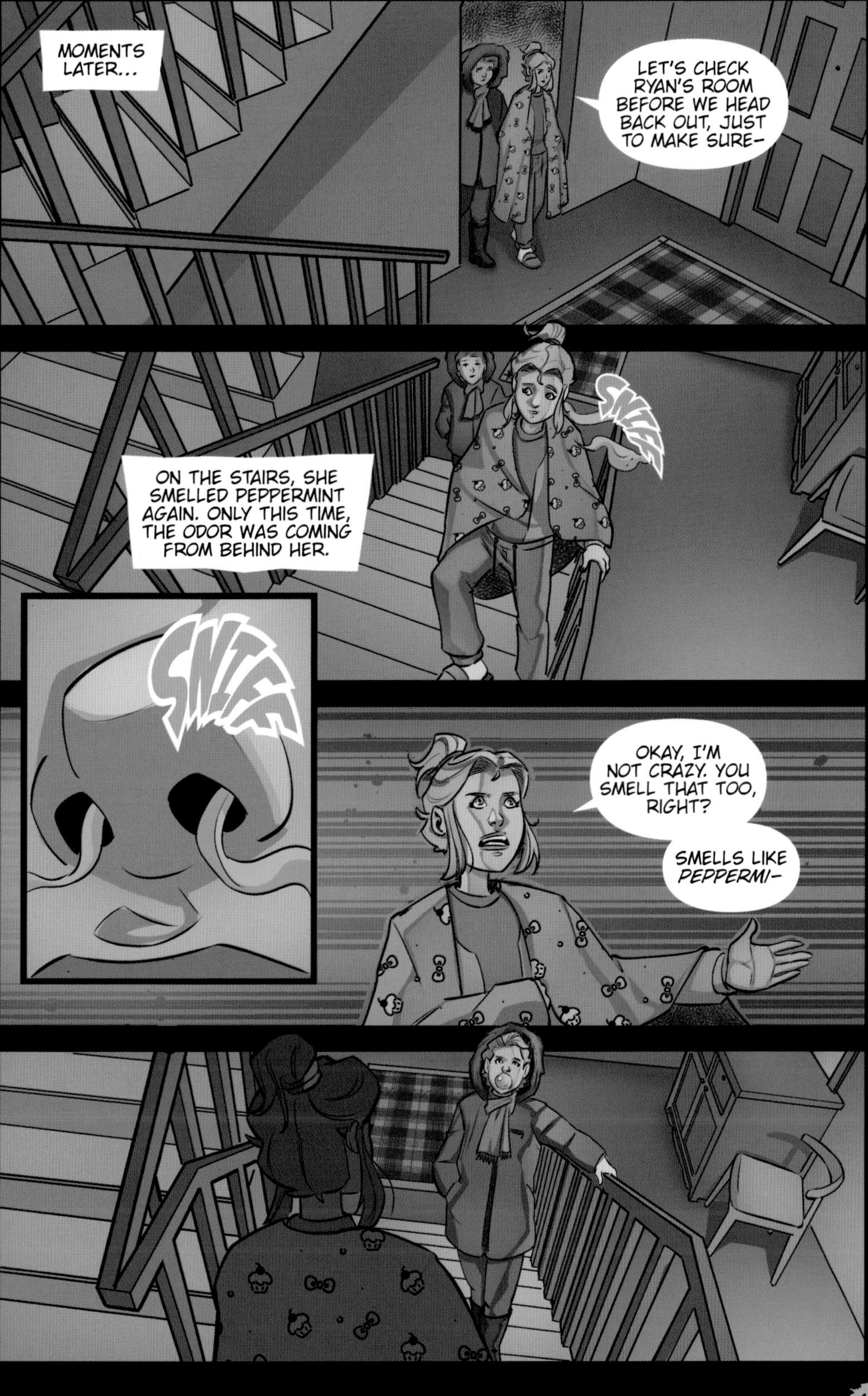

MOMENTS LATER...
LET'S CHECK RYAN'S ROOM BEFORE WE HEAD BACK OUT, JUST TO MAKE SURE—
SNIFF
ON THE STAIRS, SHE SMELLED PEPPERMINT AGAIN. ONLY THIS TIME, THE ODOR WAS COMING FROM BEHIND HER.
SNIFF
OKAY, I'M NOT CRAZY. YOU SMELL THAT TOO, RIGHT?
SMELLS LIKE *PEPPERMI—*

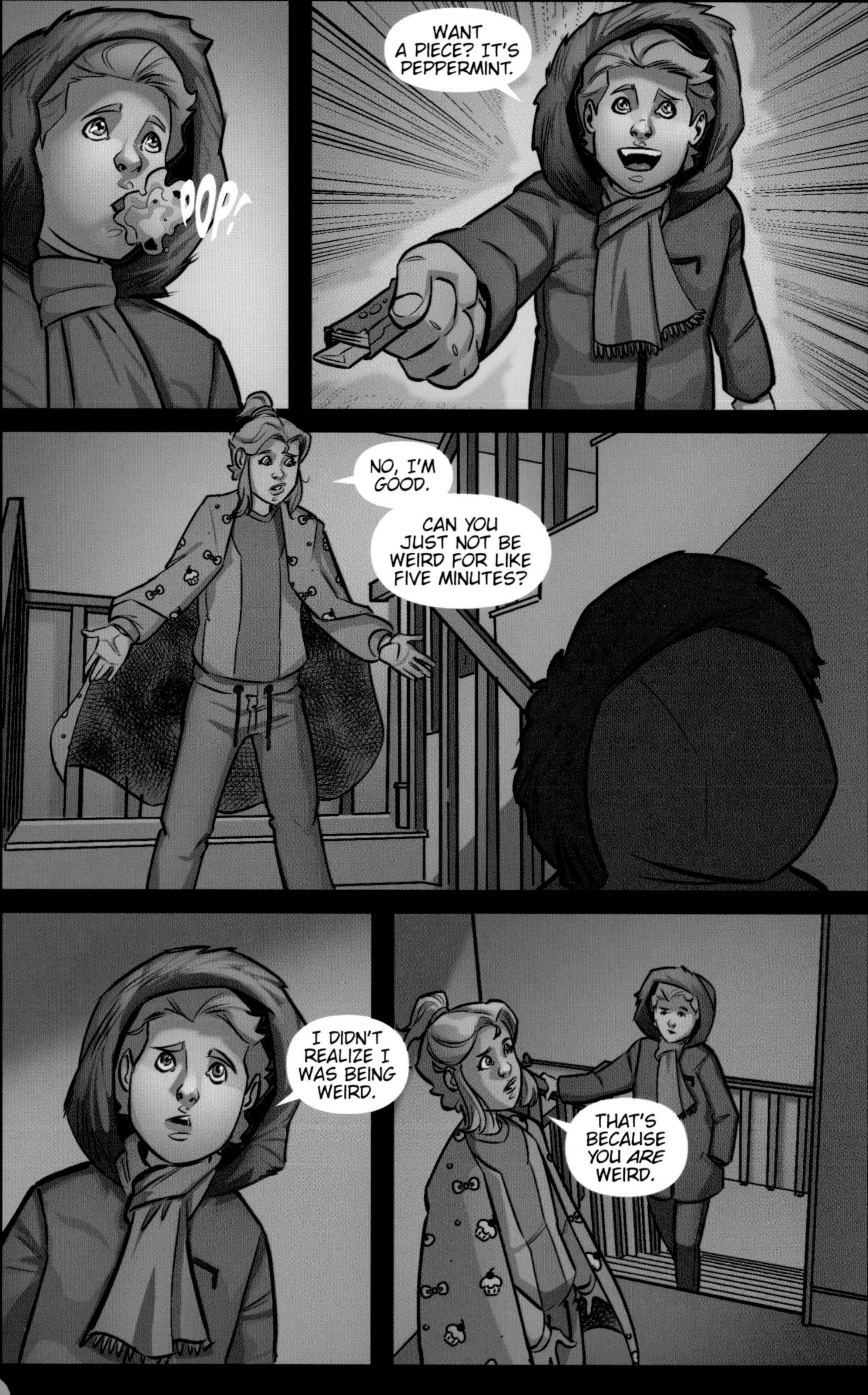
POP!
WANT A PIECE? IT'S PEPPERMINT.
NO, I'M GOOD.
CAN YOU JUST NOT BE WEIRD FOR LIKE FIVE MINUTES?
I DIDN'T REALIZE I WAS BEING WEIRD.
THAT'S BECAUSE YOU *ARE* WEIRD.

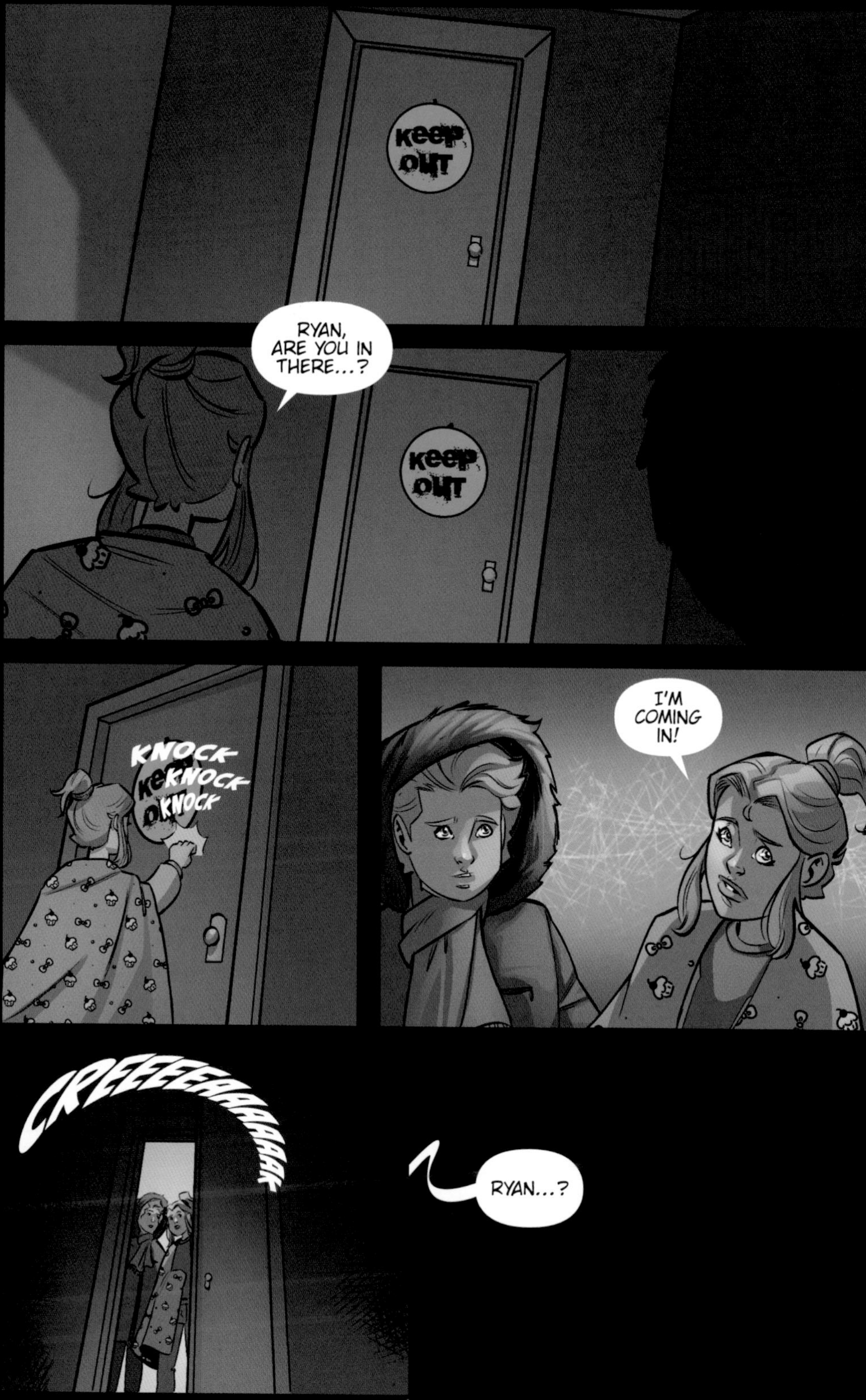
KEEP OUT
RYAN, ARE YOU IN THERE...?
KEEP OUT
KNOCK KNOCK KNOCK
I'M COMING IN!
CREEEEEAAAAAK
RYAN...?

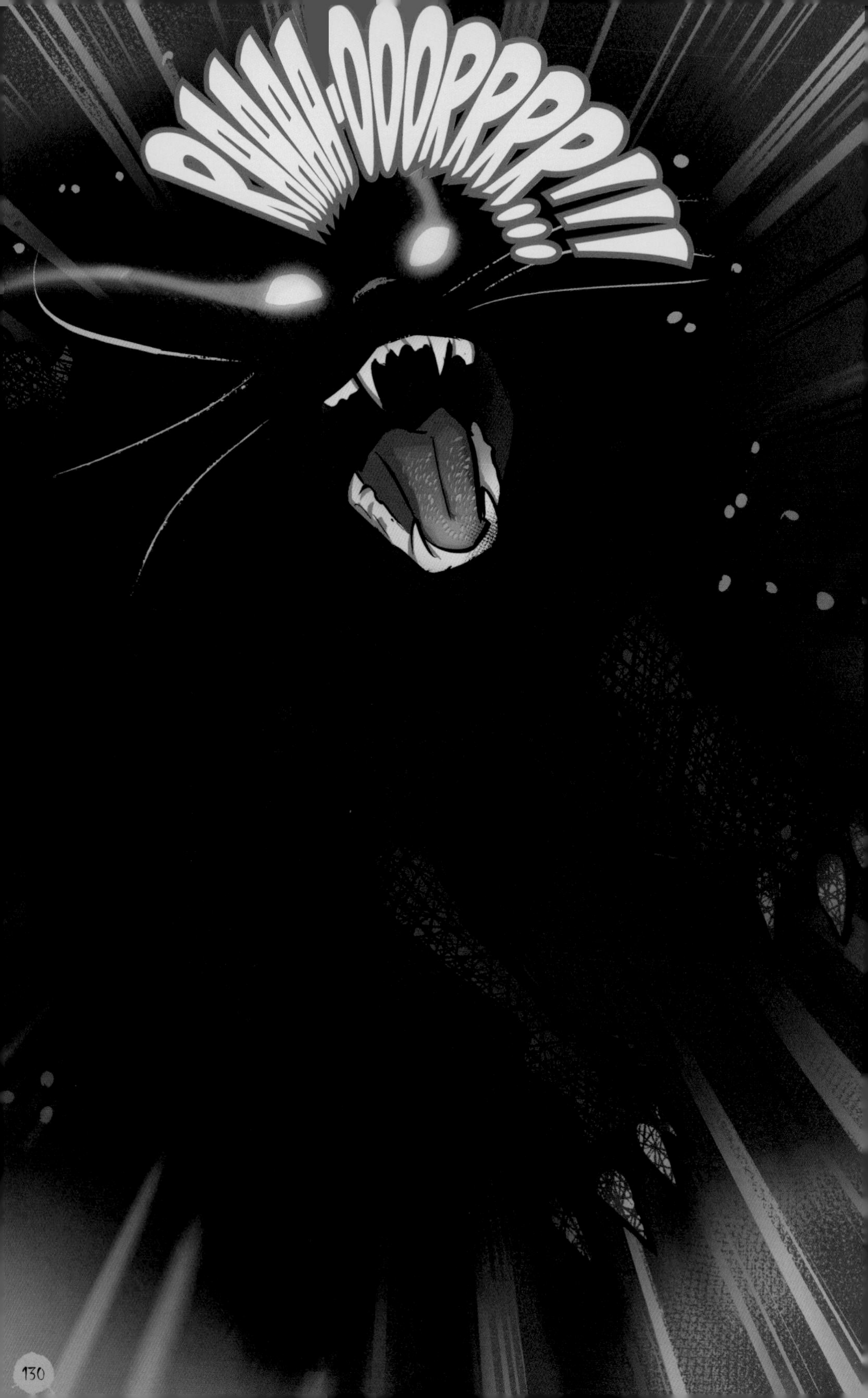
DAAAH-OOORRRR...!!!

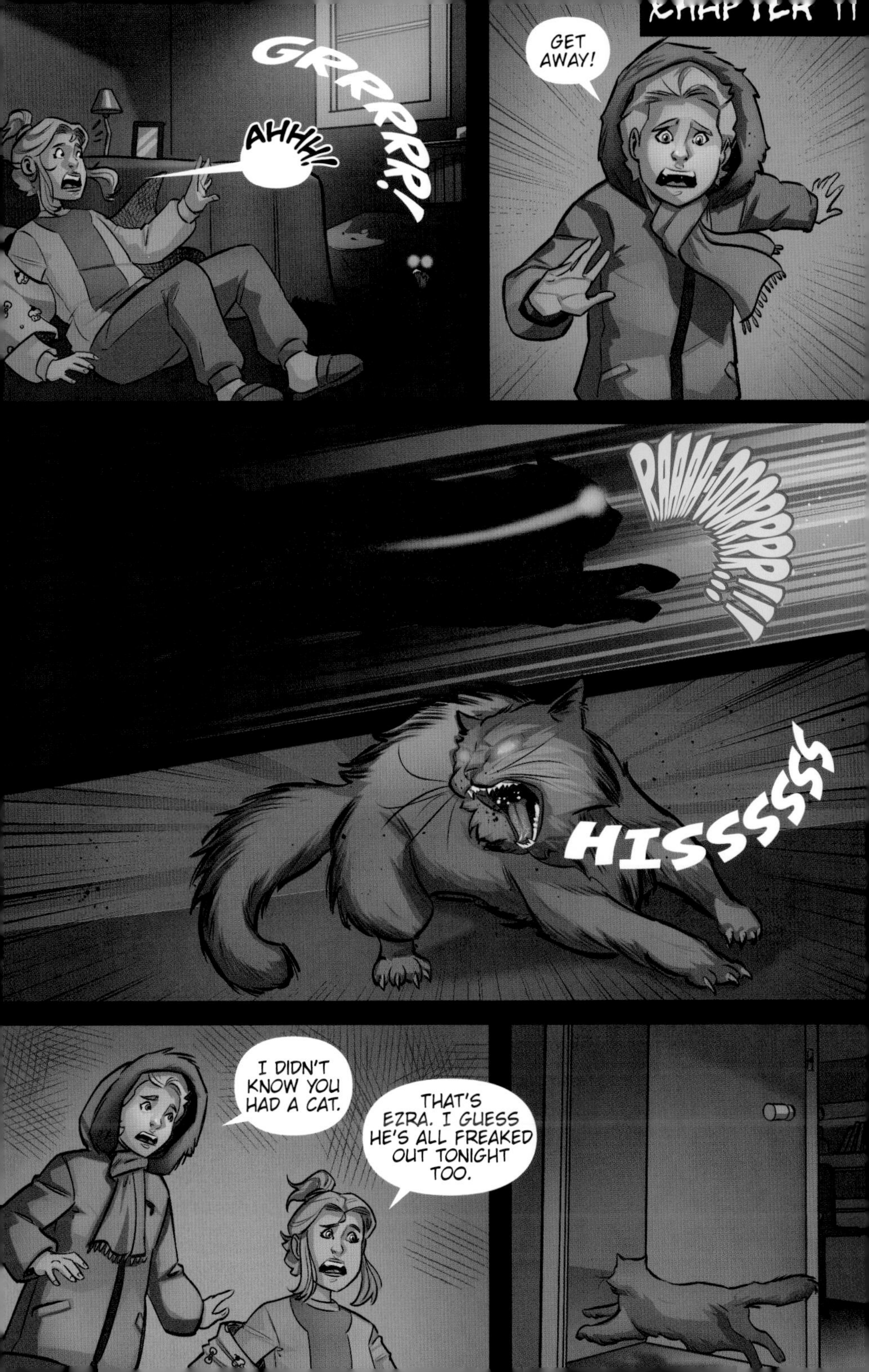
GRRRRRR!
AHHH!
GET AWAY!
HISSSSSS
I DIDN'T KNOW YOU HAD A CAT.
THAT'S EZRA. I GUESS HE'S ALL FREAKED OUT TONIGHT TOO.

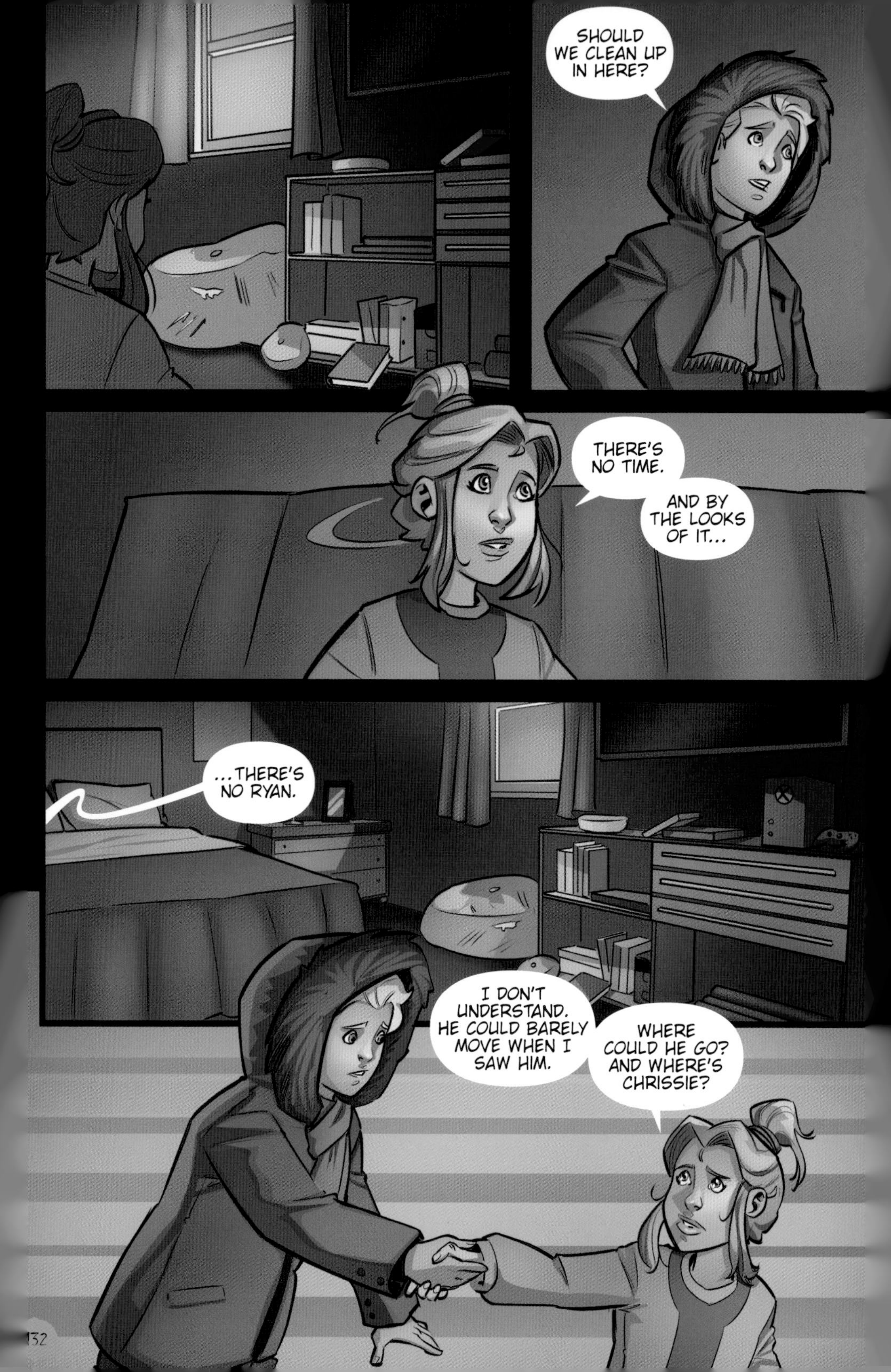
SHOULD WE CLEAN UP IN HERE?
THERE'S NO TIME.
AND BY THE LOOKS OF IT...
...THERE'S NO RYAN.
I DON'T UNDERSTAND. HE COULD BARELY MOVE WHEN I SAW HIM.
WHERE COULD HE GO? AND WHERE'S CHRISSIE?

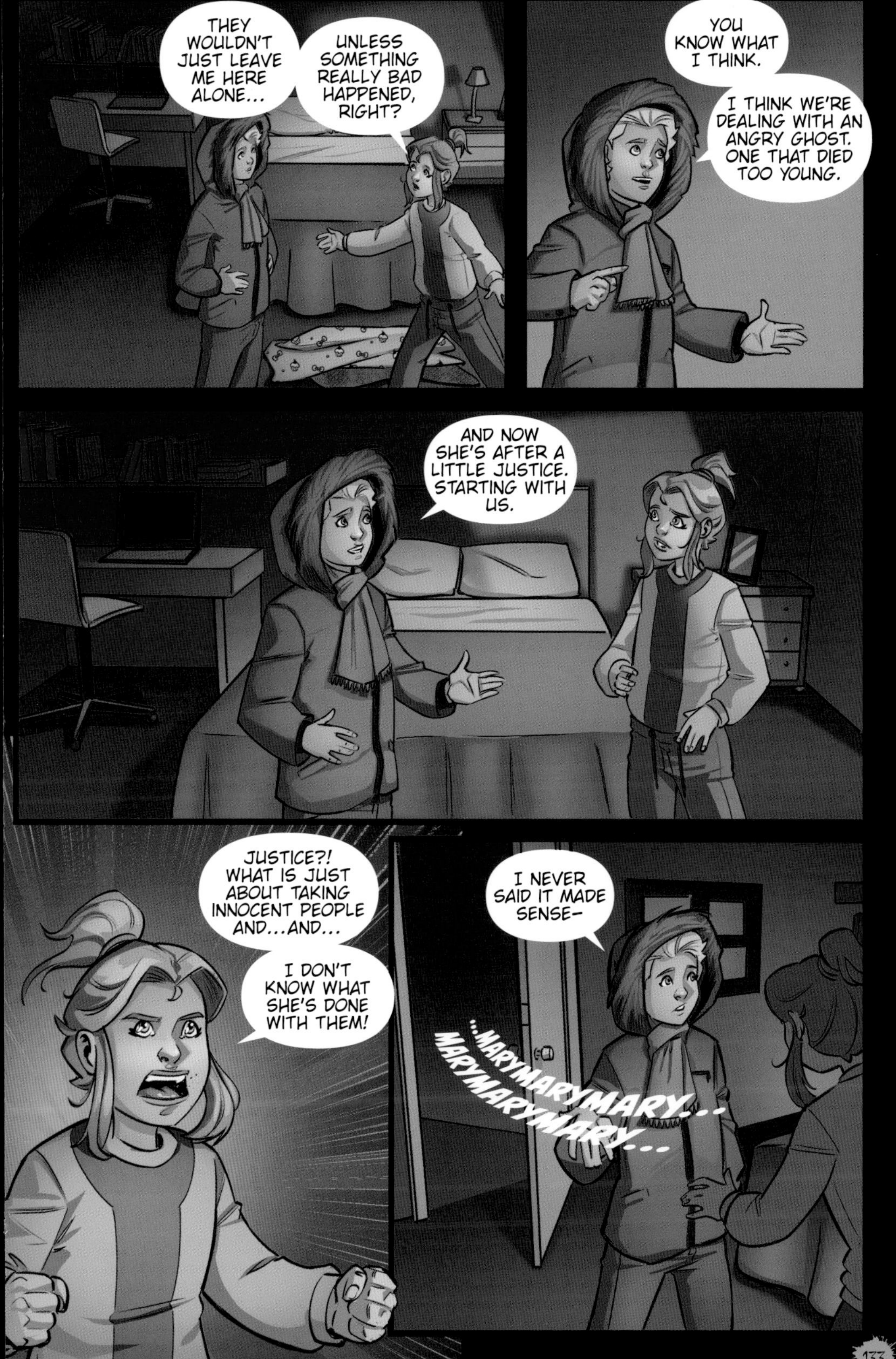
THEY WOULDN'T JUST LEAVE ME HERE ALONE...
UNLESS SOMETHING REALLY BAD HAPPENED, RIGHT?
YOU KNOW WHAT I THINK.
I THINK WE'RE DEALING WITH AN ANGRY GHOST. ONE THAT DIED TOO YOUNG.
AND NOW SHE'S AFTER A LITTLE JUSTICE. STARTING WITH US.
JUSTICE?! WHAT IS JUST ABOUT TAKING INNOCENT PEOPLE AND...AND...
I DON'T KNOW WHAT SHE'S DONE WITH THEM!
I NEVER SAID IT MADE SENSE-
...MARYMARYMARY...
MARYMARYMARY...

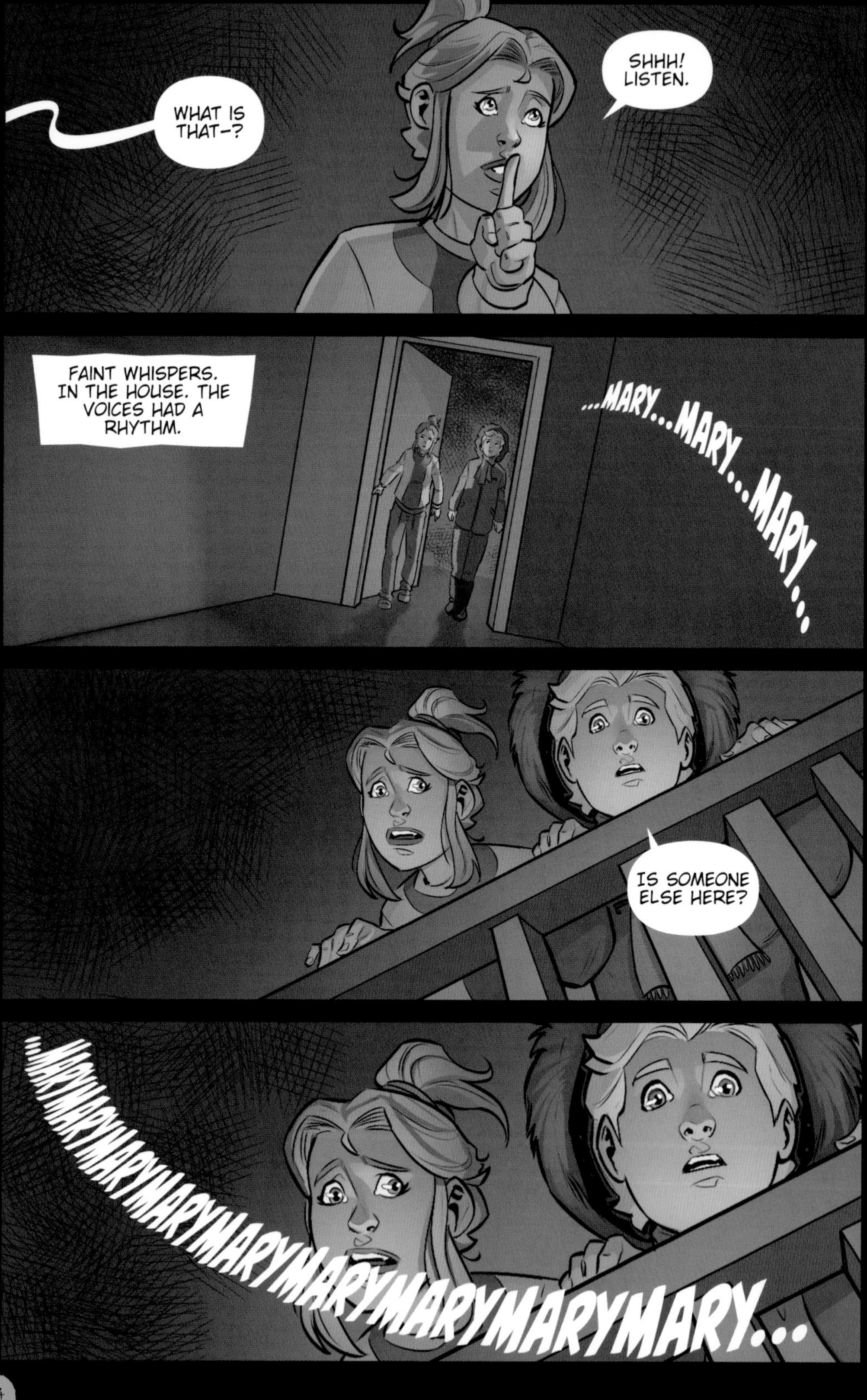
WHAT IS THAT-?
SHHH! LISTEN.
FAINT WHISPERS. IN THE HOUSE. THE VOICES HAD A RHYTHM.
...MARY...MARY...MARY...MARY...
IS SOMEONE ELSE HERE?
...MARYMARYMARYMARYMARYMARYMARY...

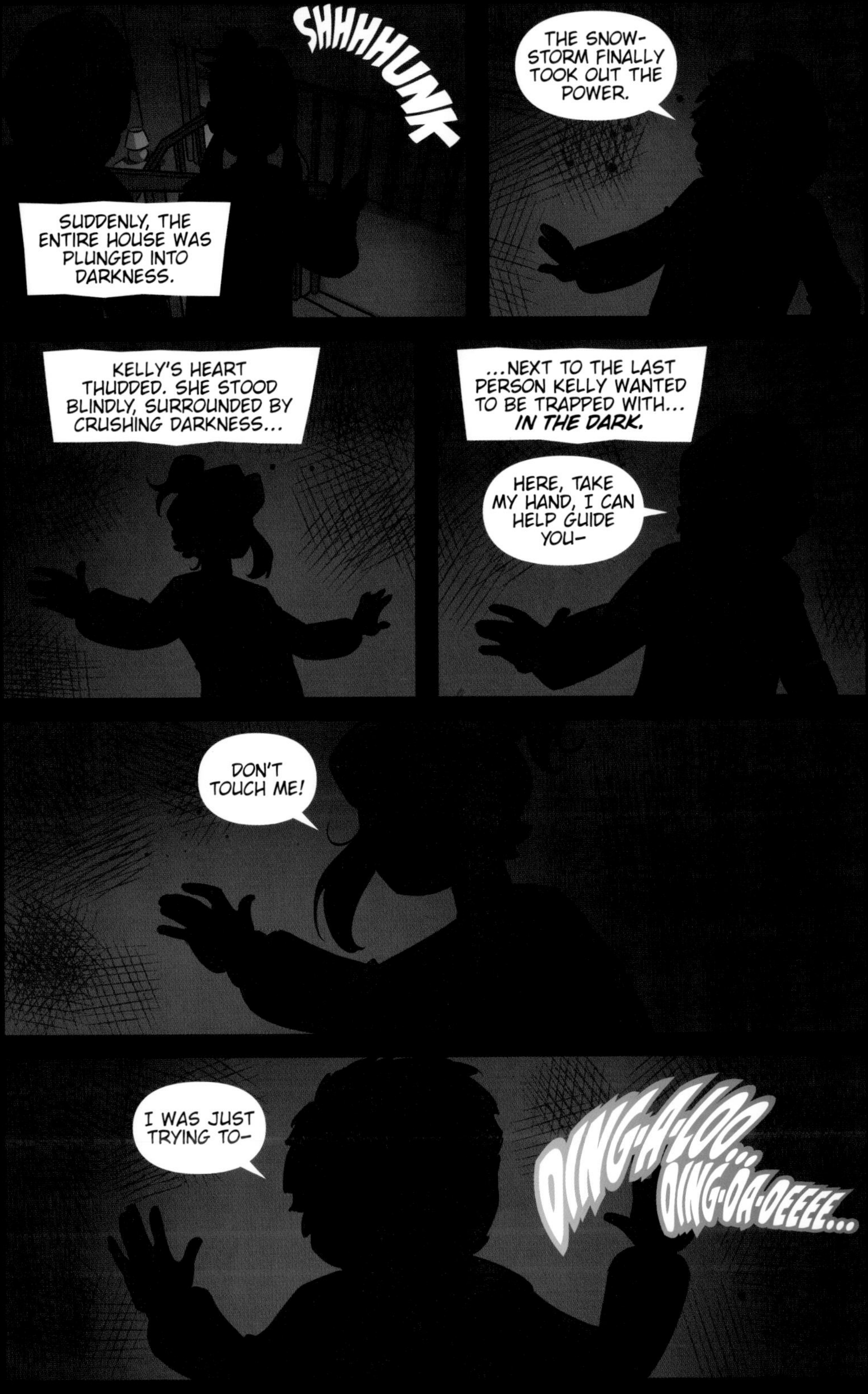
SUDDENLY, THE ENTIRE HOUSE WAS PLUNGED INTO DARKNESS.
SHHHHUNK
THE SNOW-STORM FINALLY TOOK OUT THE POWER.
KELLY'S HEART THUDDED. SHE STOOD BLINDLY, SURROUNDED BY CRUSHING DARKNESS...
...NEXT TO THE LAST PERSON KELLY WANTED TO BE TRAPPED WITH... *IN THE DARK.*
HERE, TAKE MY HAND, I CAN HELP GUIDE YOU–
DON'T TOUCH ME!
I WAS JUST TRYING TO–
DING-A-LOO... DING-OA-DEEEE...

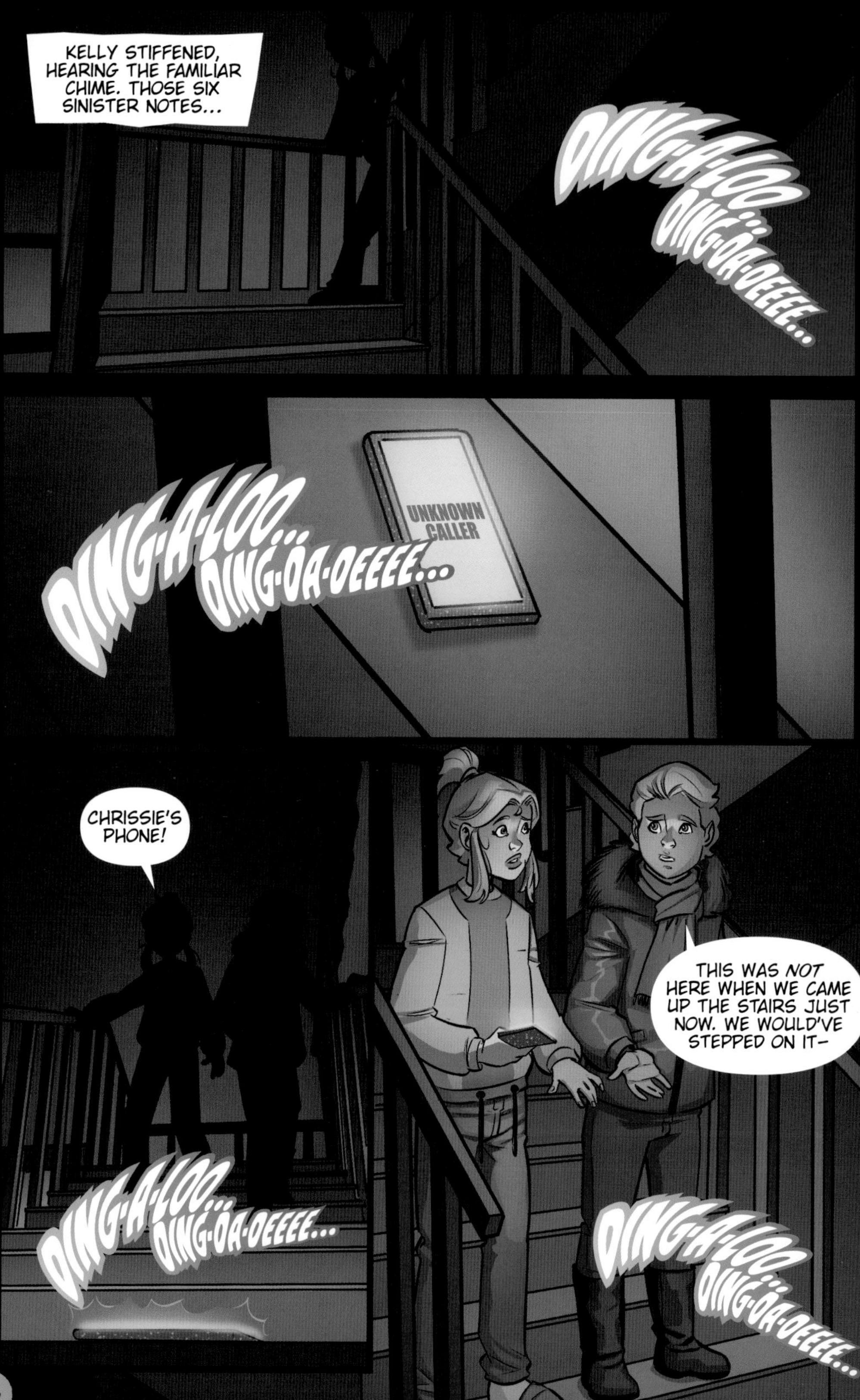
KELLY STIFFENED, HEARING THE FAMILIAR CHIME. THOSE SIX SINISTER NOTES...
DING-A-LOO... DING-OA-OEEEE...
UNKNOWN CALLER
DING-A-LOO... DING-OA-OEEEE...
CHRISSIE'S PHONE!
THIS WAS *NOT* HERE WHEN WE CAME UP THE STAIRS JUST NOW. WE WOULD'VE STEPPED ON IT–
DING-A-LOO... DING-OA-OEEEE...
DING-A-LOO... DING-OA-OEEEE...

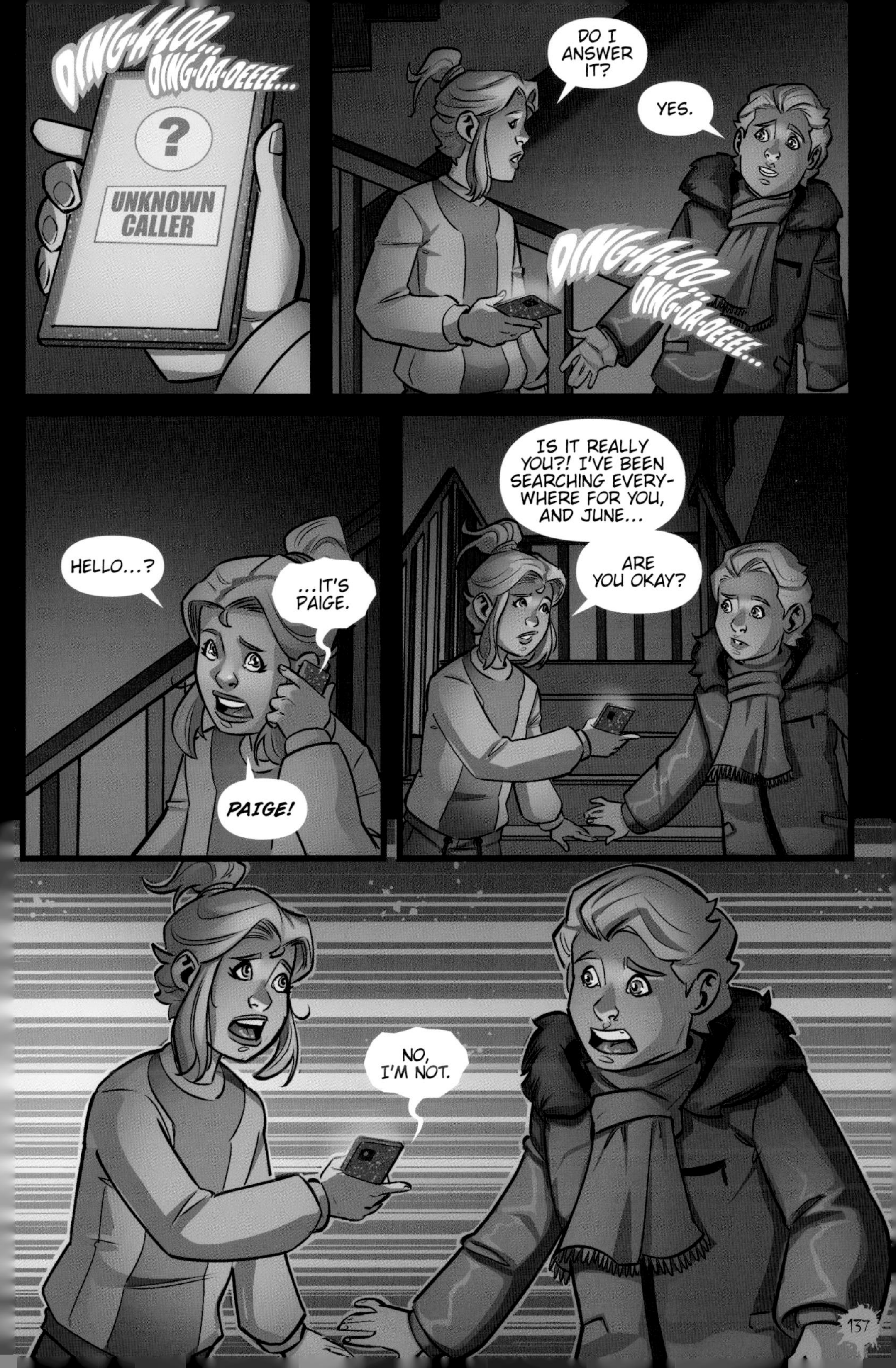
DING-A-LOO...
DING-OA-OEEEE...
?
UNKNOWN CALLER
DO I ANSWER IT?
YES.
DING-A-LOO...
DING-OA-OEEEE...
HELLO...?
...IT'S PAIGE.
PAIGE!
IS IT REALLY YOU?! I'VE BEEN SEARCHING EVERY-WHERE FOR YOU, AND JUNE...
ARE YOU OKAY?
NO, I'M NOT.

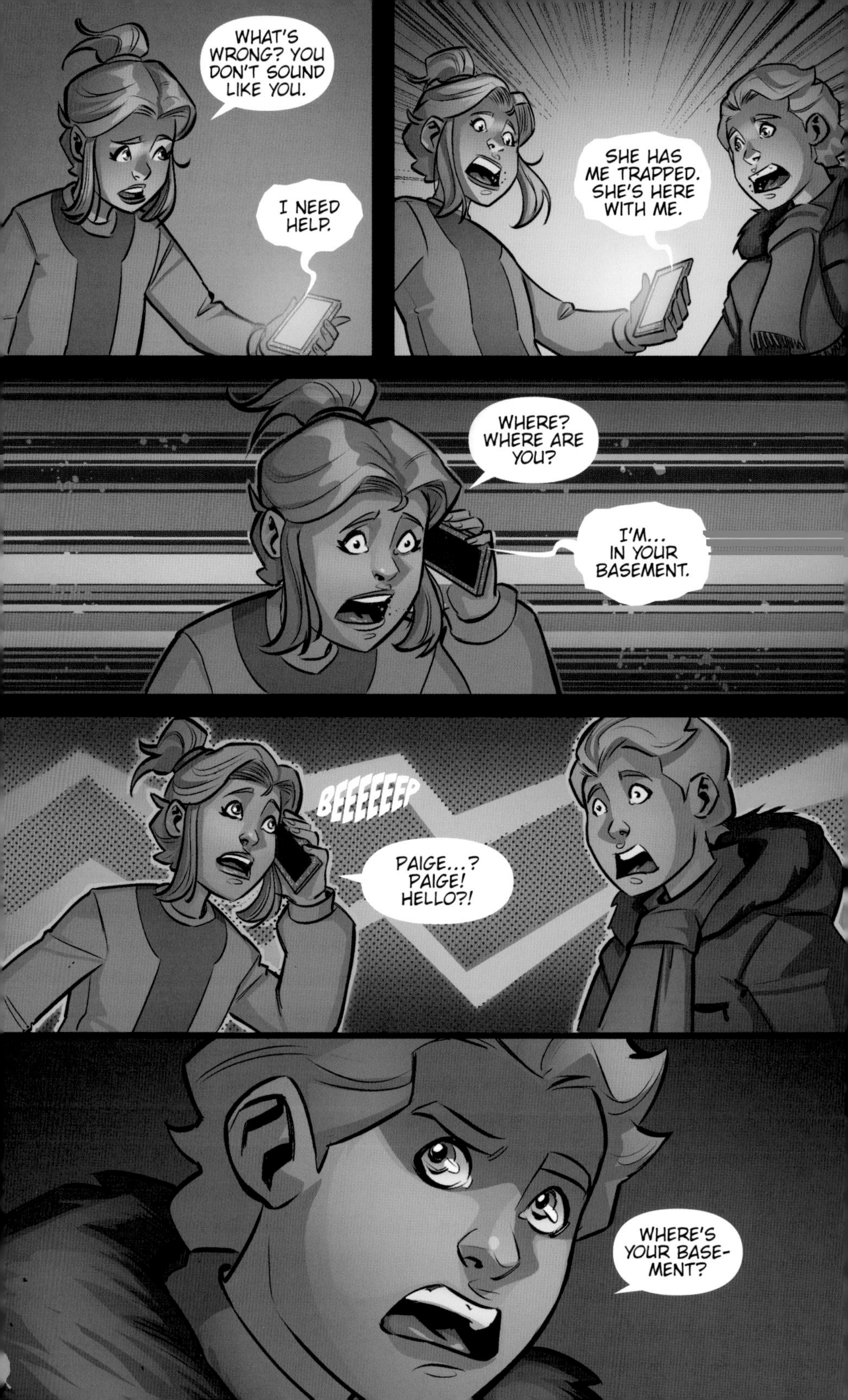
WHAT'S WRONG? YOU DON'T SOUND LIKE YOU.
I NEED HELP.
SHE HAS ME TRAPPED. SHE'S HERE WITH ME.
WHERE? WHERE ARE YOU?
I'M... IN YOUR BASEMENT.
BEEEEEEP
PAIGE...? PAIGE! HELLO?!
WHERE'S YOUR BASE-MENT?

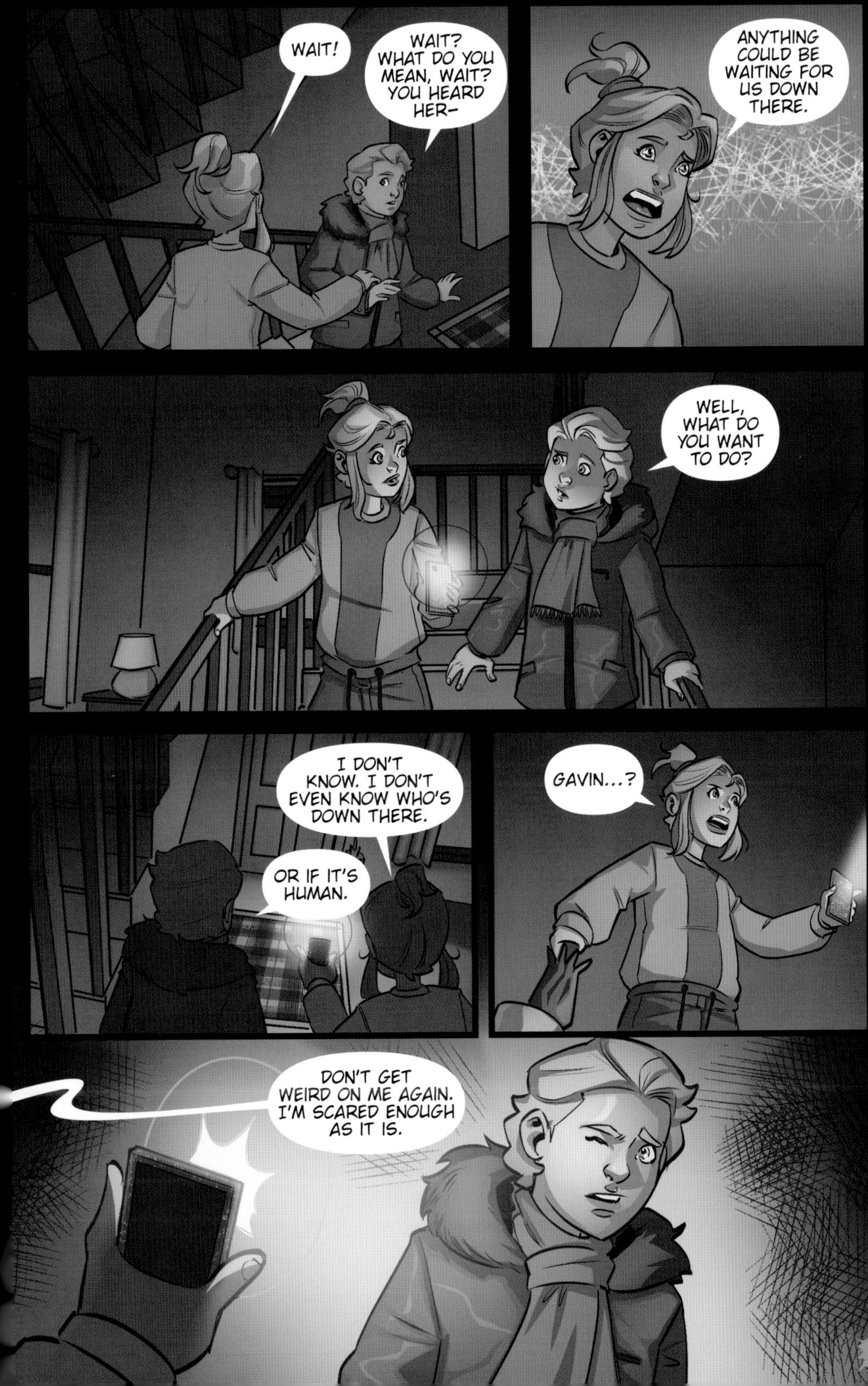
WAIT!
WAIT? WHAT DO YOU MEAN, WAIT? YOU HEARD HER-
ANYTHING COULD BE WAITING FOR US DOWN THERE.
WELL, WHAT DO YOU WANT TO DO?
I DON'T KNOW. I DON'T EVEN KNOW WHO'S DOWN THERE.
OR IF IT'S HUMAN.
GAVIN...?
DON'T GET WEIRD ON ME AGAIN. I'M SCARED ENOUGH AS IT IS.

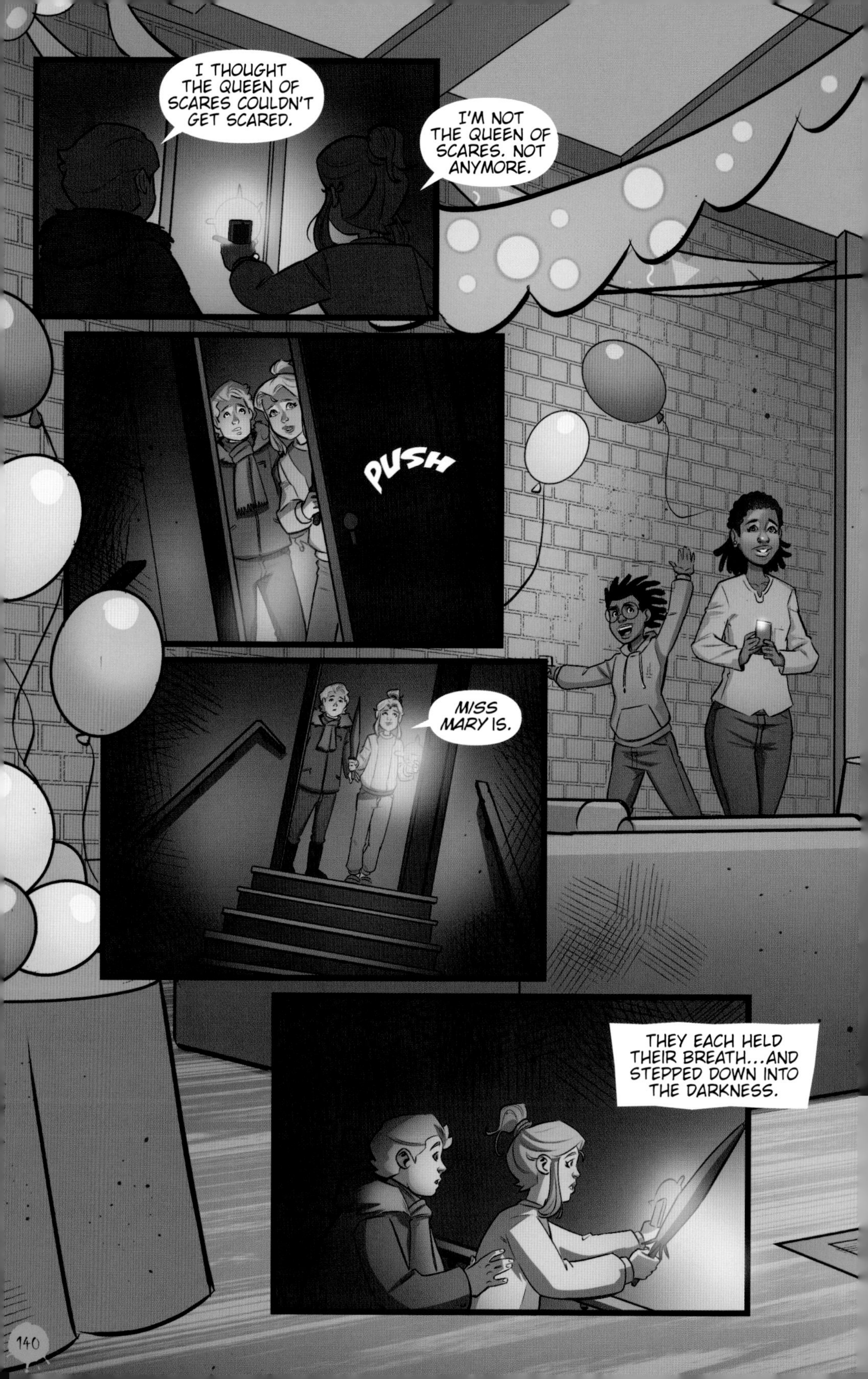

I THOUGHT THE QUEEN OF SCARES COULDN'T GET SCARED.
I'M NOT THE QUEEN OF SCARES. NOT ANYMORE.
PUSH
MISS MARY IS.
THEY EACH HELD THEIR BREATH...AND STEPPED DOWN INTO THE DARKNESS.

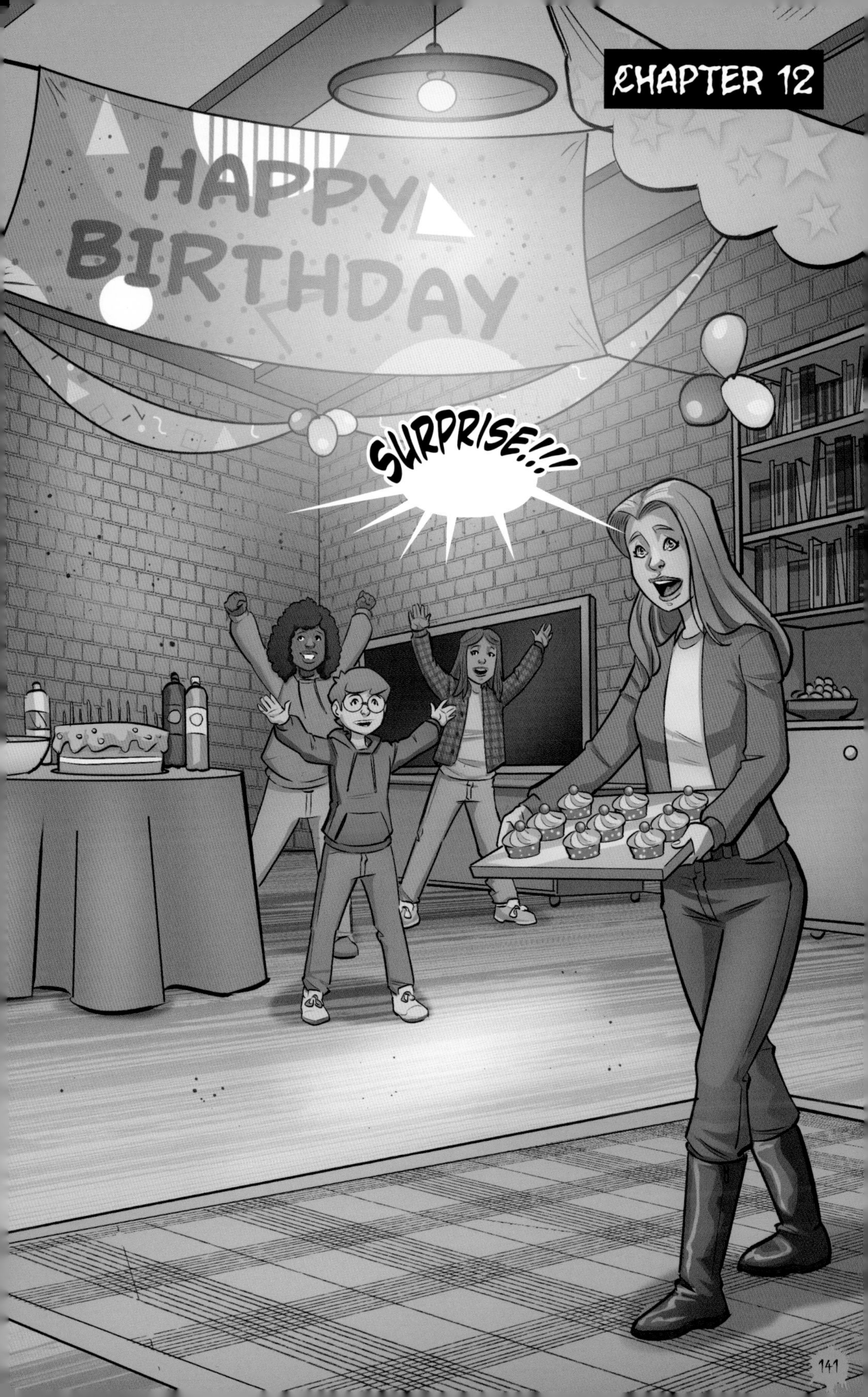
CHAPTER 12
HAPPY BIRTHDAY
SURPRISE!!!

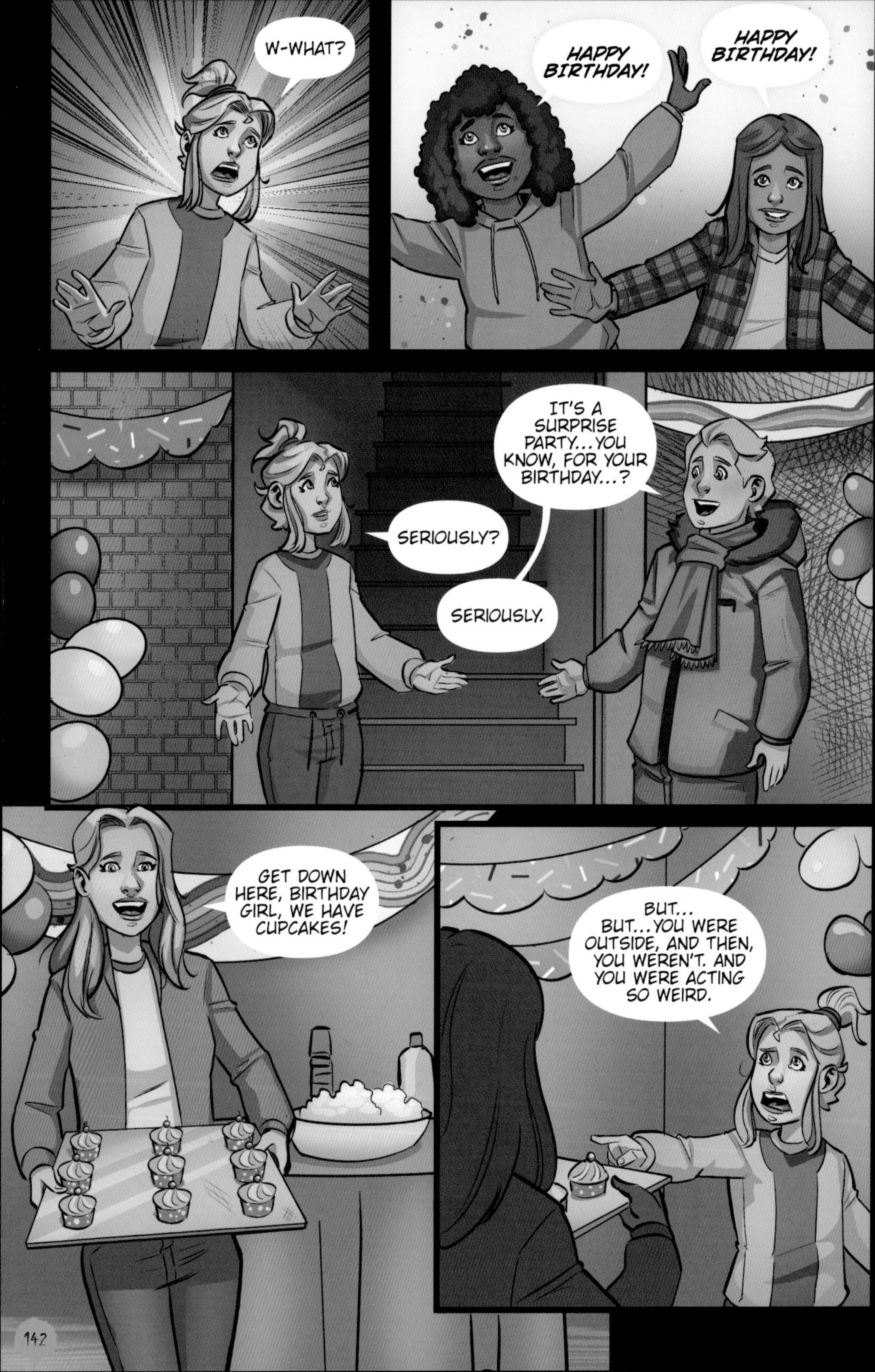
W-WHAT?
HAPPY BIRTHDAY!
HAPPY BIRTHDAY!
IT'S A SURPRISE PARTY...YOU KNOW, FOR YOUR BIRTHDAY...?
SERIOUSLY?
SERIOUSLY.
GET DOWN HERE, BIRTHDAY GIRL, WE HAVE CUPCAKES!
BUT... BUT...YOU WERE OUTSIDE, AND THEN, YOU WEREN'T. AND YOU WERE ACTING SO WEIRD.

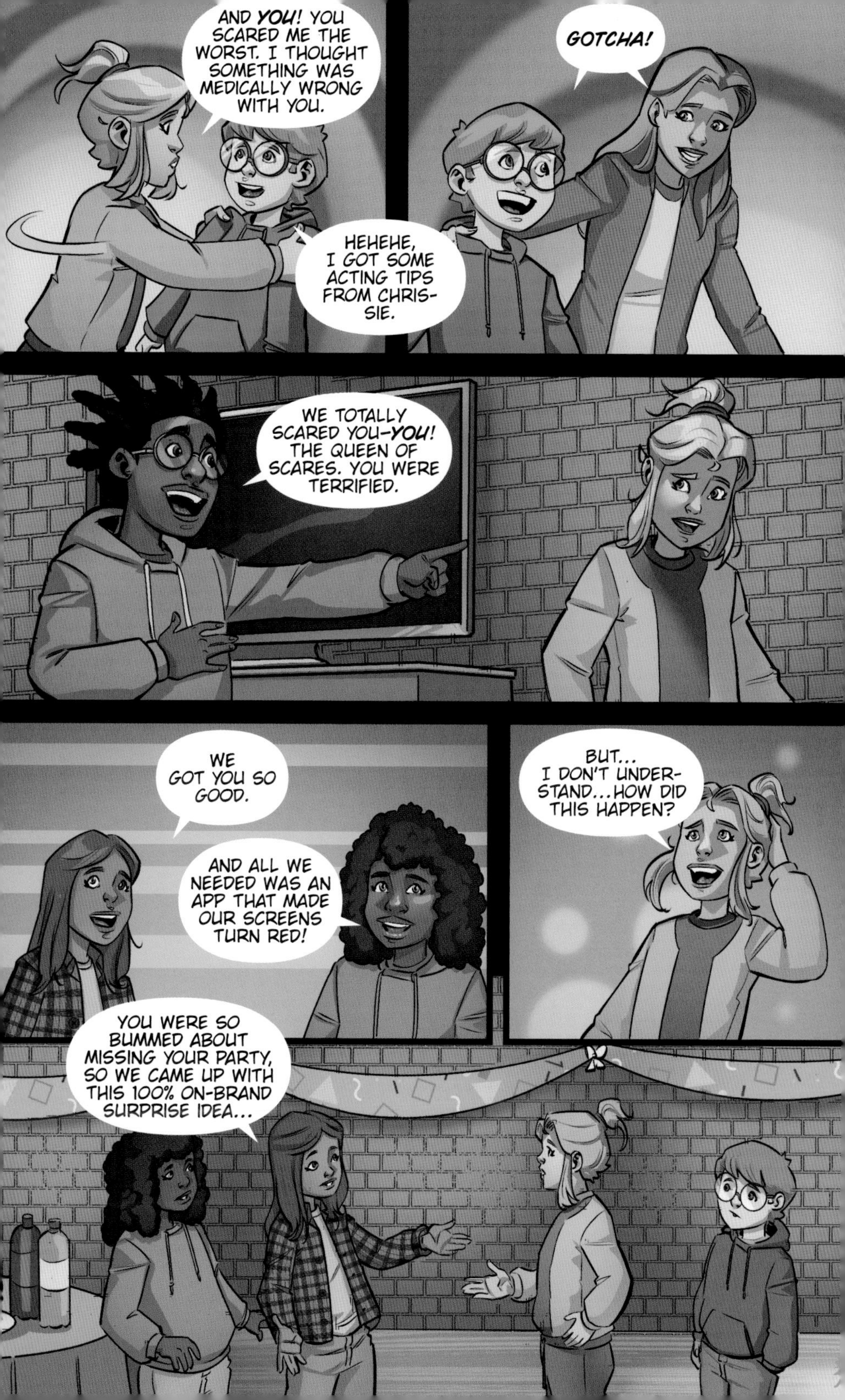
AND YOU! YOU SCARED ME THE WORST. I THOUGHT SOMETHING WAS MEDICALLY WRONG WITH YOU.
HEHEHE, I GOT SOME ACTING TIPS FROM CHRIS-SIE.
GOTCHA!
WE TOTALLY SCARED YOU–YOU! THE QUEEN OF SCARES. YOU WERE TERRIFIED.
WE GOT YOU SO GOOD.
AND ALL WE NEEDED WAS AN APP THAT MADE OUR SCREENS TURN RED!
BUT... I DON'T UNDER-STAND...HOW DID THIS HAPPEN?
YOU WERE SO BUMMED ABOUT MISSING YOUR PARTY, SO WE CAME UP WITH THIS 100% ON-BRAND SURPRISE IDEA...

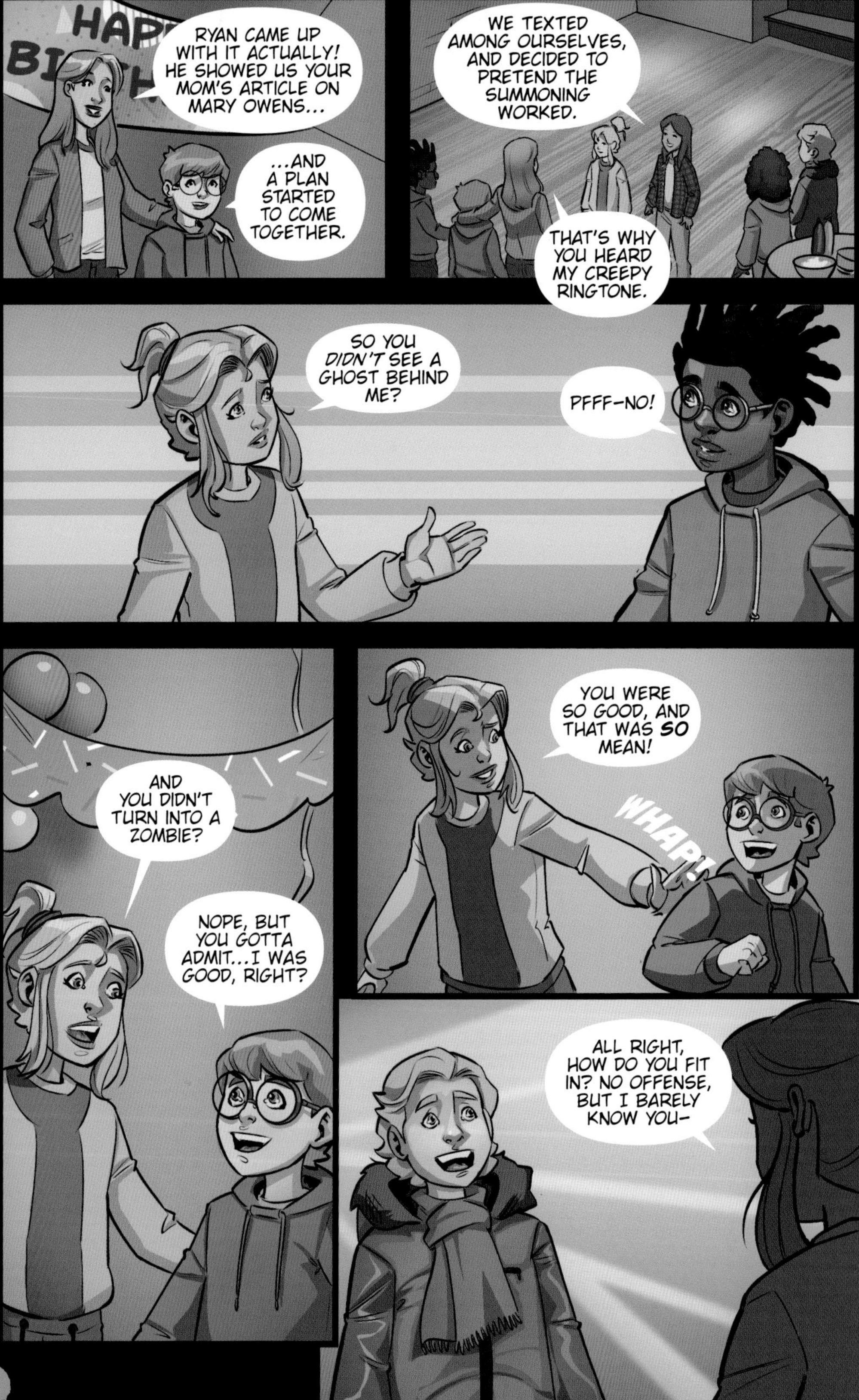
HAP
BI
RYAN CAME UP WITH IT ACTUALLY! HE SHOWED US YOUR MOM'S ARTICLE ON MARY OWENS...
...AND A PLAN STARTED TO COME TOGETHER.
WE TEXTED AMONG OURSELVES, AND DECIDED TO PRETEND THE SUMMONING WORKED.
THAT'S WHY YOU HEARD MY CREEPY RINGTONE.
SO YOU *DIDN'T* SEE A GHOST BEHIND ME?
PFFF–NO!
AND YOU DIDN'T TURN INTO A ZOMBIE?
NOPE, BUT YOU GOTTA ADMIT...I WAS GOOD, RIGHT?
YOU WERE SO GOOD, AND THAT WAS **SO** MEAN!
WHAP!
ALL RIGHT, HOW DO YOU FIT IN? NO OFFENSE, BUT I BARELY KNOW YOU–

THAT'S WHY HE WAS PERFECT FOR THIS. HE WAS ALREADY SLEEPING OVER AT MY HOUSE, AND SINCE YOU DIDN'T KNOW HIM, HE COULD MESS WITH YOUR HEAD.

YOU CREEPED ME OUT BIG-TIME. ESPECIALLY WHEN YOU CAME OUT OF THE BUSHES, RUNNING.

CHRISSIE!

WE WERE WAITING TO SNEAK IN HERE FOR THE PARTY...

WE WERE WAITING TO SNEAK IN HERE FOR THE PARTY...

CHRISSIE UNLOCKED THE SIDE DOOR FOR US...AND SPENCER'S MOM WAS ON HAND TO SUPERVISE.

I PLAYED ALONG, BUT I WAS ALWAYS LOOKING OUT FOR YOUR SAFETY, HON.

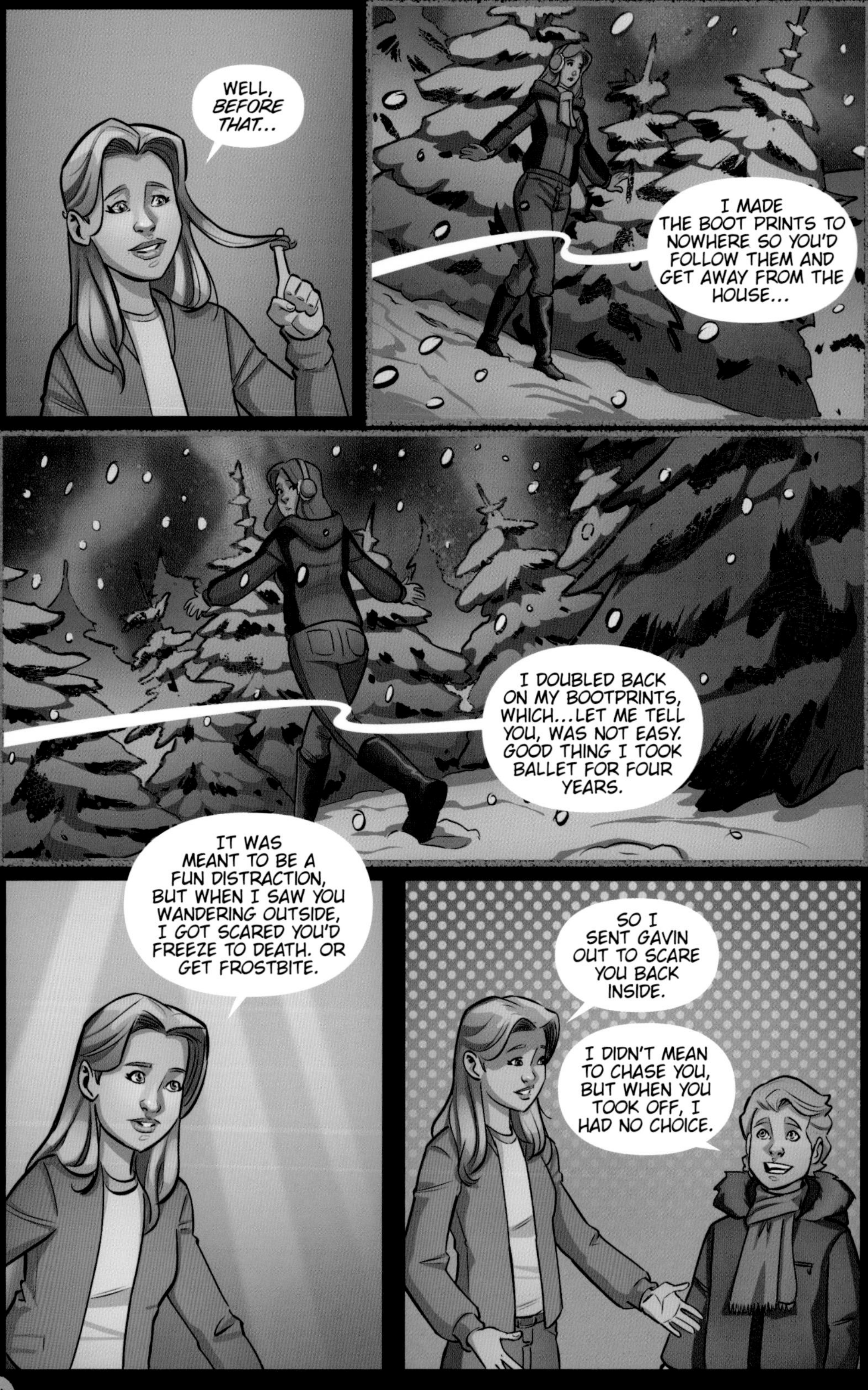
WELL, BEFORE THAT...
I MADE THE BOOT PRINTS TO NOWHERE SO YOU'D FOLLOW THEM AND GET AWAY FROM THE HOUSE...
I DOUBLED BACK ON MY BOOTPRINTS, WHICH...LET ME TELL YOU, WAS NOT EASY. GOOD THING I TOOK BALLET FOR FOUR YEARS.
IT WAS MEANT TO BE A FUN DISTRACTION, BUT WHEN I SAW YOU WANDERING OUTSIDE, I GOT SCARED YOU'D FREEZE TO DEATH. OR GET FROSTBITE.
SO I SENT GAVIN OUT TO SCARE YOU BACK INSIDE.
I DIDN'T MEAN TO CHASE YOU, BUT WHEN YOU TOOK OFF, I HAD NO CHOICE.

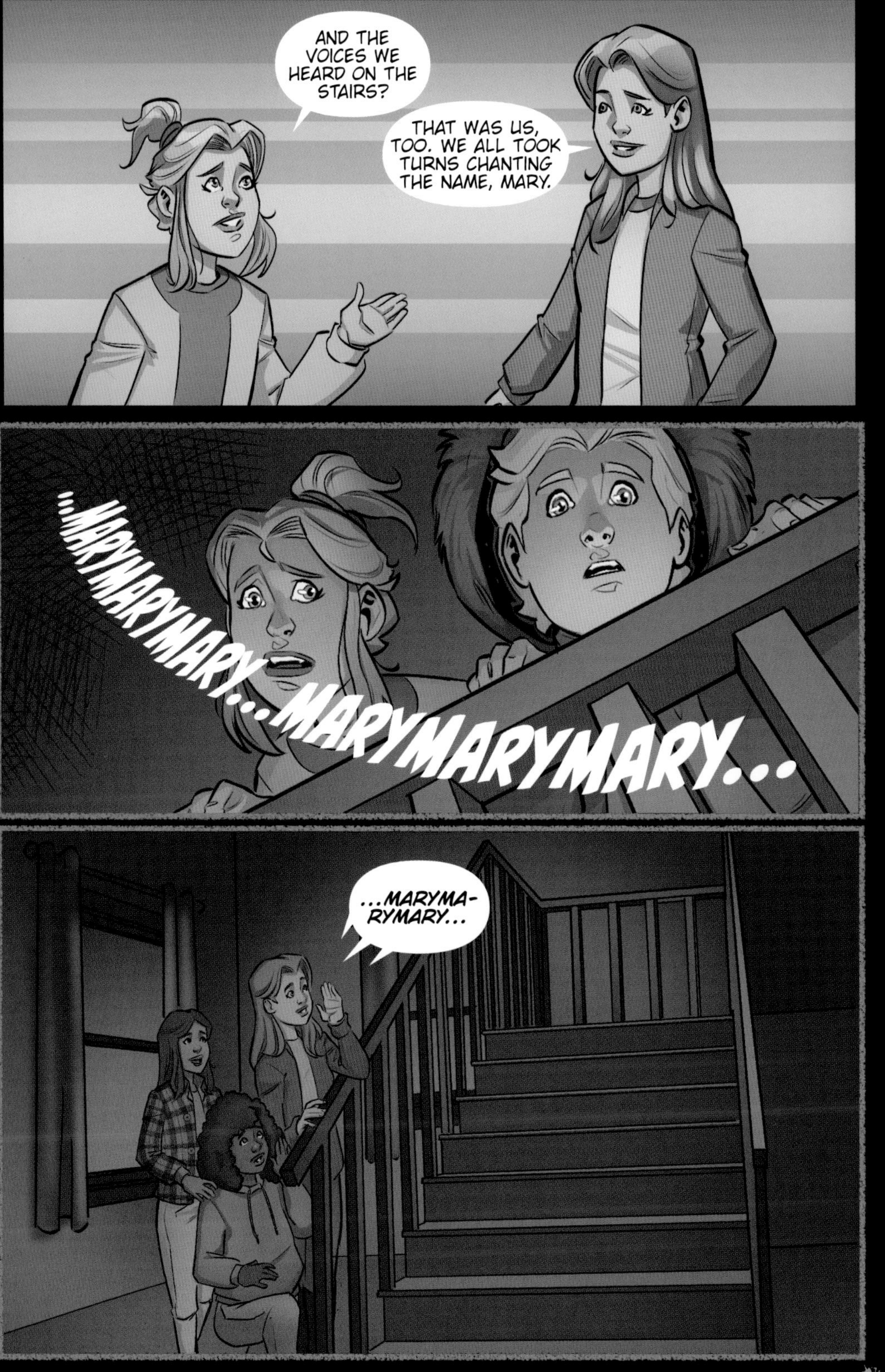
AND THE VOICES WE HEARD ON THE STAIRS?
THAT WAS US, TOO. WE ALL TOOK TURNS CHANTING THE NAME, MARY.
...MARYMARYMARY...MARYMARYMARY...
...MARYMARYMARY...

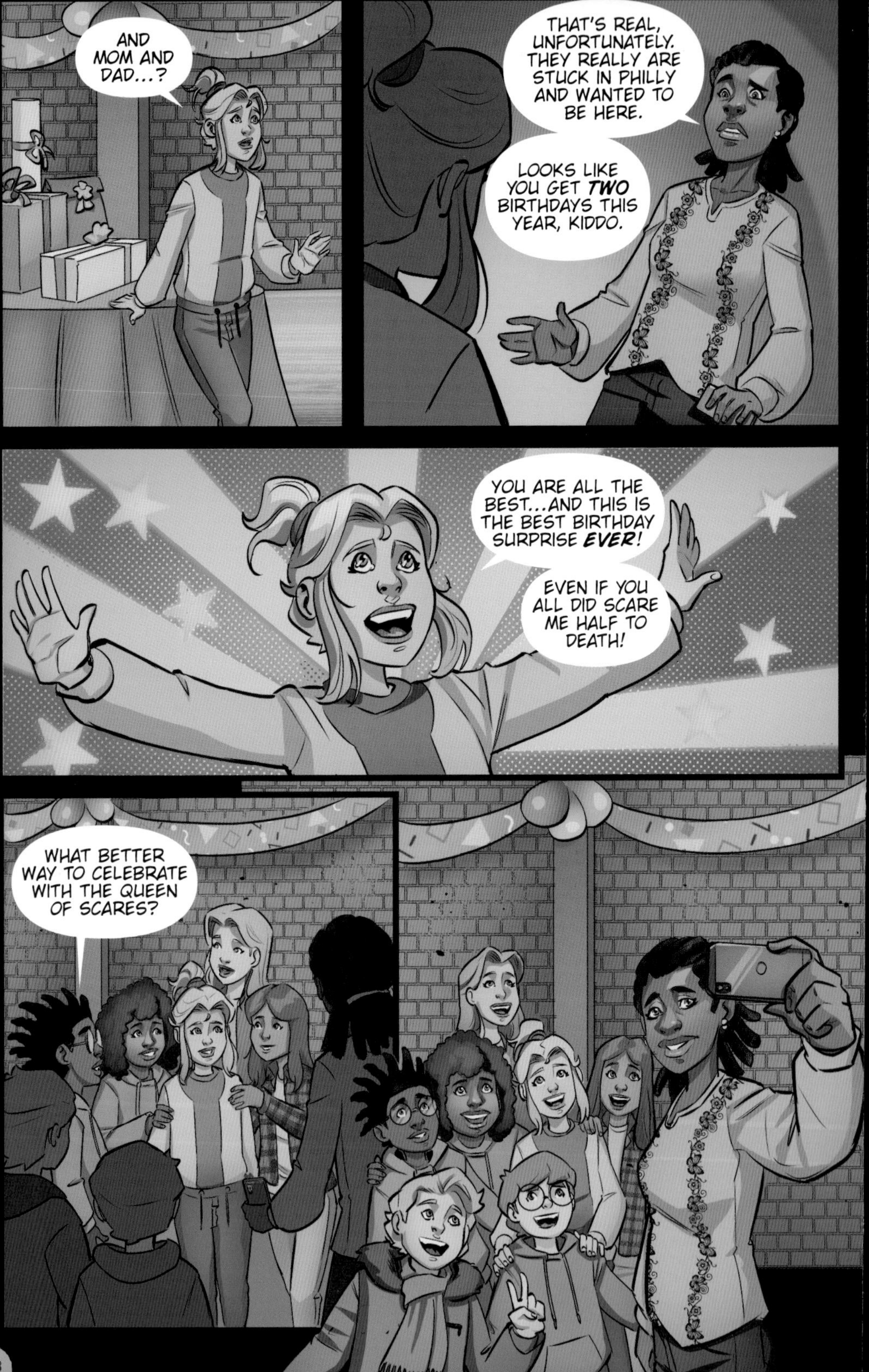
AND MOM AND DAD...?
THAT'S REAL, UNFORTUNATELY. THEY REALLY ARE STUCK IN PHILLY AND WANTED TO BE HERE.
LOOKS LIKE YOU GET **TWO** BIRTHDAYS THIS YEAR, KIDDO.
YOU ARE ALL THE BEST...AND THIS IS THE BEST BIRTHDAY SURPRISE **EVER**!
EVEN IF YOU ALL DID SCARE ME HALF TO DEATH!
WHAT BETTER WAY TO CELEBRATE WITH THE QUEEN OF SCARES?

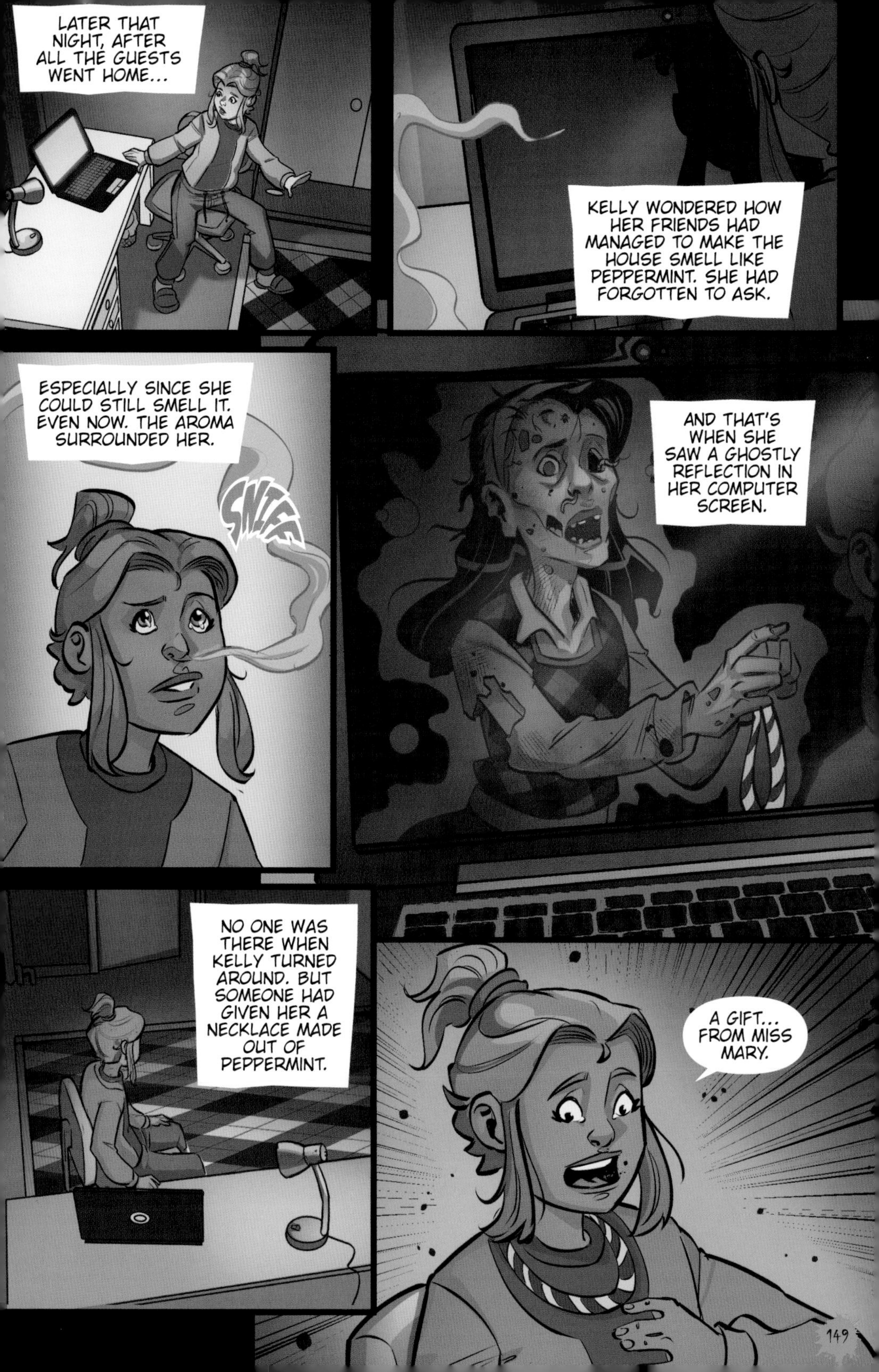
LATER THAT NIGHT, AFTER ALL THE GUESTS WENT HOME...
KELLY WONDERED HOW HER FRIENDS HAD MANAGED TO MAKE THE HOUSE SMELL LIKE PEPPERMINT. SHE HAD FORGOTTEN TO ASK.
ESPECIALLY SINCE SHE COULD STILL SMELL IT. EVEN NOW. THE AROMA SURROUNDED HER.
SNIFF
AND THAT'S WHEN SHE SAW A GHOSTLY REFLECTION IN HER COMPUTER SCREEN.
NO ONE WAS THERE WHEN KELLY TURNED AROUND. BUT SOMEONE HAD GIVEN HER A NECKLACE MADE OUT OF PEPPERMINT.
A GIFT... FROM MISS MARY.

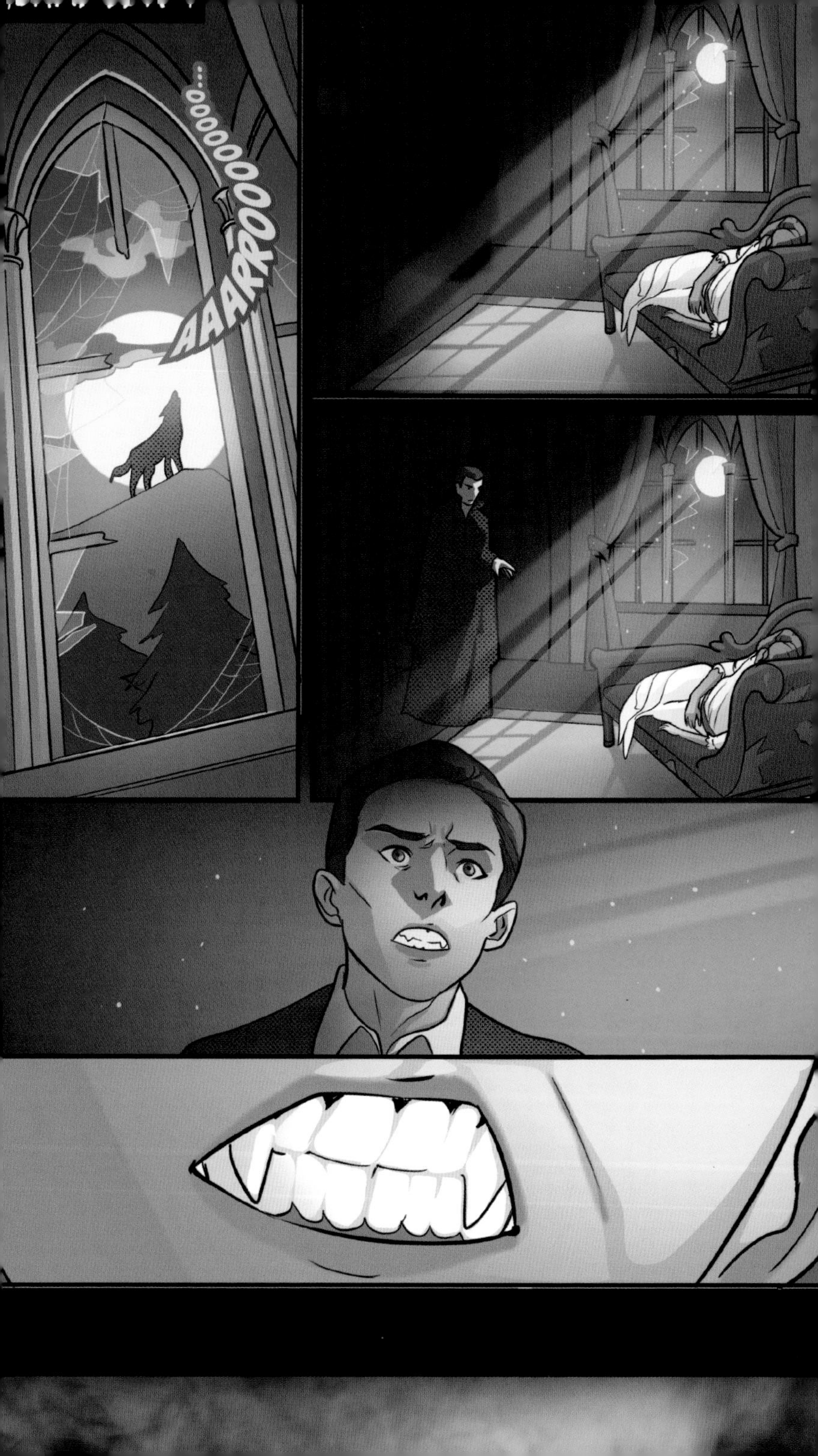
AAARROOOOOOOOO...

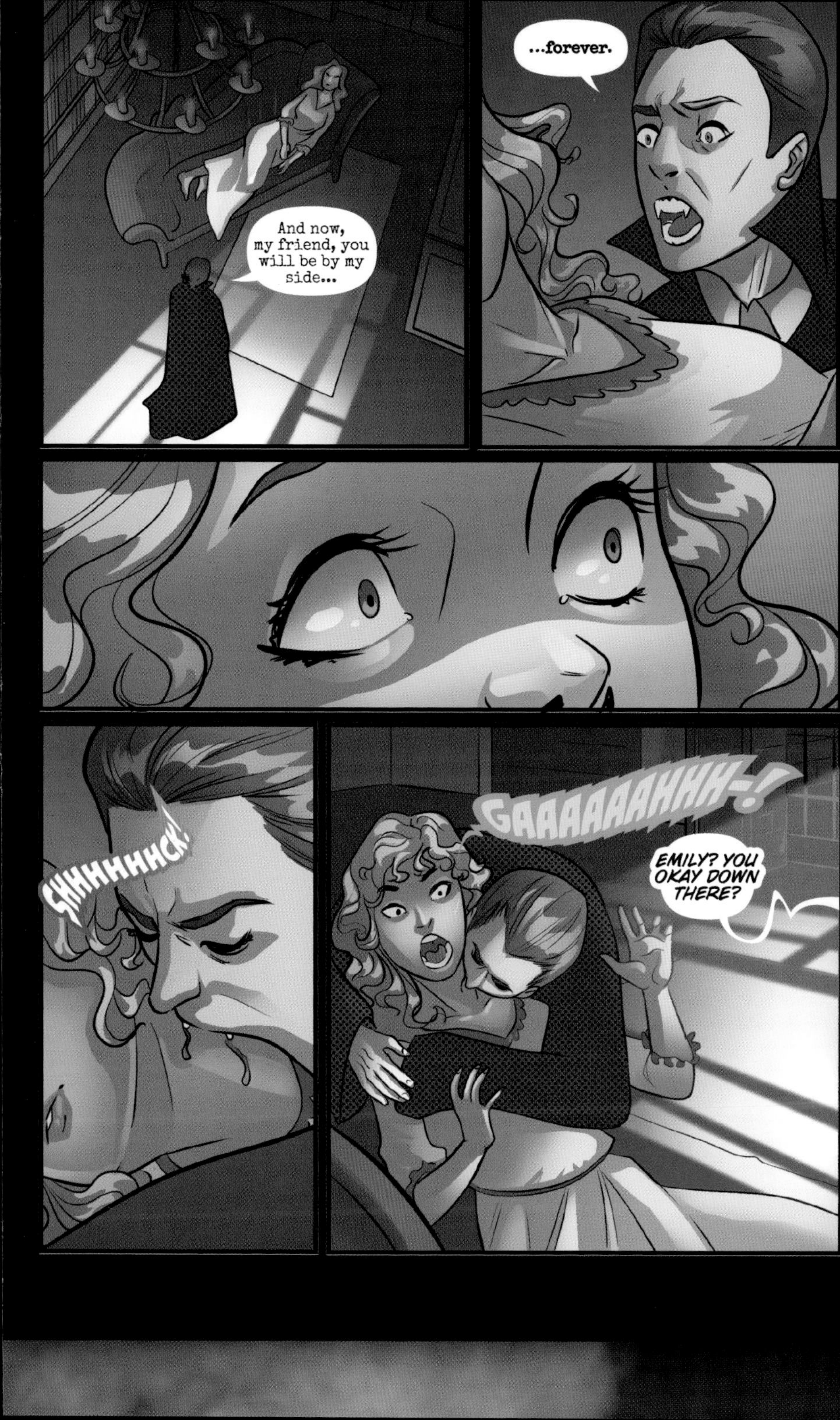
And now, my friend, you will be by my side...
...forever.
SHHHHHHCK!
GAAAAAAHHH-!
EMILY? YOU OKAY DOWN THERE?

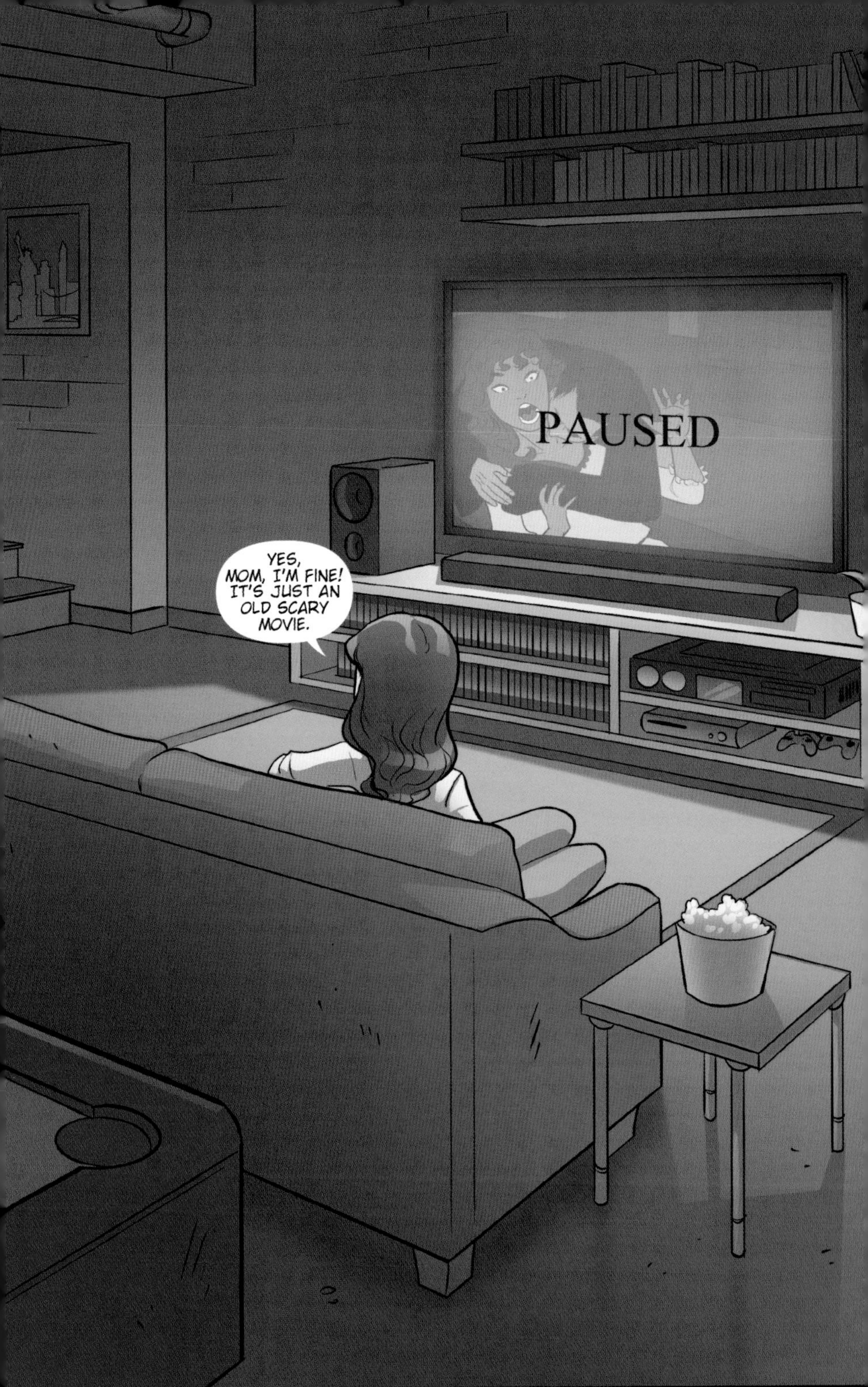
PAUSED
YES, MOM, I'M FINE! IT'S JUST AN OLD SCARY MOVIE.

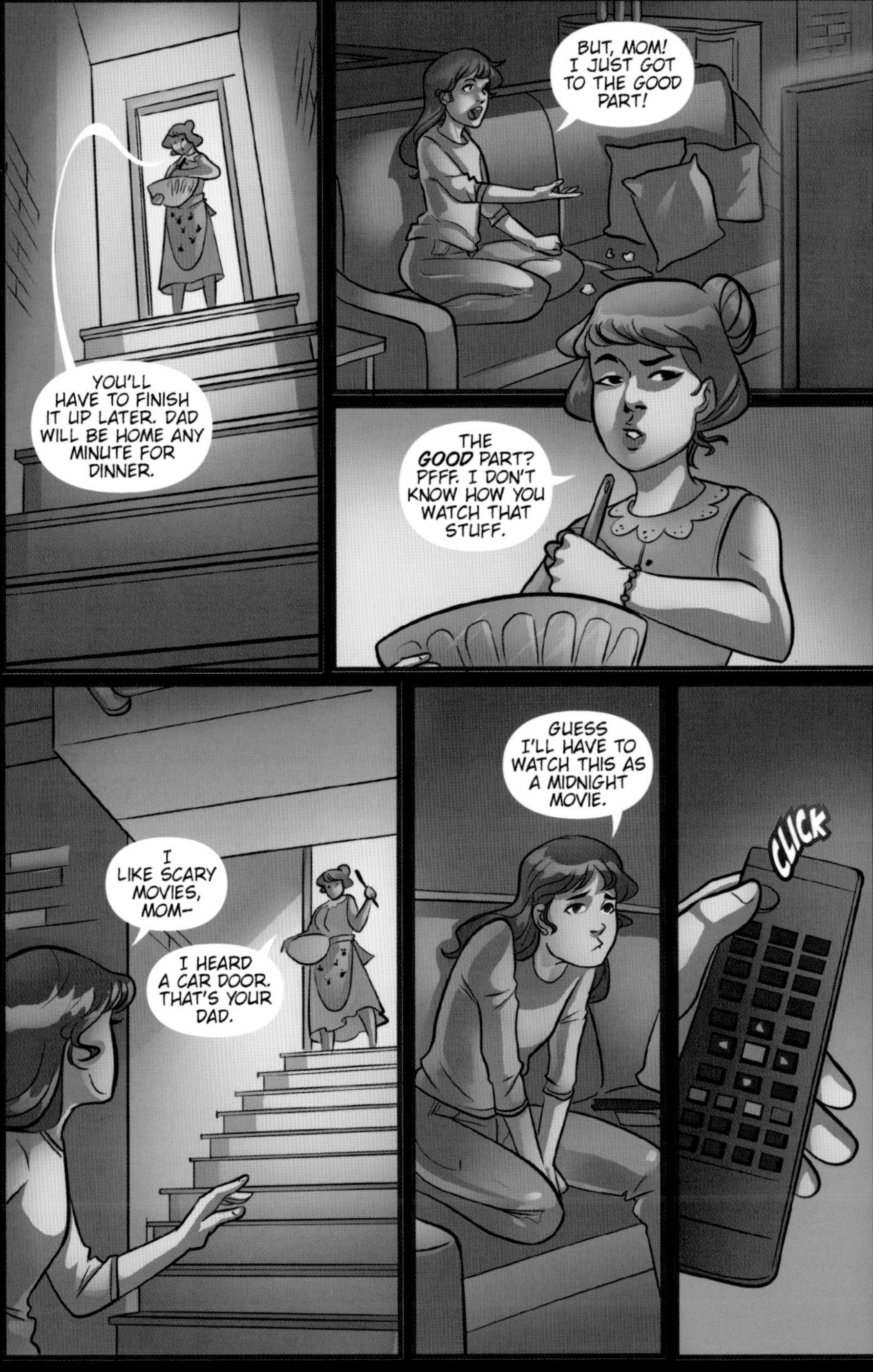

YOU'LL HAVE TO FINISH IT UP LATER. DAD WILL BE HOME ANY MINUTE FOR DINNER.
BUT, MOM! I JUST GOT TO THE GOOD PART!
THE *GOOD* PART? PFFF. I DON'T KNOW HOW YOU WATCH THAT STUFF.
I LIKE SCARY MOVIES, MOM–
I HEARD A CAR DOOR. THAT'S YOUR DAD.
GUESS I'LL HAVE TO WATCH THIS AS A MIDNIGHT MOVIE.
CLICK

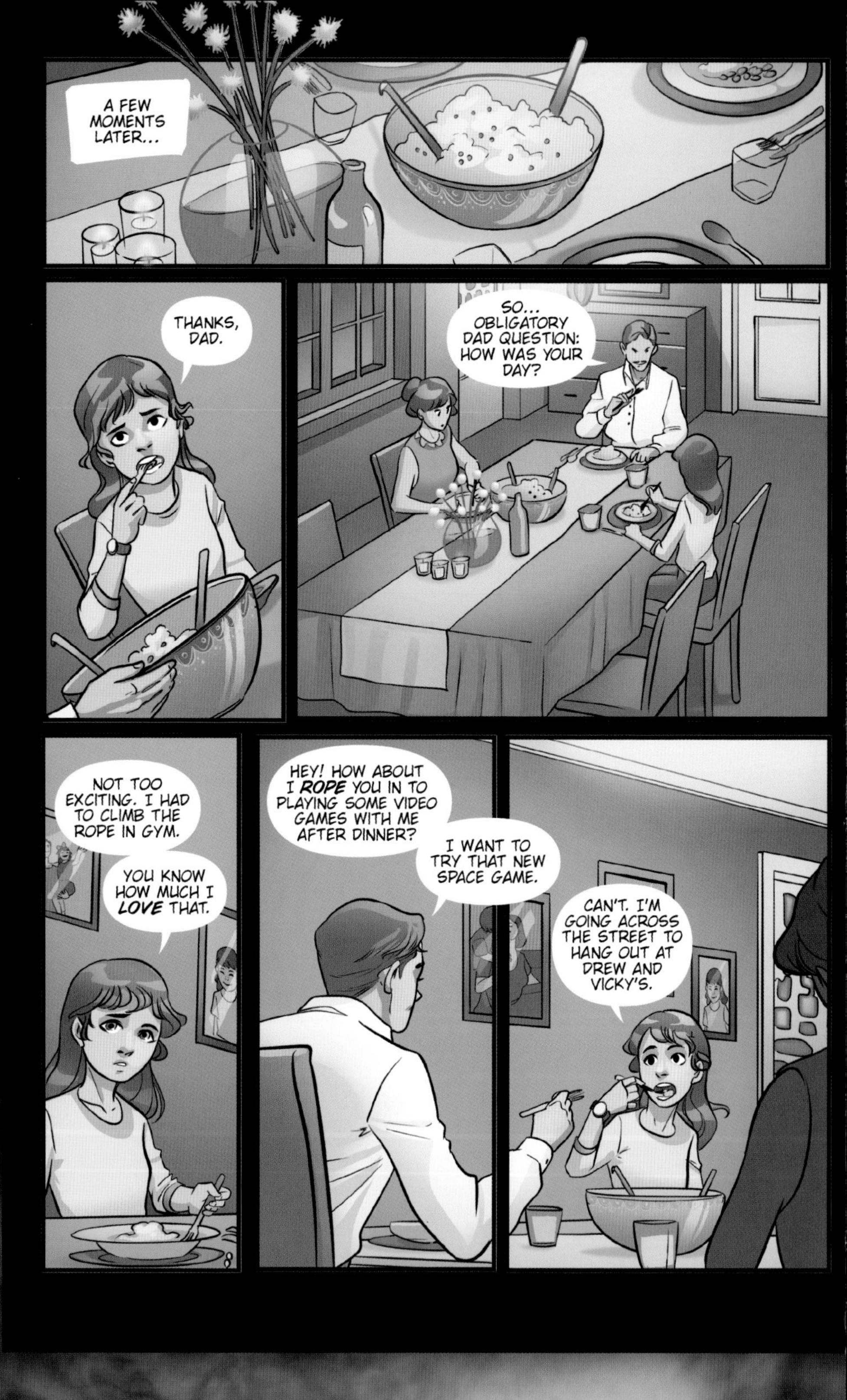
A FEW MOMENTS LATER...
THANKS, DAD.
SO... OBLIGATORY DAD QUESTION: HOW WAS YOUR DAY?
NOT TOO EXCITING. I HAD TO CLIMB THE ROPE IN GYM.
YOU KNOW HOW MUCH I LOVE THAT.
HEY! HOW ABOUT I ROPE YOU IN TO PLAYING SOME VIDEO GAMES WITH ME AFTER DINNER?
I WANT TO TRY THAT NEW SPACE GAME.
CAN'T. I'M GOING ACROSS THE STREET TO HANG OUT AT DREW AND VICKY'S.

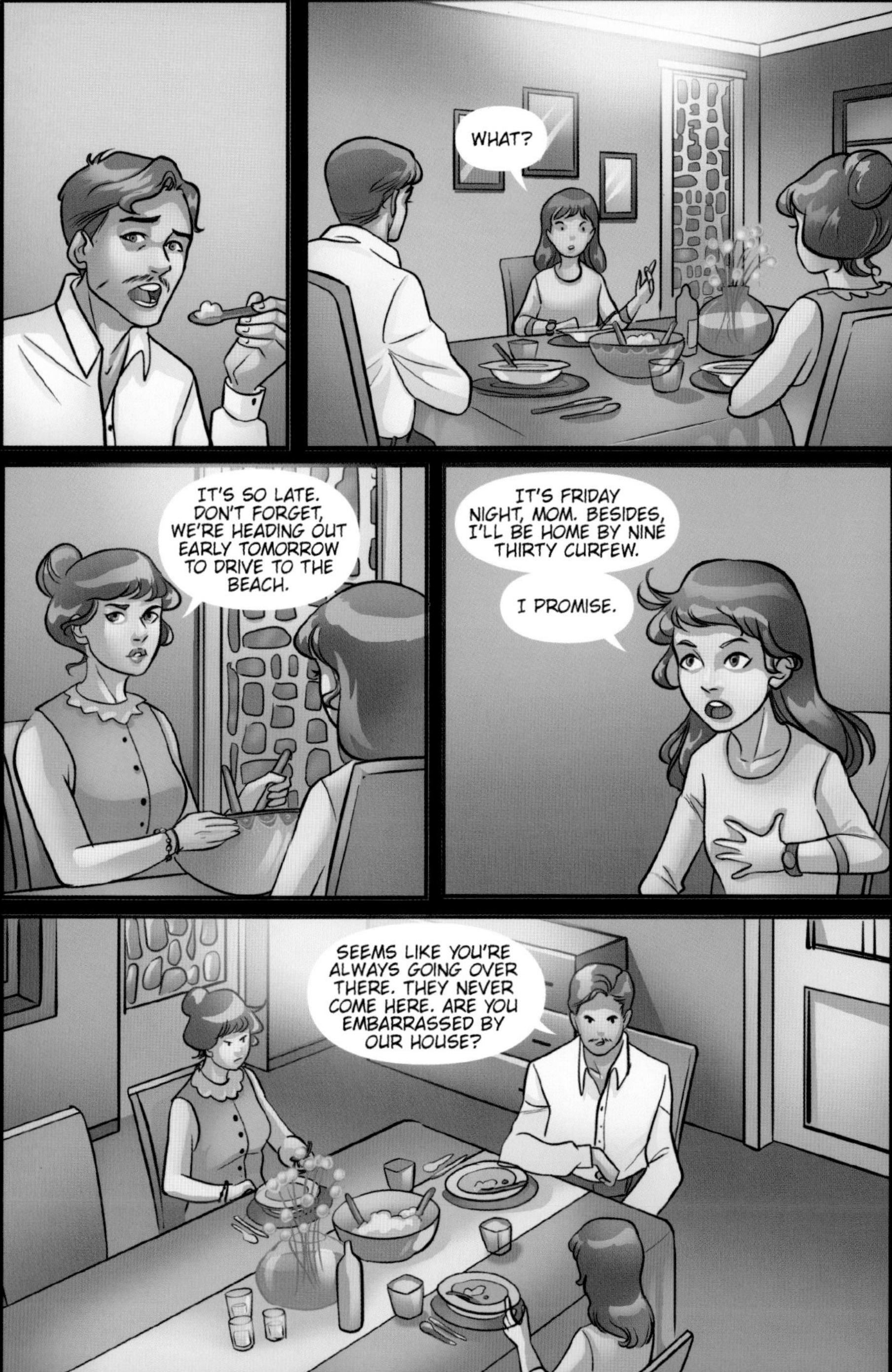
WHAT?
IT'S SO LATE. DON'T FORGET, WE'RE HEADING OUT EARLY TOMORROW TO DRIVE TO THE BEACH.
IT'S FRIDAY NIGHT, MOM. BESIDES, I'LL BE HOME BY NINE THIRTY CURFEW.
I PROMISE.
SEEMS LIKE YOU'RE ALWAYS GOING OVER THERE. THEY NEVER COME HERE. ARE YOU EMBARRASSED BY OUR HOUSE?

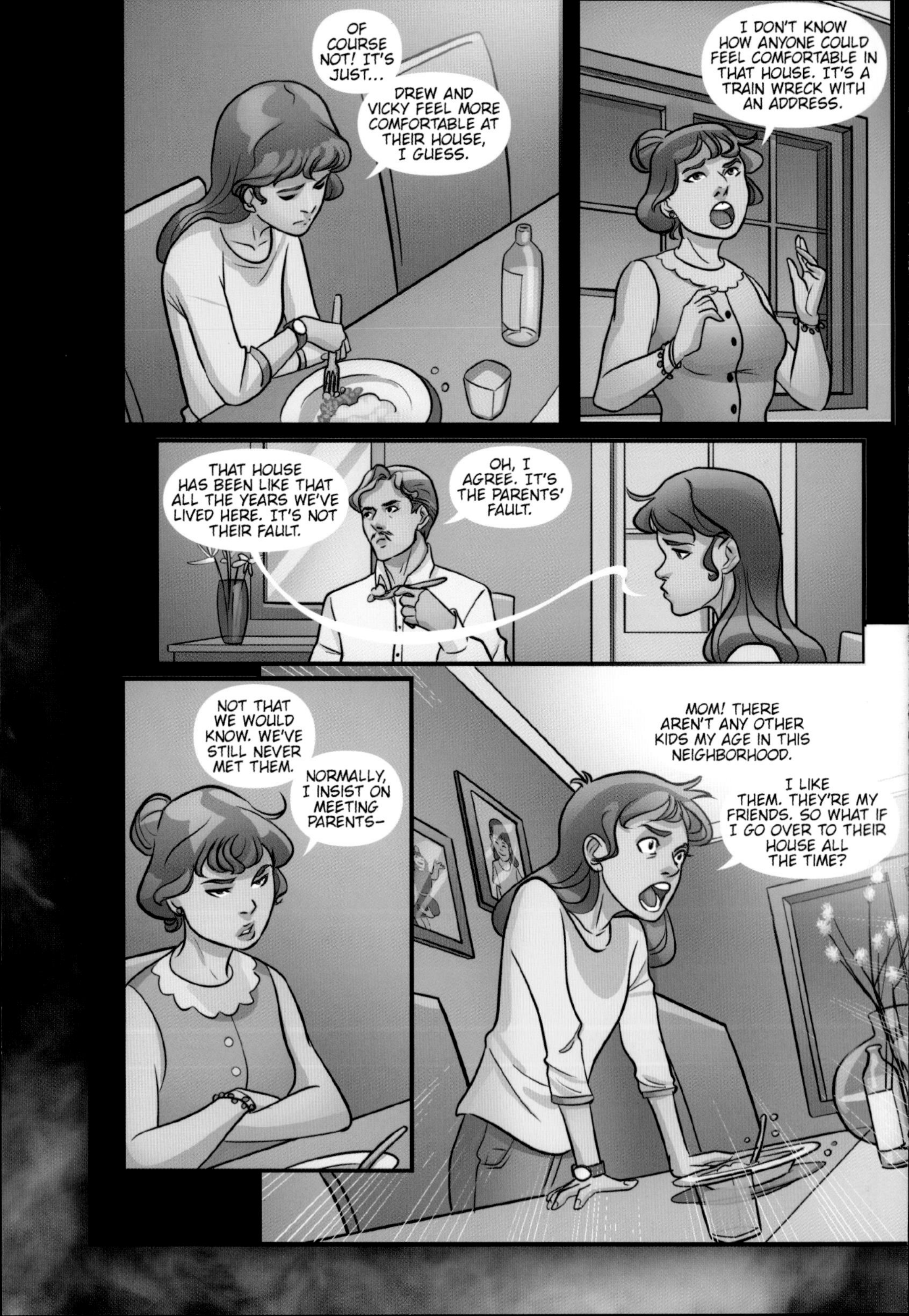
OF COURSE NOT! IT'S JUST...
DREW AND VICKY FEEL MORE COMFORTABLE AT THEIR HOUSE, I GUESS.
I DON'T KNOW HOW ANYONE COULD FEEL COMFORTABLE IN THAT HOUSE. IT'S A TRAIN WRECK WITH AN ADDRESS.
THAT HOUSE HAS BEEN LIKE THAT ALL THE YEARS WE'VE LIVED HERE. IT'S NOT THEIR FAULT.
OH, I AGREE. IT'S THE PARENTS' FAULT.
NOT THAT WE WOULD KNOW. WE'VE STILL NEVER MET THEM.
NORMALLY, I INSIST ON MEETING PARENTS-
MOM! THERE AREN'T ANY OTHER KIDS MY AGE IN THIS NEIGHBORHOOD.
I LIKE THEM. THEY'RE MY FRIENDS. SO WHAT IF I GO OVER TO THEIR HOUSE ALL THE TIME?

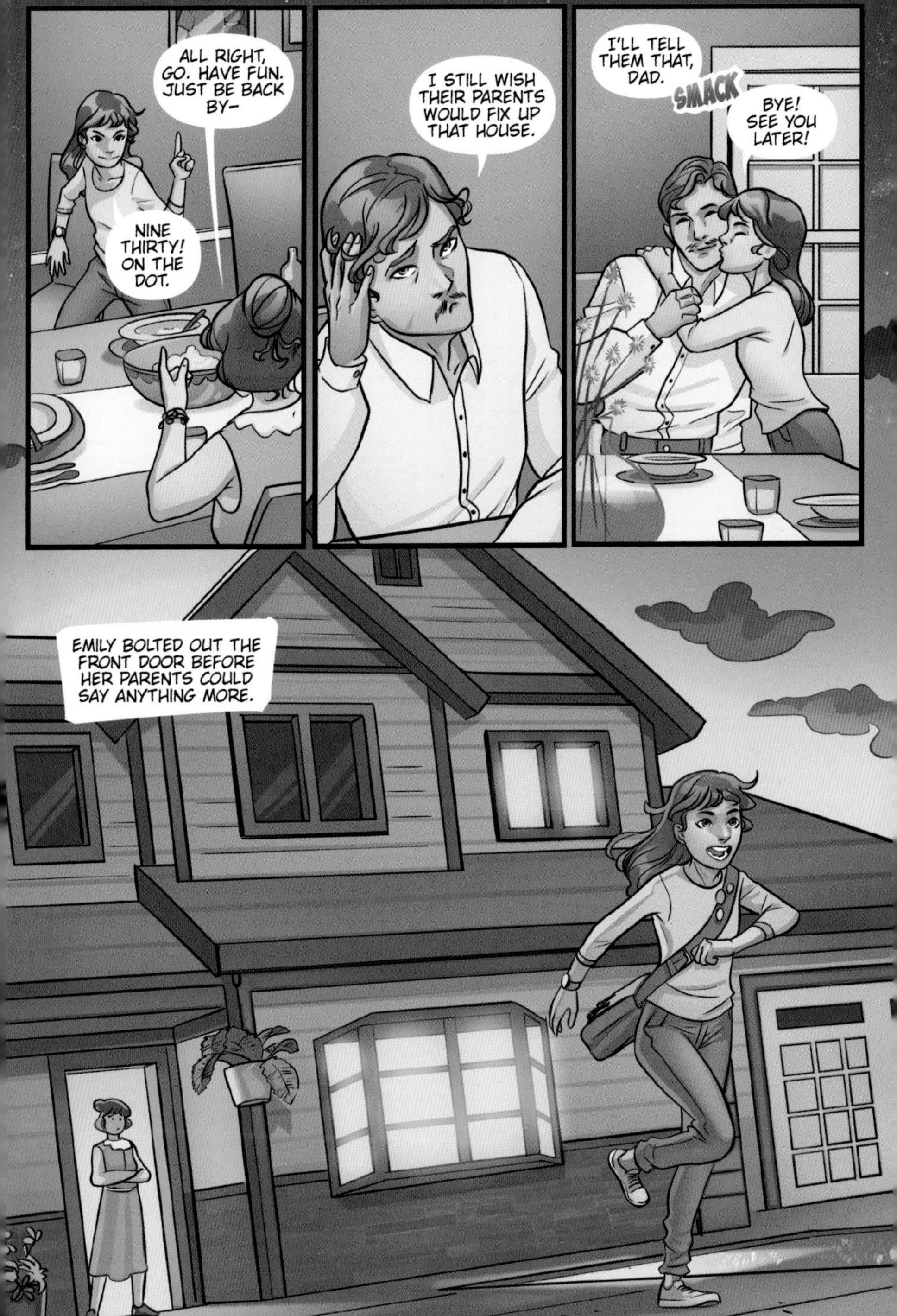
ALL RIGHT, GO. HAVE FUN. JUST BE BACK BY—
NINE THIRTY! ON THE DOT.
I STILL WISH THEIR PARENTS WOULD FIX UP THAT HOUSE.
I'LL TELL THEM THAT, DAD.
SMACK
BYE! SEE YOU LATER!
EMILY BOLTED OUT THE FRONT DOOR BEFORE HER PARENTS COULD SAY ANYTHING MORE.